Ire of Silver

Ire of Silver

As the bastard daughter of an orc chief, Thugari is nothing more than a slave. After her last beating, disguising herself as a stable boy, she escapes, stealing as she runs. Unfortunately, her victim is the orc Rukk Knaraugh, a lawbringer from the Council.

When Rukk finds her, she tries to run, fearing for her life, but he's skilled in tracking her. Claiming she is in his debt, he takes her with him, heading north as he hunts wild witches stealing babies. He agrees to release her from the debt in the dwarven city of Dussoum, where, for her, magicless people are welcome. Yet, he fascinates her, awakening something addictive within her along with the claim that she's not without magical powers.

In the sinister Chaosthane Mountains circling Dussoum, it is not shelter she finds. Despite discovering the reason behind the stolen babies, a magic blossoms within her as does her love for a lawbringer.

ALSO BY SEVANNAH STORM

The Blood of Legends Series

The Huntress

The Healer

*

The Gifting Series

Soul Forged

Fate Forged

Sun Forged

War Forged

Star Forged

Shadow Forged

Earth Forged

Lust Forged

Fire Forged

*

The Qaldreth Warriors Series

Sol Survivor

Dark Survivor (Coming soon)

*

The Space Hunter Chronicles Series

The Shikari

The Justisaar (Coming soon)

*

Standalones

Xiaxan Fox

Ire of Silver

The Crucible of the Eternals

*

Plump Playwright Series

Plump Jane

Seducing Amelia

Loving Finley

Keeping Tessa

Kissing Navy

Glossary and Pronunciations

Characters:

Thugari (*Too-Gaar-Ee*): Origin: Thoraval (human) and Ghorza (orc): Bastard daughter of a chief who slept with a dark-human (siren).

Uzul (*Oo-Zool*): Origin: Ghorza (orc): Third tier magic-user, a spellbinder.

Nerinai (*Neh-Reen-Eye*): Origin: Thoraval (dark-human): Daughter in the Macutia family, which is known for their siren females. From the Bazinhur Island, south of the Camsevair Mountains.

Varthug Nehrakgu (*Varr-Toog Na-ruck-Goo*): Origin: Ghorza (orc): Last son of the Nehrakgu lineage, which had once held moon magic, and silver eyes.

Murzush (*Mer-Zoosh*): Origin: Ghorza (orc): Wife of Varthug, and Lady of Haraton Castle.

Rukk Knaraugh (*Rook K-Narr-Rig*): Son of an Orc (that's all he'll admit to): Origin: Ghorza (orc) and elf and is a lawbringer.

Tarid Inaris (*Tare-Id In-Aar-iss*): Origin: Atrar (dark-skinned humans): Lawbringer and lawbrother to Rukk.

Sharn Tandagh (*Sharn Tan-Dag*): Origin: Ghorza (orc): Second Tier magic-user, a magus.

Borgakh Yerug (*Boar-Gag Year-Oog*): Origin: Ghorza (orc): Renowned warrior, but due to her size, and height, there are whispers her father was one of the last Hugver giants. It's false, but she lets them believe it.

Nenneg Tilly (*Neh-Negg Till-ee*): Origin: Thoraval (human): A wylder and rejected novitiate from the Council.

Mòr Guaire (*More Geh-Air*): Friend of Borgakh, and Nenneg: Origin: Dussoum (dwarf): Leader of the Geàrdan.

Geàrdan (*Geh-Arr-Dan*): A dwarven leadership comprised of female dwarves who are diplomatic, nurturing, and tasked with monitoring magic in the Chaosthane Mountains (Una, Isbeil, and Mòr).

Horknuth Knaraugh (*Hawk-Nooth K-Narr-Rig*): King of the Ghorza orcs: Origin: Ghorza (orc).

Iomhar *Eye-Om-Haar*): The all-male dwarven council specializing in war, and mining.

Iàcob (*Ay-Cob*): A male dwarven leader on the Iomhar.

Seamus (*Shay-Muss*): A male dwarven leader on the Iomhar.

Aonghas (*Ann-Gus*): A male dwarven leader on the Iomhar.

Locations:

Ainerius (*Ain-Err-Eee-Iss*): The southeastern town of Tulach.

Amarhei (*Am-Arr-Hay*): The island upon which sits the Ghorzan Royal City of Isstislaaron.

Atrar (*Att-Rar*): Realm of dark-humans.

Banach (*Baa-Nuck*): Tarid's cottage.

Bazinhur (*Bar-Zinn-Her*): The home of dark-human sirens.

Buzaram (*Boo-Zarr-Ram*): First town Rukk stops at on his way to Isstislaaron.

Camsevair (*Cam-Sir-Vare*): Southernmost mountain range.

Eral (*Eh-Ral*): Salt Plains of Eral.

Eslaniel (*Es-Lan-eel*): Tower of Eslaniel, home to the Council.

Filralad (*Phil-Rar-Lad*): A small port town north of Gallanbour Hills

Ghorza (*Gore-Za*): Realm of the orcs.

Gillanbour (*Gill-Lan-Bore*): A strip of hills east of the Chaosthane Mountains.

Haraton (*Harr-A-Ton*): Home to the Nehrakgu lineage, once a human bastion.

Isstislaaron (*Iss-Tiz-Larr-On*): The Ghorzan Royal City.

Kethil (*Keth-Ill*): All the realms combined.

Kinargun (*Kin-Narr-Gun*): The royal city of Atrar.

Kizad (*Kee-Zadd*): The Plains of Kizad where the armies camped.

Lonhuen (*Lon-Hue-En*): Second town Rukk stops at on his way to Isstislaaron.

Menoranas (*Men-Oh-Rar-Nass*): A large port town, beneath the great orc statues knowns as the Gates of Amarhei.

Mythal (*Myth-All*): The most southern town in Kethil and farthest away from Isstislaaron.

Onci (*On-See*): The main city of Thoraval.

Penven (*Pen-Vin*): A town outside the Tower of Eslaniel where the Council operates.

Sahtar (*Sarr-Tarr*): The Bay of Sahtar slithers between the island of Amarhei and Kethil.

Thoraval (*Thor-A-Val*): Realm of the humans.

Tulach (*Too-Luck*): The town north of Tarid's cottage.

Velfond (*Vell-Fornd*): The Atrarian western tribe's main town.

Monsters/Creatures/Fauna/Flora:

Malaena (*May-Lay-Na*) tree

Koveen (lamia): (*Co-Veen*): A solitary snake-tailed female that drains the blood of bairns before consuming their bodies. Lives in burrows under rocky planes or forests. Predominantly from the north, Chaosthane.

Dreshnie (*Dresh-Nee*) (camazotz): Humans bitten by immortal bats, their skin decaying slowly over time. Most dreshnies hide in caves where they form partnerships with 'pets.' Their slime is from their pours, a constant marking of their territory. They can create illusions after sifting through thoughts.

Eikusai (*Eye-Koo-Sigh*) (Drider/Inuit's Ai'Sivang): Top half of a giant spider is a human female, become dreshnie pets.

Voidwhisp (*Void-Whisp*): Wisps that take human form when the hunger is upon them. They also leave slime, ethereal plasma, behind. You cannot fight them until they take human form. To do that, you need to increase their hunger. They feed off emotions.

Bastior (*Bus-Tee-Err*): Werewolf

Steduin (*Stair-Doo-In*) (warg/nian): Has the body of an armored bear and the head of a wolf. It was said to be a ferocious animal that lived in the mountains and hunted for a living. Fears three things: the color red, fire, and noise.

Shedaji (*Sha-Dar-Jee*) (sphinx): a head of a human, a winged body of a lion.

Chapter One

Fiery agony burned across Thugari's shoulders, setting her senses alight. A grunt from the castle torturer preceded the next lash. Pinching her lips around her protruding tusks helped smother the scream tearing her throat. Another blow split her threadbare tunic and seared her skin. She lost count after her back burned, bombarding her mind with silent pleas to stop. Warm liquid dribbled to her collarbone, the stench of iron stinging her nostrils.

"Enough." Frukag, the captain of the guard, pierced the pregnant silence with a barked command. With blessed mercy, the next blow didn't fall.

Fresh pain ripped through her with each jarring breath.

"Tell us where you hid the locket, Thugari." He grabbed her hair and yanked her head back.

The violence of the gesture clattered his ethnic beads against each other and swayed them across his bare chest. Sharp darts tore at her scalp, calling forth tears, which she blinked away before he could see them. He dipped to meet her gaze, his breath stinking of old ale.

His tribal-marked face mottled red when she remained silent. "Fine. Summon the spellbinder."

She shut her eyes, dreading the soft footfalls of the ancient ether spellbinder serving her father's clan. Despite being human, Uzul was as merciless as Frukag. A breeze stung her bare back. Shivering, she tightened her arms around the stake, clinging to it as if its solid strength could pour into her. The sun began to set, ushering in cooler temperatures.

She wouldn't have to wait long for Uzul, not when he had a prior arrangement with the village healer in Bire before the evening meal.

Uzul's hem dragged on the paved stones. His impending brand of torture stiffened her shoulders, sending a renewed rivulet of blood along her collarbone to the front of her tunic. Sweat or blood stained what garments she owned. The rich, royal-blue velvet of Uzul's robe brushed her knees as he stopped beside her. Cold anise-scented air shoved her braid aside and stroked along the rune carved into her nape without his physical touch.

Activating the rune with his air magic summoned her body's memories of past lashings. Blinding agony spasmed through her, and she whimpered, not having the strength to smother the sound. As she slumped against the pole, Uzul's oily mind slithered along hers, probing her recent activities. She didn't fight him, unable to gather the will to do so.

"She's innocent," he said.

The pain ceased, and she bathed in the blessed relief like the sweetness of water after days of thirst.

"Lady Arob witnessed Thugari taking her locket." Frukag kept his voice low.

"I assumed you searched the tower?"

"Of course I did, Uzul." Hatred dripped off Frukag's tongue.

"Mmm, then consider justice served, and release the slave." Uzul's voice dwindled as he glided away with his robe trailing dirt and leaves.

Her ropes loosened, and she slumped then collapsed onto her side to coil around the base of the stake. A breeze fanned her chest. She didn't care if her torn tunic gaped, having exposed herself to the warriors before. As the illegitimate daughter of Chief Varthug, none dared to touch her. Nor was she fit for polite company.

The inner yard emptied. The darkening skies and rumbling thunder heralded a storm and left her without an avid audience. No one came to her aid, not that she expected any. As the rain splattered the sunbaked stones beneath her, she tilted her face to savor the cool droplets on her cheeks. Through those catching on her eyelashes, she gazed at the changing sky from blazing oranges to a haunting dark blue. If she lay still, her back didn't throb, and she could convince herself she didn't ache.

She whimpered, rolling onto her knees. The evening meal and her chores awaited her. Clambering to her feet, she clutched her tunic to her chest and raised her gaze to the impressive white stone façade of Haraton Castle, once a human bastion.

Peering through the stained-glass window, Lady Murzush curled her lips downward and narrowed her eyes. The fading sunlight touched on her clan markings across her bare stomach and behind her guda covering her breasts. With a flick of her gold-beaded braids, she abandoned Thugari to her suffering.

She staggered to the kitchen, hoping to slip through and up the spiraling steps to the broken-down northwest tower. It served as a room of sorts, where the wind pierced the splintered roof and missing mortar to cool her in summer, but freeze her in winter.

Belen the cook wasn't present when Thugari hesitated at the door. Tempted to drop her shoulders in relief, she caught herself in time and wove through the kitchen. Other maids shot her nervous glances as she passed them. Each step jolted her back, but there was nothing she could do and no one to tend to her.

Anger no longer settled in her soul, forcing her to react or vow vengeance. She'd fast learned it worsened her fate. Numbness claimed her emotions, nor did she fear losing her life. Frukag bemoaned her stoicism, that he couldn't discipline someone with whom he couldn't bargain. There was nothing more he could do to her besides kill her. She snorted. Death was a kindness he wasn't prepared to bestow upon her.

She climbed to her room like a decrepit elder, but the breeze sweeping down the steps cooled her damp skin. She shut the splintered door, granting herself a fragile privacy. At the task ahead, she held her temple to the coarse wood while she fought for strength. Peeling the tunic off without skinning her back took all her concentration, with each fiery twinge slowing her movements. Once free, she left the tunic where it fell on the straw-lined floor.

She crushed lavender, rosemary, and mint into her broken pewter jug, swirling the concoction to mix the herbs. On bare feet, she paused in front of the window, missing its glazing. While holding the jug to her chest, she released a slow breath then tilted the concoction over her shoulder to trickle the water down her back. Renewed fire sliced through her. She clamped her hand across her mouth to muffle her screams. Her nostrils flared, and she slammed the chipped jar on the stone windowsill, grabbing the stone to steady her.

Crimson-stained water dripped through the splintered floorboards to the abandoned guard room below where she slept in winter. The kitchen fires penetrated the southeast wall, granting her some warmth. Taking an old but clean cloth, she wrapped it around her shoulders. Biting on a scavenged black root, she rolled her back against the wall. A moan shredded her throat, and she bit harder until her teeth ached.

Not an apology crossed Frukag's wet lips. No healer did he summon. Nor could he take to task the lying bitch who accused Thugari of this theft. They believed her, for they must. The same fate awaited anyone who questioned the word of Varthug's legitimate daughter. Thugari had no rights. Her mother, Nerinai, had arrived on Haraton Castle's doorstep with her dark-skinned child. One look at Thugari's eyes and all knew who sired her.

Chief Varthug Nehrakgu's lineage sported silver-gray eyes, as it had done for thousands of years. His people were once masters of moon magic. None of her father's ancient power or her mother's human heritage had seen fit to bless Thugari with magic. Though, what knowledge she had of magic was meager.

A strange sickness took her mother when Thugari was but five summers old. Varthug welcomed her for appearance's sake but could do no more. Not without his mate, Lady Murzush, giving her permission. As constant proof of her father's blatant dalliance with a dark human, Thugari would die before receiving Murzush's kindness. Over the years, whatever obligation her father may have carried for Thugari had dwindled. Whatever love she might have had for him, he destroyed.

She peeled the cloth away from her lacerated skin and draped it over her rickety bed. After pulling on a clean tunic, she crawled under her bed, nudged a stone out of the wall, and stroked the locket lying there. She smirked. She may not have taken the locket her silly half-sister accused her of stealing, but she had stolen jewelry from Murzush. Frukag and his males never found Thugari's treasure whenever they searched her room. Only the dumbest males served her father.

The soft pad of feet on the wooden bedframe warned her she was no longer alone. She lunged for the intruder, snatching him into her arms, and crushing him against her chest for a cuddle.

Gnash, her rat, squirmed, and she giggled, releasing him. He clambered up her chest to curl into the curve of her neck. She ran a gentle finger from his gray head to his bulbous backside.

"Mmm, you've grown fat." She scratched him under his chin, and he purred, but the moment she dropped her hand, he chirped. "I'm hungry too, little one."

One more moon and she would slip out of the castle, past the gate guards, and into the southern village of Bire. She would travel through the eastern forest, circling around Haraton to head north to Chaosthane. The dwarves might shelter her for a while. They too were powerless and welcomed any creature with the same affliction. The city of Dussoum, south of the Chaosthane Mountains, might serve as a new home. The journey would take eight days, but she could do it.

The accusations were becoming more frequent, and her punishments harsher. Only a fool would remain here and court more suffering.

Chapter Two

Rukk Knaraugh swung his legs off the side of the bed with a swallowed groan, rising from the mattress to tug on his breeches, a black tunic, and a thick leather overcoat. No beads proclaimed his heritage. No war markings announced his allegiance. He was an orc without affiliation, except to the law as indicated by his black ensemble, despite the dark leaf-shaped markings along his wrists. He'd earned those during childhood trials.

As a fully clanned orc, it had taken a while to grow accustomed to garments, but now a sense of vulnerability, as if he were unarmed, claimed him when he was nude. With a soft command, white tendrils rose from his skin to sift through his hair, unravel and re-braid it. He didn't care how.

"Stay," Elanil whispered.

He grimaced. Hope poured from her blue elven gaze. He chose not to lay with a female more than once for this very reason. Not that he had found a female worthy of repeat samplings. They were a predictable and tiresome lot. Elanil had made herself available, and he was too tired to seek out another. Elves were preferable to humans, who were too weak to handle an orc at full vigor.

"Farewell." He scooped up his sword as he left her room. Once he had rutted, he never remained charming. Then again, the act itself blunted his magic and drained what energy he could muster for niceties.

She cursed his name, but that didn't bother him either. As a wood nymph with basic magic, her curses wouldn't harm an insect.

In the passage of the brothel, an Atrarian human male leaned against one wall, flicking and catching his jeweled dagger. His mannerisms conveyed impatience. His unkempt, gold-streaked brown hair fell across his dark-skinned brow, yet his vigilant gaze rested on Rukk. Tarid Inaris and he had trained together since childhood. The Council encouraged the forming of close bonds across races.

"I've summoned the healer," he said by way of greeting, sheathing his dagger into a knee-high boot. "You must be ill to have rutted with the same female twice."

Rukk scowled but ignored his fellow lawbringer otherwise.

Not needing a response, Tarid gestured at the bedroom door. "Her magic isn't powerful enough to enchant you. I considered mischievous intent, but that didn't ring true. Rukk, the imperious lawbringer, wouldn't succumb to the weak will of a wood elf."

Rukk trudged down the stairs. Exhaustion weakened his knees, and the urge to sleep on his feet bombarded him. He continued to ignore Tarid, forcing his partner to scamper after Rukk.

"Oh, ho! The silent treatment?" Tarid barked out a laugh, loud enough to echo off the narrow wooden walls of the passage. "Now that you've appeased the demands of your loins, the Council is sending us south to the bowels of Thoraval."

Frustration froze Rukk's next step, and he faced Tarid, granting him, at last, the attention he sought. "No knights available?"

Tarid leveled a serious gaze on him. "Vanishing bairns, my dear Rukk."

"Rumors," he said with a dismissive flick of his wrist.

"The cries of forlorn mothers say otherwise. Haraton Castle awaits." Tarid swept out his arm, whacking his knuckles on the wall.

"Anything south of here is unpleasant, but Haraton is hardly the bowels. It's the hours spent in the saddle, dodging ill-kept humans and orcs alike, I detest. Find another lawbringer." Rukk pulled an ebony-leather glove out of his cloak pocket to slap against his palm before gliding it on.

"The Grand Lawmaster selected you for this quest." Tarid tapped his heels against the wall. He palmed a black root and clamped it between his lips. His jaw worked as he chewed.

Inhaling in a calming breath, Rukk stared at his lawbrother, studying their differences. Tarid's more natural look contrasted with Rukk's obscured origins. Browns and golds comprised Tarid's palette, but Rukk's grays and blacks hinted at racial mix in his ancestry, if his protruding tusks and pale skin didn't. He settled his gaze on Tarid's brown eyes, forcing his friend to look away first. He did, but only for a second.

When he lifted his face, his grin brightened the dimly lit passage. "Come now, Rukk, when last have we traveled for something this intriguing?"

"Are the mounts readied?" Rukk resumed his strides along the passage and out into the quiet road, wishing he could bury his fingers in his soil pouch from his homeland. He needed a portion of his magic restored.

Rutting emptied his overflowing energy, yet laid him low for at least a day. Sleeping beside Elanil hadn't been an option. Now, he must suffer en route to Haraton.

"Of course!" Tarid bounced beside him, all joyful and excited, as if every day was a marvel and not a chore. He gestured to the local stables, built behind the tavern. "The page will meet us at the trading post with our satchels."

"How long have you known about this task?" Rukk studied Tarid's face.

Guilt twisted his features, confirming Rukk's suspicion. Tarid had hours to prepare, by the sound of things. Strolling toward the stables, darting his gaze around, Rukk was careful to hide his annoyance from his friend.

He slapped his other glove against his thigh as he walked, grateful for the thick coat shielding him from the dawn mist. The locals believed its icy fingers brought more than shivers, that curses and plagues clung to it, and any exposed skin would feel its wrath. Foolish, yes, but it was cold after the sweet warmth of Elanil's curves.

"The Grand Lawmaster summoned you after the witching hour."

Fire burned through Rukk, and he spun on Tarid, grabbing him by his fur-lined cloak. "What?"

"I couldn't find you!" Tarid raised his hands in surrender.

"Did you scry?" Rukk's voice slipped through tight lips, his jaw clenching and softening as he fought for control. Hours lost! What must the Lawmaster Janar think of him? Curse Zetar!

"You're immune to scrying!" Tarid lowered his hands as a scowl marred his forehead.

Rukk's hard-earned patience evaporated. "Not me, the female, idiot!"

Tarid snorted. "You never rut with the same female twice. How was I to know she would be so blessed?"

"Fair enough." Rukk released him without offering an apology. His friend stank of ale, which meant a dalliance at every tavern he had 'searched.' "Any further information on these bairns?" He picked off a strand of auburn hair from Tarid's cloak before marching to the stables.

He flashed Rukk a sheepish grin. "Same across the lands. Taken at dawn, burn marks on their blankets or mangers, and never seen again."

Rukk nodded. A vague memory teased his thoughts, something from his studies. It remained elusive, so he focused on the moment. "Any missing livestock? Reports of fires in forests, fields, or farms?"

"No more than usual." Tarid snuck glances at him, as if he had solved the mystery of the missing bairns.

Rukk smothered a snort. Did everyone think him the Arch-Magus? "Let's see what Haraton Castle has to offer. Lord Nehrakgu's hospitality is legendary."

"At least there will be a fresh batch of females for you to plunder."

Rukk shook his head, accepting Tarid toyed with him. All knew Rukk kept a strict schedule. Every thirteenth day meant an evening spent attending to his baser urges. To miss such an event made his magic unpredictable, his focus carnal. If his instincts were right about the cause of the disappearances, then they should return before he next needed to rut.

Tarid, however, kept no such schedule, finding any female worthy of plunder. He believed his magic lay within the rutting, despite their archives stating otherwise. Rukk envied his jovial friend's ability to deal with the energy drain. Not once had he been on the verge of losing control as Rukk had. Perhaps more frequent rutting would ease the aftermath. Or Tarid had hidden the size of his energy pool, and it would never overflow.

According to the magi, magic came from the soul—the purer the body, the more powerful the magic, no matter the energy pool's size a wielder was born with. Hence why neither of them could aspire to more powerful positions on the Council. Tarid had no inclination of mastering the art, and Rukk had declined joining the magi. He far preferred merging his powers with combat training.

"A four-day journey through the Forests of Anduia. Oh, joy!" Tarid hoisted his great bulk into the saddle. For Atrarians, Eslaniel retained warhorses—more than suitable for a male of Tarid's size.

Unsheathing his iron sword, Rukk slid it into the scabbard fixed to the saddle. Taking a moment, he patted Harpax's neck, whispering orcish words of encouragement before ruffling his mane. The ebony gelding with white socks on three of his feet had been with

Rukk for six years. His sleek lines, the ripple of power in his legs, and his stubbornness reminded Rukk of the first horse he had ridden. His mother gifted him with Telayi when he was but five.

Harpax nickered a greeting, pawing the ground to show his eagerness. Rukk vaulted into the saddle. From hours of traveling, the curved leather had molded to the exact shape of his backside.

The morning crowds parted to grant them free passage, avoiding the clumps of mud the horses' hooves flung up. Lanterns offered the illusion of warmth—the last dismal light in the gloom of the mist. He tightened the cloak around his neck, flipping his hood up to hide his pale hair, since the silver of it announced his identity.

A page waited in front of the message board outside the trading post. His gray hood was easy to discern in the lantern he held out at face-level. The lone roan to the left of him, with the Council Magus Sharn Tandagh astride it, drew a mumbled curse from Tarid. Rukk chose not to respond to this development. He didn't want his words twisted out of proportion.

The page attached their satchels to their saddles then snuffed the lantern. The gray mists shifted, lifting enough to illuminate Sharn's pristine beauty—the pale skin of her human heritage, but the bronze eyes of her orcish mother. Her pink lips pursed in a practiced pout around her tusks as she watched him. He met her gaze, assuming an expression of boredom. "The Arch-Magus insists I travel along. Something about needing a female's touch." She fiddled with the reins with her delicate fingers.

Rukk shifted his hood lower, hiding his face from the observant magus. He wished she would forsake her supposed affection for him. Even if it was true, he preferred not to rut with anyone from the Council.

"*She's a spy.*" Tarid projected his thoughts across their bond, made possible by their proximity. Neither were powerful enough to master greater distances.

"*I am aware.*" Withdrawing his dagger from his boot, Rukk pricked his thumb and cast the blood upward. His gut wrenched as he used magic he couldn't spare. "Shield me, oh, blessed life."

An expected swirl of mist carried the whispered words. The glowing droplets shot outward, slicing the air in search of vigilance. Cries in the distance confirmed the intended targets reached. Sharn slumped forward, clutching her stomach and the pommel as a soft whimper escaped her.

"Well done," Tarid said.

Rukk acknowledged his praise with a smirk, delighted to have thwarted the creatures of the night she coerced to spy for her. *"It buys us time, but she will summon more as we travel. What worries me is the Arch-Magus has never sent a magus on a mission with a lawbringer. This is an odd occurrence."*

"Mayhap the stolen bairns are more than we anticipated?"

Rukk grimaced. *"That would mean the Grand Lawmaster hasn't divulged everything. He would never send us on a task ill-informed. My allegiance is to the lawbringers and not the magi."*

The Council comprised of two factions with equal power. The magi ruled by an Arch-Magus and the lawbringers governed by a Grand Lawmaster. Within the Tower of Eslaniel, magi trained those powerful enough in the use of magic. The resolution of problems fell to the lawbringers, tasked to guard the Council and the land from unlawful or abuse of magic. It mattered not why magi rebelled, unsanctioned covens formed, or an untrained magic wielder lost control and killed their cows. Such were the norm for lawbringers, and most were resolved with the lethal use of a sword. What was unusual was the Arch-Magus involving herself in lawbringer business.

Perhaps Sharn traveling with was beneficial. Rukk would take the opportunity, so sweetly afforded him, to explore her mind in moments of weakness. After all, not even a magus as skilled as Sharn could guard her thoughts all the time. At some point, she would reveal why the Arch-Magus had thought it necessary to spy on Rukk at all.

CHAPTER THREE

THUGARI HESITATED WHEN BELEN pointed at the cold slop on the table. The female's gaze narrowed when Thugari didn't obey her. Envisioning her bowl heading for a gate guard, Thugari limp-jogged to the table and sat on the bench, swallowing a whimper when she raised her arm to cradle the bowl.

She shoveled the slop into her mouth, uncaring that it dribbled onto her chin and stained tunic. Even with no honey, salt, or anything else to add flavor, it was still delicious.

"Haraton Castle doesn't feed thieves, and if you can steal, then you have too much idle time." Belen gripped Thugari's shoulder with her dirty nails digging in above her collarbone. "Lady Arob assures me it 'twas you she saw, half-breed." Spittle layered her fat bottom lip.

Thugari muffled her moan as Belen's fingers dug into her skin. "I swear on my father's life, I did not steal it, mistress. Spellbinder Uzul agrees."

"That human!" Her top lip curled in derision. "Wearing *clothes* even as he serves Lord Varthug." She made a grating noise in the back of her throat and spat.

Thugari stared at the greenish glob on the dirty floor. Bile rose, and she almost pushed her bowl away. Not knowing when next she would find a meal, she forced the slop past the lump in her throat.

She should be thankful to Belen. Scrubbing the floors, the piss pots, and beating the tapestries lining the hall walls helped Thugari's back heal. But exhaustion had claimed her last night, and the need to sleep outweighed the hunger pangs wrenching her stomach. Gnash hadn't agreed, chirping her awake at all hours.

Each inch of her throbbed, her arm muscles too weak to lift the spoon for long. Trembling with every movement, she whimpered between mouthfuls, vowing to leave as soon as the sun set. Not another minute would she stay here.

She grabbed the stale bread, stuffing it inside her tunic where Gnash chirped. "Thank you for your kindness, Mistress Belen."

The only reason those hated words slipped out was to lure Belen into believing all was well. If Thugari didn't thank the female, she would be cleaning attics and scrubbing the guardhouse until the wee hours of the morning.

While wiping her wrist across her mouth, Thugari squared her shoulders. Decision made. She rinsed her rough-hewn bowl in the wash bucket and shook off the droplets. It would take moments to pack. Six years of planning had gone into this escape, since Uzul had first used the brand on her neck. The sweet taste of freedom coated her tongue. She sucked in a deep breath, ignoring her twinging back.

Each jarring step as she climbed the stairs lanced fire across her back. Every pulse of agony reinforced her decision to leave. As she pushed open her door, the creak announcing her arrival, the shadow of a male spilled across her floor. Stilling, she studied her father's rigid posture and his hands clasped behind him. Not that she could recall when he last visited her.

"My chief." She removed her bowl and bread, placing them on the makeshift shelf formed by missing stones in the walls.

Gnash scampered after the bread, and she gripped the ledge for him. As he nibbled on the chunk clasped in his paws, she kept her breathing even.

Her father had no reason to be there, unless he believed she had stolen her dear sister's locket and planned to punish her further.

He studied her, running his matching silver-gray gaze over her before resting on her face. His presence dominated her room. His tribal markings swirled across his bare chest, crisscrossed with leather straps. His hair, black like her own, fell down his back, braided with ribbons and beads. Bones of sentimental value peppered his adornments, and soft fur from far-off lands protected his skin from the leather belt holding up his billowing calve-length pants.

She didn't have any markings, not deserving such clanship. Nor did she have anything to spare her skin. She was an outsider, neither wanted nor valued. The distance between them was insurmountable and would remain so, no matter how much she wished otherwise.

"You look so much like your mother." His shoulders drooped into a slouch before he stiffened.

Doubtful—she had his nose. Her mother had been beautiful, before the sickness drained life's effervescence from her. Thugari remained silent, choosing not to doom herself. He was there for a reason, and guessing wrong might lead to punishment.

"Uzul told me about your...*chastisement*." He curled his lips in disgust, parting them around his tusks, and she couldn't say which irritated him more—finding out, or that she had suffered.

She suspected it was the former. For appearances, he acted the doting father. She smothered a snort. Appearances? His people had expected him to toss the runt out into the cold to die, and all knew of her mistreatment. Doting implied silks, jewels, and other expensive gifts. Curse it, she would settle for warmth, food, and Moon forbid, a little kindness.

"Should I send for the healer?" He hesitated, as if the expense, the inconvenience of it was too much.

Yet he had offered, which almost unraveled the stitched scar across her heart. A sharp pain traveled from her belly to her chest and throbbed there. The slop threatened to continue the journey up her throat. She swallowed, taking a moment to crush her hope. He didn't care, had never bothered with her before. There was no way in the netherworld she would accept help from him now. That time had passed.

"Thank you, my chief, for your *kind* offer. I am well."

"A neighboring son has shown interest in...mating you."

She froze. No, she wouldn't be chattel—bartered to strengthen his position.

He took her silence as acquiescence. "I would need to offer you clanship."

Her breath caught, and tears stung her eyes. The one thing she wanted and he offered it in lieu of her body? Pinching her lips, she fought for control, wanting to rail at him, to pummel his marked chest with her fists.

"I am a slave." She gritted her teeth as she gathered her courage. "Clanship is not required."

She met his gaze. It was disrespectful of her, but she wanted him to remember her, to wonder why she challenged him now. His jaw tightened, and a pulse ticked at its base.

When his nostrils flared, she didn't look away. This farewell might garner another bruise, a broken nose, loose teeth, but she stood firm.

Goodbye, father.

Despite the clenching of his fist, he didn't strike her but strode toward the door. There he hesitated, his grip on the doorframe splintering the ancient wood. "Instruct Belen to summon the healer if and when needed." Then he was gone. His thumping steps echoed up the stairwell.

Thugari sat on the edge of the bed, dazed by his kindness in offering a healer *twice* in one day. Fear skittered along her spine. But she wouldn't serve him, not for clanship or to bring honor to Nehrakgu. She threw a few more belongings into her hemp carry-all. Nothing scared her more than a change in the status quo. She didn't expect more from him, but hope shredded her stern admonishments and pain-filled memories. Perhaps if she stayed, he might love her? If she served him well to whoever he had sold her to? She shook her head.

Swiping away her tears, she undressed then yanked on her best pants, her cleanest tunic, and her stolen coat—thick enough to ward off the chill and hide her curves. She swept her oversized woolen cap off a hook, taking time to cover her ears and braided hair. With her worn boots pinching her feet, she grabbed her carry-all, tucked Gnash and the bread inside her tunic.

At each step down the stairs, she hesitated, listening for Belen, her heart thrumming in her ears. As Thugari passed the busy kitchen maids, she snatched a knife on the way to the medicinal garden.

Dusk was on the horizon, its stark shadows aiding her. She couldn't steal a horse. They would hunt her if she did. It was best to escape on foot. Sliding the knife into her boot, she kept her gaze on the gate guards, their axes resting at their hips. She lengthened her strides as Uzul approached them. As soon as the ether spellbinder walked through on his way to Bire, the guards would break for dinner, leaving the gates clear.

When his robed figure disappeared and the guards scampered into the hall, she slipped out of the shadows. The three horsemen riding into the inner courtyard froze her, leaving her visible to them. She gaped, drawn to the male on a black steed. His bearing was regal yet lethal. Those broad shoulders, the last rays glinting off his sword, his hood enshrouding his face mesmerized her.

She couldn't dart for cover. Any sudden movement would gain his attention. Instead, she ducked her head and gathered the reins of their horses, intending to lead them to the stables. No one noticed servants.

She peeked at the strangers. Two orcs and a foreigner in black cloaks denoting their affiliation to the Council. Rumors of an impending lawbringer visit hadn't reached the kitchen. They had to be passing through Haraton Castle. She scowled. Why did they have to choose this night?

Fully clothed orcs were a rare occurrence. Black polished boots, soft leather breeches, well-crafted saddles on magnificent war steeds spoke of wealth. This meant heavy purses. Until she reached a village where no one would recognize her, every coin would aid her. Only then could she sell her stolen treasure.

One of the strangers was a female orc, a magus in rich, deep purple. She was breathtaking. Thugari had never seen anyone quite so exquisite. She lowered her gaze and hefted her carry-all, wincing as it rubbed across her wounds. A hiss escaped her before she could smother it.

"Boy."

A deep voice thrummed through her, sparking a reaction along her skin and a whimper past her clenched lips. Gnash squeaked, and she stroked him through her tunic. She didn't want him leaping out and spooking the horses. Between her aching muscles and the new scabs on her back, she didn't appreciate the frisson of fear. Or was that a shiver of excitement? There was a dark element to the male's voice—authoritative and commanding.

"I'm speaking to you, boy."

"Yes, lawbringer?" She chuffed, deepening her voice, trying not to gape at the black-encased chest missing beads and hiding tribal markings. Nothing peeked above his collar. He must have sacrificed much to belong to the lawbringers.

"A coin for your trouble." He grabbed her wrist, dragging a yelp from her as pain shot up her arm.

She didn't raise her gaze to his, no matter how his touch burned her through his leather gloves. As he placed a coin on her palm, she unraveled his purse with her other hand, tucking it inside her coat. Even in that brief moment, she tested the hefty weight of it.

"Thank you, lawbringer." She shifted away and regathered the reins.

Keeping her head dipped, she smirked as she led the horses away. Relief warred with curiosity. She would love to sneak a glimpse of his face, to see whether he matched the smooth timbre of his voice.

Some things were best left alone, and she hurried to the stables, whispering a human poem to the horses when they whinnied in greeting. Time was running out for her. She couldn't afford to see the horses cared for other than securing them in empty stalls and slipping feed bags over their heads. A quick rummage through the saddles left her with a half-full wineskin, a satchel of food, a few silver coins, and a black medallion that pulsed a greeting.

She debated taking the sword, but in the end, decided to leave it behind before a stablehand stumbled upon her. As beautiful as the piece was, she couldn't wield it, and it was cumbersome to carry.

With one last glance behind her and the coarse wood of the southern gates under her palm, she slipped out of the castle. A skip-jog blended her into a stream of departing wagons heading for Bire. She broke off and wove between the wooden huts, cutting across the farmed land to the forest's tree line.

Running her fingers over the bark, from tree to tree, she searched for the etchings she had made on one of her many mushroom hunts. Although, she didn't go too far into the forest, not when it took hours to reach the center. If she stayed away for longer than two hours, Belen sent a warrior to find her. Hunting mushrooms meant her other chores weren't done.

The moonlight filtered through the canopy, drenching her in silver. She tilted her face to the sky. Since she was a girl, the night empowered her, imbued her body with energy, and filled her soul to bursting capacity. This night, with its sounds forming music too breathtaking for words and a sweetness to the air, she reveled in the swell of emotion engulfing her. The urge to strip gripped her, to dance naked beneath its silvery glow.

She broke the daze with a shake of her head, the sense of loss squeezing her gut. Using her fingers to find the etchings, she navigated the forest, making inane observations to a twittering Gnash. No one screamed her name or demanded she attend to her chores. No more smacks, beatings, or reprimands awaited her.

Yet as she meandered through the shadows, each sound reverberated through her, sparking her imagination. Wind rustling the leaves made her jump, sharp noises disrupting the whispers of the forest made her dive for cover, squashing poor Gnash, as well. She landed on her back, slammed her shoulders into trunks, tripped over unseen roots, and low-hanging branches snagged her cap.

As hot darts of agony and weakness assailed her, her steps faltered, and clambering to her feet became harder. On a sob, she accepted her harsh breathing and dripping sweat as demands to rest. She mumbled promises each time she trudged onward until she stumbled upon an alcove within a copse of trees.

Lying on her side, she curled into the protection of the roots and rested her head on her carry-all. The chill of the thick leaf bed didn't penetrate her jacket, but its dew soaked her pants. She didn't care. It was softer than her hay mattress, made more blissful now she was free.

With the comfort of Gnash's presence and exhaustion trembling her limbs, sleep tempted her. A few hours, she vowed. Then her bid for freedom would continue. She wasn't a slave, nor a servant. She was the illegitimate daughter of a chief, but if anyone captured her, none of that would matter.

Chapter Four

Rukk flexed his fingers, testing out the tingling numbing when all he had done was touch the boy's hand. He stared after the lad disappearing into the stables, which were larger than he remembered. A few more buildings had been added, cluttering the outer keep, proving the Clan Nehrakgu flourished. His lawbringer instincts leaped into a frenzy, and in the dusk casting its shadows across the yard, he couldn't smell magic's vigor.

He inhaled slowly, picking up an impending storm, fresh bread, and sweat. What was strange was the lavender and traces of mint trailing the boy. Judging by his hiss, Rukk would say his ribs, shoulders, or back were wounded.

He frowned, not liking that the boy suffered. As a lawbringer, he encountered many despicable acts, some tolerable, but the abuse of a child was never acceptable.

"What is it?" Sharn halted alongside him as she peered into the darkness.

Her curiosity, though appearing innocent, was far from it. During the five days it took to travel south from Penven to Haraton, she had been nothing but accommodating. He didn't trust it...her.

"Keep your ears open for any whisperings. I do not plan to stay long." Not with his instincts in turmoil.

Throwing his satchel over one shoulder, he peeled off his gloves, a finger at a time, before tucking them inside his cloak. After a final glance at the stables, he entered through the large wooden door, held open by an elderly human servant. Lamplight from behind him shadowed his face, but the light haloing his crooked form was incentive enough to enter.

"Greetings, my lady and lords. Lady Murzush and Chief Varthug welcome you to Haraton Castle. A servant shall attend to your mounts." In the flickering light, the old male's skin glowed like parchment.

"A stableboy has done so." Rukk's strides and bulk pushed the male aside. "Taking our satchels to suitable rooms would be acceptable."

"You would not prefer to freshen thyself before evening meal?" The poor male bowed with his bones cracking. Forcing a servant to work at such an advanced age reinforced Rukk's suspicions of mistreatment.

"I would," Sharn said.

Rukk scowled, not appreciating this delay. "*Tarid, go with her. See she doesn't pry,*" he said to across their bond.

Tarid nodded, slipping Rukk's satchel off his shoulder. They trailed a younger manservant, leaving Rukk with the elder.

"This way, my lord lawbringer."

Rukk strode along the short passage, the bustle and joviality of the hall ahead. Lamplight and candles illuminated a vast room with pristine stone floors and elaborate tapestries hanging on the walls. To the rear, a roaring bonfire added warmth to the room.

On a dais sat the chief and his wife, adorned in furs, intricate beadwork, and glowing tribal markings. Lady Murzush was more delicate than the average orc female, which hinted at a human or elf in her lineage. Despite the elegance of the décor and their attire, he couldn't align it to the threadbare garments on the stableboy and elderly male servant. It was the mark of a chief how he treated his lowest underlings.

The pain the boy was in still rankled. This underlying tension tightened Rukk's voice when he said, "Chief Varthug, this is not a casual visit." Not that Rukk allowed relaxed relationships with the common folk. "The Council dislikes rumors of stolen bairns."

"Clan Nehrakgu welcomes you, lawbringer Knaraugh. Your reputation precedes you, more so since your last visit. We will assist the Council, of course. Let it not be said we disrespected your authority." The male's voice reached to the edges of the hall to where his warriors ate their evening fare, which explained the lack of guards at the inner yard's gates. Some might view that as kindness in the cooling temperatures, but Rukk saw it as a lax control and an inability to lead.

"A meal in your library will do." He schooled his disgust into a firm frown. "I will interview those who lost their bairns." He scanned the hall and the various doors, implying he doubted Haraton had a library.

"I will see you to the library, my lord." A soft-spoken female orc hovered by the stairs to the side of the hall, coming forward with a practiced grace he distrusted.

It wasn't natural. He knew who she was, recalling her from years past when she was but a child. Embroidered leather clung to her hip, matching her guda, and uniform beads draped between her breasts. Nehrakgu tribal markings swirled across her bare stomach and upper arms, stating her clanship and position—Varthug's daughter.

Rukk clenched his jaw and gave her a curt nod, slapping imaginary dust off his thigh. The action kept his gaze off her and minimized what she might misconstrue as admiration or encouragement. The fluttering eyelashes she batted at him confirmed her intent, as if he would consider rutting with such an innocent. Gone were the days when a female might challenge him for a place in his bed. Only in his homeland.

His happier memories were few and hesitant to rise from the depth of sadness still coating thoughts of Ghorza. Tall trees older than time towered above the houses and palaces coerced from the roots.

Elven influence lay in the reverence shown to nature, in the beauty of the white blossoms clinging to the dark wood, against a backdrop of trickling waterfalls and streams.

Laughter had filled his waking moments, with the love in his heart balanced between his father and mother. Pale skin framed her gray eyes, and in moments like now, he caught the exact shape of her smile.

He missed her, his mother. A pang of homesickness struck, and he commanded the ill-placed emotion to fade. Home included his mother, no longer in this world. He wouldn't miss his father, think of him, or grant him another moment of his time. Not unless the netherworld froze over.

The cloying scent of flowers assaulted his nostrils as Lady Arob led him out of the hall and along a narrow, stone passage. The chill of it warred with the teasing pools of light from the lanterns.

She entered a small room lined with books and scrolls, and a solitary flame illuminated one wall. A window sat high up, a black eye filled with the night's sky.

"I'll need more light." He slapped a shelf with his gloves as if he dusted.

"Yes, my lord." She hesitated, curling a demure smile around her tusks.

With an unflinching stare, he molded his features into an expression expectant of immediate obedience. He needed her to leave, to see to his demands, to free him from her cloying scent. "Food, light, and witnesses. See to it."

She jerked back, slow to realize his dismissal. He doubted she experienced it often. He would ensure she did so during his stay. She shut the door louder than needed, but he was grateful for the solitude. Alone, at last, he ran a finger along a shelf and found it clean despite his earlier display.

Arching a brow in surprise, he scanned the decent selection of books containing history and folklore. A few showed more use, and he withdrew one on herbal applications. It fell open to a sheet of parchment, torn along the edges. On it in scratchy penmanship was a list of herbs for pain and wounds with lavender, rosemary, and mint underlined. Whoever this person was, they weren't tutored.

Lavender? His thoughts fell on the stableboy again. Wounded, reeking of lavender, suggested he had been here, desperate for help. Anyone else using the library would have better penmanship. Rukk scowled. Something bothered him. A missing piece eluded him.

A few other books held similar notations, building a story that rang with truth deep within him. As he sat on the thick-brocaded chair, he couldn't help wondering if the boy had used the chair and rested his elbows on the dark-wood desk. The cleaning of the library must have been the boy's task, and in the process, he had studied. Rukk admired that in anyone. An eagerness to learn was a rare quality.

While he waited for his meal, he scanned the book holding prominence on the desk and kept near at hand. Scratchings were on page after page of instructions on the use of weapons, how best to wield a dagger. The boy had been scared. Underlined twice were the words "get a knife." Imagining the lad clenching his jaw with determination, he chuckled.

At the knock, he shut the book with a snap. A human maid carried in an overladen tray. The aromas of rich elk stew, savory bread, and a jug of mead filled the room. As she placed it onto the desk, a male servant brought in lanterns and lit them. Perfect.

"Chief Varthug has instructed the witnesses to attend to you in a few minutes. Would that suit, my lord?" The male didn't insult him by meeting his gaze.

Rukk grunted his satisfaction, and they left, closing the door with a softer touch than Varthug's daughter had used.

Rukk ate, enjoying the thick flavor of the stew and the soft meat, as he entertained himself with the stableboy's notes. Tomorrow, he would show him a few lawbringer stances and techniques. Perhaps then, he would appease his curiosity and end this niggling fascination. Another knock assaulted his peace, and as the human maid removed his tray leaving the jug of honeyed mead, a weeping human female hovered in the doorway.

Drawing in a deep breath, he gestured for her to enter.

Chapter Five

Soft footfalls woke Thugari, along with a rustle of bushes, and the dragging of something across leaves and dirt. She lay still, choosing her hearing above eyesight as she soothed an agitated Gnash. If they were too near, sitting up might alarm them. There was no nicker of horses, only murmured voices. The softer tones of females gave her courage.

Decision made, she peered over the roots at a gaggle of heavily garbed orcs, humans, and elves meandering through the dawn-lit forest. The last female wore many layers of cloth and dragged a basket-covered travois.

Thugari stretched upward to see better, hoping to catch a glimpse of their burden. Gnash peeked out as well, his twitching nose tickling her chin. Six females out at this time of the morning and not mushroom hunting spelled trouble. A beige arm waved, the gurgle of a bairn confirming her eyes didn't deceive her. A gasp slipped out. She ducked, slapped her hand over her mouth, digging her tusks into her palm.

Their voices faded, and silence descended. As slow as possible, Thugari crept deeper under the protection of the trees, praying they shielded her once again. She tore off a chunk of bread and fed it to Gnash, hoping he didn't chirp or twitter.

Someone curled their fingers over the edge of the root—dirt embedded in the ragged nails with dark-red stains on the tips. Green smoke swirled around them, seeping from the bark into the skin. Thugari bit her lip, not willing to blink. She had never seen magic before, nor that it could be siphoned from a tree into the wielder.

"See anything?" a female whispered.

"No," another female said. "I was hoping it was a briar rabbit. We could do with a decent pot."

The voices dwindled as they debated the best methods to skin a rabbit while Thugari inhaled shallow and hushed breaths. She lay there long after they had gone. The sunlight kissed the top of the roots before she chanced to move. Gnash had escaped a while ago, scampering around, his nose twitching as he sniffed the forest air.

After scrambling out, she hesitated, nibbling on her bottom lip. Those females had stolen bairns. Their garments weren't familiar to her. Layers upon layers of crude and unfinished cloth covered their beads and tribal markings. For humans and elves, garments were the norm, but for an orc, it was disrespectful of one's clan. Hence why Frukag ensured all the servants and slaves wore clothes of some sort. The dirt-stained fingers didn't concern her, but the scars she had seen carved into the females' cheeks were unusual.

Distant yelling pushed her to decide. She could chase her freedom or abandon it out of curiosity. Even if she trailed the females, she couldn't rescue the children. And if by some miracle she snuck the bairns away, there was nowhere she could take them. A large portion of her soul pleaded with her to follow them, but the part of her that had survived so much leaned toward preservation.

The deciding factor was the direction the females had taken, north toward Chaosthane. It would do her no harm if she gathered information to pass on in the next village. That way, she would appease her soul and keep her freedom.

Crawling from the resting place, she leaped to her feet and stretched her aching body. Grabbing her carry-all, she shoved Gnash inside her tunic and barreled along the pathway, tracking the scratch marks the travois made in the forest bed.

It couldn't be the castle guards yelling. After all, she wasn't wanted nor liked. No one would miss her, and perhaps Belen would assume Thugari had gone mushroom hunting. She grinned at the image of her tormentor's bulging eyes when she realized the truth. Delicious warmth claimed Thugari's chest, filling her limbs with renewed energy and added a joyful bounce to her step.

Hours passed without another yell reaching her, but she didn't stop to rest, choosing to place a foot in front of the other, even eating from the food pouch she had stolen. The lawbringer's wineskin held the finest mead she had ever tasted, sweet and tart, but she watered it down at the first stream, hoping to prolong the flavor.

Often, she shifted Gnash from shoulder to arm, and he leaped off onto a nearby branch but found her a few steps later. If she needed to relieve herself, she did so in a swift manner, within the cover of thick bushes.

After each stream she stumbled upon, she hunted for the travois' ground scourings, torn between delight and trepidation when the tracks continued north. It was nearing mid-day when feminine voices broke the soothing cacophony of the forest. They stopped for a meal, their chatter animated as if the possibility of discovery hadn't occurred to them.

Forced to rest and grateful for it, Thugari clambered up a well-branched tree, preferring to hide where she could observe them. Her legs burned from the pace they had set, but her back didn't throb, nor was it sensitive.

Gnash scampered along the branches, testing out the bark with his paws before scurrying to her. She fed him something from the pouch, and he twittered and purred. His happiness blossomed an answering joy within her. She smiled as she scratched his back.

The bairns were quiet except for an occasional gurgle. Only magic could have kept them like this for long. In the presence of such power, she studied the females, assessing their mannerisms. They didn't have the look of the Council whose ranks had colors. According to the book in the library, the Arch-Magus wore deep red, purple for magi, rich blue for spellbinders, and dark green for novitiates.

Alongside them, the lawbringers wore black, from page, knight, lawbringer to Grand Lawmaster. The females she trailed held no such vibrant coloring. They had to be wylders. Rejected novitiates rebelling against the Council were always females. Most left the Council due to the celibacy clause. Some didn't agree with their practices or that only males could become lawbringers. Thugari didn't care either way. It was petty. Hunger would drive them to realize survival was more important.

Two females broke away from the group, walking in the direction of the stream. They held hands, swinging their arms as if they strolled through a golden meadow with yellow daylily flowers dotting the landscape. Along the way, they snuck kisses, sampling each other's lips as if stealing bairns didn't jeopardize their way of life.

There was that. No rutting, but especially with the same sex. The Council was adamant magi adhere to this commandment, which would explain why these two lovebirds were wylders. Rumor had it, the Grand Lawmaster didn't give a boar's ass about who rutted with whom, hence no wylder lawbringers. How the Arch-Magus and Grand Lawmaster ruled the Council together without an outright war was beyond Thugari's understanding.

Resting against the trunk, she tilted her head back until she stared at the blue sky. Gnash curled on her lap, napping in the afternoon sunlight. She prayed the wylders didn't tarry their mid-day meal.

By now, she should've reached a village, bartered for or stolen a horse, and galloped her way to Chaosthane. Instead, to appease her conscience, she followed addled wylders with a travois full of stolen bairns.

After choosing a Gnash-nibbled strip of dried meat from the food pouch, she sucked on it, hoping to soften it first. Listening with half an ear to the females, her mind circled to the bairns who weren't attended to, nor fed, or coddled. That didn't bode well for them. She hadn't heard much about wylders since most tended to steer clear of villages. Yet no rumors said they mistreated children.

They practiced untrained and lawbreaking magic, hiding from lawbringers tasked to hunt them. Despite this, they didn't harm people, nor steal their livestock. Villagers didn't chase them away with flaming torches and sharpened pitchforks.

Yet there sat these females, testing the stability of their community standing. Once a farmer or merchant heard of their bairn-thievery, the news would spread faster than the pox. All wylders would be subject to the same distrust and hatred, but none of that explained why these had stolen the bairns.

The females gathered to continue their journey, taking turns to drag the travois. Thugari grumbled to herself when they continued north. She was done with this nonsense to appease her restless soul. If they had headed into another direction, she would've breathed a sigh of relief. Once or twice, a wylder peered down the path, forcing Thugari to dive out of sight. They never saw her, resuming their carefree chatter. What these females found to talk about, she couldn't say. It seemed endless and pointless. Then again, no one spoke to Thugari unless to command or berate her. Wasting anyone's time with inane chatter led to a swift and painful reprimand.

So she kept quiet. It was different now when she had the choice to speak, and yet, she found she had nothing to say, even to herself or to her constant companion, Gnash. Her limited musings on the forest had long since dwindled.

The wylders stopped to rest not an hour after the mid-day meal. Thugari clambered up another tree, irritated by their dillydallying. She needed to be away from here and out of this forest before nightfall.

From this vantage point, she couldn't see them too well, so she climbed around the tree, using their voices to gauge their location.

"From here, we turn east past the village of Newhal," a female said.

She was older than the others, with an air of authority around her. Surviving all these years as a wylder meant her skill in avoiding the lawbringers was worthy. East was good news for Thugari, as was the mention of a village. She could purchase a horse there and head north.

The silence of the bairns still worried her. When the same pale arm waved, followed by a familiar gurgle, she counted the seconds until the next wave. They must have cast a time spell on the bairns. Oh, she hoped so. It meant they didn't suffer. Forty-two seconds between exact gestures.

She studied the females again. They weren't untrained. These novitiates were formidable. To cast such a spell over the basket had to require immense power, something she doubted Uzul could perform. As a magicless person, she longed for special abilities. She would have liked fire to leap from her fingertips and burn off Belen's eyebrows.

Smothering a giggle, Thugari entertained herself with the images her mind conjured as she fed Gnash strips of dried meat. Fighting Belen would've earned her more scars, though.

But it would've been worth it.

CHAPTER SIX

SCREAMING WOKE RUKK FROM his plagued sleep. Having succumbed at dawn, he didn't appreciate the ruckus that woke him sooner than he would have liked. Kicking his feet over the side of the too-soft bed, he padded nude to the window, peering at the yard below. Warriors and maids scurried about, their panicked expressions clear in the crisp morning light.

With a wince, he splashed water on his face and used the piss pot before donning fresh garments. The castle's servants would attend to his travel-worn clothing he draped across his bed. Running his hand over his satchel, he placed a spell, one too intricate to unravel with ease. The white tendrils were evidence his post-rutting magic had strengthened and restored his power pool to about a third full.

Striding to the hall, he burst in on a mountain of a female, her voice rattling the rafters. "Cease."

To drown her hollers, he didn't raise his voice but infused it with enough compulsion to silence the hall. It was Zetar's blessing to hear himself breathe. He took a moment to massage his temple, hoping to slow the impending headache.

"What is the problem?" He lowered his hand to meet the female's narrowed eyes.

"Varthugari is missing," she said, as if he knew who that was. He arched a pointed brow. "The chief's bastard daughter."

Varthugari? Rukk grimaced. I Immediate pity for the poor girl calmed his irritation. "An organized search wouldn't suffice?" His castigation was clear in his tone and the expression he leveled on the female, whose beads draped between an impressive cleavage.

"The captain of the guard is doing so." She huffed, her bosom rising and falling as if yelling exhausted her.

"Your hollering like a heifer accomplished what?" He held up a hand when she opened her mouth to speak. Her face mottled red. "I can remove your tongue, female. Do not test me." He perched on a nearby bench. "You." He chose a maid who squeaked and jerked to a halt. "Wake your lord and mistress. You?" He pointed to another maid he recognized from last night. "Bring me something to break my fast. Now, when last did you see Varthugari?" He gestured to the heifer she may now speak.

"I am Belen, the cook." She folded her thick arms across the guda covering her breasts and contorted her tribal markings. "Thugari attended to her evening chores but wasn't seen afterward. That is not unusual. In the evenings, she keeps to her tower for the most part."

Thugari? Better. "Take me to her tower."

Belen hesitated but obeyed, leading him into the bowels of the castle, through the kitchen, and into a disused guard room. She pointed up the crumbling steps. "She sleeps up there."

"The chief's daughter?" He disbelieved a chief would treat the blood-of-his-blood like this, bastard or not. Yet after the stableboy and assessing his servants, Rukk could believe this of Varthug.

As Rukk climbed the steps, he took care where he placed his feet. The thin door was ajar, which meant she had left it as such or someone had during the search. He grimaced at the makeshift bed, the lumpy straw mattress, and the bloodied, threadbare garments strewn about. She was a slave? Or had less than clan status to wear tunics. What had his heart palpitating was the fragrance of mint and lavender. He stilled, realizing who the stableboy was.

As he replayed memories of their meeting, no peace soothed his errant thoughts. More questions rose to plague him. Calming his breathing, closing his eyes, and focusing on his heartbeat until it slowed to a thump every five seconds, he summoned his magic—a finite pool of molten heat deep within him. After whispering the spell that took a quarter of his energy, he opened his eyes to the last moments the room had witnessed.

Pale-white magic bathed it with images forming out of the ether. A tense interaction played out between father and daughter, the dying hope on her face thrummed the tendrils with intense emotion. Alone, she stripped, revealing she was more female than girl. Not that the magic was clear on the exact curve of her breast. It hinted, shifting into the next movement before his gaze could fix on her nudity. In the tendrils, the stableboy materialized, her woolen cap hiding her orcish ears. He stroked the tips of his ears at the sight of hers, shivering at his touch. His paler skin denoted his mixed heritage, hers was of a darker hue. The magic pulsed, and her face formed, soft, alluring with silver-gray eyes sparking something deep inside him.

"What are you doing?" the chief asked from the doorway.

His black hair swayed and curled, unbound and beadless. Dark circles under his gray eyes spoke of over-imbibing into the wee hours. He scowled when his gaze locked onto the white tendrils in the shape of his daughter. Despite the matching eye color, the similarity was minimal, perhaps in the nose?

"Your daughter has left the castle for good." Rukk picked up a stained tunic. The blood at the collar and across the back were fresh. "It seems I'm to investigate more than the crimes against the Council." He threw it at the male, hitting him on his bare chest, jarring his beads draped around his neck. "My reputation precedes me, you said. Then what is my viewpoint on the abuse of one's authority or people?"

A surge of anger gritted his teeth, and having to listen to insincere excuses was beyond his patience. With a flick of a finger, he whispered, '*taceer*,' uncaring that the Grand Lawmaster would rain expletives upon him. The command silenced the chief. The spell wouldn't last for long, but at least the male would experience having no voice.

She had run away out of desperation, her hopeful gaze searching for an ounce of compassion or love from her father. Rukk strode past a spluttering lord, darting down the stairs to find his meal waiting. He took a long draw from the tankard. While swilling the bitter-sweet liquid, he grabbed the bread and stuffed the herb-infused cheese inside. After draining the tankard, he rose and bit into the bread, chewing as he returned to his chambers.

He wanted to find her, why he didn't know yet. It wasn't in his nature to be impulsive nor did he ignore his instincts. They clamored for attention, demanding he track her. A sense of closure lay in her whereabouts, as if finding her meant solving the missing bairns. He doubted the solution would be so swift. Appeasing his restlessness would take him a few hours in the saddle, a small discomfort should his search prove fruitful.

"Do I want to know?" Tarid leaned against the door frame.

"Did you sleep through that ruckus?" Rukk asked through a mouthful of cheese.

"I sleep through anything but Sharn's snoring." Tarid stared along the passage, intensity swirling in his eyes.

Sharn shoved past him, sashaying into Rukk's room. "I do not snore, and there was a cursed stone wall between us." "When you said a short stay, I have to admit, I didn't think it would be less than a day."

She fondled her magus pendant. It was a beautiful piece interwoven with powerful runes, magic-infused crystals, and enchantments to shield her from a physical attack. As scholars, magi weren't trained to battle, only to heal or defend themselves.

Rukk touched his chest where his lawbringer medallion rested and frowned at finding it missing. He had stashed it into his saddle after leaving Penven.

To hide his magical fingerprints, he had it enchanted so no one could scry him. He would slip it on when he mounted Harpax. Its embedded healing would ease his exhaustion and help restore his energy.

"Stay, carry on with the investigation, follow up on each of these witnesses." Rukk gestured to the list of names beside his bed. "I'm trusting my instincts, and they tell me the stableboy is the key." He faltered, wondering why he kept her identity secret. She hadn't wanted them to know, but that didn't mean he had to aid in her deceit.

"Stable boy?" Tarid arched a brow, and with a rigid posture, he stepped into the room.

Without breaching their mental connection, Rukk suspected Tarid didn't want to stand too near to Sharn. Rukk smothered a smile, expecting a harsh reaction from Tarid when he realized he would be alone with Sharn for a while.

"From last evening." Rukk dangled his cloak from one finger while searching for his coin purse. Scowling when the familiar weight wasn't present, he lifted his satchel onto the bed and rummaged through it, then flicked his spare purse onto his pillow. "Tarid, did you play Fruqa again?"

Tarid frowned. "I was too exhausted to give it a go."

Rukk held out his hand. "But you still have my coin, so hand it over."

But when Tarid shook his head, Rukk replayed when he had last registered the weight of his purse. His jaw clenched with his nostrils flaring. Anger streaked through him like a comet's tail. Disbelief coiled within him at her daring to steal from him. A faint trace of amusement tainted the edges of his memories. He admired her audacity, not her stupidity.

He lowered his hand to hold her imaginary one, his fingers tingling anew as he placed the coin into her palm, now remembering the soft flutter at his waist as she untied the purse. It must have been her thievery that triggered his heightened senses and plagued him since his arrival.

"You're leaving without us." Sharn's tone was matter-of-fact, but she cast a distasteful glance at Tarid.

The distaste's mutual, spy. Rukk nodded. "I must find him before the guards do."

"Why are you involving yourself?" Tarid asked. *"What are you not telling me?"* His concern touched Rukk's mind.

"As I said, I *need* to find him." *"If I'm not back in three days, return to Penven." "Tell the Grand Lawmaster I have the details." "Ask your brother to investigate from his side. He is next in line as Lawmaster and must have heard something."*

Tarid snorted. *"You know how stubborn Janar is. He might not want to help."*

"Sweet-talk him." Rukk grinned.

"But do you?" A skeptical expression twisted Sharn's delicate features.

"I will." The confusion he generated delighted Rukk, and he smothered a chuckle. Impulsive reactions were not the norm for him, but he had to admit, it was entertaining.

"So not yet." Tarid scowled.

"Trust me, Tarid."

Part of him understood his lawbrother's reticence. There were too many unknowns. He need not chase Thugari, yet Rukk could not explain that everything within him demanded he do so. An abused female trapped in the castle would know nothing about the missing bairns, but by the way his instincts danced, she had to know something crucial.

Sliding on his cloak, he swung his satchel over his shoulder, leaving yesterday's garments for the servants. He clipped his spare purse on his belt and glanced at Sharn. "So far, the disappearances coincide with fires, and I need you to travel to each burned house. Their positions will point us to the next target, and in the direction these thieves travel."

"You can't think it's koveen..." Tarid gaped, running a palm over his face. "It makes sense. The missing bairns were stolen in silence. The fires hid their tracks..." He grimaced. "I hate snakes, even if they're topped with full-breasted orc females. It's the hissing that gets to me, y'know, or maybe it's their forked tongues."

"I hope you prove me wrong. Finding the bairns not drained of their blood will please the Grand Lawmaster." He rested his hand on Tarid's shoulder in farewell. "If Tarid kills you, Sharn, I will claim it was an accident."

Her face paled to a death-mask of gray, but she nodded, her lips white. Tarid chuckled and nudged his head at the door.

Rukk left his chambers, darting down the steps, across the hall, and out to the stables. He waited for the stablehands to saddle Harpax, glowering at them to hurry. Holding up his palm, he instructed the servant to halt, then with care, Rukk assessed every inch of his horse, noting his ebony coat gleaming from a thorough brushing, the energy rippling his thighs, and the eagerness in his stamping foot.

Tying the satchel to the saddle, Rukk vaulted into it, patting Harpax's neck in greeting. Grabbing the reins with one hand, he guided his mount around then cantered out of the inner yard and through the village of Bire.

With it behind him, he urged Harpax to a stop and dug in his saddlebags for his medallion. Soon Rukk was cursing, and he dismounted to do a more thorough search.

It was gone.

Vaulting into the saddle, he scowled, disbelieving one of the chief's servants had stolen it. He grinned despite his moments-ago fury. Only one person could've taken it—the same female he now chased. Finding her would resolve so many issues, most she had caused.

Shaking his head, he whispered a scrying spell and laughed when a spinning ball of white hovered for a minute before fizzling out. Its inability to shoot off in any direction confirmed she had taken his medallion.

Finding her had become more difficult, and he now had to rely on archaic tracking techniques. He studied the forest to the east of the King's Way, curving north for miles. To the west was another forest, the trees less dense, and perhaps more navigable for a female on foot. He turned Harpax west.

The sun baked down on his head, beads of sweat dewed his forehead, and he had yet to find a trace of her. Cantering along the forest's edge, he searched for her entry point: a soft footprint, broken branches or twigs, disturbed leaves on the forest floor. Nothing. She might have found a wagon and traveled farther than he had anticipated. She might have veered off the King's Way or not at all. There was no evidence to guide him, no trace of her parting.

At mid-day, he had to admit he had chosen the wrong direction. Thumping his fist on his thigh, he spewed curses. He dismounted to rest in the shade of a malaena tree. Its weeping branches shielded him even as they fanned his sweat-drenched body

He grimaced, hating his garments sticking to him. After whispering *'ma'ratar,'* his relief was instant, his temperature dropping to normal. He was off his game today, and he blamed a silver-eyed lass.

Back on Harpax, he wove between the houses and across the King's Way, skirting the edges of the eastern forest. Within minutes, he found her scratchings even though the initials were that of her father.

Rukk hurried from marker to marker, a triumphant joy claiming his chest forcing him to bark out a laugh. She made this too easy for him. He was a little disappointed, but having spent longer than planned in the saddle, he was ready to have done with this.

Traces of her meanderings through the forest floor drove him to dismount. He tracked her footsteps to where she had curled up to rest. Pain scented the air, and he scowled, not liking she suffered nor that he had missed the clues where she injured herself. Around the copse of trees, six separate sets of footprints, along with the strange scourings crossed her path. She trailed after the tracks heading north. More females if he judged by their foot sizes, one dragging a travois.

He gathered Harpax's reins and inched onward, placing his feet with care as he studied the clues their passing left for him. At least he was on the right track. He vaulted into the saddle, and set his horse into a canter, not wanting to break a leg, but the path was wide and well-used.

Their chatter pierced the peaceful silence of the forest before he saw them: six wylders with a basketful of bairns.

But no Thugari.

Chapter Seven

Hoofbeats approached from the castle's direction, but no one panicked. High up, Thugari shared their nonchalance. They had set up camp alongside the path and continued to chatter regardless of the impending visitor. If this person hunted her, they would first need to go through the wylders. She may be magicless, but these females weren't.

The black horse traveling along the path was a familiar one. Her breath hitched, and she sat up, fixing her gaze on the rider, the soft, leather-encased knees with the heavy black cloak trailing him. This time she could look upon him, and he didn't disappoint. White hair fell down his back in a waterfall of braids.

She gasped, then cupped her mouth to smother further sounds. All knew who this male was. Rukk Knaraugh, the most feared lawbringer in all of Kethil. His white hair identified him, but she hadn't heard whisperings of his strong jaw, sharp nose, or brooding countenance. Curse it. She had stolen his coin purse, but hopefully someone else's medallion. She feathered her fingers over it resting between her breasts. The molded runes imprinted on her fingertips through the thin tunic.

The wylders faced him without fear, as if they thought he couldn't see them. He dismounted, drawing his sword from his saddle, all in a graceful motion. Orcs preferred axes, yet his movements were fluid, as if he had honed the skill. A great hulking brute wielded such a weapon with ease.

He didn't hesitate, slicing through the nearest female before she could react. Pandemonium struck, and spells flew, from sunlight to fire to green, all setting the surrounding forest ablaze or budding. It groaned under the barrage, and Thugari tightened her thighs around the branch. Grabbing a cowering Gnash, she shoved him inside her tunic and prepared to leap to safety as vines shot out of the undergrowth.

The spells bounced off Rukk as he cleaved through the females, their bodies crumbling behind him, bright red splashing their drab garments. The moment the oldest wylder died, the spell around the basket unraveled. Wails filled the air, forlorn and heart-wrenching. Thugari pursed her lips, fighting the urge to tend to them. Her chest ached, and she rubbed it, touching the medallion as well.

Sensing her emotional shift from fear to concern, Gnash scampered out of her tunic and buried his face in her hair.

Not an expression crossed Rukk's face. Killing six females didn't bother him. Stepping over their corpses, he approached the travois, a grimace now twisting his handsome features. He closed his eyes and whispered words she didn't understand. White magic pulsed from his fingertips, and silence descended over the basket.

He killed them! Panic gripped her, and she clung to the branches, hoping to prevent an attack of courage. She could do nothing against such a male. Killing the bairns was a sweeter end for them than what the wylders might have planned. Though, none of their whispered conversations had mentioned what awaited the bairns. She could only hazard a guess by the way they had treated the children, as if the wylders led them to the slaughter.

He bent over to sweep a curl off a bairn's temple, and it cooed a greeting. Relief was swift, gripping Thugari's chest for a split second before air rushed out of her lungs in a whoosh. His gentle touch was incongruent with the evidence of slaughter dripping from his sword. He flicked it, cleaning off the blood before sheathing it.

Dragging the corpses into a pile, he set them ablaze with a short word she assumed meant *burn*. Blue flames licked the bodies, and she covered her nose, expecting the stench of burning flesh to assault her. It didn't, and it wasn't long before only ash remained. He spread it with his booted heel, before squaring his shoulders and facing the travois.

Then he stopped and raised his gaze to the sky, his expression tense, but his face no less beautiful. Sunlight reflected off his tusks, leading her attention to his lips. "Thugari."

She jolted, and her fingers gripped the branch in dismay. Gnash squeaked and burrowed into her tunic. Rukk hadn't seen her, otherwise, he would have zapped her out of the tree. This had to be a ploy.

"I will find you, female. Don't sell or lose my medallion."

His? The threat hit home, and she found herself nodding, as if promising she wouldn't. He would hunt her until he retrieved what belonged to him. It was tempting to leave it for him to find, but should someone else stumble upon it, he would still hold her accountable. She was stuck with no way to escape him.

Revealing herself to him now wasn't wise when he could kill her outright. She had stolen from a lawbringer, after all, but he might never find her. She smirked. All she had to do was locate a village, purchase a horse with *his* coin, and bolt for Chaosthane. *Challenge accepted, lawbringer.*

She grimaced, aware it was bravado filling her with confidence. Had he been standing in front of her, after the way he took down the wylders, she would be quaking at the knees.

Under her vigilant gaze, he positioned the travois across the back of his horse, mounted, and headed along the western path to Haraton Castle. She waited until the forest obscured his broad shoulders and smothered the hoofbeats before scrambling from the tree. Ignoring the burn in her thighs, she ate while walking. She crisscrossed streams, hoping to confuse him. Often, she succumbed to the need to mislead him. She veered down a separate path for a while then forged a new one through the trees heading north. When she returned to the original path, she would leave a message taunting him, giggling to herself as she did.

The well-used path led north to the human village of Newhal. She donned her cap to hide her ears, not needing prejudice to waylay her. The centuries-old animosity between the races might still linger. Having never left the castle, she had no experience to say otherwise. experience to say otherwise. Hiding her orcish features was pointless since she had the tusks of an orc and the eyes of a Nehrakgu. Those she could do nothing about, her ears she could.

Pursing her lips, she hurried along their main dirt road, heading for the stables. Villagers gaped at her, and she returned greetings so as not to offend. She almost snorted at her silly attempts. A dark orc with silver-gray eyes in a human village? She half-expected hatred and fear bolstered with torches and pitchforks.

Slipping into the stables, she released a pent-up breath and approached the male mucking out the stalls. The stench of fresh manure pinched her nostrils. "Greetings, I would like a horse."

"Take your pick," the male said, not bothering to look at her.

She spun on the spot, creating divots with her worn heels in the straw-embedded mud. He didn't have fine stock, not like the lawbringer's mount. She hadn't expected quality, but these horses were thin, tired-looking beasts in need of care. One bay roan whinnied at her, and she offered her palm. His lips tickled her as he searched for a treat. She giggled.

Corn marks marred his flanks, darker than his white-haired reddish coat, and sorrow gripped her that someone had abused such a beautiful animal. Ignoring the tears pooling on her lashes, she whispered apologies and promises to him. He was as damaged as she was.

"I'll take him." She faced the stablemaster.

He stopped mucking to lean his elbow on the pitchfork's handle. Despite expecting the disgust curling his lips after dragging his gaze over her, it still smarted. Being half-human made their judgment worse, as if it were her fault a dark-human had rutted with an orc.

"What's a youngin like you need a horse for?"

"Do you want to sell him or not?" She met his gaze with an unflinching one of her own, determined now more than ever to buy the horse.

He huffed. "Two silver for Envis." A smirk overrode his disapproval.

Two? She fought to keep her face neutral. It was an exorbitant amount for a weathered old roan.

She tapped her chin, pretending to consider his offer. "Throw in a decent saddle, and you have a deal, sirrah."

He jerked back, taken by surprise at her quick agreement, extending his palm for the coin. Showing him her back, she opened the lawbringer's purse and grimaced. The idiot only had gold coins, and offering the stablemaster one would either mean no change or he might hunt her down to steal from her. It would happen at dusk and far from the eyes of Newhal's law-abiding folk, according to the stories told by the castle guards.

But she didn't have a choice, so she dropped a coin onto his palm and unlatched the door to her horse. He nudged her, and she patted his neck in greeting. They would have plenty of time to bond. The stablemaster stood there biting the coin several times to ensure its authenticity.

"I don't have change for this," he said. "But I can give you six silvers, a bag of oats, a food pouch, and the best tack I have."

Thugari smothered a chuckle, burying her face in her horse's neck to hide her amusement. "If you hurry."

As the male rushed around her readying her horse he called Envis, he scratched his balding head. Something bothered him, and she doubted she would leave here without him asking.

Grabbing the pommel, she struggled to pull herself into the saddle, managing by the fourth attempt. Perched on the saddle, the height flicked her gaze forward. She had never been on a horse before. If she fell off, she would die.

Everything inside her screamed this.

"Are you all right, miss?" He arched a brow at her.

Instead of answering, she thanked him while he tied a traveling pack behind her. The quality was better than she had expected, and for him to do this implied a personal integrity she could admire.

"Miss, how did you come by your coin?" He tightened his fingers around the reins he was halfway to handing her.

She lowered her chin to her chest to hide her smile. Many would ask her, so she needed to perfect her story. Summoning as much lost hope as she could, drenching her chest with the pain of neglect, she raised her gaze to meet his, hoping the familiar ache thrumming through her reflected on her face.

"I am the bastard daughter of Chief Varthug." All who met her would guess as much with her silver-gray eyes and dark skin as evidence, so there was no point in lying about it. "My father tried to welcome me into his home, but his lady wouldn't allow it. At dawn, he shoved the coin into my hand, and escorted me out of the castle." She caught her voice on a shuddering sob, which she thought was a nice touch. The stablemaster handed her the reins and gave her knee an awkward pat.

"Did she want your life?" he whispered.

She bit her lip to hold back a giggle, nodding instead.

"Heartless hussy." The stablemaster glanced around his stables and raised worried eyes to hers. "Will she send guards after you?"

"Worse, good sir." She shook her head. "Yesterday, two lawbringers and a magus arrived at the castle." As soon as she reached the outskirts of the village, she would pat herself on her back for that masterful twist. Should Rukk meet the stablemaster, he might struggle to gain information from him.

The old male sucked in a sharp breath. "Have no fear. You did not buy Envis from me. May Zetar bless your journey, child." He shuffled back to allow her to leave.

Guilt struck her, a sharp pain slicing her chest as bile rose to choke her. It was true. Lady Murzush had shown her no kindness, but the reason the lawbringer hunted her was Thugari's fault. Still, having an ally would cost neither of them, and it might hinder the great Rukk in his promise to find her.

She made a show of wiping her tears, gracing the stablemaster with a watery smile before urging Envis out of the stables and onto the dirt road. By the time they reached the outskirts of the village, her tears had dried. She laughed—the joy of the open road before her with freedom bolstering her spirits.

Gnash scampered out of her tunic, across Envis's crest to settle between his ears, which twitched at the intrusion. No matter how her horse snorted and stamped his foot, Gnash clung on. As did Thugari, expecting to be thrown at any moment. She pleaded with Envis, but to no avail. When her voice croaked, she resorted to humming a song. She blinked when he calmed.

Tentatively, she inched backward until her backside filled the saddle. Patting his neck, she smiled at the birds in the sky, the white clouds, and the cool breeze toying with her hair. All was right in her world.

CHAPTER EIGHT

RUKK ENTERED THE INNER yard, dragging the travois behind him. He had a sizable entourage of giggling, weeping orc and human females, hoping to find their bairns. Riding through the village on his way to the castle had garnered their attention.

He leaped out of the saddle, tossed his reins to a stableboy before striding to where Tarid and Sharn waited.

Females gathered around Harpax, their chatter loud under the vigilance of many males. A few were the castle guards. Others were the fathers.

"You found the bairns." Tarid gave him a disgusted look.

"Sharn, you're a female and a magus. See to it the bairns go to their real mothers." Rukk arched a brow when she opened her mouth to argue.

She pursed her lips and hurried toward the travois. He fell into place beside Tarid and lowered his voice, recounting what Rukk had done since he had ridden out that morning.

"Once again, you had an adventure without me." Tarid scowled. "You should not have killed all the wylders. We need answers. What if they served the koveen?"

"They did, for not a single female tended to the bairns, which they would've done had they taken them to raise as their own." Rukk rubbed his jaw, fighting the exhaustion from a day spent in the saddle. "They kept the bairns in a time-state."

Tarid gaped. "Holy Zetar, 'tis unholy power required to perform such a spell."

"We can. Does that make us unholy?" Rukk couldn't resist teasing him.

"Did you find your stableboy?" Tarid kept his gaze on the arguing females.

Rukk knew better than to believe his false disinterest. "Yes, in a way. He has my medallion." He grinned when Tarid swung to gape at him. This time, Rukk faked his nonchalance. "Any news on the fires?"

"Those causing them travel northwest to Dussoum." Tarid gestured north.

This was good and bad news. Rukk frowned. "The dwarves are magicless, so it must be something they disturbed in the bowels of their mines that summons the koveen."

Tarid remained silent for a while, then shook his head. "Or the trail goes past Chaosthane to Ghorza."

Rukk accepted his task was not yet complete. "The wylders were heading in a north-eastern direction, perhaps toward a separate lair."

"Northeast is still north," Tarid said. "To Penven to report our findings?"

Rukk chuckled as Sharn snatched a bairn from a female's arms, her face flushed in anger. "Yes, then I must return to reclaim my medallion."

"I can meet with the Grand Lawmaster." The offer was to save Rukk time spent in the saddle.

"I doubt he would forgive my absence. Let's keep my missing medallion between us." To lose one's medallion was a punishable offense.

Rukk preferred to retrieve it before anyone discovered its disappearance or his health deteriorated to a point where he would need to travel to his homeland. He grimaced.

Tarid observed Sharn interact with the females, his focus unwavering. "When do you wish to depart?"

"As soon as we can." Rukk scanned the yard in search of a Nehrakgu. "How fares the chief?"

Tarid huffed, making his displeasure known. "His voice has returned, but he is furious, demanding an apology. Word of this will reach the Grand Lawmaster's ears before we arrive."

"I cannot regret my actions, Tarid. He wounded his daughter without remorse."

Tarid's brown brow shot up. "Daughter?"

"The stableboy." Despite his attempts to remain stoic, Rukk smiled.

Tarid formed an 'o' with his mouth, his eyes widening with disbelief before narrowing in anger. "I do not doubt your word, nor your reasons. It is the impulsivity of your actions that irritates me. How did you know hunting her would lead you to the bairns? Oft times, your intuition is too mysterious for me to accept."

"Blame it on my elven heritage, my lawbrother." Rukk shrugged.

Tarid frowned, studying Rukk's face. "If I didn't know your schedule, I would accuse you of succumbing to an attraction."

Rukk grumbled, not liking the implication. Thugari was, in a way, striking, but stealing from him, twice, placed her in the never-to-touch category. He would rather rut with Elanil again. Finding Thugari would be difficult with his anti-scrying enchantment on his medallion. Difficult, but not impossible, and therein lay the attraction. She challenged him, his skills, his authority, and he had to admit, he liked it.

"You finding the bairns is the only reason you weren't barred entry," Chief Varthug said as he joined Rukk's side.

"Tell me, Chief, have you heard of the watch list?" Rukk strolled off, not waiting for the male's response.

His spluttering was enough to delight Rukk, despite Tarid's hasty assurances he hadn't meant the implication. Rukk had every intention of placing Varthug's name on the list. The Council shouldn't consider a male worthy if he mistreated those of a lower stature to him. The hurried tread of Tarid followed Rukk until his solid weight fell into step beside him.

"We'll leave after a bath and a meal," Rukk said. "Tell your female to prepare."

"*My* female?" Tarid gaped seconds before his face twisted and anger darkened his brown eyes. "I wouldn't touch Sharn if—"

"Protestations?" Rukk grinned.

Having completed the first part in this hunt, the joy of accomplishment pulsed through his chest despite missing his medallion. He had thwarted a koveen without having to encounter it. That was something to celebrate.

"You." Pointing at a female drew a squeak of surprise, and she almost dropped the bundle she carried. "I want a bath and a meal brought to my chambers." Under his stern gaze, she nodded, her skin paling further. "Make haste. I'm not a patient male."

Not that he was a monster or enjoyed scaring people. He didn't tolerate tardiness or the performing of tasks in a haphazard manner. Having the Council's might behind him wasn't the reason for his arrogance. He had earned the fear and respect afforded him, even if they exaggerated the rumors of his achievements.

He bounded up the stairs two at a time but didn't make it to his chambers.

"Did you find my *sister*?" Lady Arob pushed away from his door, swaying her hips.

She was but a child in a female's body. At the sight of her tribal markings, he wondered why he hadn't seen any on Thugari, or had his magic not delved to that detail? He frowned. No, Chief Varthug had never initiated her into his clan.

Hatred burned through Rukk, so sudden he clamped his lips shut to smother a growl. To not have tribal markings meant an orc had no identity, no loyalty. Not only had Varthug mistreated his daughter, but he had made her an outcast, reviled by all orcs, in his clan or in others. The female before him hadn't shown Thugari compassion, either.

"You have a sister?" He couldn't bring himself to add her title. Never again would he call her 'my lady.' "Are you referring to the female who has the misfortune to have your father's blood running through her veins? Or the female you've abused her entire life? Or the female who will receive more attention from me than you ever will?"

Gasping, Arob's face burned red. He slipped around her and shut his chamber door in her face. Dropping onto the bed, he removed his boots, his thoughts drifting to the upcoming meeting with the Grand Lawmaster. Facing Venec Galand was never pleasant. The male could see through Rukk, his motives, and his arrogance to the meat of the problem. He hoped Venec didn't notice his missing medallion.

If the koveen's involvement hadn't been important, Rukk would track Thugari first. A shadow lingered in his soul, warning him of a threatening darkness. He couldn't sense from where, although, the direction the wylders traveled was north. He grimaced, peeling off his tunic to drape it over his cloak.

He granted permission to enter when the knock came. Servants rushed to fill the wooden tub with steaming water. A maid held out clay jugs of scented oils, and he shook his head. Few knew he had sensitive skin, a condition from his elven mother. Unless the soaps and oils were made from the purest ingredients, he couldn't bear it touching his skin.

Twisting his lips, he acknowledged the affliction, but it didn't mean he had to like it. With a flick of his wrist, he opened his satchel, and dug out a cloth-wrapped bar of soap. The potent scent of lavender greeted him.

After the maid shut the door behind the departing servants, he stripped out of his breeches and sunk into the water, moaning when the heat soothed his aching muscles.

He leaned his head over the tub's edge and considered his next steps. Five days to return to Penven, and from there he would travel back to Haraton, but via the eastern villages.

Someone was bound to have seen her. She was on foot, but if she were smart—which he suspected she was—she would purchase a horse with his gold.

He did not fear she would rid herself of his medallion. She had to realize he would hunt her first and wouldn't believe her if she said she had left it on a boulder next to a footpath. There had to be a way to track her without relying on footprints and painstaking investigation. He needed magic, but there were few ways to thwart his own anti-scrying enchantment.

If he had something of hers like a lock of her hair and a powerful spellbinder or magus, then perhaps a hunting spell might overcome his medallion's influence. Lathering his soap, he washed, pondering how strong Uzul's magic was. Rukk wouldn't dare command Sharn to cast such a spell. He didn't trust her, and sharing the loss of his medallion meant he was beholden to her for her silence.

He whispered to his hair to unravel, then lathered the soap to wash it. A knock interrupted his thoughts, and he commanded the intruder to enter. A maid scurried in, placing a tray on the table. She left as fast, squeaking when she bumped into Tarid on the way out. He flashed her a charming smile and whispered in her ear. A giggle escaping her, she nodded. He shut the door, dropping into the chair to pick at Rukk's meal. He scowled at Tarid's audacity but said nothing, since it was pointless.

"The bairns are with their mothers." He bit into a hunk of bison.

The aroma of it made Rukk salivate. He didn't rush his bath, preferring to soak with the suds on the surface hiding his nudity. Accepting the offered goblet of mead, he sipped from it, swirling the honeyed sweetness around his mouth before swallowing.

"I doubt the Grand Lawmaster will find this surprising." Tarid sucked the juices off his thumb.

"He sent us here for confirmation. You and I both know this isn't the only rumor of stolen bairns. Koveen aren't this productive." Rukk splashed water over his face, rinsing off the lavender soap. The fragrance of it sent his thoughts to Thugari.

"You sense it too?" Tarid stilled, the jug of mead resting on his bottom lip. Without another cup, he would show his nature and gulp from the jug.

"Yes. Something's brewing." Rukk rose from the bath, grabbing the toweling cloth to dry off.

Tarid tipped the jug back. His sensing the changes too was alarming, not that Rukk didn't respect his lawbrother and his skills. Rukk's mixed heritage made him more sensitive to the flow of magic. Then again, if he could sense the imbalance, then Galand could, as well.

Rukk hurried through dressing and handed the maid his dirty clothes when she delivered a fresh platter of food. "We leave as soon as my garments are clean." He dismissed her and the seductive glance she threw at Tarid.

Rukk sat on the chair, taking a moment to inhale the tantalizing smell of braised bison drenched in an onion-rich sauce. He refilled his goblet before Tarid emptied the jug, then ate, eager to assuage the sharp twists of a ravenous belly.

"Sharn seems to have realized her presence was pointless." Tarid tore off a chunk of seed bread to soak up the remnants of his gravy. "Grand Lawmaster and the Arch-Magus must be arguing again."

"Regardless, it shouldn't impact the tasks of a lawbringer." Rukk arched a brow. "Did Sharn reveal the reasons for traveling along?"

"Her questions revolved around you and your limitations. The koveen kidnapping the bairns was a trivial excuse behind her accompanying us." Tarid's gaze lingered on Rukk's food, as if he could eat another serving.

"Mm." Rukk hummed around a mouthful of succulent bison. "I'll raise the Arch-Magus's interest with Galand." He finished his meal in relative silence, broken only by the infrequent burping of his lawbrother, intermittent with bites of an apple Tarid pulled from his pocket.

They would set out by sunset after Rukk had a chat with Uzul. He planned to rest the horses as many times as needed, but he would push through to Penven. Grand Lawmaster, then Thugari, in that order, and as Zetar was his witness, Rukk would give that female a tongue-lashing for her audacity.

Chapter Nine

If it weren't for Envis, Thugari would hide up a tree. She couldn't bring herself to abandon the old horse, so she cowered in the tall bushes, praying to the Moon above they wouldn't see her. Separate groups of wylders had crisscrossed her path since she left Newhal hours ago. The first encounter before Newhal had been an anomaly, but this? More stolen bairns headed north. What plagued her was the horrible end that might await these children.

Gnash squirmed inside her tunic, and she undid a few ties so he could poke his head out for a scratch. She stroked him as he sniffed the air.

There wasn't a lawbringer to save the bairns this time. At night, curled against a tree, with Gnash on his own adventure but within sight, she stared at the star-filled sky and imagined traveling to the Council's Tower of Eslaniel outside Penven. Getting them to open the doors to her would have been her first hurdle. If they did, they would dismiss her concerns as the ramblings of a mad female. So she would continue north, dodging the wylders. At least with their constant presence, no bandits loitered.

The next day, the forest's eerie silence enhanced her footsteps as she led Envis along an overgrown path. Gnash snuggled in his mane, the two having formed a bond of sorts. Envis snorted, nudging her shoulder as if in warning. No insects chirped, and no birds sang in joyful homage to the sun. Into this came slithering, grating, and hissing, spiking the forest's tension and thickening the air. Her breath caught, and she fumbled for her knife in her boot. Spinning in a slow circle, she scanned the trees. The path she chose was the least traveled, and she had hoped to avoid meeting wylders.

The thing slithering across the path sent chills down her spine. She tightened her grip on the knife, raising it as if to ward off the creature. Not that it paid her any attention. That didn't matter, not with the ice tingling her scalp and pooling in her belly. It had looked like a shirtless female with unkempt black hair. Dirt marred its upper body, and muddy smears covered sagging breasts. Thugari couldn't tell what it had been when its stringy hair hid its ears.

She shook her head. The torso had lacked the defined ridges of muscle, so whatever it was, it had never been an orc. It was minutes later she remembered seeing a snake body, thick and powerful, gliding the creature over the forest bed.

Bile rose to choke her, and she threw her arms around Envis's neck, needing his soothing presence. Gnash's beady eyes peered at her from within the horse's mane.

The creature also traveled north. If Thugari didn't need to reach Dussoum, she might have chosen the opposite direction.

"Oh, Envis, Gnash," she said, her voice hushed. "What do I do?"

She was ill-equipped to handle this, with no magic, no fighting skills other than what the book had taught her. Sparring with an imaginary opponent didn't prepare her for an actual fight. Stopping at each village would garner too much interest, but keeping to the forest wasn't wise either.

Envis nudged her again, and she stroked his neck. Regular feedings and fresh air would improve the look of him, but he was far from ready to gallop any distance. She would head northeast, still north, but not in the direction of the snake-female and all those wylders. Wherever they were heading, Thugari didn't want to be there.

Grudging respect grew for the lawbringer's skills. She had never thought she would need Rukk. She dropped her knife back into her boot, and pondered a thought growing in the dark recesses of her mind. If she waited for Rukk Knaraugh, she could return his medallion to him and steer him north, hoping he didn't skin her hide for stealing from him in the first place.

The fear coursing through her, paralyzing her, was the only reason she considered facing the lawbringer sooner. These sightings haunted her sleep, and she jerked awake often. Into the daylight, nervousness followed her until exhaustion pounded at her senses, draining her. As the sun set, darkening the shadows in the forest, so did her eyelids droop.

She stood there, undecided. Pressing a hand to her temple, she squeezed her eyes shut to ease the burning as she weighed her options. Find someplace to bed down for the night or push through by moonlight. She had stuck to the stream meandering through the forest. Perhaps by night, she could skirt the edges of the forest and cover more ground.

"What have we here?"

She squeaked, having fallen asleep on her feet. Jerking backward, she bounced off Envis to land in a heap, digging her fingers into the rich forest floor.

"A stray girl," a female said, crouching in front of Thugari to sweep her hair off her face. "A Nehrakgu too. Pity, you looked like you needed help." She rose, but stared at her.

Thugari sucked in a startled breath, recognizing the female. The number of weapons littering her body could mean only one person, but the confirmation came from the jagged scar marring the side of her face and sagging one eye... Borgakh Yerug—an orc of great renown. Guda covered her chest and other strips saw to her muscled body, her height that of a full-grown orc male. Her tribal markings etched into her skin solidified her Ghorzan identity.

"And?" Borgakh glanced behind her.

"I sense something. If she has magic, it's weak." A petite human female stepped from the shadows with a bright face, as if illuminated by an unholy light.

Thugari scrambled backward at the sight of the wylder's clothing. She threw out a hand as if to ward off an attack, almost snorting at her stupidity.

"She has seen my kind." The female twisted her lips in displeasure.

"How many and where?" Borgakh crouched again.

For a female her size, Thugari had to peer up at her to maintain eye contact. Obsidian eyes blinked at her, dark against her pale skin. A hood hid her hair color, but judging by the slashes of crow's wings as her eyebrows, Thugari assumed it was black, as well. Lip piercings clinked against her tusks, glimmering in the light, distracting her.

She cleared her throat before stuttering, "Many covens and a snake-female too."

"A koveen? Oh, this doesn't bode well." Borgakh's scowl was ferocious to behold, yet Thugari found comfort in her presence. Nothing could harm her with the orc maiden nearby.

"We should notify the Council," the wylder said.

Borgakh snorted, rising to her full height once again. "Walk right to their door with a wylder in tow? Once was enough, thank you." She extended a hand to Thugari, who studied it for a moment before accepting it. Seconds later, she was airborne.

"So, little one, why aren't you curled up in front of the castle's fireplace?" Borgakh bypassed Thugari to whisper to Envis.

The traitor whickered and nudged the orc in what Thugari perceived as a smitten gesture. Gnash bolted out of Envis's mane, scampered along the horse's neck, and leaped onto Thugari's shoulders to burrow in her hair.

"Is that a...rat?" The wylder leaped away.

"This is Gnash. We're heading to Dussoum." Thugari chose not to confirm her origins. "The wylders have stolen bairns and were taking them north."

She dusted off her baggy breeches to hide her trembling fingers. There were tales of hideous creatures, but seeing one had rattled her.

"Nenneg?" Borgakh arched a brow at her wylder companion, who held a palm out. Emerald smoke swirled from it, reaching toward Thugari. She tumbled back, bumping into Borgakh this time. "Relax, she's making sure I can trust you."

The tendrils sharpened into points but didn't come closer than a foot. Gnash dived inside Thugari's tunic.

"She's cursed and protected," Nenneg said. "I can't sense how to unravel either." She dropped her arm and shrugged. "Trust or don't trust, I'm tired and starving."

Borgakh sighed. "Fine, we camp here tonight. Join us, Nehrakgu."

Thugari hesitated, considering offering a fictitious name. "The name's Thugari." Lying now might lead to death. Wylder Nenneg might realize Thugari's deception, and trust would fall to the wayside. Not to mention the lure of a good night's rest was too tempting to sacrifice for anonymity.

"Thugari Nehrakgu? As in Varthug's daughter?" Borgakh guided her horse into the clearing. She tethered it to a nearby tree and rummaged in her satchels, before pulling out a brush to run along the horse's flanks.

"He's my father by blood only." Thugari gripped Envis's reins in a tight fist and mimicked Borgakh's example, tethering her horse before digging in the satchel for a brush.

"It might be best to choose another name. Just Thugari would raise suspicion." Nenneg whispered a word, and fire leaped to life in the center of the clearing.

"My mother's last name was Macutia," she said. "Is Thugari Macutia better?"

"It does have a lyrical sound to it." Nenneg cast a concerned brow at Borgakh, who patted her horse's neck then marched across the clearing to sit in front of the fire.

She spread out a cloth, on which she placed food items from her satchel. Thugari gathered her food pouch and joined her, although she chose to sit opposite the intimidating female.

"Tell me, how much do you know about your mother's family?" Borgakh sank her teeth into a boar's leg the length of her arm, tearing off a mouthful.

Gnash poked his head out, the temptation of food too irresistible for the coward. Thugari bit into her black-peppered cheese and chewed while she dug in her pouch, searching for the last piece of dried fruit she had thrown in there.

"Not much. I was six when she died, but what I know is what I've gleaned from the whispers circulating the castle. My grandparents weren't happy with her choice of lover, nor with her condition. The castle folk claimed Varthug had no intention of laying with her, but she enthralled him with her powerful magic." Thugari snorted. "A magic she didn't pass on to me." With deft tugs, she tore off chunks of bread, laying them in a row on her thigh. She'd given up on finding the fruit, suspecting a certain rodent had eaten it. "My mother loved him. He must have done something to encourage her affections." She chose a piece of bread and popped it in her mouth.

"How did she die?" Borgakh took a long draw from her waterskin.

Thugari scanned through her faded memories, trying to recall that day and failing. "Within hours, she went from rosy-cheeked to gray-skinned. It wasn't until years later I realized her death might not have been natural."

"Lady Murzush," Nenneg mumbled.

Thugari met Nenneg's gaze, unable to see the color of her eyes in the flickering flames. Striated-green tendrils swelled out of her fingertips, and a patch of strawberries grew at her hip. She plucked one and bit into it. Magic made life easier. If only Thugari had any talent for it, then she wouldn't have gone a day hungry.

"It's all rumors and nothing tangible. It's also plausible my mother contracted a disease and died." She fell silent, remembering the pain of loss crushing her chest, the fear for her future, and the cold comfort of her threadbare blankets.

An unknown female's face shimmered across her mind, and the pain was gone. If only she could forget crying herself to sleep, her sobs hindered by her chattering teeth.

"Your life didn't improve." Nenneg tossed an arcing tendril of green magic at Thugari, and a patch of strawberries grew beside her.

"No." Plucking a plump one, she bit into it as Nenneg had done. "Thank you for this," Thugari said around a mouthful of tart fruit, the juice of it dribbling from her bottom lip. She wiped it away on the sleeve of her tunic.

"I wouldn't choose Macutia until you know more about your family. They might be brigands or wealthy merchants."

Borgakh didn't catch the startled look Nenneg threw at her. Thugari did, and she cycled Borgakh's words through her mind, trying to understand what had alarmed Nenneg.

"You've escaped. Choose a new name."

Thugari smiled to herself, imagining choosing Knaraugh just to irritate him. The expression on his handsome features would make the consequences worth it. "Any suggestions?" she asked, aware they waited for her to answer.

"Vitanor? It means new life in old orcish." Borgakh offered her waterskin, which Thugari rose to accept.

"I like it." She tilted the skin to her lips.

Sweet water drenched her tongue. It bubbled as she swallowed. She giggled, holding the bag away from her in surprise.

Energy exploded, from stomach to limbs, draining the exhaustion from her. "What *is* this?"

"Water from the Well of the Mothers in the center of Isstislaaron." Borgakh smirked. "A sip or two at night, and you will awaken refreshed."

"I *feel* it working." Thugari carried the waterskin with care, handing it to Borgakh before returning to her side of the camp.

Thugari unraveled her bedroll, then made sure Envis was well tethered. Nenneg rose as well, circling the camp while muttering words and streaming green smoke. Something shimmered overhead, and Thugari threw a worried look at Borgakh, who had climbed into her bedroll, her sword stretched alongside her. Nothing to alarm her then. Feeling like a fool, Thugari lay down for the evening with Gnash curling into the curve of her neck.

She had never encountered this much magic before. With only Uzul as her source growing up, it was understandable. Seeing the various kinds, she had to admit she was curious. The wylders had green and white magic. Rukk's had been white. Green must mean earth power, since Nenneg had such magic, but Thugari didn't know if Nenneg was limited to one color. Nor did Thugari know if a person was born with magic or gifted it. Regardless, magic wielders were expected to attend training, hence the existence of the Council's tower.

If she stayed with them, she would find out. Nenneg might reveal to Thugari a world she had only heard whispers of. Her eyes drooped, and she sighed, contentment softening her muscles, sagging her bones into the welcoming arms of her bedroll. Nothing had ever felt this good.

Chapter Ten

Gripping the hood of Uzul's cloak, Rukk yanked the man's head back, pressing his dagger's blade into his skin. A trickle of blood pooled at his collarbone.

"I'm not asking again, spellbinder. What hold do you have over Thugari?" Rukk studied the male's human features, the translucent skin, yellow hair, and *gray* eyes, now understanding why he had a position at Haraton. "Magus Sharn Tandagh said you were exiled, you were a coward, and your name is a curse."

The male trembled, slicing the blade deeper.

"Careful, spellbinder, or you will slit your own throat. I will not be held accountable for an exile's death. Would you prefer I summon the magus and have her deal with you?"

Uzul shook his head, careful not to move his neck. "Pocket." He gritted the one word through his clenched teeth.

Flicking the blade away, Rukk waited until the male dug in his pocket and withdrew a lock of black hair. He snatched it off Uzul's palm and tucked it inside his cloak.

"If this is anyone else's hair, other than Thugari's, I will return and kill you."

Rukk strolled out of the male's chambers, puzzled by how hard Uzul had fought to cling onto a bastard daughter's hair. Rukk galloped Harpax east to the nearest Fountain of Sound.

Tarid had reminded him they *did* exist, and using its services wouldn't mean a four-day delay in finding Thugari. Galand would see Rukk's face as they discussed the koveen problem, so at least a mollified Grand Lawmaster was in Rukk's future and not extra days spent in the saddle.

He approached the Fountain with caution. Few weary travelers used them, as it served as an ambush point. The white stone was of unknown origin, but nature didn't care, splitting its seams, and weathering its edges. A haypier vine had a chokehold around the Fountain's base with its tendrils almost dipping into the brown murky waters.

He dismounted, unsheathing his orcish dagger—a gift from his mother when he was younger and the same one he had held to Uzul's throat. Guilt twinged his heart, and he sighed. He had to visit his mother, perhaps after solving this koveen-wylder-bairn mystery. He could sneak in without his father knowing of his presence and press a kiss to mother's tree.

With a flick of his wrist, he removed the offending plant, and any of its seedlings, shoving it aside. He muttered 'burn' in old orcish. Blue flames consumed it as it had done to the dead wylders. The setting sun hurried him. He would prefer not to light a torch to see the Grand Lawmaster's face.

The cost to use this ancient magic was a drop of his blood. Wiping the blade on his breeches, Rukk sliced his palm and clenched a fist to drip blood into the scum-layered water.

He scowled at the murky waters—the Fountain's defense mechanism. It didn't sparkle or trickle in enticement, and drinking from it promised a painful death.

A circle formed around the ripples his life's blood had made, clear, crisp, so he whispered the Grand Lawmaster's name. "Venec Galand."

"What is it?" Venec's voice boomed, agitating the waters around his image.

His flushed square face, lined with age and scars, peered at Rukk, his gaze darting down even as his mouth parted. If Rukk didn't know better, he would say his Grand Lawmaster was rutting. Which was impossible for the male wouldn't retain his power if he did.

"An update, as requested." Rukk arched a brow, implying he could end this and cease giving the male feedback. It had inconvenienced him to travel to the Fountain in the opposite direction to Thugari.

"Get on with it." Was there a hitch to Venec's voice? A gasp?

Rukk shook his head, clearing his ears and fighting for focus. "Koveen ally with wylders, sending bairns north. We will follow and inform as we travel. Expect delays, depending on available Fountains."

"Good." Venec waved his hand, and the image shimmered, but Rukk would swear he heard the word 'harder.'

Scowling, he sheathed his dagger and mounted Harpax. Fountains often carried old messages. They said it never forgot a conversation, so whispered words sometimes echoed in the background of active sessions. Still, the Grand Lawmaster's behavior bothered Rukk. Spinning toward the castle, he would unite with Tarid and Sharn, and they would head for the forest.

Sharn did not know that part of the hunt was for a stableboy, and neither of the lawbringers would inform her of such. She was a spy for the Arch-Magus.

Come to think of it, Galand hadn't seemed alarmed by the news of the koveen involvement. He might have known about it before sending Rukk to investigate. The suspicion Venec wanted Rukk out of the way gripped him, and he couldn't shake the truth of it, ringing like a death knell.

As soon as Tarid's visage came into focus, Rukk conveyed his concerns to his lawbrother through their connection. Tarid's brows shot up, and he shook his head in denial.

"It can't be. Why would he send us here? I will admit you do pose a threat to his reign. After all, you are the most revered of lawbringers, not him." Tarid's warhorse fell into a gallop beside him, but Rukk slowed Harpax, not wanting to overtax their mounts.

"He hasn't been active in maintaining his training, is all. The Council of Lawbringers still reveres him." Rukk trusted the male more than he did his father.

"If what you say is true, then why this subterfuge? If he's aware of the koveen's antics, then what else isn't he sharing? I will speak to Janar. None of this makes sense." Tarid narrowed his eyes, slicing a concerned look at Rukk. *"You're weakening."*

Rukk pursed his lips. He hadn't meant to reveal what he had guarded for so long. *"I need my medallion."*

"You tied your lifeforce to it?" Horror flickered over Tarid's face.

Rukk didn't respond. It was best to let Tarid think he had done that when in truth it was far worse. Crafted from Ghorzan soil and Rukk's mother's heart, it was the perfect replica of a lawbringer's medallion. He needed it to keep him well.

The Ghorzan people thrived on their magical island, north of Dussoum—the soil rich, the plants almost sentient. His father had formed an alliance with his mother's people, who lived in peace and harmony, strengthening their magic from generation to generation. So leaving the island was decided death, and the medallion was his stay of execution. The pouch of soil all traveling Ghorzans carried maintained their life, but didn't bolster their health.

But added to this was the anti-scrying spell. Without the medallion, he was vulnerable to being hunted. He patted his pocket, hoping Thugari's hair would bypass all those enchantments.

They breached the forest as the shadows of night claimed it. Sharn summoned a sphere of light. It guided them along the paths and illuminated the first batch of wylders they came across.

He loved to regale lawbrothers of epic battles, but this wouldn't make his list. The wylders fought without heart, as if they didn't mind dying. His experience with their kind had been impressive, their battle skills worthy, yet now, there, they succumbed to his and Tarid's swords.

Their magic used to be powerful, not the pathetic balls of light and fire thrown and so easily thwarted.

Wiping the blood off his sword on one of their tunics, he studied their faces wearing death's unkind masks. These were young females, girls still eligible as novitiates. Yet, they had forsaken the Council before final judgment. The wylders must be recruiting them from villages and training them.

Such a waste.

He pointed at his lawbrother with his sword, then sheathed it. "Tarid, head to the nearest village with the travois. We'll reunite in the next town."

"Which is Lemfor," Sharn said, leaning over the bairns. "Time-stated, and judging by these wylder corpses, they do not have the talent for such a spell."

"I agree." Tarid hitched the travois to his warhorse.

He vaulted into his saddle but paused, his reins in a tight grip when Sharn stopped beside him. She placed her palm on his knee, and he jerked, his jaw hardening. Her eyelids fluttered as she chanted a lyrical spell, forming a sphere of light that bobbed and weaved in front of him.

"It will light your way until you reach the village." She offered Tarid a shy smile.

"Thank you, Sharn." *"Why would she spy on me?"* He arched a brow at Rukk, who shrugged.

"Be grateful for the gift." He mounted Harpax, following their sphere north even as he listened for Tarid, heading path east from them. The forest fell silent, sensing their presence. Rukk didn't instigate conversation, preferring to mire in his thoughts, which ricocheted between the koveen, wylders, Sharn, Venec, and often ending with Thugari.

Days ago, his only concern was who to pick for his scheduled rutting, and even that had gone awry.

They rested alongside a stream, allowing their horses to drink or nibble at the surrounding foliage. As Rukk chewed on dried fruit, he wondered why the stream whispered its way through the forest as if it feared discovery or disturbing the peace. Squeezing his eyes shut, and with the tart apple coating his tongue, he listened with more than his ears. Old magic lingered in the surrounding trees, this spot having had meaning for someone ages ago.

"Do you sense it?" Sharn's usual lyrical voice grated him this night.

He fixed his gaze on her.

She raised her face to the heavens. The moonlight peeking through the dense canopy coated her skin in silver. "The stone against which you rest was once drenched in the blood of virgins."

Rukk smirked. This wasn't evil magic or the slaughter of innocents. He trusted his senses more than her tongue. Why not come right out and admit her reasons for accompanying them? Or was it tied to Venec's strange behavior?

Taking a long pull from his waterskin, Rukk sloshed the water to clear his mouth of apple while studying her. She had yet to reveal her motives for coming with, so until she was truthful, he couldn't trust her. So much for catching her thoughts unguarded. She had thwarted his attempts better than he had expected.

"I am certain it was for a noble cause." He shrugged in fake-nonchalance. "Ready?" As he rose, he hid his grin since her face had crumpled into a scowl. *I'm not a fool, Sharn.*

Chuckling to himself, he stowed his food pouch, ran a hand along Harpax's flanks, then adjusted his saddle before mounting. When Harpax tossed his great head and pawed the ground, Rukk vaulted off, unsheathing his sword in the process. Two koveen slithered past, dragging a travois. Sharn reacted first, casting two lilac balls, slowing them as if they crawled on ice.

He lunged forward, swinging his sword, dodging a crossbow bolt as one koveen thawed. It ducked his downward slice and lashed out, its claws tearing through his leather tunic exposing skin and marring it with crimson streaks.

He grunted, dropped into a roll and rose, thrusting upward with the dagger he drew from his boot. Slashing in a wide arc, he hoped to catch the other koveen by surprise, but its scream pierced the night. Flames of lilac and blue hardened its outer skin before it cracked and exploded.

Wiping koveen innards off his face, he glared at Sharn, who dared to giggle. "For that, you're taking the travois to the nearest village."

"Worth it," she sang.

As she tethered the travois to her horse, Rukk jumped up and down, hoping to dislodge as much gore as possible. The stench curled his lips, furrowing his nose until he wished he could stop breathing.

She neared, watching him with a smile. "For a renowned lawbringer, your mannerisms are too feminine."

"What?" He cast a baleful stare at her, cursing her under his tongue.

She giggled again, which grated more than her voice did. Then as she clicked her fingers, frigid air rushed over his body, and he was clean. "Can't do much for your ripped tunic. That you'll have to tend to yourself."

"Thank you." He wanted to stamp his foot like a child, show ingratitude for this gift, but common courtesy cost him nothing but his pride. "You need to teach me that spell."

She shrugged, pouring water out of a waterskin onto the ground, then with her eyelids fluttering, she hovered a hand over the puddle. Lilac strands rose like tendrils of smoke to melt into her skin. Pink splashed her cheeks when she looked at him. Sunlight restored his magic, still, it took days to return.

"See you in Lemfor." She mounted her horse. "I'll keep a lookout for Tarid and other koveen along the way."

"Mark their locations...please. We have to know where they're coming from and where they're heading." He listened as she meandered east through the forest with a new sphere. She had left one for him, but he wasn't pleased about it. Her thoughtfulness went against his opinion of her.

He splashed water on his face in defiance of her gift of cleansing. As droplets dribbled off his chin, he washed his sword, wiping the blade across his breeches before sliding it into its saddle sheath. More life drained from him, not aided by the koveen's venomous claws. He stumbled, grabbing hold of Harpax's neck, and sucked in deep breaths, fighting the spots around his vision. A fumble later, and he scrambled for the pouch holding a little of his homeland. He buried his fingers into the cool soil. Energy flowed up his arm and into his chest, bursting outwards with fire. His vision cleared, but not without tinging his world in grays.

He needed to find his medallion—soon.

Chapter Eleven

Thugari fell into a routine, straggling Borgakh and Nenneg as they meandered through the forest. At some point, they transitioned from Clegloch Forest into the weeping Forest of Anduia. The trees grew together, forcing travelers to stick to the narrow paths. Yet the flora fought to reclaim those, as well. Many a time, Borgakh had to hack through creeping vines and reaching branches.

As the sun set, they would unpack for the night and leave Thugari alone by the fire to wander off, whispering words while holding hands. She took it as a good sign, trusting their satchels and mounts in her care without a backward glance.

As she chewed on a strip of dried meat and watched Gnash scamper about, she pondered their attraction. Nenneg was sweet, her character gentle. Thugari had never known a female like her. No one at Haraton valued kindness.

Once they'd accepted Thugari, that kindness flowed over to her. Small things like waking her up with a hot cup of tea. Tears burned behind her eyes each morning as she sat up to accept the offering. She dipped her head after each sip, hoping to hide how much she appreciated the gesture.

Into this were the constant reminders they were on a mission. Borgakh would roar a battle cry that chilled Thugari's blood, charging down the pathways with bloodlust trailing her in the form of a timid wylder. Thugari followed, but not on their heels because involving her unskilled self in a battle with koveen or wylders would endanger her friends.

Friends? Her breath hitched. A tight pain crushed her chest, and she bit down hard on her bottom lip. She scooped Gnash off the bedroll for a cuddle, squashing the wiggling rat to her chest. She had never thought anyone would find her worthy of their time. Because they had included her without hesitation, she wouldn't jeopardize their trust.

Gnash tore free and scrambled into her food pouch. She giggled, expecting to find gnawed bread and sampled fruit when next she was hungry. Rising, she tended the fire Nenneg created. Thugari spread out their bedrolls, placed their food pouches and waterskins alongside, then washed her hands in the pool behind the campsite. Pressing her cool fingers on the back of her neck, she studied the moon's reflection on the water's surface, finding the murmur of the waterfall soothing.

Raising her face for the moonlight to drench her, she inhaled a slow breath, as if she could suck in enough air to satiate her starved lungs. Which was strange, since her breathing was fine. Yet, with each moment spent under Moon's embrace, a sense of completion engulfed her as if she was well, whole.

"Take a bath." Borgakh entered the clearing without Nenneg.

Thugari peered around the tall orc for her lover, arching a brow in silent query. "I can't swim."

A rustle in the bushes foretold Nenneg's arrival. She adjusted her garments, implying she had relieved herself. "It's not deep. You can see the bottom. Besides, we have mint soap." She scooped up her satchel and rummaged in it, then held out a cloth-wrapped bar.

Thugari hesitated, so Nenneg stomped across, grabbed her hand, and thumped the soap onto her palm. Heat inflamed Thugari's cheeks. It wasn't the soap she feared. She couldn't imagine bathing in front of anyone. The bucket-baths were in private, and she had never wet her body from head to toe, or as Nenneg had implied, toe to hip.

"In the morning, we'll leave you with our things and visit the nearby village west of here." Borgakh collapsed onto her bedroll and sprawled back on one elbow, spreading out her length. "We need to replenish our supplies, and Fentley is as good a place as any."

"Do you think they're missing bairns, as well?" Thugari sat and placed the soap beside her. "If so, where are the koveen and wylders taking them?"

"Chaosthane." Nenneg crossed to the pool to splash her face. Drying it off on her sleeve, she faced Thugari with a frown marring her delicate features. "It bodes ill for Kethil."

"You know what's behind this," Thugari whispered. The sad acceptance of the thefts and a sideways glance at Borgakh gave Nenneg away.

"Seven months ago, I was one of these deluded wylders." Nenneg paced around the fire. Her swirling skirts sent embers and flames spiraling upward. "I encountered something in the caverns of Chaosthane, and when I tried to warn the Council..." She shuddered, rubbing her arms as if the fire couldn't warm her. "Borgakh captured me outside Penven, pinning me to a tree to demand an explanation. Of course, her reputation does precede her, and I trembled in my boots. I stuttered like a youngling." Nenneg's forced giggle sliced through the tension in the air.

"It didn't take her long to charm me." Borgakh flashed a tender smile.

"Having the orc maiden at my side when I faced the Arch-Magus and the Grand Lawmaster bolstered my voice." Nenneg puffed up her chest.

"Did they listen to you?" Thugari asked, wondering whether she would have had the confidence to face such legends.

Nenneg shook her head. "Even with Borgakh beside me, they dismissed my experience as impossible."

When Thugari had thought to deliver her version of the events, she hadn't considered whether they would take her at her word, only whether they would grant her an audience. Respect for Nenneg's courage rose within Thugari, and she altered her opinion of the wylder as braver than herself. Come to think of it, she preferred to cower behind boulders, peer through bushes, or burrow into groves than face koveen.

"What's the best way to kill a koveen?" she asked.

A slow smile softened Borgakh's face. "At last you ask, little one. Any sharp blade, but you are not made for such skills."

Cold drenched Thugari's scalp, and she fought back a wash of tears. "But—"

"I do not doubt your heart, nor your ability to learn what is needed. It is the koveen I am wary of. Best to avoid them at all costs."

She sighed and accepted the waterskin Borgakh offered. Thugari had hoped the orc maiden would teach her how to at least defend herself. Straightening her shoulders, she vowed to pursue this, but not now. She would wait until Borgakh was in a happier mood before she asked again.

Chapter Twelve

Silence gripped the forest in anticipation of dawn. Shadows deepened as dew coated leaves, vines, and petals, and the temperature dipped. Sharn's orb pulsed as it led north. In its pool of light, Rukk saw far enough ahead to eradicate his fear of Harpax breaking a leg. The trees thickened. A scowl formed. He hated traveling through the Forest of Anduia.

As a half-elf, he sensed the lost souls, the whispers of the dead beneath the decaying layers softening the ground. As a half-orc, his clan spoke only of conquered wars. Few knew of its history, of failed battles, of shared goals, of united races, and how much such wars had cost Kethil.

If he dug beneath the decaying plant matter, he would discover the translucent bones of his ancestors, millions having sacrificed themselves to stop the Ravenous Dark. Yet the archives weren't forthcoming on what the Dark was. Battling a faceless enemy, something feared and dreaded would be difficult for any male. It rose from the bowels of Chaosthane like a storm cloud every few centuries, having fed on the evil deeds saturating the soil.

Orcs, humans, elves, and dwarves had forgotten all they had lost. Such legends were whispered around evening fires, and as a child, he had drifted off to dream of epic battles like the Battle Denui. Wave after wave of thousands of warriors had thrown themselves against the might of the Dark. Each death fed the Dark, strengthened it.

Perhaps only he saw the shadows, the shifting figures still in their full regalia. Only he heard their battle cries and pleas for mercy. Harpax snorted, sensing the forest's unease.

Rukk silenced his thoughts and forced himself to focus on Harpax's gait and not the centuries of heartache lingering in every creature's soul.

They had thwarted the Ravenous Dark, thrusting it into the bowels of Kethil. Not that the magi or lawbringers knew how this was accomplished. The archives carried no such knowledge. He doubted the Dark would remain underground, and even if it did break free of the eternal chains restraining it, there was nothing to feed on. Harpax snorted again, dragging Rukk from his thoughts. He dipped his fingers into his hidden soil pouch, needing to touch his homeland. Warmth pulsed along his arm and soaked into his skin.

Exhaustion trudged through him, dulling his senses until even blinking became laborious. He approached a small village, Rontler or Ventley, he couldn't remember. An elf's innate sense of direction guided him truer than a magus could, although, nowadays, most magi relied on charts sketched by merchants. He had managed to hide that aspect of himself from Tarid. Because of Rukk's elven mother, he was sensitive to magic, to time, to history.

Hopefully the village had a decent inn. As much as a lawbringer traveled, he had never grown fond of sleeping on the ground. If circumstances forced him to do so this day, it would be another complaint to lay at Thugari's feet. She had to be sleeping in luxury and using his coin to do so. And Zetar forbid, what if she stole from someone less forgiving than Rukk?

A surge of something sharp and alarming settled over his heart, thumping its beats out of rhythm. Not recognizing it, having never experienced the emotion before, he dismissed the vise-like grip on his chest as indigestion. Still, his mind whispered the symptoms stemmed from fear. He shook his head. There was nothing to fear, and certainly not from a half-orc thief like Thugari.

Breaking into his thoughts came a splash northeast of the path, triggering a flurry of hekle birds leaving their nests. The jagged, iridescent wings of the raucous and cumbersome creatures dotted the sunrise like downward arrows pointing to the disturbance. He wavered, not sure he wanted to investigate. The yellow tainting the majestic indigo sky would soon smother the shadows and voices haunting the forest.

He halted Harpax and dismounted, tethering him to a nearby branch. Sharn's orb hovered above the horse. She hadn't tied it to Rukk's movements, yet another thing to be grateful for.

Layers of wet leaves, moss, and soil softened his footsteps as he wove through the trees growing in tight formation. Silver bark scarred with growth and memories hindered his vision. The final row hid him from view as he peered into the clearing. Stacked to one side of the camp were satchels and three bedrolls. A fire burned in the dawn light. He waited for movement.

A waterfall trickled into a pool, its rumble softened by rocks until it splattered on the surface, rippling outward. Sliding his hood back to expose his twitching ears, he held his breath and listened. Frowning at the silence, he doubted his hearing and sanity. There was no one here despite the evidence of a campsite. Rolling his shoulders to relax his tense muscles, he turned for Harpax, not wishing to dally further.

Bubbles disturbing the mirrored surface of the pool caught his attention, and he froze when something burst out. A female. She flicked her molten black hair in a wide arc, spraying droplets with the length of it. Her threadbare tunic clung to her breasts, the dark areolas visible in the soft morning light.

Thugari. Not that he recognized her by her nipples, but by the obsidian medallion nestled in her cleavage. Satisfaction swept through him. At last! He need not search for her any longer. A breeze tickled the leaves, tantalizing him with the fragrance of mint. He scanned the rocks and located the bar of soap. A maiden bathing, and not just any girl, but the female he hunted.

She waded toward the bank, rising out of the water with a grace he paused to admire, for he couldn't recall seeing such fluidity in motion. Yet, she had masqueraded as a stableboy, mimicking their mannerisms and fooling two lawbringers.

She gathered her braids in her hands and twisted them over one shoulder, rivulets of water streaming over her curves and down her bare legs. He drew in a slow, silent breath, the burn in his lungs demanding he breathe. He lingered on the indent of her waist, the wide arc of her hips, down to thick thighs and defined calves. He clenched his jaw.

Anger replaced the fiery addiction of arousal as he fought the lust. When she peeled off her tunic to wring out and drape over a boulder, his emotions catapulted through him with an explosion of fury he hadn't experienced in a while. Scars—pink, ivory, and ebony—marred the smoothness of her skin. Nehrakgu had done this to her. His way of marking her without giving her the protection of his clan. And Rukk had let the male off with a silencing spell. What kind of a lawbringer was he?

An incompetent one.

She jumped as she pulled on fresh breeches, her enticing breasts bouncing. On went a tunic, the hem snagging her hard nipples as she adjusted the cloth in place. When his ears twitched again, he glanced east to the rustle of leaves and hushed giggles.

She heard it too, peering into the forest before rushing through her tunic's ties. He darted through the trees, his braids whipping the trunks as he ran. Yet he remained hidden from her, his focus on the intruders, but his thoughts on a dark-orc thief with irresistible curves.

A hundred yards southeast, two young woodcutters huddled beside a boulder, unaware of the temptress in the pool. They cradled the wineskin as if they had stolen it. Shaking his head, he summoned his magic, and diaphanous white tendrils circled his fingers. With a whispered word, he fired bolts at them and waited for them to collapse in slumber. He peeled the wineskin from their fingers and sniffed it. Grimacing at the watered-down mead, he poured it over their sleeping forms before grabbing each one by their pant legs to drag them east, farther away from the pool and toward the nearest village.

Navigating his way to Thugari, Rukk considered what he should say to her. Demand his medallion? Of course. Did he want her to apologize and beg for forgiveness? Drop to her knees? Grunting, he tried to smother the image of her on her knees for a more pleasurable reason. He was sicker than he thought, to succumb to the sight of a naked female so easily. Healing would be swift once his medallion hung from his neck, and this unexpected attraction would vanish.

"Thugari." He stepped into the clearing and swore in Elvish.

The pool was serene and the campsite abandoned.

Chapter Thirteen

THE TOWN OF LEMFOR was a bustling one, boasting a store, a tavern with an inn above it, and a livery. It wrapped around a Fountain of Sound in the dead center of the market. Stalls selling a variety of items snatched Thugari's attention from side-to-side until the muscles in her neck throbbed. Fresh fruit, cured meats, pipe tobacco, and leather goods from sellers calling out their wares. Scurrying folks dodged horse shit on the cobbles, and some allowed their fur-lined cloaks to drag through it. Yet, despite the vibrancy of life, sharpened spikes lined the entrances, human males with pickaxes, rusted swords, or pitchforks watched with distrustful, narrowed eyes. Hushed wailing merged with the burble of activity.

"Thugari, refill our pouches and wineskins. Nenneg, find us lodgings. I'll take the horses to the stables and meet you at the tavern for a meal." Borgakh shoved coin into Thugari's hand before gathering the reins and striding off.

She didn't stare after the tall orc for long. Tantalizing aromas from a nearby stall had her feet sidling across. Thugari's stomach pinched then growled, so she handed over a copper for honeyed apple rings. Tearing one off with her teeth, she chewed and ogled, keeping one hand on her coin just in case. As she ambled along the stalls, she lowered her apple to a gap in her tunic for Gnash to have a quick nibble.

Merchant after merchant offered her bargains, throwing in extra despite her attempts to refuse. A smile from her, and their prices dropped. She would ask Borgakh if that was normal for town markets. With such variety, she bought too much—cheeses, large hams, dried fruit, and too many wineskins, though she doubted the contents would taste better than Borgakh's water.

Remembering its flavor soured the apple for her, and she threw it away, licking her fingers as she meandered the stalls. Tunics, cloaks, and boots tempted her to part with Rukk's gold. Overburdened as she was, she headed for the tavern, the sun's position reminding her that she had dallied.

The stench of unwashed bodies, stale mead, and roasted boar slammed into her as she slipped inside the tavern. A few patrons halted their conversation, running narrowed gazes over her, but she ignored them, weaving through the crowds to where Borgakh and Nenneg sat. Borgakh held the young wylder's hand, stroking her thumb across it. Nenneg's eyes sparkled, and a teasing smile lingered.

If Thugari hadn't heard their whispered endearments, giggles, and moans at night, or seen their open affection for one another, she would have found their proximity curious. Borgakh was a striking female. Even Thugari thought the orc maiden's plump lips pretty.

"They saw you coming, Thugari." The warrior female's bold laugh sliced through the deafening din.

"I spent less than needed. Too many lowered their prices or gave extra." She pushed Borgakh's coin pouch across the scarred wooden table. "It was most strange, Borgakh."

Nenneg glanced at Borgakh, who flushed. The orc maiden coughed. "We'll send you for supplies more often." She laid out two keys, then gathered the coin pouch, tucking it into her armor. "Yours and ours."

Thugari swallowed past the lump in her throat. Tears stung her eyes at their kindness.

She blinked them away, grabbed the keys, and raced up the stairs. Slamming her back against the wood-paneled walls, she juggled the pouches and wineskins to wipe away the tears. She hadn't cried in years. Well, not since her mother died. Gnash rubbed his cheek along her neck, offering comfort.

Sniveling, she held up the unmarked keys and groaned. Doors lined the passageway on both sides, and she would have to test each one.

She cursed under her breath at every failed attempt. Moon above, if anything became squashed in the juggle she would throw something. Gnash tickling her as he scurried from food pouch to food pouch served to distract her. The click of a matched key echoed in the quiet of the upper floor with the muted hum of the tavern below. Stumbling inside, she spotted their satchels alongside the bed and placed their purchases on the table.

The next door was hers. The key slid in with a satisfactory click, lifting her spirits and transforming the hum below into a welcoming murmur. She lowered her purchases to the floor, settled Gnash on the pillow, then threw herself onto the massive bed, squealing as she sank into its soft mattress. Borgakh and Nenneg waited for her. She leaped to her feet and left, dropping the key into a separate pocket and trapping Gnash inside the room.

She skipped down the stairs, the aroma of boar tempting her as she rounded the landing. The sight of silver hair jerked her to a halt. Rukk? She sidled backward, squeaked when she stumbled over a man's foot and bounced off a robust farmer—who reeked of onion—to land at his feet. Crawling along the mead-saturated floor, she ignored the farmer's bark of surprise. She would swim through manure as long as Rukk didn't see her.

Clambering up a wall, she kept her back pinned to it, peeking through the crowd to make sure her eyes hadn't deceived her. His braided hair fell over the back of the chair. He stretched out his long legs and tapped his thick fingers on the table. An unrestrained smile softened his features into something breathtaking. Her heart drummed to deafen her, and something tight squeezed her chest.

He chatted with Borgakh as if they were friends, or he had tracked Nenneg from Penven. Thugari chewed on her bottom lip as she wondered how to rescue her friends. A shiver slithered down her back, sending goosebumps along her arms and up to her temples. He said he would find her, find his medallion. If she gave it back to him, he would leave them alone.

When she ran her trembling fingers across the medallion, she sniffed. Once more, tears stung her eyes. She didn't want to part with it, but it wasn't hers to keep. To save her friends, she would sacrifice much. Throwing out her arm, she snagged a passing tavern maid.

"Do you have a cloth?" she asked.

Frowning, the poor female held out a dirty rag.

Thugari snatched it. "Wait." She turned away, dug inside her tunic to unloop the medallion, then wrapped it inside the cloth. Shoving the bundle into the female's hands along with a coin, Thugari pointed at Rukk.

She refused to blink as the tavern maid placed the bundle in front of him. He arched a brow at her before dragging it onto his lap to unravel it. Then he straightened in the chair, darting glances around the room. Thugari ducked away, sucking in calming breaths. She snuck a peek to find him rising to his feet, and with a startled cry, scurried up the stairs.

She fumbled with her key, cursing in a breathless voice when she missed the keyhole. At last, it clicked, but the sound of approaching footsteps thrust her into her room. She slammed the door and bolt home before stumbling away from it. The bed at the back of her calves tripped her, and she fell, bouncing twice on the bed before landing on the floor with an *oof*.

Lying behind the bed, she prayed and peered over it, hoping he didn't find her. Gnash scampered across the bed, twittering loud enough to wake the dead. She shushed him, scooped him, and tucked him into her hair.

Borgakh wouldn't rescue her, but Thugari didn't expect her to when the orc maiden didn't know why Rukk hunted her. The tips of her ears burned at the conversation between them, imagining him mentioning why he was in the area.

Moon above. Thugari's heart thumped, echoing the pounding outside her room, as if someone knocked on the doors. She clapped a hand over her mouth to smother the squeal when her door rattled. He could use magic to unbolt it, and he was strong enough to break it down. His pursuit made no sense. She had given him his medallion. Shit, his coin pouch. She hadn't spent any of it since buying Envis, not wanting to owe the lawbringer more, preferring to sell the stolen lockets instead. As it was, he could take her life, and no one would bat an eye.

"Thugari." His rasping voice penetrated the door. She sucked in a breath and held it. Gnash burrowed deeper. No, Rukk couldn't know this was her room. He had to be guessing. "I can smell you, my little thief."

Smell her? She sniffed her tunic and grimaced at the stench of tavern clinging to her hands and garments.

"Thank you for my medallion," he said, startling another gasp from her. "Please open the door."

No way under the sweet moon would she do such a thing. He would kill her for sure. Using kind words didn't render her stupid. A sob escaped her, and she smothered her face in the blanket. Gnash darted for the pillow and burrowed under it. She couldn't stay there tonight. Rukk might enter her room when she was most vulnerable.

Almost weeping like a child, she cursed him under her breath for ruining her first time in a real bed. A night in Envis's stall was her only option, and she hoped the stablemaster didn't discover her until morning. She hurried to wash her hands in the clay water bowl the inn had provided. Patting her palms dry on her breeches, she shoved her food pouch and wineskin inside her satchel. Gnash?

She flipped the pillow away and found nothing. Spinning on the spot and not seeing him, she pressed her cheek to the floor to peer under the bed. Panic hit her, and she bit her lip to stem the flow of curses. She would have to sneak into the room in the morning and find him.

She pushed the window open. If she hung from the windowsill and dropped down, she could survive the fall. Or worse, break a leg, but it wouldn't kill her.

"Thugari, please, open for me." He tapped the door.

She hesitated, taking a step toward him before realizing he seduced her with his alluring voice. Decision made. She placed his coin pouch on the table, careful not to make a sound. With a final glance at the door, she looped the satchel over her shoulder, then climbed out the window.

As she peered at the ground, fear slithered through her like the first chilled winds of winter, and she castigated herself for her foolishness. She didn't need help from Rukk to be an idiot. She managed fine without him. As she twisted, intending to climb into the room, white gossamer tendrils pierced the cracks of the door and glided the bolt aside.

She let go of the window's ledge.

CHAPTER FOURTEEN

RUKK STOPPED OUTSIDE A door where Thugari's crisp fragrance of mint was the strongest. Any words he spoke, he did so out of desperation. In his search for her, she had become important to him. When she didn't respond, he considered she might fear retribution for the theft. He was a lawbringer known for his harsh judgments.

Movement from inside the room forced him to summon magic and open the door. With two fingers, he pushed the door open. His coin pouch snagged his attention from where it sat on a table alongside an open window.

It proved his senses correct. This was Thugari's room. Striding in, he scanned its empty contents and scowled. A whimper from outside whipped his head around, and he lunged for the window, grabbing his still-warm pouch as he dove through the narrow opening.

He somersaulted in mid-air to land in a crouch. Her climb out the window to escape him demonstrated her fear. Pocketing his coin pouch, he waited for his eyes to adjust to the darkness. A smothered sob and a limping figure slipped around the corner of the tavern, heading in the direction of the stables.

He sprinted after her. She kept to the shadows, surely hoping to hide. He found her and pinned her to the wall. Golden light pooled from the windows, raucous laughter served as background noise to his pounding heart and her ragged breathing. He layered his body over hers, imprisoning her trembling form, and shuddered. Her softness molded to his harder edges like the welcoming embrace of a lover.

"Thugari." He cupped her face to catch her tears.

"Get off me." She struggled, every wriggle nestling his hips against hers.

He sucked in a sharp breath, willing her to cease, desperate to stop the torment. "I vow not to harm you, little thief."

She stilled. "Returning me to Haraton will harm me."

Her apple-scented breath wafted over his chin and mouth. He choked back a groan, anticipating how delicious she would taste.

"I-I won't go back, lawbringer. Kill me and have done with it."

"The Council will deal with your father." Anger tightened his jaw, sharpened his voice, and he fought to soften it, lest he frighten her further.

"I doubt that." Her fingers fluttered against his chest where they rested.

Feeling her touch to the depths of his soul, he wished no garments separated their forms.

"I know what he did to you, Thugari, and the Council will hold him accountable for abusing their trust." He swept her hair off her temple, marveling at its silkiness.

Sucking in a deep breath, he savored her enticing scent, allowing it to fill every inch of him. Silence descended, thickening the air between them, firing his senses, which made outrageous demands for relief.

"Release me." Her soft-spoken words ran along his skin as if she caressed him.

"I can't." He couldn't command his body to step away from her and let her leave him.

She was magicless, yet in some strange way, she had bewitched him. Arousal pounded at his focus, his control, tightening his body. Like a bastior—the ancestor of wolfman creatures—once he fixated on her, she was at the core of every decision he made.

She gasped, fighting his embrace. An ache spread outward from his loins, wrenching his stomach, squeezing his lungs until he thrummed with need.

"You had better release her, Rukk." Borgakh's voice sliced through the darkness and the lust clouding his mind, seconds before an orb of light illuminated them.

She balanced an elbow on the hilt of her sword, its point buried in the cobbles with her implication clear. Thugari relaxed, and her body molded to his even more—her breasts, her curves, the feminine mound of her stomach, the length of her thighs. A moan slipped past his clenched lips.

"Thugari and I have a *history*." Rukk chose to word this thing between them as such.

It was orc custom not to involve oneself in something of a personal nature. How his senses pulsed, as if he had overindulged on his father's fine wine, made this more than personal. It made this intimate.

"You owe him, Thugari?" Borgakh's pseudo-casual pose stiffened.

Rukk faced Thugari for the first time since the orb of light's illumination. He studied her, memorizing her features inches away. Her silver-gray gaze met his. His heart skipped a beat as he drowned in those swirling depths. Time slowed, enhancing the gentle rise and fall of her breathing, the splash of color blooming across her cheeks, her lips parting, tempting him to kiss her.

"I..." She bit her bottom lip. "He could ki... Yes." Her gaze traced a path down his nose, lingered on his lips before flicking up to meet his again. "He helped me escape Haraton and paid for Envis."

Her words tore through him. She could have inspired Borgakh to champion her, forcing him to kill his old friend or forfeit Thugari. Nenneg hovered behind Borgakh, her raised hands swirling with green magic, which meant another protector might have died. Borgakh protected Thugari, and Nenneg guarded her lover.

He dipped his head, bringing his lips to within an inch of hers. "Envis?"

"My horse." She pushed against him with her hands and hips, a torturous plea to release her, which only served to fire his blood more.

"Don't move." He used compulsion and his full authority in his voice.

She listened, ceased her wriggling even as her heartbeat skittered. Her nostrils flared as she studied him. She squeezed her eyes shut and tilted her head back against the wooden wall, yet curled her fingers into his tunic as if she wanted him to remain in place.

"Where are you heading?" Borgakh sidled to them while sheathing her sword. He wasn't deceived into complacency. She was lethal with or without weapons.

"Chaosthane." He ran his fingertip along Thugari's cheek, capturing a stray curl to loop behind an ear. When he stroked the orcish tip, she gasped and squirmed beneath him. He flashed a smile, delighted to find her sensitive to his touch.

"Travel with us." Borgakh spun on her heels to head for the tavern. "Let's discuss why over roast boar."

"We head for the Peaks of Gill-Eòin." Nenneg uncurled her fingers, dissipating her magic and the orb of light as her gaze trailed Borgakh.

After peeling himself off Thugari with much reluctance, he dipped to slide his arms under her knees and around her back. He hadn't forgotten she had hurt herself jumping from the window. Her breath feathered across his neck as she clung to him, holding as much of her body off him as she could. Nenneg, who had watched him carry her, rushed to unhook Thugari's satchel.

"Put me down," Thugari said from between clenched teeth.

He ignored her, jostling her to silence her before weaving through the crowd and placing her on a chair. Removing his medallion, he slipped it over her head and tucked it inside her tunic to find its natural resting place between her breasts. She jerked back, reaching for it, but he captured her hand in his and held firm.

He shook his head. "It will reduce the swelling and start the healing process until I can look at it later."

"*Later?*" she mouthed, darting a glance at Borgakh and Nenneg. "Why would I go anywhere with you?" Fear darkened her eyes.

"You're with me now, Thugari." He sat and faced Borgakh, rather than analyze why those words spread joy through him.

"I *am* glad to see you, Rukk. We considered sounding the Council with our findings, but the sightings are increasing, and we haven't had a chance. More or better news would aid the Council's decision, and Zetar willing, spur them into action." Borgakh drank from her wooden cup, draining it before she waved over a tavern maid.

He waited for the maid to leave to fulfill Borgakh's request. "I follow the koveen north, though why and what they're up to, I cannot say." Thugari's skin tingled his fingers as per the first time they touched, now more potent skin on skin than when his gloves had separated them. "I have encountered many in my hunt for this one." Gesturing with his head at his thief, he smiled at her. "We have crossed paths, have we not, my little...doe."

Her shoulders slumped. She had thought he would call her a thief in front of her champions.

"We track the koveen too," Nenneg said. "I didn't relish killing my sisters, but their blind obedience deserves death."

"You know why they travel north." His body tensed as if preparing to battle, but he didn't crush Thugari's delicate hand with his. Brushing his thumb over her knuckles, he hoped such an action would calm him even as he cherished the softness of her.

"I do, and I will share why when we are far from listening ears." Nenneg clasped Borgakh's hand.

"Does the Grand Lawmaster know? If so, did you address the Council?" He quieted his inner turmoil.

Nenneg's answer would determine how much Galand withheld from him and would prove whether Rukk could trust the Grand Lawmaster. He couldn't recall in their history when last they had declared a lawmaster unworthy.

Though, what their laws and rituals dictated for such an occurrence, he would need to research. Ousting Galand wasn't an enviable task. Perhaps Rukk needed to seek guidance from the Arch-Magus Erwana Le Fevre.

The young wylder nodded while accepting the bowl of fresh fruit the tavern maid placed before her. Thugari tried to wiggle her hand free. He glanced at her, not wanting to cease touching her, but she shifted closer to the table and the plate of boar placed before her. He released her and waited as she bit into the meat, her eyelids fluttering in bliss.

To say he tasted his meal would be erroneous. To say he drank more mead than he should have would be an accurate assessment. Every move Thugari made snagged his attention, even when his gaze wasn't upon her. He'd never been more aware of a female.

"We leave as soon as my companions arrive." He swirled the honeyed mead in his cup. "They delivered reclaimed bairns to their villages."

Borgakh dropped a bone and sucked on her fingers. "We can't wait. We'll travel ahead and meet up at the next town."

"Thugari stays with me." His tone was adamant.

Nenneg opened her mouth to argue, but Borgakh shook her head.

He didn't care what they discussed. Only Thugari's opinion mattered since she stiffened beside him. Reaching across, he laced their fingers and leaned in. With his lips brushing her earlobe, he said, "We'll discuss why in your room."

She jerked away from him, fear darkening her eyes. Her reaction brought him to his feet, lifting her, as well.

"Good slumber," he said to Borgakh and Nenneg in passing.

Thugari dug in her pockets and placed a key on the table. She gathered her satchel and limped up the stairs. He didn't speak as she entered her room—the door open from when he had intruded. Closing it behind him, he glided the bolt home and, with a whispered word, placed a ward of protection.

"Summon the town guard, charge me, or kill me. Just don't harm my friends." She set her satchel on the bed, then faced him with her fists clenched at her sides. A breathtaking beauty stood before him.

He forced himself to look away, hoping to bolster his waning self-control. "It doesn't work like that, Thugari."

"No mining the salt plains, no death?" Her expression switched from distrust to hope, then to fear. "My body?" Her question came out on a squeak. She was so easy to read, his doe.

He ran his gaze down her body, lingering on her curves with a deep longing. Fighting sudden breathlessness, he shook his head. "I will explain."

"Where are your things?"

He appreciated the courage she displayed, but her strong tone didn't mask her trembling limbs. The change of subject would only buy her time, but if she thought she could attempt another escape, she was in for a harsher lesson.

"The innkeeper has them in safekeeping." He sat on the only chair and gestured to the bed. "Owing an orc is a serious matter, Thugari, you know this."

A pulse worked at the base of her jaw, but she sat, her fingers gripping her knees. "I'm sorry. I wanted to escape, and the more coin I had, the farther I could outrun my father."

He smiled, finding her honesty enchanting. "I understand your motives, little one, and had you taken just my pouch, I wouldn't have pursued you. My medallion, however, is far more precious to me."

Her fingers stroking the medallion through her tunic mesmerized him. He would like nothing more than to bury himself in her, his medallion nestled between her bouncing breasts. He blinked to clear the image from his mind. She wasn't ready for rutting. Innocence bathed her, her reactions guileless.

Excitement skittered through him, and he bit down hard on his inner cheek, needing the sharp pain to ground him. If he wasn't on a task, he would be the one to introduce her to the pleasures of the flesh, but he couldn't afford the delay.

With Thugari, he sensed rutting with her would mean more to him than just tending to an urge. It would take longer than an evening and incapacitate him for more than two days.

"How long will I owe you?" Her soft voice called him from his delicious thoughts.

"Until you *want* to remain with me. When that happens, you are free to choose your own destiny." He scanned her expressive face, resting on where she nibbled on her bottom lip. Then a smile burst to life, growing until she chuckled.

"So like the orcs not to have definitive laws. At this moment, I want to be as far away from you as possible." She gaped, slapped a hand across her mouth, and her eyes widened. "Not that I don't like you...or don't find you attractive. Moon above. I mean, I have plans this will delay."

He grinned. Her hurried yet revealing words burrowed into his chest and radiated warmth outward. "Thank you." He rose to his full height, only to kneel at her feet to untie a boot. "Tell me what a free Nehrakgu has planned."

She scowled, falling back on her elbows as she studied him through half-lidded eyes. "I don't like Nehrakgu, and I have yet to choose a last name. I thought of using my mother's, but Borgakh said it wasn't wise to do so when I know nothing of my lineage."

He frowned, finding Borgakh's advice strange. Claiming one's lineage was the first step to self-discovery and finding a clan to belong to. All orcs knew this. "What's your mother's name?" Sliding off the boot on the healthy foot, he untied Thugari's other boot, more careful this time. Although, since she hadn't complained, either the injury was minor or his medallion had done well.

"Macutia," she said as he peeled her boot off.

He froze, raising his gaze to look at her. She *had* enthralled him. A shudder tore through him, and he released a slow breath. He could work with this, thwart her influence.

"They say my mother was a powerful enchantress who ensnared my father, but it wouldn't surprise me if they lied. Dead people can't defend themselves." She sat up, her shrug wooden, belying her casual tone.

"Choosing another name is wise." He summoned his magic to wrap around her bruised ankle. The medallion had brought down the swelling. "So, why are you traveling with the orc maiden?"

"They're heading north to Chaosthane. I hope to find shelter there among my kind."

"And your kind is?" He hadn't heard of orcs dwelling anywhere near the dwarves. They tolerated each other at the best of times and only as allies in war.

"Magicless."

"A Macutia without magic?" He fought for focus when his magic wavered.

She didn't know. No one had told her about her mother or any Macutia, for that matter. For his sanity, he wouldn't be the one to enlighten her. As she was, sitting there, her breasts pressed to her knees, her tunic gaping, she enticed him more than he could bear. He, a lawbringer, was jealous of his medallion cocooned in her cleavage. If she knew of her magic and how it manifested, he would be unable to resist her.

No one could.

"I'll take you as far as Dussoum." He leaned back on his haunches after her bruises faded and only smooth dark skin remained. Trailing a fingertip around her ankle, he marveled at the softness even there. "Along the way, I'll teach you to fight. I would like to see how much you learned from your book."

Her head whipped up. This close, the pink on the underside of her bottom lip snagged his gaze.

He frowned. "Do I frighten you, Thugari?"

She clamped her lips shut over her tusks and straightened, her focus never leaving his. "I'm not scared of anything." Color stained her cheeks.

"Don't lie to me, little one. It's disrespectful." He grabbed her hands and urged her to her feet.

Then with as much care as he could muster, he slipped his arms around her and gathered her against him. He trembled at having her curves touching him again, but he stood there, didn't say another word, just held her and waited.

She kept her body rigid as if she expected a slap or a harsh word. Time ticked by. She relaxed, raising her arms from his hips to his back, then they tightened as she burrowed her nose into his neck. She was a skittish creature, fearful of kindness and distrusting affection. He would have to whittle that away, and by then, when she trusted him with her life, perhaps he would no longer yearn to find pleasure between her thighs.

CHAPTER FIFTEEN

It took Thugari ages to fall asleep, what with the change in her circumstances and listening for the familiar pitter-patter of little feet that never came. When she did drift off, she rested for too short a time. In the moonlight ghosting the room, the bulge of Rukk's shoulder filled her vision, his hair pooling on the pillow. She buried her fingers in the silken tresses, unable to resist the allure. What an odd evening. At least she could sleep in the bed, but therein lay her dilemma. It was too soft, and if her movements wouldn't awaken him, she would sprawl on the floor.

She considered escaping, but climbing out the window again was foolhardy. He had used his magic on the door which shimmered white, so leaving that way was impossible. She was trapped. Fear had faded after his long hug, as he showed his intentions were good. He had sprawled out on the bed and fallen asleep, not fearing an attack from her, either. She cherished trust given. His was breathtaking.

In the soothing silence of the night, with the old tavern creaking in the wind, she relived the last few hours—seeing his face, running up the stairs, hiding in her room only to throw herself out the window. Of course, she had hurt herself, and for nothing since he had caught her with ease.

Strange emotions had assaulted her. Blurring with her fear, ever on the surface, was this coiling heat in her belly and lower. She ached, compounded when he touched her or leveled those dark-brown eyes on her. They pierced through her, to her core, and revealed her motives, sifted through her thoughts and deepest desires.

He was kinder than she expected, keeping her with him instead of killing her, chopping off her hand for stealing, or worse, sending her to mine the salt plains. A tear slipped out, surprising her since she hadn't sensed its buildup.

Wiping it away, she smothered a snort. As if hiding the evidence of her tears could erase her intense gratitude. She didn't deserve his treatment of her. The great Rukk wasn't known for his kindness. The way he looked at her, touched and held her, engulfed her in a cloud of safety. She was a fool if she ran from that, from such an escort north.

She tested her ankle, swirling it in slow circles. He had healed her too, and that had bound her to him far more than his silly orcish vow.

"Thugari."

She yelped, jerking back, and fell off, hitting the floor. Rising to glare at him over the edge of the bed, she squeaked, finding him sprawled on her side with her fingers entangled in his hair.

She released him, scrambling to her feet. "Sorry, you startled me."

"I can see that." His sleepy smile creased his upper lip. "Why are you awake?"

"The bed's too soft." Heat scorched a path up her temple and down her throat as mortification claimed her. "I didn't mean to wake you."

He rolled off his side of the bed, ripped off the blanket, and spread it on the floor. Throwing the pillows down, he spread out, stretching his long legs as he peered at her.

"Well? What are you waiting for?" He gestured with a flick of his wrist for her to lie next to him.

Bolting forward, she hastened to obey, not sure what her chores were, how much of a slave she was, and what the consequences were for disobedience. She lay on her left side, watching his profile kissed by the moonlight even as it emboldened her. He was asleep already. She shoved her palm between her cheek and pillow and forced her eyes shut. They fluttered open, not willing to succumb to sleep no matter how exhausted she was.

"I can sense your gaze, little doe." He flipped onto his side to look at her.

"Am I a slave?" She winced when anger crept across his face, hardening it. Here lay the male most feared. "I need to know what my chores are, and how you will reprimand me if I disobey."

His eyes widened, and his hand darted out, cupping her cheek. Having expected a slap, she jerked away. His fingers stroked her chin and hovered in mid-air before he retracted his arm. "I won't harm you, little one. Do you believe me when I say so?" He fixed his gaze on her, his intention clear. There would be no sleep for either of them until she responded.

Seconds dragged by, so she hurried to answer. "I do." She did. He hadn't hurt her yet. Anyone with malicious intent would have revealed their baser character by now.

"You're not a slave. If you promise to travel with me to Dussoum as my...friend, I will consider your debt paid in full."

Tears stung her eyes, bombarding her control until they slipped through, her eyelids unable to hold back the deluge. Whimpering, she rolled over onto her other side, giving him her back, trying to swallow past the raw lump in her throat. He didn't need to see her fall apart. Any weakness she showed garnered mockery or intolerance. Despite not knowing how to handle his gentleness, if he was harsh with her, it would tear her apart. Yet, cruelty she could deal with, couldn't she? She scrubbed her eyes, willing the tears to cease falling.

He shuffled across the blanket until the heat of his chest warmed her back without touching her. "Sweet Zetar, Thugari, please...don't cry."

"I'm not crying. I'm fine." She ignored her strangled voice and garbled words. He brushed her shoulder and down her upper arm to her elbow. "Don't be nice to me, please." She clambered to her feet, hurrying to the bowl to splash water on her face. Cool air caressed her stomach when she raised her tunic to wipe off the droplets. "Tell me my chores, give me boundaries, a time when I'll be free, and I can live with that. As your friend, you expect nothing of me. I'm not someone to pity, lawbringer."

He scowled but didn't rise from the floor. Sprawled on his back, he folded his arms beneath his head and sighed. The action shifted his tunic up, exposing his ridged torso, every mesmerizing inch of it. "I don't pity you, Thugari." He leveled his gaze on her, clear in the streaming moonlight. "Treat me as you would Borgakh."

She shook her head. Borgakh didn't scatter her senses, thoughts, and focus. Borgakh didn't summon this excitement raising the hairs all over her body, didn't snag her breath with the barest of touches.

"Am I so different? Or am I unworthy of your time?" His voice pleaded, then hardened on the last question. He sat up and patted the blanket. "Let me tell you a story."

She hesitated, but saw this as an opportunity to prove she could trust him. Dropping beside him, she folded her legs beneath her. He gathered one of her braids to unravel, his thick fingers gentle as he finger-combed through the strands.

"It is I who should ask for your forgiveness. Years ago, I visited Haraton. Your father and Lady Murzush spared no expense in entertaining me." He lowered his gaze to the task at hand, saving her from their dark depths.

"I don't remember your visit." She shifted across to grant him easier access to her hair.

No one had braided it since her mother died. It was strange, unnerving to allow Rukk to perform such an intimate act. His focus was distant, his eyes glazed as if he relived an event.

He brought the tip of her braid to his chin and feathered it back and forth. "Lady Arob wasn't there, either." A moan escaped his parted lips.

Something addictive coiled in Thugari's belly, and she struggled to breathe. "Um, she has left the castle once to visit her cousins. It was the harvesting season, which meant days spent out in the sun."

She picked at the nodules on the blanket, desperate to look anywhere else but at this captivating male. The sunlight, as wonderful as it was to be outside the castle, had blackened her skin. For days, castle-folk avoided her, spat at her, or cursed her. She shivered, hearing their whispered words as if they were in the room.

"If I hadn't indulged, if I had done my duty, I might have ended your torment sooner. For this, I ask your forgiveness, little doe." His dark gaze was on her again, his sincerity clear.

"That's not much of a story." A chuckle snuck up on her. "No dragons or vicious monsters? Yes, there was a damsel-in-distress, but since you didn't know who she was or where to find her, I would have to forgive you." She wagged a finger at him, giggling as she did so. A smile crawled across his face, as if she surprised him by daring to tease him. "I trust you won't let that happen again, fair lawbringer?"

"I vow if the damsel promises to remain by my side. I cannot make amends otherwise." He dropped her braid to cup her cheek, burying his fingers in her hair. His palm was hot and rough, yet tied to it were her heartstrings.

"I don't blame you, Rukk." Seeing this discussion continuing until sunrise, she gathered her courage and took the first step. "For Borgakh and Nenneg, I set up camp and all it entails, in thanks for their protection. I could do the same for you?"

She tried to smother the hope in her voice. Having a usefulness and being more than a slave or a burden mattered to her. And with no other valid skills, she could at least make the journey bearable.

"I believe we have reached an agreement. I will protect you from the wind and rain, from the monsters and dragons." He withdrew his dagger from his boot and sliced his palm before offering her the blade. His intense expression stuttered her heartbeat.

The sight of blood wasn't new to her, but it meant something to him. She reached for his dagger with tentative fingers, then snatched her hand back, offering her palm instead. Not knowing how sharp the edge was could lead to a deeper than necessary wound.

He cupped her hand in his and flicked the blade across, forming a thin crimson line that stung. Her blood pooled in her palm as he sheathed the dagger into his boot and clasped her hand, palm to palm. As he chanted lyrical old orcish, his magic—cold yet burning—swirled around their clasped hands. Tingling scurried up her arm and into her chest, nestling there. Something intense engulfed her heart, wrenching and haunting.

"Your life is tied to mine," he said.

"What?" She gasped, pulling her hand free to rub a fingertip across the blood smear on her healed palm. It was all that remained. "Why? Why would you do such a thing? I'm nobody." Curling her fingers into her palm, she fought the urge to smack him.

"How else am I to know when you're in danger?" He stretched out on the blanket again, tucking his arms behind his head.

"Let me die, you idiot." Lying next to him, she gave him her back. Tying his life to hers made him vulnerable. She was a weakling. Anyone and anything could kill her to harm him.

"Quit grumbling. It's an unbreakable bond." He repositioned her until she sprawled over him, her cheek on his chest, her leg over his. He looped an arm around her, cupping her elbow. "Rest, little one, for tomorrow we might depart."

Rest? She couldn't find peace when his life lay in her hands. The steady rhythm of his heart and his soft breathing fluttered her eyelids shut. She blinked them open, threw a glare at his stubborn chin, and despite her best efforts, her eyes closed moments later.

Releasing a long sigh, she ignored the pulse of her heart beating in her palm, mimicking his, thump for thump. Slipping her hand over his taut stomach to his side, she tightened her hold and vowed no one would use her to get to him. No one would know they could.

Chapter Sixteen

Rukk awoke with a feminine body curled around his. Thugari clung to him, nuzzling his chest, her arm thrown over him. Unable to resist the temptation, he gathered her against him, burying his face in her hair.

Sighing, he tilted his body to better embrace her. In doing so, something at his neck twittered. He hesitated, torn between gawking like an idiot or shoving Thugari aside as he shook off the creature.

She moaned, rubbing her leg over his thighs. His heart, which had stopped beating at the discovery of an intruder, now danced at her seductive movements. An exotic scent rose when she shifted and ran her hand up his belly to dig her nails into his chest. He swallowed a groan, not wanting to scare the creature, nor could he hold back the lust shredding his control.

"Thugari." Her name slipped from his tongue like a lover's caress.

He cleared his throat and nudged her. A tiny head popped up, its whiskers twitching. Summoning his magic, he waited until it burned his palm before striking.

"Morning." She stretched, thrusting her breasts out as she arched. A sigh slipped from her plump lips as she settled her hooded gaze on him. "What's the matter?"

"Creep away. I don't want to harm you when I kill the thing at my neck." His tone was level, his words gritted out through his clenched teeth.

"Kill?" She gaped. "Don't you dare." Leaping across him, she snatched the thing from his neck. "Gnash, where have you been?"

Rukk grunted, sucking his magic into his body as he clambered to his feet. "Of course you have a pet rat."

She stroked the brown head, then cuddled it to her chest. The gesture notched the level of irritation fast gnawing at his patience. He didn't bother asking her how she slept. Not when he had a raging arousal to deal with. Her scent thickened, calling to him, pounding at his senses.

Splashing his face with water from the pewter bowl, he dried himself on his tunic since his satchel was still with the innkeeper. Without a backward glance and an instruction to come down to the common room when she was ready, he stomped off.

He had just ordered the food when she appeared, slinking between the males starting on their hangovers early. A fire flickered in the hearth, drenching him with unneeded heat. Still, the mead soothed his frazzled nerves.

Males raised their heads when she passed, casting longing gazes at her in mid-sip or chew. She didn't notice, dropping onto the chair in front of him, bringing with her forest-fresh scent. A pair of beady eyes peeked at him from her thick hair.

He downed his mead and ordered another, preferring to stare at her without speaking. She plowed through her breakfast of dark bread, thick butter, and strips of meat. The fork beside her platter remained untouched, yet for once, he didn't mind, not with the way she licked her fingers.

The slow sweep of her tongue along each finger and the soft sucking noises she made would test the strongest warrior. He was a fool, all kinds of one. Not that he regretted tying his life to hers. As an impulse decision, he couldn't deny the strange compulsion and hoped doing so would diminish her allure. As naïve and unprotected as she was, the bond had been necessary, but it had yet to ease his arousal. He shifted in his chair, the ever-present ache a constant reminder.

It was days before his scheduled rutting. Another week of this agony. He searched the tavern, assessing the females present. A few were pretty and cleanish, but he couldn't summon the enthusiasm to pursue one. Perhaps at the next town, he might find something more to his taste. Scowling, he reminded himself he hadn't broken his self-inflicted tradition in years, yet now he considered doing so, yearned for it.

Thugari stroked her cleavage where his medallion had rested until this morning. "This is yours."

She offered him his medallion, tearing her tunic in the process. It gaped even more. Yanking his gaze away as he looped his medallion over his head, he scanned the patrons and their lingering glances. She did affect more than just him.

"That was delicious." As she leaned back to pat her belly, her collar tore, exposing the curve of a breast.

He raised his gaze to meet hers. There wasn't a hint of seduction in the bright smile she shared with him.

"Where to now?"

"The marketplace to spend coin." He led her out of the tavern into the morning light, glaring at any male gawking at her. His tolerance would be low until he had her better clothed. He couldn't endure more nights like the last, nor did he know how long it would take for her influence to wear off.

A blue tunic caught his eye, and he stopped to test its cloth. It was of excellent quality and small enough to fit her. "What other colors do you have?" he asked the merchant, who hurried to show him an off-white, a rich burgundy, and a dark gray. "I'll take all of them. Three sets of breeches in butter-soft leather for the lady." He turned to find Thugari four stalls back running a tentative finger over a dagger. "That lady." He gestured with a flick of his thumb. "That fur-lined cloak, those leather gloves, and a pair of boots."

"The boots will need fitting," the merchant said, accepting the coin Rukk dropped onto his palm, even as his gaze lingered on Thugari.

Rukk scowled and folded his arms across his chest as she meandered through the stalls. When she realized he waited, color stained her cheeks, and she skipped to him, trailing her hair behind with her breasts bouncing as he dreamed they would. He squeezed his eyes shut, sucking in calming breaths.

"Sorry," she said, her breathlessness uncoiling heat in the pit of his stomach.

"Try on those boots." He lowered his gaze to her patched 'footwear,' not willing to dignify them by calling them boots.

Frowning, she opened her mouth to argue, but he shook his head. Clamping her lips, she slumped onto a stool. After trying on two sets of boots, she found a pair that fit well.

"Here." He flicked out the cloak, opening it for her to slip in. By now, her scowl was ferocious to behold, not diminishing her beauty in the least. Tucking her pet rat inside her tunic, she gathered her hair off her shoulders and offered her back.

He fumbled, almost dropping the cloak. There, burned into the back of her neck, was an ancient sigil in the shape of a heater shield. The Stone Cage required great skill to weave the spell and was painful to apply. Horror tore through him. His fingers gripped and released the cloak as he fought to remain calm. He wanted to throw her over Harpax and hurry her to the Council.

Whoever had cast the spell or ordered it done hadn't wanted her magic to manifest. Too long unbroken, the power would build and either leak out or explode, harming the individual. Magical explosions tended to drive the magic-user insane or endanger those around them. The Council had banned the use of the Stone Cage two centuries ago. How she had come to bear it was a mystery.

"How does it feel?" He gave up on regulating his voice.

She threw a glare at him and stormed off, her cloak billowing behind her. The merchant looked nervous, his hand tightening around his purse as if Rukk would demand his coin back.

With the bundle tucked under his arm, he straggled after Thugari to the inn. Perfect, he needed to sit her down and ask her about the sigil. Every part of him dreaded the discussion. How could he explain her life was in danger? Worse, he'd life bonded with a female he might have to kill. Whatever had driven him to act impulsively, he prayed Zetar had a plan.

"I don't need your coin." She paced inside their room. The cloak draped the end of the bed, and on top of it, curled her rat. Her new boots squeaked on the wooden floors with each directional change.

"Wind and rain, Thugari." He placed the parcel on the bed. "Enough about the garments, tell me about the sigil on your neck."

Color drained from her face, turning her rich brown skin ashen. "I've had it for as long as I can remember. In the last few years, Uzul has used it to force me to relive past punishments." She hesitated, betrayal merged with fury in her silver-gray eyes. Trudging the distance between them, she knelt before him and flipped her hair out of the way.

Fire exploded through his chest at her expectation he would hurt her as Uzul had done. He should have slit the male's throat! Not a breeze teased her hair, her breath caught and held as she awaited punishment. Here before him was the beaten female who'd fled her home. Her stillness tensed his muscles and crumbled his resolve. He fell to his knees and wrapped his arms around her, surrounding himself with her exotic fragrance.

"I vowed not to harm you, little doe." He kissed her hair.

She sobbed, her shoulders sagging, then rising and falling as she sucked in gulping breaths. "I thought my ingratitude offended you."

"New garments because your breast peeking out of your tunic was too tempting even for me." He chuckled, but it was self-deprecating. His lustful thoughts were his burden to bear.

"Oh." Her face flushed, and he wanted to cup her cheeks, to feel the heat of her embarrassment under his thumbs. She grabbed her gaping tunic, holding it closed.

Too late, sweet Thugari.

Despite the shimmer of tears on her eyelashes, she smiled. "I would have let you hurt me this once, but would have slipped away from you soon after."

He grunted. "I would have hunted you again. We made a deal. Now...your sigil. When did you receive it?" He traced the pad of his thumb along her jaw.

"After my mother died. I don't remember much. I mourned my loss with a numb heart." She narrowed her eyes, her gaze distant. "A female stranger removed the pain."

"Did Uzul or your father explain it to you?" He scowled, with anger coursing through his veins.

Varthug Nehrakgu would receive a harsher judgment than his name on the watch list. If Rukk had his way, the Council would strip him of his titles, his wealth, and Rukk would ensure his dignity suffered, as well.

"No." She tilted her face, peering into his eyes. "Why this interest? Isn't it used to hurt people?"

"It's called a Stone Cage, enclosing your magic until the sigil is removed or your trapped magic severs your mind. Lawbringers kill the magic-user when that happens." Succumbing, too weak to resist, he cupped her face, and buried his fingers in her silken strands.

He traced her eyes, the flutter of her eyelashes, along her button yet adorable nose to rest on her parted lips. Zetar save him.

"I have magic?" She layered her hands over his, gaping at him with a mixture of awe and dismay.

"By now, you should know magic is neither good nor evil. Where you relived pain, it can also invoke pleasure." Drawing in a calming breath, he pressed his temple to hers. "There's more, Thugari."

He leaned back, hoping to avoid her warmth seeping through his garments. One sensuous caress across her sigil, and she would find lust to be a harsher tormentor than pain.

"More?" she mouthed, her eyes widening until he could see the gray and silver merging.

"To rid yourself of the sigil without knowing the unraveling spell requires powerful magic and your...virginity." He squeezed his eyes shut, not wanting to see her reaction or to beg her to choose him.

Curse it.

What he endured wasn't a natural attraction, but fighting it was proving difficult. If his lawbrothers ever found out, he would never live it down.

She squeaked. "What? How?"

"A magus might be able to undo the sigil, after which you have a day to rut with someone. The spell needs an intimate blood sacrifice. It will be easier than you think, Thugari. Once the seal is removed, you will fight off males and females."

"Me?" She snorted, her shoulders shaking as she laughed. Such sweet joy tinkled off the wooden walls.

"You're a Macutia, renowned human sirens who still bear old magic." He released her, shifting away from her tempting form.

"This is nonsense, Rukk. Sirens are sea myths." She flicked a dismissive hand.

"Centuries-old myths still apply, land or sea."

"Why would you say such things?" Her smile teased her lips, but fear-tainted hope he deceived her reflected in her eyes.

"Please don't make me prove it, Thugari. For my sanity, I beg you." He rubbed his face, imagining touching her, envisioning her arching and writhing on the bed in ecstasy. "I cannot bring you relief. Not that I don't want to, because holy Zetar, I would kill for a taste of you. The throes of passion take your will, leave you at the mercy of your body's demands."

He took another step back and another until his backside bumped against the door. "Choose when and with whom."

She squared her shoulders. "Fine, say I believe you. Will you at least tell me when we meet a magus powerful enough?"

"Yes, of course." He slumped. One kiss from a Macutia could fell a mountain of an orc. No wonder Varthug had succumbed and Lady Murzush hated Thugari for it.

"Can we discuss your rat?" Pulling the knife from his belt, he gestured to the sleeping bundle of brown fur on her cloak.

She darted to him and cupped his hand, as if to prevent him from using his blade. "Gnash? He's my pet."

Rukk gripped her shoulders, peering into her eyes. "He can't go with us, Thugari, not to Dussoum."

"What? Why not?" She scowled and pinned her hands on her hips, challenging him.

Heat exploded in his chest, and he wanted nothing more than to kiss her until she bowed to his will. Sweet Zetar, she rattled his belief in his abilities. But he doubted he could stop at a kiss.

"Do you have something against rats?" Clenching her jaw, she narrowed her eyes.

He laughed. Him, afraid of rats? "No, but dwarves prefer them skewered and roasted."

She gaped and sat on the edge of the bed, fear twisting her features. "I can't leave him behind, Rukk. He's been with me for three summers, the one creature I could talk to." She gathered the ball of fur for a cuddle. "He was there for me when I froze in winter, his tiny body helpless against the frigid nights, but his company more precious."

"It's in danger of becoming a stew. Maybe we can find it a home here, a family, Thugari. We'll keep an eye out for its kind."

"Gnash is a boy rat, not an it. And if we find no rats? Or they don't accept him?" The poor creature squealed as she crushed it in a hug Rukk envied.

"Then it...*he* can come with. There's bound to be a few safe havens on our journey north." Rukk handed her the parcel, forcing her to return Gnash to the cloak.

She raised her shimmering, mournful gaze to his and sighed. "What else did you purchase?"

"See for yourself." He gave her his back to stare out the window, needing it to calm his ardor. As a cool breeze teased his hair and seeped into his skin to refuel his ether magic, he listened to her exclamations of delight over her new breeches and gloves.

"Don't look, I'm pulling on a tunic." Silence followed, and he returned to study the townsfolk as they went about their business. "What do you think?"

He looked, obedient for the moment. She had chosen the blue one, setting the silver of her eyes ablaze, with the opening parting to reveal the delicious swells of her breasts. Curse it. Growling something at her about needing mead, he did what any hot-blooded male would do when faced with this much temptation. He ran.

Chapter Seventeen

Thugari held her braids over one shoulder while feathering her fingertips along the ridges of the sigil embedded in her skin. Tingles rippled down her neck, her chest, and coiled in her stomach. She couldn't remember when the sigil had happened or who put it there. Her father must have requested it so she wouldn't seduce his males or tempt them to rise up against him. She wanted to snort in disbelief, but Rukk acted as if she could ensnare him with a look.

Bolts of joy bounced through her and nestled in her chest, a bold heat spread outward. She smiled, recalling his compliment. *I would kill for a taste of you.* Her heart leaped, clogged her throat, and hindered her breathing. Her supposed magic, older than time and Kethil no doubt, could seduce everyone. She couldn't convince Belen to give her more broth or a chunk of bread, nor stop Frukag from delivering another blow. Preventing Uzul from inflicting the memory of past punishments had been beyond her *siren* abilities.

Let Rukk believe whatever he wanted as long as he escorted her to Dussoum. She wouldn't mention it either, lest anyone think he had lost his mind. Tugging off her new boots, she dropped her loose breeches and slipped on the soft leather ones he had bought for her. They hugged her legs, backside, and hips, but not in an uncomfortable way. Tucking her tunic in, she pulled her boots back on, offered Gnash a strip of dried meat, and shut the door behind her.

With his nose buried in a cup of mead, Rukk cast a worried glance at her as she approached him. His ebony eyes scoured her form, and his cheeks darkened. His eyes fluttered shut as if he were in pain.

"I'm going to the stables to check on the horses." She waited for him to speak, but he didn't, nodding at her, instead. "I don't have a disease, Rukk, and I can travel north without you. I was fine with Borgakh before you charged into my life." She took two steps and peered over her shoulder. "Let me know what you decide."

Thugari stomped along the dusty road, dodging merchants, horse shit, and the occasional cart. A fire burned in her belly, rising to fog her thoughts.

She wanted to arch her back and scream out her frustrations, as if the billowing clouds could solve her problems or the way Rukk treated her. The problem was, she liked him, even when he irritated her.

When she entered the stables, Envis whickered a greeting, and she hurried over, cooing and jabbering nonsensical words. The stablemaster hovered, then scurried away when someone led two horses in. Grateful for the solitude, she grabbed a brush off the wall and ran it along Envis's neck, shoulders, and back, patting and stroking him as she did so.

"So tell me, what have you heard?" She giggled, rubbing her forehead along the bridge of his nose, wondering what tales horses shared amongst themselves, for they traveled as far and wide as their masters did.

"There are myths about talking animals." The tenor of the deep voice rumbled through her.

Her curiosity forced her to face the speaker. A tall male, dark of skin and broad of shoulders, flashed a bright tuskless smile. She blinked, scanning his features, searching for his orcish ears. His were rounded at the tip, so not an orc.

"Are you a dark human?"

He laughed, the sound echoing off the wooden confines of the stables. "Yes, I'm from Atrar. My people are as dark-skinned as you. Though, my brother Janar is fairer. I often tease him that his virginity bleaches his skin." He chuckled

"Does it?" She frowned, glancing at her arms. Wouldn't she be paler then?

"Not at all. To my kind, virginity strengthens the magic within the wielder. The purer the body, the stronger the power." He patted the neck of his horse.

"Is there a nation of people who look like me?" She gripped the brush to her chest and approached him, peering into his brown eyes softened with mirth.

His off-white tunic contrasted with his coloring of browns and golds. A thick, fur-lined, black cloak hung off his broad shoulders, and she might have thought him a lawbringer if it wasn't for his brown leather breeches.

"Two nations. Your Bazinhur hasn't gone anywhere."

"Bazinhur," she said, pronouncing it with care. "I know *of* my people but not where." She pointed to the north, arching a hopeful brow.

He laughed again, the sound warming her more than this morning's sunlight. "South, past Haraton, the Camsevair Mountains, and across the Bay of Herynd."

Disappointment hit her, and she frowned, fighting off the surge of doubt. Perhaps she headed in the wrong direction. She shook her head, biting on her lip. Knowing nothing of her people meant an unpredictable welcome. North was safer, but if what Rukk said about her magic was true, the dwarves wouldn't allow her entry into Chaosthane. She would have wasted all this time traveling. Her fate rested on whether or not she had magic, but she hoped with all her soul the famed Gates of Chaosthane would prove Rukk wrong.

"Your people, are they welcoming of strangers? If I hide my ears, I could almost pass as an Atrarian."

Patting his horse, he offered her another smile. "That is a long discussion."

She jerked back, realizing her rudeness in bombarding him with her questions and assuming he would share. Ducking her head, she buried her face in Envis's neck, hiding her inflamed cheeks.

"I can regale you with tales of my homeland over mead?" He ran his large, scarred hand over Envis's forelock. It seemed as if mirth rippled under his skin. The crease lines around his eyes and mouth attested to the joy he often found.

"The tavern's roast boar is good."

He grinned. "Are you hungry?"

"No, thank you. I have eaten this day." Remembering her meal, what followed, and Rukk's revelation, she frowned, glancing outside to learn the time. He might not have left the table and would be elbows deep in his mead by now. She grimaced. More time away from each other would be wise. "I'm trying to avoid my...traveling companion."

"Me too." The Atrarian laughed, his great shoulders shaking. "Stablemaster, where can we find good mead without visiting the tavern?"

"I keep a barrel out back for when I tend the stables." The male removed his cap to slap on his thigh, his balding head blinding in the sunlight. "For a price, of course."

"Lead the way, good sir," the stranger said, gesturing to Thugari to join him.

She did, placing the brush on a nearby stool before hurrying after the stablemaster. "My name's Thugari, by the way." She sat on a rickety chair in the livery's backroom, wiping her palms on her thighs.

The stablemaster raised the casket to pour honeyed mead into a jug. He placed it alongside the wooden cup and held out a palm into which the handsome stranger dropped a silver. The stablemaster beamed, bowed, and shut the door behind him.

Silence descended in the room, but she wasn't frightened to be alone with the Atrarian.

"A pleasure to make your acquaintance. I'm Tarid Inaris of the Clan Marwirn," he said, pouring the mead into both cups before offering her one as he assumed the other chair.

"I have no last name. I'm not affiliated with my father, and I've been warned not to use my mother's." She sipped the mead and sighed. Its sweetness coated her tongue, then left a tart aftertaste after she swallowed.

"Intriguing," Tarid said. "What brings you to fair...?" He frowned and glanced around the room in confusion. "Where *are* we?"

She giggled, which ended in a hiccup and a realization she had drained her mead. "This is Lemfor." Her lips tingled, so she feathered her fingertips over them, testing whether she could feel anything. "It's a long story. I stumbled upon Borgakh and her companion, Nenneg, traveling through the woods. Everyone I've met is heading north."

He arched a brow. "Borgakh Yerug? The orc maiden?"

"You know her?" Thugari rose onto unsteady legs and wove the short distance to the jug.

She shouldn't have anymore, but it was delicious, and she was too happy to worry about later or tomorrow. Slamming the cup down harder than planned, she gestured to his. He drained it, and handed it to her. She poured with care, making sure she didn't spill.

"Yes, she's a friend. Where is she now? I would love to share stories and a good meal with her around a fire." Tarid accepted the offered cup, taking a long drink from it.

"She left this morning, I think. We saw her last night, but she didn't save me this time. I suppose I couldn't expect her to since it was my fault in the first place."

"You're speaking in riddles, my dear."

She shrugged, sipping her mead. Her tongue almost entangled itself, and it felt swollen. It wasn't a sensation she liked. "Dodging koveen and wylders with stolen bairns."

Tarid stilled with the rim of his cup resting on his bottom lip. He sipped then lowered it, keeping his gaze on her. "You've seen this?"

She nodded, then gripped her head, trying to stop the dizziness. "Yes, Nenneg's a wylder too."

"Does she know why this is happening?" Gone was the laughter from before. There sat a male, skilled in who knew what, serious and determined, waiting for her to speak.

"She saw something in the mountains of Gill-Eòin. After meeting Borgakh, together they sought the Council's guidance. Now they head to Chaosthane, killing koveen and wylders along the way."

"Meeting you was fortuitous." Tarid shifted in his chair with a polite smile. His furrowed brow defied the joy in his expression.

She straightened too, peeked at the backroom's door, and weighed whether she could make it there before he caught her. The air was hot, oppressive, and she was alone with this male without her trusty kitchen knife. Cursed Moon, it was still in her old boot. Sadness swept through her, as if she had lost an old friend.

He made no sudden moves, sitting there sipping his mead. "Why didn't you leave with Borgakh?"

"Um…" She dragged herself from her mourning. "I have a new traveling companion who will escort me north. Once we reach Dussoum, we will split ways." She clamped her mouth shut as a precaution against revealing more. There were daggers in his boots, and a sword sheathed at his side. His jovial personality had distracted her from noticing how well-armed he was.

"I hope for silence on the next leg of the journey." He glared at the bottom of his cup. "I cannot bear another day alone with my companion."

"How bad could he be?" She took a casual sip, savoring the mead. The buzz blurring her hearing had diminished, and her nostrils had ceased to sting. If this was what becoming drunk was like, she didn't see the appeal.

"He? *She*, little one." Tarid chuckled, but it was a cold, sad sound, lacking his earlier mirth.

Little one? She jerked, sloshing mead over her trembling hand. It was a common enough endearment.

He rested his head on the wooden wall. "You seem nervous. Are you forced to travel with this person?"

"In a way. Although, I've seen him take down a coven of wylders, so he can protect me as he promised to do." Her face burned as she recalled Rukk's hair swirling around him, as bright as the silver of his sword. Gulping down her mead, she prayed it cooled her parched throat.

"If you were reluctant to travel with him, Borgakh wouldn't have left you." Tarid refilled their cups, his hand steady as he poured.

"He said something about owing an orc was serious business, and she agreed."

"Don't I know it." Tarid snorted. "Both my companions are orcs."

"Two companions? Where's the other one?" She swirled the mead, mesmerized by the lamplight reflecting in its honeyed depths. Tension eased from her body as if every bone had softened. Even though she was alone with a stranger, she wasn't as alarmed by it as she was moments ago.

"We're meeting him here."

"If you're heading north, Tarid, let's swap companions." She giggled at the expressions sure to twist Rukk's face when she told him she had exchanged him from someone more jovial. "I'm a quiet traveler, preferring not to announce my presence."

"I'll protect you better." He thumped a fist against his barrel chest before grinning. "I wish we could, sweet Thugari, but alas, I am duty-bound."

"I understand, and I owe a debt to an orc."

They sipped their mead in silence. She studied his expressions, for deep within his brown eyes was a yearning that echoed within her.

"I'm starving," he said, breaking the thick silence consuming the room. "Shall we head to the tavern?"

She drained her cup and placed it alongside the jug. As she tried to rise, she teetered. He lunged for her, holding her up with an arm around her waist.

"Sorry." She hiccupped. "I don't drink mead often."

"I've got you, little one." With a swing of his arm, he swept her onto his back. By the time she could squeal, it was too late. All she could do was cling to his shoulders. "Wrap your legs around my hips."

She did so, dropping her temple to his shoulder as her world spun in dizzying circles, threatening to spill the mead and her meal. "Tarid, thank you for the mead."

"You won't thank me in the morning, Thugari."

"Rukk won't either," she mumbled as he jostled her, and she bit down on her innards rising to choke her.

"Rukk's the orc you owe a debt to?" Tarid laughed all the way to the tavern.

CHAPTER EIGHTEEN

Rukk sloshed his honeyed mead over his hand, startled by Tarid's mental voice. The cup raised halfway to Rukk's lips had remained untouched. Thugari's threat to travel without him plagued him since she left him. No matter how her presence tormented him, he couldn't bring himself to part with her, not yet. As he sat there, wallowing in self-pity, a solution to thwart her siren wiles was an elusive one.

"Tarid, it's about time I heard from you. How far away are you?" Rukk was desperate to see his lawbrother who had experience in dealing with this level of temptation.

"Won't be long now. Have you seen Sharn?"

"No, why? Did you two separate?" Silence met his question, but the bond between them revealed his lawbrother's anguish. Something had happened to alter Tarid's pleasant mood. *"I need an inquest. I fear I'm losing my mind."*

Tarid mulled that over before he said, *"I'm on my way."*

Rukk's sucked in a breath and leaned back, allowing the tavern maid to clean up his mess. He requested two meals in case Thugari returned. He couldn't tell how long she had been gone, and the thought of her running again troubled him. Panic gripped him, and the icy tongue of fear licked his spine. He shouldn't have let her leave. Vaulting to his feet sent his chair toppling. *Cursed female.*

He hadn't made it out of the tavern when her laughter rang through the village. Despite appreciating the joyful sound, he resented she was happy when he suffered so.

"Stop it." Her garbled words between giggles and outbursts of laughter reached his orc ears. "I'll cover you with half-digested mead."

"It's called vomit, plain and simple," a male said in an all-too-familiar voice.

Rukk lunged through the door, grinding to a halt in the bright afternoon sunlight. He didn't want to believe it. The female who tortured him—mind, body, and soul—had her legs wrapped around his closest lawbrother.

Undecided was whether the red around Rukk's vision and the fury tensing his muscles were from anger or jealousy. He opted for the former because he didn't experience the latter.

Tarid might have a simple explanation for this. Rukk parted his mouth to speak. "What—?"

"Does she have a room?" He nudged Rukk out of the way, silencing his demand for answers.

Rolling his lips into a grimace, he led Tarid to their room, opening the door for him too. With a flick of his shoulders, Tarid tossed Thugari, sending her flying. She landed on the bed amid laughter and braids then snuggled into the mattress, tucked her hands beneath her cheek, and with a satisfied sigh, fell asleep.

"The little one can't handle her mead." Tarid chuckled. *"Just like Janar."*

Rukk folded his arms across his chest and intensified his scowl. As usual, it made no impact on Tarid.

"Fine, don't talk to me, Rukk. Just listen. I won't ask why you insisted she travel with us—that's none of my business. I will tell you Nenneg shared with her what's behind the koveen and wylder alliance."

His shoulders slumped. Tarid, in his not-so-subtle way, pointed out they had a task to perform, and this—whatever it was between Thugari and Rukk—he should put aside...for now.

"She's the stableboy." Without waiting for Tarid's response, Rukk strode out of the room, bounding down the stairs to his table where his meal waited.

"That explains it." Tarid trailed him to the common room.

Sharn sat, steepling her fingers in front of her chin. "Who is she?" She rested her room key on the table.

Rukk glared at her, not appreciating her annoying appearance when he had yet to pacify his anger. "A debt," he said, and she clamped her lips shut. He almost praised Zetar, grateful for the silence.

"Your medallion?" Tarid dragged a bowl of boar stew across to him and chose the seat farthest from Sharn.

Rukk arched a brow, then shrugged, having expected their relationship to deteriorate. It wasn't as if Tarid kept his distaste for Sharn hidden. Rukk tapped his chest where his medallion rested. *"I have it."*

Tarid nodded. "Thugari tells me you saw Borgakh. How fares she?"

Borgakh had almost skewered Rukk. Thankfully, his obsession with Thugari hadn't cost him his life...yet. "She is well and awaits our arrival in the next town."

"Borgakh Yerug?" Sharn waved to a tavern maid and pointed to Tarid's meal.

"She's an old friend." Rukk pursed his lips. It was thanks to that friendship, Borgakh hadn't killed him first and asked questions later. "As to the female upstairs, she travels north with us to Dussoum."

Sharn opened her mouth to speak, but when Tarid shook his head, she fell silent. The tavern maid placed a steaming bowl in front of Sharn who dipped her chin to hide her pink cheeks.

Rukk fought the chuckle bubbling up his throat. Something had happened, but unlike his uncouth brother, he wouldn't pry.

"We leave in the morning?" Sharn asked around a spoonful of stew.

Rukk hadn't formulated a plan to survive another night with Thugari in his arms. Perhaps Sharn could share her room? He scowled. As a Knaraugh and a lawbringer, he'd trained to handle anything, and he had dealt with creatures far worse than an innocent, desperately needing his help, dark-orc siren.

Although not a fool, he wouldn't place himself in the path of temptation if he could help it.

He ran a hand over his face, exhaustion pounding at his senses. His thoughts should be on the koveen, the journey, and confronting Galand.

"I can spend a few more hours in the saddle if you wish to leave now." Sharn's offer was his saving grace. "We did sleep in this morning and didn't overtax our horses."

"I agree. I would've appreciated a soft bed, but a night under the stars isn't unpleasant." Tarid pushed away his empty bowl. *"I have a pressing need to see my brother."*

"And I have questions for Venec." Rukk held Sharn's gaze the longest, conveying his sincerity. "Thank you."

"I'll gather our things and meet you at the stables." Abandoning her half-eaten meal, she leaped to her feet to race up the stairs.

"I'll fill our food pouches and collect the horses. Sharn takes long to pack." Tarid rose and flashed Rukk a mischievous grin. *"I know which one is Thugari's horse, so don't fret."*

He forced himself not to react to Tarid's jibe. "I'll collect our satchels and bundle her up for the journey."

"Rather you than me." Tarid laughed as he bounded out the tavern, leaving Rukk to settle with the innkeeper.

Packing Thugari's things didn't take long since she didn't have much. Her food pouch overflowed, a sign of having experienced extreme hunger. He dressed her in her cloak, bending her arms to slip them in. With both satchels slung over his shoulders, he settled Gnash into the curve of her neck then scooped her into his arms.

This time she curled around Rukk without fear, her cheek to his chest, and her arms circling his waist. She mumbled something that sounded like his name, but when she said no more, he navigated his way down the narrow stairs and out into the sunlight.

Sharn had mounted her horse but hedged in Tarid's. He opened his arms to take Thugari, but Rukk hesitated. He didn't like his brother touching her. That reaction was illogical, so he handed her over. Harpax whinnied in greeting. Rukk whispered to him in orcish while he looped their satchel straps through the D rings. With a final pat to Harpax's neck, he vaulted on.

Tarid draped Thugari over her saddle. He tucked her cloak around her before gathering Envis's reins to offer to Rukk.

"My thanks." He hoped Tarid hadn't picked up his earlier reticence.

"Scout ahead, we'll catch up," Tarid called to Sharn, slowing his horse into a walk. *"Now tell me why you need an inquest?"*

"Let me show you." Rukk chanted, summoning his magic as he held out his arm.

Tarid did the same, pinning the underside of his wrist to Rukk's where their matching Aymer sigils rested and now glowed white. The pinch of magic draining from his core was worth it when Tarid would understand what Rukk was suffering through.

Tarid's eyes shut as Rukk bombarded him with memories, from his sounding with Galand and his suspicions, to this morning when he sulked over his mead. Yanking his wrist away, Rukk ceased chanting and drew in steadying breaths as he raised his sweat-drenched face to the night's cool breeze. The emotional drain churned nausea in his gut, threatening to toss his mead.

"It's not Thursday." Tarid stared at Thugari, who slept on, despite what was an uncomfortable position. *I suppose your schedule doesn't matter if she's a siren of old, albeit a restrained one.* He raised his gaze to where Sharn waited for them.

"Does Thugari tempt you?" Holy Zetar, please say yes. No, wait. Rukk gnashed his teeth as he tightened his jaw. He didn't want Tarid to find Thugari tempting, even though it would prove he was sane.

"No." As Tarid lingered on Sharn's face, a theory formed within Rukk.

Would Thugari's allure affect those whose hearts weren't free to claim? Borgakh and Nenneg hadn't succumbed, and it seemed Tarid's interest lay elsewhere.

"Rukk, you don't need an inquest. You're not losing your mind. What you're experiencing is either the influence of a powerful siren or potent lust. Since we cannot confirm her siren heritage without Sharn or the Arch-Magus assessing her, I would suggest you treat this as the latter. Find a female and see if she eases the tension in your loins."

Rukk snorted, doubting such a simple solution would work and wished he hadn't said anything to Tarid. *"Mistaken lust?"*

He arched a brow, not about to mention how much Thugari fascinated him. How he admired her whenever she touched her hair or licked a spoon. But for the sake of his sanity, he would peruse the available females in the next town.

Gnash scampered along the reins to nestle in Harpax's mane. His ears stiffened, and with a toss of his head, he bucked, attempting to dislodge the rat.

Rukk considered tossing the rat off, but it would only scamper after them. Sighing, he spoke one word. Harpax calmed for a moment then pranced on the spot, struck out with his forelegs, and pawed the ground.

"Tooleea," Rukk repeated. "Be still."

Harpax snorted but calmed, twitching his ears in a show of displeasure.

When Rukk nudged his flanks, Harpax broke into a trot.

Rukk glanced at Sharn as they joined her, acknowledging he needed to ask for a favor. Grimacing, he prayed she didn't hold his past treatment of her against him. Regardless, whether Thugari was a siren or not, he had no intention of releasing her from the debt. Not anymore.

Chapter Nineteen

THE RAUCOUS CAW OF a hekle bird jerked Thugari awake. Notorious late sleepers, its cawing meant she had overslept. Struggling to swallow past her swollen tongue, she scrambled to her feet, throwing out a hand to stop the world from spinning. Nausea hit her hard, and she gagged, bending over as bile rose to choke her. She collapsed onto her bedroll again, lying still as she blinked at the blue sky.

After her stomach settled, and after forcing herself to sit up, she pulled on her boots. She furrowed her brow as she scanned the camp. She had no memory of this place or how she arrived here. Rukk must have snuck her out of Lemfor.

Twisting, she searched for Gnash, sighing when he scampered up her leg to dive inside her tunic. Horses nibbled on low-hanging branches, picking at the guilo berries, and the fire roasted a few pigeons.

To awaken alone, she fought the bile churning her stomach. Slapping it down while sucking in calming breaths, she poked the fire with a stick. That in itself was odd. Leaving a fire unattended was dangerous. But perhaps, they had not meant to be gone for long.

After turning the pigeons, she tidied the camp and brushed down the horses, raising her head at every rustle or squawk. Four bedrolls meant four travelers, the same number of horses and familiar ones—Tarid's and Envis. Rubbing her temple, she tried to recall the events of yesterday. She and Rukk had argued, and Tarid had plied her with mead. Oh, yes, honeyed mead. She gagged, vowing never to drink again.

"Morning." An orc female sauntered into the clearing. "How are you feeling?"

Thugari tensed then relaxed, rolling her shoulders. Magus robes adorned a lithe body, and the beautiful face was one she recognized from the castle. She was Rukk's travel companion.

"Like a dead fish." Thugari crouched to tend to the fire again, needing something to occupy her hands. Sharp movements heaved her stomach, so she stayed on her haunches to suck in calming breaths. The ground spun, and she squeezed her eyes shut, tightening her hold on the stick she'd stoked the fire with. The wood bit into her palm, but she couldn't bring herself to unfurl her fist.

Hands gripped her shoulders and guided her back to her bedroll. The touch was gentle yet forceful, brooking no argument. She curled into a ball, shivering against the morning's cool breeze as sweat formed on her forehead.

"You've never over-imbibed, have you?" The female's voice came from far away, as if she spoke to Thugari through a cavern.

Ice hit her, engulfing her until her muscles froze, petrifying her. But when she peeked at the source of the cold, the magus hovered a hand over Thugari's stomach. The female must hate her. Rukk had promised to protect Thugari, then left her at the mercy of this sadist! Her teeth chattered, garbling her curses.

"Quit complaining, I'm stripping your body of the poison."

"Who poisoned me?" Thugari forced the words through her clenched jaw. No sooner had she decided to climb inside her bedroll, the cold vanished, and delicious warmth seeped into her bones. A moan of pleasure ripped from her.

"Feeling better?" the orc asked.

Thugari frowned. Her roiling stomach had calmed, as did the shivering and dizziness. "Thank you. It was kind of you to help me."

The female huffed, stomping away to rummage in her satchel. Thugari had the impression she had helped her out of obligation and not out of the kindness of her heart. Standing, testing her weight on her legs, Thugari sighed. She scooped Gnash out of her hair and placed him in front of her open food pouch.

"Where's Rukk?"

"Now you ask?" The orc flipped her black hair off her shoulder, flashing her eyes in dismissal. "We encountered koveen, of course. Since we're near a village, they're returning the bairns. Rukk wanted to task me or Tarid to do so, but he changed his mind, and left me to tend to your sad state."

Dropping her satchel with a thump, she unclipped her dagger and let it fall onto her bedroll. "I don't appreciate this misuse. I'm a magus, not a nursemaid. Come closer." Pushing up the sleeves of her robe, she flexed her fingers.

Thugari lurched back from the female who hissed like an agitated snake. With a flick of her delicate wrist, Thugari found her feet moving of their own accord, despite her attempts otherwise. Then, as if she were the prized heifer at the village fair, the orc poked Thugari's cheeks, stroked her ears, and grabbed her chin to peer at her teeth. She waved her hands over Thugari's face, a frown furrowing her brow. Magic sparked to life, sizzling as it licked her skin. Thugari couldn't step away from the acrid smell of it even if she wanted to.

"I sense no magic. What in cursed hell is Rukk concerned about?" The magus summoned more magic.

An ethereal glow coated her body, shimmering in the midday sunlight. The hairs on Thugari's skin rose, sending shivers and tingles through her. The magic stung and twitched her muscles.

"Please...stop," she gritted out through the pain.

"Rukk believes magic lies deep within you. I don't sense it. Now, show me this sigil."

Heaviness returned to Thugari's limbs, releasing her from the enthrallment. She wanted to run from this uncaring female but wouldn't make it out of the clearing. Spinning on her heels, she lifted her hair, exposing the mark burned into her nape. The magus gasped, running her fingers along the shape. Fresh agony swept through Thugari, weakening her knees.

"The Stone Cage." The magus echoed Rukk's assessment. "No wonder I feel nothing. I need to use the power of revelation."

Thugari didn't like the sound of that. Visions of writhing on the floor burned behind her eyes, and she stumbled away, throwing out a hand to hold the female back. "No more."

"It's painless," she said. "For the most part."

The unrepentant smirk on her delicate features flooded Thugari with anger. Rukk said he would protect her, which should include from his companions. Her body tensed as she dreamed of hitting him when he returned from the village.

Wait, there were four horses. "If they took the bairns to the village, why are their horses here?"

She counted them again to make sure her earlier dizziness hadn't added to their numbers.

"Spotted that, did you?" The silly orc giggled. "What else is amiss?"

"Amiss?" Fear trickled down Thugari's neck, pooling in her chest as it tightened her spine.

She spun in a slow circle, assessing the clearing, the campsite, and the surrounding forest.

The bedrolls, other than her own, had an untouched look. The satchels alongside them were new, no weathering of the leather, no personal details. Her kitchen knife that was no longer in her possession lay on the moss-lined floor beside the fire.

"What are you?" Dread strangled her throat, rasping her voice.

"At last. I find your pain entertaining, dark-orc, and deceiving your friends was a pleasure." Her face contorted into something elongated, razor-sharp teeth descending past its rotting bottom lip.

Thugari shivered, fear having formed pins and needles in her extremities. Rukk! Her scream remained silent for she dared not anger this *thing*.

"What are you?" she asked again.

"A dreshnie, ignorant one. The last of my kind you shall ever meet. Today, we feast on your remains."

"We?" Thugari swallowed past the lump in her throat, her voice squeaking in alarm.

"My pet, of course."

Her pet? Thugari gaped at the dissolving camp-mirage. Slime lined the walls of a dark, dank cave. The stench of decaying undergrowth mingled with a sweet floral fragrance, sickening yet enticing. The cave's roof remained shadowed from the green-flamed sconces mounted to the rock walls. A normal fire was in the center, so at least one thing was real.

"How did you create the illusion?" Thugari circled her finger, indicating the cavern.

"From yours and your companions' memories. I'm delighted you made this fun for me. Most meals scream, plead, whine, or try to escape. It grows tiresome."

No rock lay about for her to throw, no weapons rested against the walls. Only bones and glowing skulls peeked out from the slime. She had nothing with which to defend herself. A worn path led to the right, and if she inched toward it, she might make a run to sunlight or death.

"Where are my companions?" Gnash wasn't with her, and she prayed the dreshnie hadn't eaten him. Scanning the bones around the fire, she searched for fresh ones, with something heavy squeezing her chest.

"Dealing with those slithering witches and their narrow-minded plans. Your mate left you against a tree, so I snatched you." The dreshnie rubbed her hands together in glee. "Naruzee will be ravenous." She gestured with her elongated fingers, the narrow black nails extending like talons. "You've been obliging so far. Sit alongside the fire. I would like Naruzee to see you as soon as she returns."

"Will she be gone long?" Thugari shuffled around the fire, needing its warmth, but also wanting to maintain distance between her and the decaying female.

Skin sloughed off her limbs, giving Thugari glimpses of sinew and bone. Her hair draped around her in a tangled mess with bare patches of her scalp and skull.

From the chill of the cave, along with the stench, uncontrollable trembling claimed Thugari's limbs. She preferred the image the dreshnie had created—a disgruntled orc magus healing her and Gnash stuffing his adorable face.

Death was imminent for her, but she would go down fighting or running. Though the latter was far more preferable.

Rubbing her arms, trying to keep warm, she snuck glances at the dark passage. "Am I facing the right direction?" she asked. "Why is Naruzee delayed?"

"My, you are an eager one. Yes, stand just so. She's tending to her children in the bowels of this cavern. Carved by an underground river, it extends for miles and miles. Plenty of space for her hungry young."

Silence coated the cave, except for the hissing of the fire and a constant dripping echoing—its origin unknown. Thugari now knew to escape, she needed to run in the opposite direction. Moon above, when she had run from Haraton, she never imagined such a gruesome death awaited her. But she refused to regret leaving her so-called home.

A steady *tick-tick* reached her ears first, joined by skittering that reverberated through the dark passage. A foot stepped into the flickering green light, then retracted. Thugari narrowed her focus as she peered into the darkness, trying to discern other shapes in the shifting shadows. She stopped breathing as her lungs refused to work. Dark flecks circled her vision, but she dared not blink.

Black eyes flashed red, and a cackle accompanied the giant spider scampering toward her. Her legs splayed out—two to each side, two to the front, and two gripping the ceiling of the passage. Then as she skittered into view, the pristine-white, naked torso of a female appeared, her human eyes bulbous.

Thugari froze. Her instincts screamed to run, but her muscles petrified, trapping her to the spot.

"She reeks of fear, Lhazara. What did you do to prepare this one? Spin a web of lies? Deceive her into believing her freedom is nigh?" Naruzee giggled, patting her belly with a human hand, while her spider-legs tapped in impatience.

"Her company has been entertaining," Lhazara, the dreshnie, said. "It's a pity we need to eat her."

Naruzee jerked, stepping more into the light. Patterns glowed on her dark carapace. The hairs on her legs were as long and thick as Thugari's forearm.

"It's a pleasure to meet you," she said as if on cue. Amazing she could form words with her throat too tight to swallow.

"Manners?" The genuine smile splitting Naruzee's deformed face wasn't a pleasant sight. "It's been a while since we had someone interesting to talk to. My children are well-fed for this day. We can hold off nibbling on your limbs for now."

Hope pierced Thugari's chest. It was no more than a stay of execution, but any delay in her death was a welcome one. Drawing in a shallow breath, she bowed in thanks, hoping to impress the spider into allowing her to live.

"Oh, I was hoping you would say that." Lhazara scurried around Thugari, gathering items hidden from view. Within minutes, she had spread out a tattered blanket beside the fire.

Naruzee tucked her legs beneath her spider-abdomen and lowered herself to Thugari's eye level. "Tell me your life story," she said, accepting the wineskin Lhazara offered her.

Thugari started from the death of her mother, exaggerating each emotion and event, butchering her father and his sycophants in their eyes until he became a true villain. She left out no details, conveyed her growing desire for Rukk, the longing to live away from her father's influence, and her supposed trapped magic. Naruzee and Lhazara's reactions were passionate in her defense, and for a while, Thugari pretended she sat around a fire with friends.

If she had siren magic as Rukk claimed and the Stone Cage had begun to unravel, then she should be able to seduce these creatures to let her leave. Yet, no matter how sweet she was, how she smiled and charmed, it made no impact on either of them.

Lhazara draped a molding cloak across Thugari's shoulders, the stench of blood and piss wafting from its damp cloth.

"Thank you," she said even as she shivered in disgust.

She wanted to fling the thing off, but doing so might offend her captors. Faking a yawn, she drooped her head as if she fought sleep but peeked to see if her ruse was working. If she lured them into a false sense of security, she could sneak out while they slumbered.

"Oh, look how exhausted the poor dear is. Let her rest, Naruzee. We can have her for breakfast while her heart is still bleeding." Lhazara raised eager eyes to her pet, who, as far as Thugari could tell, was the mistress in their partnership.

Naruzee tapped her chin as if she gave the dreshnie's suggestion earnest consideration. "Tie her up, Lhazara. Exerting myself to track her used to please me, but I was younger then."

Shit, Thugari hadn't planned on that. She didn't jerk away when Lhazara approached with rope no matter how much she longed to do so. Instead, Thugari held her wrists to be 'helpful' when it forced the dreshnie to tie her up the way Thugari wanted. Familiar with all manner of restraints, she had much to say about the knot Lhazara used. Clasping her hands against her chest with enough wiggle room to slip free, Thugari curled onto the blanket and closed her eyes.

She didn't know how long she needed to pretend to rest, but time dragged as the fire died down. The toughest challenge was resisting the lure of sleep when her captors didn't speak loud enough to help her. The repetitive dripping lulled her, and she jerked awake, holding her breath as she listened for their murmuring. When no mumbled words reached her, she popped an eye open and raised her head, scanning the cavern.

Lhazara hung upside down from a stalactite while Naruzee hadn't moved from her previous spot by the fire. Wiggling her hands free, Thugari lowered the rope and rotten coat to the blanket, then sidled toward the passage she identified earlier. Flicking her gaze between their faces, she clutched the base of a torch nestled in the sconce and lifted it, needing the light so she didn't plummet off a precipice.

Then with the careful placement of each foot, she exited the cavern, green flames illuminating her way.

Chapter Twenty

Linked to Rukk's fury was the sensation crippling him at the knees and tying his tongue. That was all his hazed mind could grasp. The intensity paralyzed him, but he didn't have the time to ponder what it was. At first, seeing the camp empty made him spew curses at himself for leaving Thugari alone, for assuming she wouldn't run. She had done so before, and as a dark-orc ignorant of her heritage, she didn't place as much importance on a debt as he did.

If it wasn't for Envis nibbling on guilo berries, Gnash sleeping on Harpax's withers, and the slime burrowing into the tree's gray bark, Rukk would have believed she had escaped again. But she would never leave her horse and rat behind.

"Pack up camp and catch up," he called as he crossed to the horses.

"To hell with the camp," Tarid said, untethering Harpax's reins.

With Thugari's cloak in hand, Rukk vaulted onto his mount. Broken branches, scorched trees, and a lingering sickly scent marked the trail. As he urged Harpax on with Gnash clinging to the mane, he fought the panic rising to choke him, strangling his throat.

"Are you serious?" Sharn asked from behind him minutes later, gesturing to the rat peeking out. She had muttered to herself when he had discovered Thugari missing. "Tarid, please, talk sense into your lawbrother. We can't chase after a childish dark-orc who doesn't have the sense to stay put."

"Shut up, Sharn." Tarid's tone brooked no argument, and gratitude swirled in Rukk's chest, so he snapped a nod at him. "Thugari is a part of our group. Something has happened to her, and by Zetar, I pray it isn't what I think it is. She's defenseless, and as lawbringers, we vowed to aid those in need."

"Your magus vows must be different. Should you prefer to remain behind, I will not mourn your absence." Rukk kept his gaze ahead. The life bond between him and Thugari proved she still lived. "Know this, should you need my help in the future, it won't be forthcoming."

Rounding a grove of trees, he halted Harpax. Before him, delving into the depths of the forest floor, was a cave opening. Air, permeated with the stench of rotting meat, gushed out. He dismounted, tethering Harpax to a tree a distance from the cave before withdrawing his sword from the saddle sheath.

Gnash leaped off the horse's brow to land on Rukk's shoulder. He scooped the twittering rodent and dropped it onto the saddle. It scampered across, clinging with its paws to his forearm. Sighing, he let it climb up his arm to his shoulder. It would trail him into the cave if he left it behind.

"Fine, but if you die, it's on you," he whispered, then snatched his hand back when he realized he stroked its head.

"I won't wait outside like an obedient bride." Sharn jumped off her mount. Once she tethered it, she summoned an orb of light as Tarid readied himself. He gripped his sword and rested his crossbow against his back, its bolts nestled in slots on his belt.

With the two of them behind him, Rukk faced the gaping cave and expelled a long, controlled breath. He rolled his shoulders back, released and regripped his sword, taking comfort in its familiar weight. Not that he feared for their lives. No, only Thugari mattered, but he did not have the time to poke his emotions regarding her.

"The spiderwebs give me hope." He gestured with his sword at the gray threads clinging to the rock walls.

Tarid nodded. "I'm glad she wasn't taken by a voidwhisp. Although taking on a dreshnie and its pet isn't an easy battle."

Sharn froze. "A voidwhisp?"

Tarid frowned and crowded her, keeping his voice low. "Do you not remember your nature studies?"

"Old Macgell had a voice that droned," Sharn mumbled.

Tarid gave her a longsuffering sigh, overdoing it a little. "Voidwhisps take human form when the hunger is upon them. They also leave slime behind, part in this world, and part in the ethereal realm. You cannot fight them until they're human. To force the change, you need to increase their hunger. Lust and fear are their preferred food."

"They feed off emotions?" She gulped, raising wide eyes to Tarid. "What's a dreshnie?"

"We don't have time to explain." Rukk threw a scowl at her, then approached the tunnel on silent feet. "Just don't anger one. They go berserk and use their talons to shred every part of you."

"They keep pets. In this case, I would say we're dealing with an eikusai." Tarid shivered. "I hate spiders more than koveen."

He took position behind Rukk, his footsteps as quiet as he could make it for an Atrarian. Sharn straggled, gripping her dagger in one hand and a staff in the other. Despite threatening her, Rukk appreciated her presence. If Thugari needed it, Sharn could heal her while he and Tarid battled.

A cold heaviness plunged into the pit of his stomach. He prayed Thugari was well. Pulling her lock of hair from his coat pocket, he held it to his lips as he whispered a seeker spell. It burst into purple flame, the scent of mint and lavender burning his nostrils. A puff of lilac smoke glowed, then meandered ahead of him, leading the way.

His boots squelched on the slime and moss lining the floor of the cave as he ventured deeper in. The orb prevented him from falling to his death, but also acted as a beacon to whatever lived within the caverns. Rukk wasn't concerned. An eikusai was territorial, its children created from male victims it enchanted into mating it. A dreshnie aided in the illusion since millions of eikusai meant more pets to entrap victims to feast on. Yet, by all indications, this dreshnie had hunted alone.

Rukk couldn't tell if that meant bad luck on Thugari's part. Every decade or so, a dreshnie left its home, sneaking through the forest to gauge the state of the world, its current events, and the proximity of victims, as if it didn't trust the news its pets brought. Perhaps they investigated due to boredom. It had found an unprotected, innocent, and too-trusting Thugari. Fresh anger slithered through his blood, urging him forward with fueled determination.

The coolness of the cave contrasted with Gnash's warm body at his throat. An image rose of Thugari cuddling the rat for heat. It had been there for her when she had needed it the most. He would never admit it, but its presence comforted him.

The tunnel opened into an enormous cavern, as wide as it was tall. Sunlight streamed through the cracks in the ceiling, too high for even his elven eyes to discern. Along the side was a narrow path hewn into the rock eons ago. He grimaced at the stench of decay thickening the farther he traveled. No one spoke, for which he was grateful. Dealing with the dreshnie and its pet would be difficult without adding other creatures to the melee.

The lilac tendrils curled around the cliff, disappearing along another tunnel. *"Tell Sharn to snuff her orb."*

A whispered comment from Tarid later, and the orb faded. The glow of the lilac smoke brightened. Something slithered down the rock walls, dripping and plopping. Water and slime, Rukk guessed. A chill ran from his neck to the base of his spine, but he squared his shoulders, ignoring the sensation something watched their progress.

"We're not alone." Tarid words were unnecessary, but Rukk nodded, assuming his brother could see him in the dark.

Up ahead, the lilac tendrils split along two tunnels. He hesitated, not sure which one to choose. He faced Sharn and Tarid, impatience hardening his jaw with his brow furrowing.

"The seeker split into two. Which must mean the passages merge farther on. Thugari's at the end of them both. I would recommend we not separate." He kept his voice soft, his gaze meeting Sharn's over the blinding glow of her staff.

He had been so focused on the lilac seeker that he hadn't realized she had commanded her weapon to shine. He scowled. Its sphere of light was smaller than the orb, and on the slippery floor, he couldn't begrudge her the need to see. Still, she had disobeyed him.

"The cavern is to the right, so I would choose the left path. Less chance of falling into the void." She gestured with her dagger to the narrow passage.

Rukk arched a brow at Tarid, who nodded and curled his arm around Sharn's waist to pull her against him. He nudged her in front of him, positioning her in the middle with him guarding her back.

Hurrying after the lilac tendrils that hadn't waited for him, Rukk stumbled on a rock. He thrust out a hand to regain his balance. It sank into layers of spun web, piercing through the damp to the slime-lined rock beneath it. His fingers burned, as if he had shoved them into a fire. The agony gritted his teeth, but he forged onward. If all went well, he could heal himself when they were once more en route to Chaosthane. For now, he dare not waste time and his energy on it.

Firelight flickered on the tunnel's walls. Sharn's breath blew across the back of his neck. Ahead, curled into a ball was the eikusai. Behind it hung the dreshnie, and to the rear of the cave disappeared the lilac tendrils along another passage. On a blanket in front of a fire was a rope and a ragged cloak with no sign of Thugari. Discarded garments from previous victims lay in a pile, but none of those looked recent. She had either escaped or the eikusai had eaten her somewhere else. He shook the dark thought from his mind. With their bond, he would have felt her death.

Gnash's nose twitched as it sniffed the air. It glanced at him before burrowing into Rukk's hair. He smiled at how not-so-brave the rodent was.

With no other choice, he followed the seeker. Its lilac glow was bright, confirming Thugari lived. Perhaps a cocoon entombed her where she waited for him to rescue her. He raised his foot, planning where to place it when Sharn grabbed his shoulder, swirled her staff, and silence echoed in his ears. Nodding in thanks, he circled the sleeping eikusai, careful not to brush the hairs on her legs. Even though their passing would be in silence, touching it or a disturbance of the air would awaken it.

He broke into the passage, forcing his shoulders to relax. Sharn didn't cancel the silencing spell until they had traveled the new passage for a while. Fissures in the floor slowed their pace. He peered into a gorge below, the depths beyond his ability to see, and prayed Thugari hadn't tumbled, trapping herself.

Sharn summoned an orb again, and it trailed them, ensuring nothing surprised them from behind. When the tunnel broke onto a platform, steps carved into the rock led deeper into the underground caverns. It was the only path Thugari could have taken, instead, the lilac seeker flew in the opposite direction.

Gnash's whiskers tickled Rukk's neck before it scampered across his shoulders to leap off. At first, panic that the creature might kill itself froze him in place. But when he trailed it, the orb shifted as well. Its light touched the smooth rock, caressed the dripping stalactites, and settled on one wall, clear of slime and cobwebs. There, slumped against it, was his female.

Bolting forward, he threw himself beside her. He swept a chirping Gnash aside to grab her shoulders. She wasn't an illusion. Relief was like sinking into a hot bath, engulfing him with heat in the chilled cavern. He cupped her face, wiping away the tear stains with his thumbs. Alongside her lay a burned-out torch.

"Thugari?" His whisper was loud in the cavernous silence.

She jerked awake, throwing up her hands as if to ward off an attack. The smile bursting across her face was more beautiful than the sun rising on his home. He yanked her into his arms, uncaring that she stank of rotting flesh. She shivered and burrowed into him, rubbing her cold nose across his throat. Gnash chirped and twittered, scrambling from her to him and back.

At having her in his arms, alive, joy ricocheted through Rukk. He bounced on his haunches, excitement overwhelming his instincts. Skittering and the flapping of wings approached, but he ignored it as he helped Thugari to her feet, trusting his party to protect him.

As he draped her cloak around her, Tarid unholstered his crossbow and faced the direction of the eikusai. Rukk picked up his sword where he had dropped it and ushered Thugari behind him. She buried her fingers into the back of his cloak. Sharn's orb enlarged and illuminated the platform, which was empty except for the eikusai stepping from the tunnel.

"You've done well, polite one. You have brought more food for my babies." The spider giggled, coming into the light to rise to her full height. From around her flapped a bat-like creature, landing on the platform before furling its wings.

"You were right to wait, Nazuree. Was it her memories that aided you in this plan?" The black-taloned dreshnie sidled to the right, cutting off the exit down the steps.

"Someone must cherish such a pretty thing." The spider scurried to the left. A few legs and part of her carapace cut off access to the passage behind her.

Rukk raised his sword, gripping the leather-bound hilt with both hands. His burned palm cracked, with blood staining it. Clenching his jaw at the fresh wave of pain, he pressed his lips to Thugari's ear. "I have a dagger in my boot."

She snatched the weapon, raising it in front of her as her book must have taught her to. "Thank you for finding me." She sliced a nervous glance at him. "My torch died, and I was too scared to go anywhere without light, not when the last thing I saw was that." She gestured to the vast cavern surrounding the platform. He couldn't see the other side, the ceiling, or the bottom.

"Let us not dally any longer." The dreshnie flicked out her hands. Her talons doubled the length of her fingers.

She charged, but Sharn struck her with a fireball. Tarid shot a bolt at Nazuree's eye, who swept it aside as if it were an annoying insect. She scurried forward, aiming for Rukk, undeterred by Tarid's second bolt. Rukk spun his sword, forming a shield between him and the eikusai. It thwarted her striking legs, their sharp points lethal.

Sharn threw more balls of fire, while Tarid dropped his crossbow to unsheathe his sword. Thugari dove for the crossbow before hiding behind Rukk.

She called to Tarid to throw his bolts over. He did so, undoing his belt with one hand. She scrambled for it, and her curses accompanied her efforts to load the crossbow. Rukk grinned, admiring her determination. He lunged at the eikusai, deflecting her attacks while thrusting his sword at her, hoping to slice off a leg. When he struck one, his sword bounced off, the reverberation running up his arm to his shoulder, numbing it. He hadn't realized how impenetrable she was.

His studies had mentioned this, but the reality of it was alarming. Her weakness lay in her eyes and abdomen. Fire also burned her kind, although she didn't fear it. Sharn cast ball after ball at the dreshnie, who cackled as she fought. Tarid dodged her swinging claws and the slime she spat at him.

Rukk faced his opponent. He needed to abandon Thugari to kill the eikusai. He would have to be under her, dig his sword into her abdomen, and run it along the length of it. On his back, he would be defenseless.

The other option was to vault to eye level, using her legs for added height. He could swing his sword to blind or behead her. Neither attack guaranteed success. *"Tell Sharn to fire at the eikusai. I want the light to dazzle her. Then I need you to leap up and attack her eyes."*

"Why? Aiming for her abdomen?" Tarid swung his sword at the dreshnie, who dodged but not soon enough. He sliced through one wing. Both fluttered, and she cried out, floundering away.

"Ready?"

Tarid spoke to Sharn, and she turned, firing flames at the eikusai. It stumbled backward as Tarid leaped into the air. Rukk dove under its abdomen, sinking his sword in. He didn't need to force it along. The eikusai screamed and thrashed, aiding the sword's journey. The dreshnie cried out, rushing to help her pet.

"Cease!" The dreshnie's shrill command sliced through the chaos.

Rukk rolled out from under the collapsing spider and clambered to his feet. Chilling horror coiled and released within him at the sight of the dreshnie's talons buried in Thugari's shoulder.

CHAPTER TWENTY-ONE

In Rukk's arms, Thugari had known true happiness. Never before had a person inspired such joy that it filled her with light from her toes to her ears. For a moment, she had thought him a figment of her imagination, as if the desperation and despair seeping into the marrow of her bones had summoned him. She fell asleep repeating his promise, castigating him for failing her, and pleading with him to find her.

When he dove under Nazuree's body to bury his sword into her, Thugari cried out, expecting one of the spider's legs to skewer him. At the same time, as if he had wings, Tarid leaped into the air and blinded Nazuree. One slash across her eyes and she thrashed, her legs splaying out as she screeched. Lhazara cried out, drawing Sharn's attention, but by then the dreshnie had vaulted into the air—weaving from a bleeding wing—to land behind Thugari.

Before she could raise the crossbow, or drop it and grab the dagger, the dreshnie sank her talons into Thugari's shoulder. Fire stabbed through her like hot skewers with heat leaking down her chest. She screamed, the agony more than she could endure despite the warmth of her spilled blood holding back the cave's chill.

Gnash dove inside her tunic, shivering against her belly.

Thugari tried to shuffle away, but Lhazara yanked her back, eliciting another scream from her. She froze but whimpered, not wanting to anger the dreshnie or bring on a wave of agony.

"Cease!" Lhazara's fury shrilled her voice until it pierced Thugari's eardrums.

She flinched then moaned, for even that small movement spiked agony and leaked tears down her cheeks. The cavern was behind them, and with a flick of her wrist, Lhazara could throw her over the edge.

Rukk clambered from under the crumpling Nazuree. He rose to his feet and paled, taking a step toward Thugari. She shook her head, pleading with her eyes he stay back. He had tried to keep his promise to her, and for that, she was grateful. Once she plummeted, her death would null whatever debt she owed him.

"Killing my pet is unforgivable." Lhazara sniffed, her distress rippling through her body and along her talons.

Thugari clenched her lips to smother the scream crawling up her throat demanding release. Dipping her chin, she didn't want to focus on the anger and sadness on Rukk's face. He must know there was nothing he could do to save her. But she wasn't helpless. With one last shove, she could plummet to her death, taking the dreshnie and Gnash with her.

"Release her, dreshnie." Tarid shifted.

Lhazara curled her fingers into a fist, drawing more blood and another scream from Thugari, who couldn't bear much more of this. Icy numbness slithered along her right arm, rendering it useless.

Tarid froze, holding up a hand in surrender.

"Release her, and we won't hunt you, old one," Rukk said. "You can find another pet from one of the eikusai's children."

"I can kill you where you stand, beast." Sharn's voice dripped with disdain.

Lhazara faced her, while Rukk growled at Sharn. "You care not for your companion?" she asked Sharn, darting a surprised glance at Thugari.

"She's an obligation, nothing more. No matter what you do with her, know this—you will die." Two balls of fire burst into life, swirling on Sharn's splayed-out palms, painting her delicate features in gold. "My magic knows the taste of your blood. There is nowhere in this cavern you can hide."

Each step Rukk took snatched Thugari's breath. Lhazara's grip loosened in her distraction. Thugari was so close to freedom, the agony excruciating with the talons shifting and the tips scraping the wounds. She smothered a sob, keeping herself still.

Tarid darted a gaze between Sharn and the dreshnie. Thugari wanted to wail in anguish, to curl into a ball as she whimpered and sobbed. Instead, she needed to focus, to stay calm even as her vision blurred around the edges. Heat burned across her face, as she blinked away the tears.

Peeking at Lhazara's profile, Thugari measured whether she could twist free, dive for the loaded crossbow, and fire. This short a distance, she couldn't miss the dreshnie, but with a useless arm, she couldn't load another bolt. This would be her last chance.

Drawing in a calming breath, she wrenched her shoulder back and stumbled out of Lhazara's reach. She garbled a scream as fiery agony bent her over. The dreshnie froze for a moment, gaping at Thugari in horror, then launched herself upward. Thugari stagger-fumbled for the crossbow, and swung it, aiming for the dreshnie's chest as Sharn released balls of fire.

Lhazara squealed when they struck her, and she plummeted, landing with a sickening thud on the platform. Flames engulfed her unmoving body, and with a sob, Thugari fell onto her back, cradling the crossbow to her chest. Tears of relief, pain, and happiness slipped free, trickling into her ears.

Rukk's face appeared in her line of vision, and she had never seen anything more beautiful. He smiled, cupped a cheek, and wiped away her tears with the pad of his thumb. "You did well, little one."

She would cherish the look on his face, a mixture of pride, exhaustion, and contentment. Scooping up a scrambling Gnash, he settled her pet on his shoulder, then leaned back on his haunches to summon his magic. He held his glowing palm over her wound. Cold heat burned, and she arched, writhing under the agony, whimpers escaping her clenched lips. He muttered words of apology and encouragement, but his voice sounded far away, the pain transcending this world and dragging her into the depths of the netherworld.

"How is she?" Sharn's fake-concern brought Thugari back to the moment.

She glared at her, not wanting the female near her. "Don't," she said when Sharn summoned her magic. "You're not my nursemaid. You owe me nothing."

Sharn flinched, smothering her magic. "How did you know—?"

"The dreshnie told me." Thugari looked away not wanting to see the magus's face. At Sharn's retreating steps, she opened her eyes to admire Rukk's features and smiled. "Thank you for keeping your promise."

"Let's see if you can move." He looped an arm around her back and helped her stand.

The pain had lessened to a dull throb, but blood loss affected her balance. She stumbled, falling onto a knee before she was airborne. He carried her too often, but she had to admit, she needed his warmth, his strength, and the intoxicating scent of him.

"I will light the way." Sharn summoned an orb of light.

"I'll guard our backs." Tarid brandished his sword. He took the crossbow Thugari clasped to her chest and holstered it on his back.

As one, they meandered along the passages, across the dreshnie's campsite, and up to the entrance. Thugari grumbled at having chosen the wrong direction to run. The distance from the campsite where the horses waited was shorter with a path climbing out of the caverns. Sunlight streamed into the tunnel, blinding her, and she burrowed her face in the curve of Rukk's arm, shielding her eyes. Yet the rays' warmth was delicious, licking across her head and cheeks.

Before Rukk released her, Sharn ran her magic-laced hands over them both, ice chilling Thugari despite the sunlight. Since he didn't say anything, neither did Thugari, but she planned to ask him about it later.

He hoisted her into Harpax's saddle, then deposited Gnash between the horse's ears. Smiling at her, Rukk launched himself into the saddle, tugging her against him until the V of his legs cradled her backside. The trip to their campsite took an hour, not that she cared. She melted to his chest, content to drift off with his arm looped around her waist.

Never again would she take this sense of safety for granted. She would tell him that too. As the trees passed by in a blur, he shifted behind her, as if his backside was numb. At one point, he buried his nose in her hair or kissed the crown of her head.

She couldn't be sure she hadn't dreamed it. A part of her lumped it under her hopeful imagination.

"Is she asleep?" Tarid's voice came from the left.

"Yes, why?" Rukk's arm tightened around her, pinning her against him.

"I would like to tell her that her bolt struck true. It hit the dreshnie in the heart."

"Lucky shot," Sharn said.

Thugari was too delighted to care. She grinned and peeked at Rukk. His gaze met hers, the expression in the ebony depths intense. His focus dipped to her lips and rested there for a while. It made her chest explode with something hot enough to snatch her breath. She looked away, content to leave that emotion alone for now.

She replayed Tarid's words with hope piercing her self-doubt. If she understood him, her bolt had made a difference, perhaps even saved their lives. All she had was the book's instructions on how to wield an eating dagger, but she wasn't as useless or defenseless as she had once thought.

"Will you teach me to fight?" She kept her voice low.

"Yes," Rukk said. "We'll add crossbow to your training." He buried his face in her hair again and shifted his arm, his wrist rubbing the underside of a breast. Tingles shot outward, and her nipple puckered.

She gasped at the new and pleasant sensation but said nothing, in case it was an accident. Moon above, her body's response was hot, delicious, and addictive. He had mentioned pleasure, so this must be it. If so, sacrificing her virginity wouldn't be a hardship.

Now, all she needed to do was find a powerful magus and convince Rukk to teach her more than the crossbow.

Burrowing into his embrace, she pondered how best to tackle such a monumental task.

Chapter Twenty-Two

THE MOMENT SHE GASPED, he zeroed in on her heartbeat, the rise and fall of her chest, and her slight trembling. Sharn had cleaned them both, so Rukk wasn't prevented from cuddling Thugari, though he doubted any stench would stop him.

Her backside nestled against his cock, and the softness of her thighs rubbing against his kept his focus on carnal activities he would rather be doing with her.

Yes, he would train her, and he looked forward to it, wanting to spend time with her. Each moment would be an opportunity to seduce her, and soon, she would lie beneath him, her breathless moans music to his ears. Sigil willing, of course.

His determination fueled his amazement at how this female had snuck under his defenses.

"You're sighing." Tarid chuckled, breaking the silence of the surrounding forest.

"I still desire her, so leave me be." Rukk released Harpax's reins, trusting his mount to lead him true.

He wrapped his arms around Thugari's waist and buried his face in her neck. With the sun setting, they would stay camped until tomorrow morning. The temptation of her asleep in her bedroll would be enough to plague his dreams. If he slept alongside her, he could restrain himself by being near her, able to scent and touch her if need be. Though, that might increase the temptation.

"When we reach the next town, Rukk, find a female. I don't think you will make Thursday."

The image of burying himself in another female made him shiver with revulsion. His lips curled in distaste, and he shook his head. *"I want Thugari. No other female will do."*

"Fine, then find a magus powerful enough to remove her sigil. Ask Sharn tonight when Thugari's asleep."

"I promised her I would let her know if the removal of her sigil was possible." Rukk had planned to ask Sharn, but the dreshnie-eikusai incident had delayed it. He conveyed as much to Tarid.

"Do so when you know for sure. It isn't necessary to raise the girl's hopes after the day she's had."

"True." Rukk kissed her temple, inhaling her scent until he believed it filled every inch of his lungs.

He would ask Sharn and inform Thugari if it was good news. He feathered his lips across the tip of her ear peeking through the wealth of her dark braids. She trembled in his arms, and a glance revealed pebbled nipples tenting her tunic. His pulse leaped in eagerness, and he released her, needing to calm himself before he yanked her off Harpax and rutted with her under the nearest bush.

"I'll ask Sharn while you find dinner. When you return, perhaps I'll have news for you."

"Very well." Rukk agreed to the hunt because he needed time away from Thugari. The lust driving him overrode his thoughts, his intentions.

Alone, he could ask the forest to aid him, trust the loitering ancestor spirits to calm him. Unable to capture Harpax's reins, he gripped his knees, hoping to keep his hands there. He trapped his thumbs between their thighs and found himself stroking her through her breeches.

He gathered her braids onto one shoulder to press his forehead to her back, then his lips. It wasn't enough, didn't satisfy this need driving him. With a groan, he captured her chin with his fingers and tilted her face to him. Brushing his lips across hers, he drowned in the molten silver depths of her eyes. She gasped as he hovered his mouth over hers, letting their breaths mingle. Rubbing his lips across hers again, he tested the pliancy of them with the tip of his tongue. She was sweet, with a hint of tartness that lingered and urged him to take more.

Harpax lurched to a halt, and Rukk flung his arms around Thugari in reaction. The camp lay before him. He swung his leg around to dismount, then held up his arms. She leaned into them, placing her palms to his shoulders, her touch searing through his tunic.

As she snuck her hands under his cloak, her fingers burned a trail along his neck. He stared at her, mesmerized by the darkness of her skin, the brightness of her eyes, and the tempting pink of her mouth.

She slithered down his body. When he moaned, she raised a concerned gaze to meet his, her palms resting against his chest.

Tarid shoved his crossbow between them, along with his belt of bolts. He flashed an unrepentant grin when he looped an arm around Thugari and led her away. Glaring at his lawbrother, Rukk stormed his way into the forest, managing to give Sharn a nod of thanks for tethering Harpax.

When he hadn't seen deer, hare, or hekle, he forced himself to pause, drawing in the cool forest air until he stopped announcing his presence. The quicker he hunted dinner, the quicker he could defend Thugari from Sharn's icy demeanor. Tarid would protect her on Rukk's behalf, but he pined for Sharn. Rukk couldn't expect his brother to remain fair.

He clenched his jaw, checked on the cocked bolt, and squeezed his eyes shut, listening with his being. The scratchings of a pair of weasels reached him from the east. A young deer pawed the floor to the south, breaking off branches as it chewed on berries. He crept in that direction. A deer would take time to skin and prepare, but it would feed them for a while.

On silent feet, he stalked it, freezing when its pawing ceased. Taking careful aim, he released a slow breath as he fired. The bolt struck true. The deer collapsed, the moss of the floor softening its fall. Unable to sense its life pulse proved it was dead. Placing a palm over its still heart, he thanked the spirits for the gift. Grabbing it by its short antlers, he dragged it back to the campsite.

He made sure to stomp as he approached. Sharn and Tarid didn't need him to do so, but Thugari did. She had yet to train her orc ears. Part of him was eager to hear Sharn's findings, but he dreaded a confirmation.

If his assessment was wrong, then Thugari would be free to choose the life she wanted, away from him. She wouldn't need him anymore.

He shivered, having not expected the temperature to drop when there was a fire, but falling snow wouldn't surprise him.

"What in cursed hell happened?" He released his prey, wiping the sweat off his brow. Tarid stood there, arms spread wide as he held two females apart.

"Thugari won't let Sharn anywhere near her." He threw a pleading look at Rukk.

"I wouldn't use the power of revelation for such a simple discernment," Sharn said, her face mottled. "I'm the magus, not you, you piece of dark-orc wastrel."

"I'm telling you, if you lay a finger on me, I'll bite it off." Thugari snapped her teeth for emphasis.

Rukk charged, wrapping his arms around her trembling form and dragged her aside. He spun her, presenting his back to Sharn, granting Thugari privacy, even as he relished her curves rubbing against him.

"Why won't you let her look, little one?" He cupped her cheeks when she twisted to meet his gaze, her anger setting her eyes aglow.

"Lhazara showed me what will happen. Before you ask whether I believe a dreshnie over Sharn, she sifted through our thoughts and memories. I told Sharn this, that she needed to use the power of revelation. She dismissed it as if I was an idiot."

"That spell uses the magus's blood, and for orcs, our blood is precious. Let her discover this on her own, then the sacrifice will be her choice."

Thugari layered her hands over his, her silver eyes unblinking. They cooled to swirling gray, and she nodded, chewing on her bottom lip. His gaze dropped there, lingering on a habit he found irresistible. He dipped his head, planning to snatch another kiss, but she left his arms to face Sharn.

"I'm sorry, I didn't know how much the power of revelation would cost you." Thugari gathered her braids over a shoulder and offered her back.

Sharn hesitated, pulling out of Tarid's embrace to run her fingers over Thugari's sigil. "It is a Stone Cage." Awe laced her voice as it had Rukk's. She summoned her magic until it spiraled around her hands before spreading it over the sigil.

Thugari flinched away as if she expected it to hurt, then sighed. Her tension eased. She flashed a smile at Rukk, her shoulders relaxing as Sharn assessed her.

"It was painful in the dreshnie's illusion," she said by way of explanation. "I'm delighted she was wrong."

"It's an ancient sigil. Rukk was correct. A powerful magus must have woven it. At the next Fountain of Sound, we will contact my Arch-Magus. Erwana will know who did it, or how to undo it."

"Oh, but Rukk said something about whispering the words to unravel it and finding someone to lose my virginity to."

Sharn gaped, glanced at Rukk, then giggled. "It seems Rukk knows of something lying beneath the sigil he chooses not to share with us. We will ask Erwana, and follow her guidance."

"If anything has taught me I know nothing about such matters, it is the past day. I'll listen to Erwana's findings, but *I* will determine if I adhere to them." Thugari squared her shoulders as if she prepared for another battle with Sharn. "Thank you for your assessment."

"Let us prepare dinner." Tarid steered Sharn toward the deer carcass Rukk had left at the edge of the campsite.

"How's your shoulder?" Rukk laced his fingers through Thugari's to guide her onto her bedroll.

"It's better." She released his hand to undo a braid, then another. "Why did Sharn use magic on us outside the cave?"

"To clean us." He sat on the bedroll beside her. "It's a spell taught to magi able to summon more than one type of magic."

"Oh, well, it was sweet of her. I had to wear this disgusting cloak that stank so bad it made me gag. I couldn't appear ungrateful since I was wooing them with my politeness." Her face twisted in a grimace.

"I thought I had deceived them into believing me submissive, meanwhile, they were waiting for me to lure you into their snare. I'm such a fool." She released her hair to grab his knees, her touch burning him through his breeches. "Will I always be this naïve? Tell me your training will open my eyes."

Rukk laughed—it tumbled from his belly to shake his shoulders and bring tears to the corners of his eyes. "Yes, in a way, but I like your naïveté." He covered her hands on his knees with his. "You didn't crumble under the strain, you planned, then acted on it. That takes courage, Thugari."

"Stupidity in this case," she grumbled. "You could've died because of me."

"We're hard to kill. Besides, you killed her with her talons buried in your shoulder. Now, remove your cloak and open your tunic so I can assess your wound. My magic may bring you from the brink of death, but I'll need to do more healing sessions if the dreshnie poisoned you."

"I feel well, though." She flicked her cloak off her shoulders, exposing the unstained tunic.

Four tears marked where the talons had pierced Thugari's tunic and cloak, proving the incident had happened. Under Rukk's fixed gaze, she undid the ties enough to push the tunic off her shoulder. He had sealed the four wounds but hadn't fully healed her. He wanted nothing to mar her silken skin, and he needed to make sure no internal injuries remained. Summoning his magic, white circled his healed hand before he pinned his palm to her shoulder. He placed his other hand on her back, holding her near as he leaned in, his focus on the fading scars.

"You have to stop saving me, Rukk. Every rescue extends my debt." She nibbled on her lip again, snagging his attention when he glanced at her. "I don't want to be a burden, and you *do* need to reach Chaosthane to find out why the koveen steal bairns. Please don't let me delay you." A tear slipped down her cheek, but she didn't wipe it away. "I've cost you a day as it is."

"You've saved the future victims of the dreshnie and her pet." Rukk captured her tear with his lips, unable to do more with his hands busy. He could've sworn his skin tingled, the salty taste of her addictive. "Tomorrow, we will leave to meet Borgakh, and now you have battle tales of your own to share around a fire."

"How can you find humor in this?"

"I have seen much, killed many. Without humor, I would descend into the netherworld in despair. And, Thugari Dark-Orc, I find your smiles more beautiful than a full sky of stars."

She gasped, raising her gaze to meet his. "Why do you say such things, Rukk?"

"My new tendency to spout poetic words is why I believe your lineage is that of a siren. I'm not one to sweet-talk a female to lay between her thighs, yet here I am, doing just that." He removed his palm and shifted her tunic in place. With trembling fingers, he did her ties, ending the temptation to rip her garments off and taste those dark nipples he had seen in the pond. "So forgive me while we discover what lies in your mysterious past."

"Very well, as long as you don't expect me to spin poetic words about your moonlight-kissed hair and obsidian eyes."

"My what?" Rukk dropped onto his backside, struggling to understand her.

He was aware he affected her, made her shiver and gasp. Yet he had never considered what she thought of his appearance.

She laughed, shrugging on her cloak before braiding her hair. "Or would you prefer I compliment you on your broad shoulders and how tight your backside—"

"Thugari." He growled and placed a finger to her lips. Heat hit his body hard. He bit his inner cheek, fighting the urge to lunge for her. "Vixen."

Scrambling to his feet, he offered her a hand. She slid hers into his, and he lifted her, taking a moment to steady her with a grip at her hip. Every time he touched her, no matter how innocent, the heat of her burned into his memory, tightening the connection between them.

"Do we have salt?" She stepped around him. "I know how to cure meat, skin a deer, braise it over a fire, and if we can find sutar mushrooms, make a wonderful broth." She accepted the bag of salt Sharn held out to her and set to work rubbing it into the chunks of meat Tarid sliced off. "I'm not as wonderful a cook as Belen, but I did learn a thing or two from...*helping* her."

"I saw mushrooms south of here." Sharn cleaned the blood off Thugari's hands.

Within minutes, Rukk escorted a rat and Thugari—the female haunting his dreams. While she crouched and brushed bushes aside, Gnash scampered along branches, between trunks, and across the dense forest floor.

It didn't take her long to find what she sought. She bounced on her toes like an excited child. Around her, he smiled more than he used to. In the shadows of the forest, he didn't judge himself for it.

"*I do.*" The humor Tarid conveyed wiped the smile off Rukk's face.

"*Quit listening in on my thoughts.*"

"*Quit sharing them. Hurry back, we have visitors.*" Tarid's thoughts darkened in warning.

"*What now?*" Silence met Rukk's question. He scooped Gnash off a boulder and tucked it into his neck. Hurrying past Thugari, he kept her behind him.

"Be on your guard," he said, raising his sword.

CHAPTER TWENTY-THREE

THUGARI TRAILED RUKK. HE reached behind him to see how far she was, and often pulled her closer. Something awaited them at the campsite that necessitated protection. Gnash's eyes peered at her from within a wealth of silver hair.

In the scoop of her tunic lay the picked sutar mushrooms, sweet enough to flavor the wildness of the venison. Excitement bubbled within her at the thought of cooking for their party. It was a service she could provide if she could remember the steps.

In the camp, two human males stood, with three horses overburdened with goods. Merchants, if she had to guess. The older male pleaded with Tarid.

Thugari studied the travelers, resting her gaze on a younger version of him. His yellow-haired son had an appealing face, one prone to good humor if his laugh lines were any indication.

"I apologize for intruding, but the sun took its light earlier than we anticipated, stranding us in the forest," the old male said. "We only ask to share your camp until daybreak, then we will be on our way."

"What frightens you?" Sharn snuffed her magic and lowered her hands.

"It's the Forest of Anduia. Something watches from the shadows." The young male tossed a nervous glance at his father.

"A band of well-armed travelers was the safest option." The old male raised his hands in pleading. "No matter the cost."

"We are grateful to find lawbringers." The young male cast a wary gaze at Sharn.

"Welcome." Tarid grinned, opening his arms wide. "We have a deer to share if you're hungry."

Thugari slipped around Rukk, dodging his outstretched hand. Yet he grazed her belly, leaving exploding butterflies in the wake of his touch. He tried to stop her, but she couldn't see these strangers as dangerous. After the dreshnie and eikusai, the human males would have to be ferocious to frighten her.

"Why didn't you stick to the King's Way?" She knelt beside the pot of boiling water. With the tail end of her cloak, she cleaned each mushroom before plopping them into the pot.

"Bandits target us when we travel by road." The older one rummaged in a satchel, then scurried toward Thugari, carrying a small box.

Leveling the tip of his sword on the old man's chest, Rukk halted him. His magic swirling around his palms served as an additional warning.

"I but offer herbs and flavorings for your use." The old man flipped the box open for Rukk's inspection. "Please. I am Binidig Kerrien, and this is my son, Devan. We don't mean you harm. You have a magus with you. Ask her to test my word."

Devan lunged between Rukk and his father, as if to protect him, bringing the tip of the sword level with his bobbing Adam's apple. "We only want to avoid the koveen and wylders swarming the forests. Never before have we seen so many."

Plopping the last mushroom into the water, Thugari rose to press a palm to Rukk's chest. His gaze dipped, traversed her face, then with a fierce scowl, he lowered his sword. She patted him then reached for the box. This posturing might cost them a delicious meal when on the evening breeze, a hint of rosemary, chives, and sage teased her nose. Not all of those herbs went well with sweet mushrooms, but Binidig might have others.

"Tarragon, ginger, thyme, and rosemary? You wouldn't happen to have garlic, wild or otherwise?" she asked Binidig. Excitement made her bounce on her toes as she flipped the box's lid shut, dreading a spill if she stumbled. She hissed at Rukk to stow his sword. He ignored her.

"Indeed I do." Binidig chuckled. "Devan, grab a handful for the young lass."

Accepting the pungent bundle, she beamed a smile for obedient Devan. In the firelight, his yellow hair turned to molten gold, and she had to force her gaze away.

"Some of your mead, please, Tarid." She hurried to the cauldron. Humming to herself as she made dinner, she threw in pinches of various herbs, crushed garlic, and a good pour of the honeyed mead. Strips of meat followed.

As she worked, Tarid and Sharn helped set up camp for the strangers, while Rukk carried Thugari's bedroll next to his. He sat with legs akimbo, sharpening his sword. Whenever she peeked at him, he either glared at Devan or scowled at Tarid. Once, she caught Rukk looking at her with an unreadable expression as the firelight glinted off his tusks. His intimidation was ruined by the nuts and cheese he fed Gnash when he thought no one was looking. When he stroked Gnash's head, her heart stuttered, before leaping to catch up.

"It's ready." Smiling, she spooned into each person's bowl before carrying hers and Rukk's to him.

She watched with bated breath as everyone took a bite, and their surprised cries of delight shot pride through her. With flushed cheeks, she dipped her head, fighting an attack of shyness. Scooping in a mouthful, she sighed, wiping the tears forming with quick flicks of her fingers.

It tasted like Belen's. She had seen the female prepare it so many times, but here and now, Thugari had only memory to guide her. Rukk rested his palm on her back, then rubbed it up and down. He offered comfort, though she hadn't made a sound. When he removed his touch, a sense of loss gripped her, like a stray breeze chilling her skin.

As the forest settled for the approaching witching hour, silence settled on the camp.

The one to break it was Rukk, surprising when he had been sullen since Binidig and Devan's intrusion. "We are near to the Heart of Anduia, where spirits roam in eternal discontent and some remain mischievous. It is they who watch you."

He glided his stone along his sword's blade. Spread out in front of his bedroll were everyone's weapons due for a clean or a sharpen. The arsenal was threatening, as if he needed to declare his abilities or keep weapons close at hand. She studied the Kerriens, trying to see what bothered Rukk.

"They will bear witness to any nefarious plans strangers might have." His message didn't appear to miss the mark. Devan winced while Binidig peered into the shadows of the forest.

Eager to escape the tension in the camp, Thugari hurried to wash the bowls in the nearby stream. Each move she made, every gesture or word spoken was under Rukk's vigilant gaze. She flopped onto her bedroll and selected a dagger to polish. He flicked a surprised glance at her but said nothing. She ought to trust him and his instincts as a warrior. He had yet to fail her. As she glided the cloth along the blade, careful to mind the edge, she studied their guests.

Binidig regaled Tarid with stories of the finest meads and distilleries he had encountered as a merchant, traveling from the south of Thoraval, near where they mined the endless plains of salt. His destination was Dussoum to sell his wares and purchase dwarven crafts. From there, he would return to the biggest city of Thoraval, Onci. It was a journey he had done a thousand times, if not more.

Sharn sat in silence, her eyes shut as magic spiraled around her form. In the flickering flames, tendrils reached from the fire toward the magus.

"What is Sharn doing?" Thugari kept her voice low.

Rukk raised his gaze for a second. "She is replenishing her magic. Fire requires fire, light requires sunlight, earth magic—"

"Requires earth?" Thugari teased.

A smile twitched his lips. "And moon magic?"

She gasped, raising her face to the moonlight. No wonder she loved the silver light bathing her, as if it empowered or healed her. "It feeds my soul." She lowered her chin to meet his gaze. Something intense swirled in his eyes, and he parted his lips as if he couldn't breathe.

She hurriedly looked away and caught Devan staring at her again. He flashed a sweet smile. What that meant, she didn't know, but she didn't like the way his attention made her feel. Sweat trickled down her spine despite the cool breeze circling the camp. Disorientated moths swarmed her stomach, churning her meal. There was a marked difference between what Rukk called forth in her and those frenzied moths. She swallowed past the nausea crawling up her throat. Keeping her focus on the dagger in her lap or on Rukk's carved visage, she forced herself to ignore Devan.

"Tired?" Rukk asked. The steady back and forth of his whetstone on his blade soothed her nerves, and she smiled despite Devan's gaze having not left her.

"Yes, and you?"

Nodding, he returned Sharn and Tarid's weapons. Striding to Thugari, he gestured to her to stand, then shifted her bedroll, laying his between hers and the fire. No warmth or light would reach her, but it granted her a blessed break from Devan's interest.

"Thank you," she said, wiggling into her bedroll.

Exhaustion melted her bones when she sprawled onto her back. A sigh of contentment escaped her. In the presence of the dreshnie, she hadn't slept well, but tonight, with Rukk near, that would be different. He climbed into his bedroll, flipping onto his side to face her with his broad shoulders casting her in shadow.

She may have escaped the stare of a golden-haired male, only to fall under Rukk's ebony gaze, evocative and as confusing. Rolling onto her side, she gave him her back, lifting her hip to free her trapped cloak from under her. Now would have been the time to cuddle Gnash, except he peered at her from the curve in Rukk's neck.

The sounds of the forest in perpetual repeat lulled her as she drifted between oblivion and consciousness. She surfaced when Rukk looped an arm around her waist, crushing her against his chest and engulfing her in warmth. His presence was more comforting than she would ever reveal to him.

It must have been her mind toying with her, planting memories of his lips brushing her ear or a kiss pressed to her neck. Perhaps it was longing throbbing in her core, one that yearned for a smile from a taciturn lawbringer.

Her deepest wish manifested during the night for when dawn greeted her, she had her nose buried against Rukk's chest, his arms wrapped around her, and her knee clenched between his thighs.

She froze, despite basking in the masculine scent of him. Her fingers had sunk into his tunic, wrinkling the cloth under her grip. Drawing in a slow breath, she raised her gaze to his face, praying he slept on.

His focus was on her, unflinching. Sliding a hand up her back, he tangled his fingers in her braids and tugged to tilt her head back. Trapped, her ability to breathe elusive, she peered at him through half-lidded eyes. No expression crossed his face, yet his ebony gaze traveled over her, lingering on her mouth before flicking up to meet hers.

"Rukk?" Sharn's voice didn't alter his expression or the intensity of his single-minded attention. "If we leave now, we'll make the nearest Fountain before midday."

He released Thugari's hair, stroking his fingers across her ear to cup her cheek. Her heart rose to choke her, skittering without rhythm. She was tempted to nuzzle his rough palm. Something hot and needy uncoiled in her core, thrumming through her.

"We're meeting Borgakh in town." He rubbed his thumb across Thugari's bottom lip.

She parted her mouth to speak, but he pinned his forefinger across it, his eyes conveying the need for silence. She nodded, not understanding why she had to remain quiet, but trusting him regardless. A part deep inside of her wanted to stay in his embrace and investigate these volcanic sensations bubbling in her belly. The pleasurable heat originated from his touch, intense expression, and breathtaking focus, which meant she was a step closer to finding out what these feelings meant.

"I will awaken Tarid." Sharn's footsteps faded.

Thugari arched a brow, a silent request to explain why she couldn't speak. He withdrew his finger and feathered his thumb across her lips to pinch her chin.

He dipped his head, slow in his descent, then captured her mouth with his, inhaling her breath. She trembled. Her heart pounded in her ears, deafening her as her fingers tightened, digging into the flesh of his chest. This was...kissing, something she had never experienced.

Closing his eyes, he tasted her with tentative flicks of his tongue, and she smothered a moan that rose without her approval. His eyelids fluttered open, and there, within the depths were his intentions. He knew what he was doing to her, where he was taking her, and what he wanted from her. She was adrift, in thrall to his will.

She tilted her head, needing to taste him too, to test the softness of his bottom lip as he had done to her. He tensed, and she worried if she had offended him or done it wrong. He released her chin, and she lowered her gaze, wanting to hide her dismay and the embarrassment scorching her cheeks.

He untangled her fingers, kissed their tips, then rolled away from her, exposing her to the sunlight, and the weak warmth of the dying fire. She shivered with the loss of his intense heat more noticeable.

"You're awake too?" Sharn smiled at Thugari, which had her wanting to look behind her as if the magus addressed someone else. "Would you like a tisane? It's Binidig's personal brew."

"Please." Thugari sat up to unravel her cloak tangled around one leg.

With Gnash sniffing the air from his shoulder, Rukk disappeared into the trees to relieve himself, as she would soon. After she clambered to her feet, she stretched, reaching to the clouds feathering across the golden sky.

"Morning." Devan flashed a charming smile.

She buried her nose in the cup Sharn handed her, avoiding eye contact. "Did you sleep well?" she asked, choosing politeness.

He arched a brow in surprise, and shame burned her. She had been rude to him the night before. Though to be fair, she still didn't understand his earlier fascination. Sharn was more beautiful by far. The magus should garner more compliments.

Thugari was content with that. Drawing attention left a trail if her father decided to search for her.

"You have dark human in your blood, right? Not Atrarian like Tarid." Devan gestured to Tarid, who stood by the fire glowering at Sharn.

Thugari nodded, then sipped her tea, savoring the spices coating her tongue, and the hot liquid gliding down her throat to warm her belly. Cinnamon? It was an expensive spice and scarce, yet Binidig drank it in his tea.

"What is your family name?" Devan offered to refill her cup, and she handed it over with a tentative smile. "Perhaps my father and I have met them."

"I doubt it." Rukk stomped into the camp with a scowl.

He took the cup from Devan, emptied its contents, shoved the cup into Devan's hands, then laced his fingers through Thugari's, dragging her toward Envis. She was too stunned at his rudeness to offer Devan an apology.

"Envis is hurt. His front leg is swollen below the knee. He could've bumped it or something bit him."

Fear tightened her throat and, with a cry, she tore her hand from Rukk's, running to assess Envis's injury. Crooning in hushed tones, she stroked his muzzle to his forelock and down his neck. He tossed his head, then nudged her shoulder in greeting. Gnash nestling between his ears clung on for dear life, chirping in admonishment.

"I'll heal him." Rukk dropped to his haunches.

Stunned to find an angry gash, she crouched beside Envis. Her neglect slumped her shoulders. "I'm sorry, my friend." She rose to pat his neck as Rukk summoned his magic. "Don't try to be brave. I need you well." Envis snorted, shifting in position, as if he understood her. "Did you see if the same thing hurt Harpax, Rukk?" She studied the other mounts.

"He is well," he said.

She crouched again, watching him work. His focus wasn't on the wound though. He switched between it and her face, as if he wanted to say something, but hesitated.

Pausing, with his magic curling from his fingers, he said, "I don't trust them, Thugari. Please, don't encourage familiarity."

She met his gaze. Part of her wanted to rebel, to tell him he was paranoid, but after what she had endured, here in the forests and at the castle, she chose to listen to him. "I won't be rude, but I won't seek them out."

"Fair enough." His body relaxed, betraying his concern.

She peeked at Binidig and Devan. What did Rukk see that urged caution? Ice drenched her face as a slow realization dawned. She leaned toward Rukk. Her mind painted every glance and gesture from the merchants as suspicious. "Do you think my father sent them?"

He pursed his lips. "They travel between Onci and Dussoum, so the odds of them knowing Varthug are high."

She gaped and raised a shocked gaze to Rukk. "He never wanted me when I was a child. Why now? I mean, I planned for the possibility he would search for me, but thought it a slim one."

Rukk didn't respond, not that she expected or needed him to. He released Envis, a slight swelling remaining. "Envis should be fine to ride, but stay close to me."

He slid his palms down her raised arms, along her exposed torso to grip her waist, spinning her to face him. "They will travel with us to Vangate, where we will reunite with Borgakh and Nenneg." Rukk's breath fanned her ear.

She shivered. A tingle traveled to her nipples, as if fire connected them.

Meeting her gaze, he stroked his thumb along her cheek. "Thugari, I—"

"What's wrong with the horses?" Tarid asked, receiving a glare from Rukk.

They stared at each other, eyebrows arched, lips pursed, and ended with Tarid chuckling, tossing a grin at Thugari. It was then she realized they communicated without voices. She tried to hide her surprise, having never considered that was possible with magic.

"I will help Sharn pack up camp." She slipped past Rukk, his touch burning her hip when he tried to stop her.

"Hungry?" Sharn asked.

Thugari hurried toward her, surprised the orc female was her refuge. Gnash scampered across the camp, dodging feet to reach Thugari. She offered him a piece of an apple and scooped him onto her shoulder. She ate as she rolled bedrolls, secured satchels to saddles, and watched Sharn snuff the campfire by sucking the flames into her body. Her cheeks glowed pink when nothing but embers smoldered in the pit.

"What's wrong with Rukk?" She ran her glowing hands over Thugari, Gnash, and their cooking equipment—the cold gush of air refreshed as it cleaned.

Thugari narrowed her gaze at the silent-arguing lawbringers. "He distrusts everyone," she said, not wanting to reveal too much lest Rukk meant it to be private. And suggesting 'everyone' was vague enough.

"Yes, he does." Sharn sighed. The pots clanged as she stowed them away. "Except Tarid."

"Does Tarid not like you?" Thugari received a glower for her curiosity.

Sharn stomped off, leaving Thugari alone with the merchants.

She smiled at them but her twitching fingers revealed her anxiety, so she dropped the pretense and disappeared into the bushes to relieve herself.

Chapter Twenty-Four

THE TOWN OF VANGATE loomed on the horizon, smoke billowing from its chimneys blurring into the gray of the dismal sky. It was bigger than Thugari had expected, but she was grateful for it. Devan's constant attempts to talk to her angered Rukk, who sat like a washboard.

Like Lemfor, there was a strong town guard presence, vigilance against the theft of their bairns. Many glared hatred, distrust, or fear at her, as if she would steal a precious little one. In their places, she might have been the same—helpless, lost, and devastated. Did they blame the orcs, or distrust all travelers regardless of race?

Rukk dismounted then lifted her down. The hard edge of his jaw could chisel rock. Tarid led the horses to the stables, and she helped carry their satchels into the tavern, stashing Gnash inside a food pouch lest the innkeeper deny them service.

Rooms were scarce due to the Festival of Oranges, leaving Thugari to share with Sharn.

A thunderous expression flitted across Rukk's face, but it vanished, his stoicism once more in place.

"I smell roasted goose." Sharn bounced, her ebony hair swirling around her as she placed her satchel on one side of the bed.

Thugari dumped her things onto the bed. Gnash made chirping noises, shuffling inside the food pouch so that it looked like a bag possessed. "I'm starving too."

She rubbed her rumbling belly. The rich aroma when she had entered the common room had her salivating. Ignoring her hunger, she had scanned the common room in search of Borgakh or Nenneg. She was eager to see her friends.

"Do I look presentable?" Sharn's question widened Thugari's eyes.

"You're beautiful, as always." She unpacked her tunics and breeches, running a palm over them to iron out the creases.

Pink burst across the magus's skin. She fidgeted, plucking at the purple robe clinging to her curves. "Always?"

"Yes." Thugari unraveled her braid with the vain hope to untangle the mess with her fingers.

Sharn slapped her hands away and sang a short lyrical song. Her magic's touch was gentle, untangling the knots and forming fresh braids. Thugari wished she had such a talent.

"Then why does Devan pay you more attention? Tarid nitpicks everything I do or say. Rukk tolerates my presence, so that's normal." She huffed as she fluffed her hair. "Thank Zetar, *he's* not acting strange."

Thugari shrugged, accepting her taciturn lawbringer as he was. *Her* lawbringer? Moon above. "My father might have sent Devan to take me back."

She chose to share Rukk's suspicions rather than dwell on the churning, crushing sensations in her chest. Desperate to think of anything other than what Rukk invoked within her, she drew in steady breaths and focused on Sharn's despair. Allowing the female to suffer under the misapprehension Thugari was prettier meant the souring of their blossoming friendship.

"Your father?" She frowned.

"Yes, Varthug Nehrakgu."

Sharn jerked back, her mouth gaping as her gaze traveled over Thugari, who wore the gray tunic today. "Your silver eyes. What an oblivious fool I am." She paced the room, muttering furious words. "He had the sigil burned into your neck? What a monster."

Thugari's stomach gurgled, and a fresh blush stained Sharn's cheeks. She opened the door, and gestured to Thugari to lead the way, then shut and warded the door, securing Gnash and their belongings.

Down in the common room, Borgakh charged through the males, shoving them aside to yank Thugari into a hug. Nenneg slipped between them, not holding back.

Thugari laughed as tears spilled at such a welcome. Never had anyone been pleased to see her. After introducing Sharn to the orc maiden and her lover, Tarid left them alone to order food from the innkeeper.

Borgakh grabbed Thugari's wrist, her grip firm but gentle, and leaned into whisper, "Are you well, little one?" She threw an assessing glance at Sharn. "Has Rukk treated you well, or will I be killing him in the morning?"

"The dreshnie and eikusai would've eaten her if it wasn't for Rukk." Sharn gave a brief overview of how he had searched for Thugari in the cavern. "He ignored any of my suggestions to abandon Thugari to her fate. That was before I realized how much you mean to him." She reached across to squeeze Thugari's hand.

"What?" Her heart danced at Sharn's implication. Rukk's opinion of Thugari shouldn't matter, but it did.

"As a debt, she's valued." Borgakh beetled her brow in confusion.

"There's that too." Sharn accepted the tankard Tarid offered.

The harried server placed platters of meat and fruit onto the table, and the subject turned to the upcoming journey north. They were five days from Chaosthane.

Sharn mentioned stopping at the Fountain but didn't say why. Borgakh searched the tavern door as many times as Thugari did. For her, it was Rukk's absence and the overwhelming urge to find out where he was.

Who Borgakh was on the lookout for, Thugari didn't know.

"Shall we take a walk?" She arched a brow at Borgakh, who pursed her lips before nodding. The warrior dipped her head to whisper in Nenneg's ear before leaving.

Borgakh cleared a path to the tavern door with her intimidating stature. The evening air was crisp, refreshing, and Thugari sucked in great gulps, raising her face to the indigo sky. The colors of the rainbow twinkled in the stars, and the moon's gentle touch filled her with its power.

"Did you wait long?" She fell into step beside the warrior female.

"No, and we didn't encounter any bairns, only a nest of koveen. They're solitary creatures, so finding them in a group worries me, Thugari." She ran her scarred hand over her face, scrubbing hard before dropping it with a sigh. "It did make killing them easier." Her smile was bright in the moonlight.

"They've been scarce for us, nothing since we left Lemfor."

Borgakh lips whitened. "The forests have grown quiet. There are fewer animals to hunt, as if they sense what's coming. Whatever it is has the spirits agitated. I fear what awaits us is worse than what Nenneg saw."

"Evening, Thugari." Devan smiled as he strode toward her. "I'm delighted to stumble upon you."

At the sight of the strange male, Thugari struggled to hide her frustration. "Do you need something?" She searched for his father but found him missing.

"I thought to buy you an ale." Devan frowned at Borgakh, as if he disliked not finding Thugari alone.

She made the introductions but coughed to hide her smile when Borgakh ran her gaze over him, almost in a dismissive manner.

"That's a kind gesture, Devan, but as you can see, I'm enjoying a stroll with my friend."

Thugari bit her lip, forcing herself to remain polite. Not once had she encouraged his attention, and she didn't know how to dissuade him without hurting his feelings. Yet, if he persisted in ignoring her gentle rebuttals, she would have to be firmer with him.

"My apologies. I didn't mean to intrude." He darted around her, heading for the tavern. "I'll keep an eye out for your return."

"Curse it all, what was that?" Borgakh's shoulders shook with laughter.

"A problem." Thugari huffed. "He appears sweet, but I don't trust his intentions."

"Why not?" Borgakh gripped the dagger on her belt. "Has he done or said something to lead you to think he would harm you?"

Thugari frowned as she recalled the past day. He had been polite, endearing, and helpful. There were no hints in Devan's character to lead Rukk to believe her father had sent him.

She said as much to Borgakh, who laughed until tears dripped off her chin.

"Rukk said so?" Another round of laughter followed.

What was so amusing? She folded her arms across her chest and waited, tapping her foot.

Between wheezes, Borgakh wiped her cheeks, a grin lingering.

"I don't see the humor," Thugari said.

"I can see that, little one. Do you trust Rukk?" She led Thugari along the cobbled road toward the market square.

"Of course," she said.

"Even if what he says is wrong?"

"Wrong? Why would he lie to me?" That made no sense. She threw a scowl at Borgakh, not appreciating their subject.

"Why indeed. To keep you safe?" Borgakh raised her face to the sky and sucked in a huge breath, as if she held back another round of laughter. "Who am I to reveal Rukk's motives? I can hazard a guess, but anything I say may lead you down the wrong path. Talk to him when next you see him."

"He hasn't been approachable the entire day, not since he kiss…" She bit her lip and lowered her chin with embarrassment burning her cheeks. It was futile.

Borgakh guffawed again, spewing indiscernible babble at the same time. She staggered back to the tavern, clutching her stomach, having managed to say if they didn't return now, Thugari would have to carry her there.

Borgakh collapsed beside Nenneg and leaned in to whisper. Nenneg's gaze rose in surprise to meet Thugari's. Her wide-eyed expression was almost one of pity, as if Thugari had mortworm on her feminine bits. She didn't appreciate the implication.

A tankard of ale landed in her hands, and she faced Devan. He wrapped his fingers around her wrist and ushered her toward an empty table at the back of the common room. She could swear she heard Borgakh's laughter above the din of the tavern.

"I'm glad to have this moment to talk to you *alone*." He bumped his shoulder against hers when he chose the chair beside her. With a charming smile, he ran his brown gaze over her face.

"What did you want to say?" She made to take a long draw of her ale, then hesitated, choosing instead to set it aside. Who knew what lay at the bottom of the tankard.

"I want to know everything about you." He dipped his head and caught her gaze. "Your favorite color, food, or flower. Do you like amulets or rings?"

"I don't know." She scowled. Rukk's warning rang in her ears, and she distrusted Devan's insincere interest. They headed in different directions, a future between them impossible. Besides, she didn't know how to answer his questions.

"Why do you have lawbringers guarding you? Are you nobility?" He sipped his ale, his shoulders hunched.

She shifted on the seat, creating distance between them. "My father awaits me in Dussoum." Lying to him was easier to stomach.

"They escort you as a favor?" He gestured to the tavern maid to refill his tankard.

"I don't know the details." Thugari threw a longing glance at Borgakh's table. "Thank you for the ale, Devan, but I need to return to my party."

She pushed the untouched ale across the table, placing her palms on the surface to boost her departure. He gripped her wrist, digging his nails into her skin. She cried out, glaring at Devan, whose charming smile had vanished.

"Sit." He yanked her to the bench. She yelped, pulling on her arm, trying to free herself. "If one person comes to your aid, I'll snap your bones."

She blinked at him as if she had misheard him. "Are you insane?" Panic crawled up her throat and numbed her limbs. "I'm friends with the orc maiden Borgakh Yerug and lawbringer Rukk Knaraugh. What do you hope to gain by this?" She nudged her chin at his bruising grip.

"Untold wealth, Varthugari Nehrakgu." His smirk twisted his features into something evil.

Memories flashed of the dreshnie on fire, a reminder she had survived so much. A human male was nothing compared to that. Right at that moment, he squeezed her wrist so hard she expected to hear it snap. She whimpered, biting down on her bottom lip to smother it.

The ass laughed, delighted to have caught her, or he enjoyed the pain he inflicted. It didn't matter which. With her back to the common room, she had to twist to grab someone's attention.

"Go ahead and break my bones. They'll heal me, but you will die by sword, magic, or arrow. Pick one or leave." While the anger burned with the pain, she glared at him.

He laughed. "I didn't believe him. Lord Varthug warned us your beauty would entice, your voice sweet to the ears, but to guard against such wicked magic."

"Why would my father pay for my return? He never wanted me, so sending you is confounding." She bit her lip, willing to endure Devan's nails digging into her skin for a moment longer if it granted her answers.

"You shamed him, as if he were the monster. By fleeing, you rejected the mate he found for you, one willing to ignore your..." Disgust twisted Devan's face, "less than desirable lineage. What awaits you is untold punishment." He tightened his fingers. "You *are* a cruel, heartless abomination, twisting a man's desires against him."

She flinched as those tormenting voices from her childhood sang her shame. Shaking her head, she banished those memories to the dark recesses of her mind. She was free, and there was nothing in Kethil that would send her back to Haraton.

"I may be, but you're an idiot." She rose to her feet, tears escaping as his nails drew blood.

One moment she was in agony, and the next, yanked away from the table and thrown over a shoulder. Air rushed out of her lungs, and she fought for breath. Black spots blurred her vision, but the nip in the air told her whoever he was, he had carried her outside uncontested.

Chapter Twenty-Five

Thugari raised her arms to ward off a blow. They were in the shadows where the moonlight dared not trespass.

"I'll scream." She gasped for air, then stilled.

The man's scent upon the breeze was familiar. She shook her head. Rukk pinning her to a wall with such aggression was illogical. Her longing for him must be playing with her senses.

The male flicked her hands aside and cupped her face.

She struggled, bringing up a knee, aiming for his groin, which he easily dodged.

"Thugari."

She recognized that voice. Rukk. Joy and relief engulfed her, and she cried out, throwing her arms around him. Clinging to him, she buried her face in his neck.

He pulled her arms down, holding her away from him with a bruising grip on her shoulders. "What were you doing with Devan?" His hoarse voice was intense with emotion.

She frowned. He must have seen how Devan was hurting her and stormed in to rescue her. That happened far too often for her liking, but Rukk had saved her again.

"Nothing." She shook her head, despite knowing he couldn't see her. "Moon above, Rukk, I'm so glad you found me."

"Lies. He was all over you, smiling and whispering in your ear."

"What?" He sounded like he had gone mad. "Why would I? You said he was from my father and—"

"You used your siren ways on him, lured him." Rukk gripped her forearms and yanked her against his body.

Fresh fire splintered her wrist, canceling her outrage. She screamed, struggling to pull away. When he released her, she whimpered with the cool air sharp against her wet cheeks.

"You're in pain." His voice softened.

"Who are you?" She stumbled away from him, cradling her wrist to her chest.

Her mind whirled in shock, not holding any thought long enough for her emotions to settle on a reaction. Anger returned, now directed at Rukk, but deeper lay disappointment. Both intense emotions pooled tears on her lashes.

"Curse it, Thugari. Curse your allure, your beauty, your innocence. Curse the danger that follows you." He stomped as he paced, then silence fell. Drawing in a deep breath, he crowded her. She flinched, expecting to suffer more pain or even worse, a gentle touch. "Who hurt you?"

"As if that matters now." She didn't know him, this volatile male with his stoicism and steadfast integrity absent.

"It matters to me." His voice spiked. "Follow me. If you do not, I'll throw you over my shoulder again." He disappeared around the corner of the tavern.

She considered running in the opposite direction. Abandoning Gnash was out of the question, and the part of her that had grown fond of Rukk rebelled. With a huff, she hurried to catch up.

Through the tavern's rear entrance and up the stairs they hurried until he opened his room door, gesturing for her to enter. She peeked at her door—a beacon of safety—until she recalled the last time she had tried to hide from him.

With his door shut and the lantern lit, he faced her. His obsidian gaze traveled over her, then rested on her arm still clasped to her chest. His touch was gentle, breaking her determination to remain firm against his attraction, as she had feared it would.

Tears stung behind her eyes, and she lowered her chin to her chest, hoping to hide how his behavior had hurt her. He grumbled, and the cool caress of his magic wrapped around her wrist summoning a sigh of relief from her.

"Did he do this?" he asked, as if he hadn't just manhandled her himself.

"My father sent him," she said, unable to raise her voice past a whisper. Her wrist no longer burned, but her chest throbbed with a mixture of despair, sadness, and longing.

Worst of all, her understanding of Rukk was forever altered. "I thought you had sensed how much pain I was in, you know, because of our bond. But you didn't, Rukk."

Silence met her declaration, and he wore the same expression as if he spoke to Tarid. A ruckus rose from the tavern below. She didn't ponder the cause when Rukk's gaze filled with unspeakable turmoil. Perhaps she wasn't the only one to suffer tonight. Something must have driven him to act as he had. He might have received terrible news, and she judged him for it.

"He won't bother you again." A pulse ticked at the base of his jaw. "Tarid has dealt with it."

She didn't care about Devan or whether she saw him again. What she wanted was to understand what had affected Rukk's behavior. "What happened tonight, Rukk?" She hoped his explanation made sense.

He didn't respond, focusing on her wrist until the bruising faded. Snuffing his magic, he glided his hand up her forearm to her elbow, then with a twirl, pinned her to the door. His lips on hers melted her resolve. The heated taste of him demanded a response. He buried his fingers in her hair, layering his hard body over hers, trapping her.

A predatorial groan tore from him, and he pulled away, snatching quick kisses before pressing his temple to hers. "I thought he had charmed you with his boyish looks and smile. I saw the way he admired you today, tried to talk with you, and tonight, with his body nestled against yours...I'm sorry, Thugari. The taste and scent of you has lust gripping me, throwing logic to the four corners of Kethil." He put distance between them, running his hands over his face and into his disheveled hair. "It's not an excuse for the way I acted. So, as a plea for forgiveness, I release you from the debt."

Running away of her own free will was different from having someone push her away. His words didn't bring her joy or relief, but a dark hollowness reverberated with fear—that she would never see him again, never share these remarkable kisses. She didn't want him to leave her.

She cupped his cheeks, forcing him to meet her gaze. "There is no debt, remember? We have a bargain I won't release you from." Taking another step brought his warmth closer, reaching her through their garments. "Besides, who else will help remove this sigil? Who else will kiss me like you do?"

"Thugari." He grabbed her hand to kiss her palm. "You don't know of what you speak, innocent one. Kisses lead to more, for they must, and more is what I need from you."

Drawing in a sharp breath, she acknowledged that every part of her body wanted more too, whatever that meant. "Are you applying for the position of my first lover?"

Where she found the nerve to ask him, she didn't know. It had to be the intense burning in his eyes, or the way his body called to hers, or his fingers reaching between them to stroke her neck, sending tingles to her breasts and lower. Something breathtaking churned inside her, and she ached, throbbed, needed his touch or his mouth on hers.

His smile was swift and breathtaking. "There is no first lover position if we cannot unravel your sigil."

"Here you are." Tarid burst into the room.

"You know damn well where I am." Rukk glared at Tarid as he gathered Thugari near. "I asked you to stay away."

"I would have if the Grand Lawmaster hadn't sounded me."

Rukk stiffened, and their expressions morphed as they communicated in silence again. Thugari said nothing, choosing to burrow into his embrace. She dug her fingers in his tunic and rubbed her cheek across his chest. There was something to being held as if she mattered, as if he loved her.

Swallowing past the sudden lump in her throat, she shuffled back. He and Tarid needed to discuss lawbringer business, judging by their continued silence.

Rukk's arms tightened, his focus dropping to her upturned face. He glowered at Tarid, who threw his arms in the air. Returning his gaze to her, Rukk said, "The Grand Lawmaster has summoned us to the Tower."

"Why?" She bit her lip, hoping to quiet her curiosity. "It's none of my business."

"I would obey him in an instant, but this time, I mean to ignore his summons and discover what lures wylder and koveen alike."

"They serve the owner of the voice." She hurried to share what Nenneg had told her—the voice in the Chaosthane caverns, the hordes preparing for war. Rukk's expression darkened as she spoke.

"It cannot be." Tarid collapsed onto the chair, his face pale. "There's no mention in the ancient texts of the Ravenous Dark returning this soon."

"We need to travel to Penven after all." Rukk swept her hair off her temple, tucking it behind her ear in a delicate caress.

"Good. Perhaps Janar can shed some light. The history of the Dark is his passion, after all." Tarid touched her forearm. "Thugari, I have a cabin a friend left to me. It's northwest of here and ramshackle, but it's yours if you choose to wait for us."

"Don't worry about me. I can travel with Borgakh." In Dussoum, she would find out once and for all whether she carried her mother's powers.

"I will speak to the Arch-Magus about your sigil. If I cannot find you in Chaosthane, I will sound you." Rukk cupped her cheek and stroked his thumb across her chin.

She gaped. There were rumors of such shrines. "A Fountain of Sound?"

He nodded and hugged her, as if he didn't want to release her.

She slipped her arms around his waist and squeezed, assuming he would be gone by morning. Silent communication passed between the lawbringers, then Tarid stormed out, mumbling something about telling Borgakh and Sharn the change in plans.

Rukk leaned away from her to dig in his cloak. Gathering her hand in his, he dropped his coin pouch onto her palm and curled her fingers around it. "Take it. Obey Borgakh in tense situations."

She thrust his pouch at him, but he cupped her fist, pressing a kiss to her knuckles. "I don't need your coin, Rukk." She did, but she couldn't accept his generous gift. With her heart aching and her chest tight, she couldn't laugh at how things had changed. She had stolen his pouch yet was resistant to take it now when it was freely given.

"You could travel with me, but my Grand Lawmaster hasn't been himself of late. I'm not certain what reception I'll receive, let alone with a dark-orc siren bearing a Stone Cage." He stroked his fingers up her neck to caress the sigil, eliciting a startled cry from her. His touch had her clenching her thighs against the throbbing ache she now knew was lust.

He growled, dipping his head as if to kiss her. Freezing midway, he squeezed his eyes shut. His expressions changed, his jaw hardening as Tarid spoke to him. "Tarid's cabin is called Banach Cottage. Ask the stablemaster in Tulach for directions." Rukk shifted until their bodies aligned. "Sweet Zetar, Thugari, I don't want to leave you."

He dusted kisses from her ear to her mouth, setting fire to her senses. Her knees crumpled, and she clung to him, parting her lips when he feathered kisses across them. She hoped to capture his breath and a little of his soul.

Instead, he teased her tongue with his. She reveled in the taste of him and at his intrusion that boiled her insides into pure need. Unskilled, she didn't know what to do.

His swirling, teasing tongue overwhelmed her, consumed her thoughts. Using her tongue to push at his, she warred with him, learning the crevices of his mouth in the process.

A groan rumbled through him, vibrating her sensitive nipples crushed against his chest. Every part of her overheated. Added to this was a desperate need to remove her garments, to feel his bare skin against hers.

He tilted his head, and the kiss deepened. Her world narrowed to this moment and her inability to consume him.

He wrenched away from her, throwing out an arm as if to hold her back. His breathing labored, and his hand trembled. "I shouldn't have kissed you like that. I'm sorry, little one."

Sorry? She frowned, fighting for breath. The kiss was wonderful, and she wanted, no, *needed* him to do it again. His clenched jaw warned her not to ask.

She headed for the door, pausing with a hand on the frame. "Travel well, Rukk."

Walking away was harder than escaping Haraton or pretending to sleep beside an eikusai. Every part of her wanted to turn and throw herself into his arms. He had obligations. She was a runaway. That he had shared any of his time with her was a miracle.

In the privacy of her room, she sobbed in silence, wailing in whispered screams of agony. Her shoulders shook, the turmoil in her chest was of loss and despair. She couldn't shake the thought she might never see him again. Lying on the hard, wooden floor, she fought for each breath. Footsteps passed her room.

She clambered to her feet, splashing water onto her face, and praying Sharn didn't arrive soon. She didn't know how to explain her swollen eyes.

With his coin pouch clutched to her chest, she stared out the open window, sighing as the breeze cooled her flushed face. She leaned out, catching a sliver of moonlight, and prayed for strength. Imagining him returning to her, a silhouette on the horizon riding Harpax, placated her broken heart. The illusion wrapped her in his embrace, kissed her hair, and declared his undying love. She would wait for him at Tarid's cabin even if the dwarves welcomed her.

Sharn entered their room as Thugari buried the coin pouch at the bottom of her satchel. Gathering Gnash off the windowsill, she rubbed her chin across the top of his head.

The beautiful magus huffed as she paced, gesturing with her arms in her agitation.

"Sharn?"

She faced Thugari, tears on her eyelashes. "I'm such a fool."

"Why would you say that?" Thugari had never seen the female without her self-assurance.

Sharn wiped her cheeks as she curled her trembling lips into a watery smile. "I've received no instructions to abandon my task, so I travel where Rukk and Tarid go."

"You spy on them?" Thugari sat on the edge of the bed and rocked a sleeping Gnash. "Why them, and how does that make you a fool?"

"Arch-Magus Erwana has her reasons, which she's keeping close to her chest. Returning to the Tower of Eslaniel will afford me an interview. I might learn more, but I won't forget about your sigil."

"Thank you." Thugari didn't mention Rukk had made the same offer. Moon forbid something should happen to him, but if it did, Sharn's help would be welcome.

"I thought I was in love." Her lips contorted, her derision self-directed. "With Rukk, of all lawbringers." She snorted even as her tears formed fresh rivulets. "I hoped this task would force him to realize how wonderful and capable I am. Instead, it's not Rukk who noticed."

Shock sealed Thugari's tongue, and she could do nothing but gape. Her silence must have encouraged Sharn to continue.

"He never behaved toward me as he does with you. Rukk tolerates me, which is progress from his initial distrust." Sharn resumed her pacing, her agitation returning. "When we reach Penven, my task might end, and my time with Tarid will too." She laughed, high-pitched and hysterical. "I *am* a fool, right?"

Ah, now Thugari understood. "Does Tarid feel the same way?" She smothered a smile, having never expected Sharn to develop feelings for Tarid, let alone share them with her.

"I don't know. His treatment of me was abysmal, but after battling for the bairns together, we developed a comfortable rapport." She dabbed her cheeks, staring at her damp fingertips with surprise.

"Do you think he believes you are still in love with Rukk?"

Sharn chuckled, slapping her palm on her thigh. "Curse it all. You're right. I was so blatant with my unrealistic affection for Rukk." She nodded as if she formed a plan. "Tarid says you'll continue with Borgakh?"

Thugari jerked back, startled by the change in subject. "Yes, to Dussoum. I was hoping to find a home among the magicless."

"If you're without power, they *will* welcome you. Should the Gates of Chaosthane deny you, don't linger." Sharn gripped Thugari's healed wrist, her touch far less painful than Devan's. "The dwarves can be cruel to those who contain even an ounce of magic. Oh, and hide Gnash. They're rather partial to rat."

Thugari smiled. "Tarid has offered the use of his cabin. I'll go there, whether the Gates grant me entry or not. Time on my own might be what I need." She marveled at the decision she made. The warmth of certainty and the freedom to decide her own fate spread outward to fill her with peace.

Sharn hurried to her satchel to pack.

Unbuckling her boots, Thugari snuck a peek at her. "I hope you'll consider me your friend."

"Same," she said, her smile exploding with joy across her face. "I'm sorry for judging you."

"I'm a lamb amid the lions, so yes, my presence should've raised questions. I stole Rukk's coin pouch when you arrived at Haraton." She didn't mention the medallion, not out of distrust this time, but out of respect for Rukk. He had said it was precious to him.

Sharn stopped, her gaze assessing her. "You're the stableboy?" She giggled, undoing her robe to reveal the cotton slip beneath. "I didn't suspect a thing. Well done, Thugari." She climbed into bed, spreading her braid upon the blankets.

"Promise me you'll take care of them both." Thugari peeled her breeches off and hung them over the back of the chair. She climbed into bed, flipping onto her side to peer at Sharn.

"A vow easily made."

Thugari slipped her clasped hands under her cheek as Gnash curled against her neck. She had to find contentment in Sharn's promise, even though their circumstances could change. She might never see any of them again.

Chapter Twenty-Six

Rukk withdrew his fingers from his cloak pocket. The two days to reach Penven had blurred for him, and at last, they waited outside Venec's chamber. His thoughts were never far from Thugari, his fingers always reaching into his pocket where he kept a lock of her hair. He remembered standing over her sleeping form. Sharn and Tarid had gone to fetch the horses, granting him this moment to bid Thugari farewell.

In sleep, he could admire her features, her silver-gray eyes not distracting him. She slept with her mouth parted, the pink of her tongue visible. He bent to brush her lips with his for one last taste of her. Since then, at inopportune times, and most often when sleep eluded him, his tongue recalled the sweetness of her. What he recalled the most was her unfettered laughter, her sweet smile, and her kindness despite how abysmal life had treated her.

Leaning against the wall, he unsheathed his dagger, hoping to keep his fingers from reaching for his pocket. This was the weapon he had used to slice off locks of her hair. The emerald gem in its hilt winked a greeting as he spun it. Exhaustion hounded him since they had pushed their horses to reach the Tower. Yet tension had him wound tight, not understanding why Venec had summoned him.

Tarid paced, shooting glances at the chamber door every few steps. *"What's taking so long, Rukk? I am eager to find Janar. He did not greet me as he used to."*

Rukk forced a smile. *"When will you cease teasing your brother about his virginity? It is revered, honorable. Go easy on him."*

Tarid chuckled. *"Never."* His laughter dwindled. *"His achievements are whispered around our tribe with reverence."*

"So are yours, brother." Rukk patted his pocket holding Thugari's lock of hair.

Tarid snorted. *"As in, there rides Tarid the Atrarian, friend to the rutting Rukk."*

Rukk grinned. *"Save your silliness for Janar. He is far more tolerant than I am."*

The soft footsteps of females whispering along the passage forewarned them. They raised their patient gazes. Arch-Magus Erwana glided into view first. Trailing her was Sharn's familiar figure. Neither spoke, but Erwana gestured to them to follow her onto a secluded balcony.

Tarid arched a brow at Rukk. *"Let us hear what she has to say."*

Rukk nodded. *"As long as we don't venture far."*

She stared out at the surrounding lands, the snow-capped Camsevair Mountains far to the south. Her burgundy velvet robe was rich in color and hugged luscious curves. Down her back fell a waterfall of golden curls, but when she faced Rukk, her human features twisted in concern.

"Sharn tells me you're steadfast, and for that I'm grateful. I've sent magi to test how deep the rot goes. I apologize for doubting your loyalty. Much has happened in your absence, and it is worse than I feared." Her lips twitched, as if she debated what to reveal.

He remained silent, waiting for her to say her piece.

Her expression soured. "A month ago, Venec went north to Dussoum to meet with the dwarven senate, the Iomhar. They alerted the Tower of disturbances in the bowels of their mines. Something stirred, killing their scouts and spreading darkness, climbing the mine levels reaching toward life. Nothing the dwarves did halted the spread."

"The Ravenous Dark?" He needed her to name it.

At the same time, he prayed she mentioned something else—an unknown disease, a scourge of mutated creatures, anything but the Ravenous Dark. The last time it had risen was seven centuries ago with Kethil younger and less corrupted. Core values had changed since then with greed, selfishness, and perversion now in control. It would find willing sycophants. Once it conquered Kethil, evil would destroy everything of worth—family, friendship, love—and plummet nature into chaos. Restoring the balance was why all the realms united to battle it, time after time.

Erwana didn't hesitate. "Yes."

"Zetar spare us." Tarid gripped his head, his mouth twisted in horror. "How long have they known?"

"What can we do?" Sharn asked, blushing when her question merged with Tarid's.

Erwana maintained eye-contact with Rukk. "I didn't travel with Venec, and for that, I take full responsibility. He returned a changed male. Gone was the pillar of strength I revered. The male in that chamber isn't my old friend." Her nostrils flared before she dipped her head, not before he caught the glimmer of tears. "Please, when you meet with him, be vigilant and judge for yourself. See me after he dismisses you."

She patted Rukk's shoulder on her way past him. "I have sounded the leaders, calling them to arms, and we head for Chaosthane before the full moon. I have done this without the other half of the Tower's authority. Your lawbrothers do not know of the threat growing in the north. You, Rukk Knaraugh, need to deal with your Grand Lawmaster out of respect for who he was."

"Me? My lawbrothers will decide his fate if what you say is true." Rukk inhaled a slow breath, not focusing on how he had sensed something had changed and done nothing about it.

His last sound with Venec had left him uneasy. Venec wanted to see Rukk, and he would soon discover why.

Until then, he would withhold judgment. "The koveen and wylders prove something is amiss. I will sound my brothers. We need to plan our response."

"*If* the Dark rises, the ancient texts must have documented how to defeat the darkness." Tarid straightened his shoulders in an aggressive posture Rukk recognized. Having something to do empowered Tarid, gave him focus.

"Our scrolls might shed light," Sharn said.

"See to Venec, and Tarid, meet Sharn in the archives afterward." Erwana abandoned them on the balcony, and the air cooled, as if the weight of truth impacted the weather.

Tugging Thugari's lock of hair out of his pocket, Rukk held it to his lips, believing her scent clung to it. She headed for Chaosthane and into the belly of an evil he couldn't protect her from. Her innocence alone would call to the Ravenous Dark and its minions to her.

With a groan, he darted after Erwana, catching her at the stairs leading to the lower levels of the Tower. "Arch-Magus, forgive me. I have a personal matter I need to discuss with you."

She paused with her hands clasped in front of her. Her expression was one of patience as she waited for him to speak.

"On my last task, I encountered a dark-orc with a Stone Cage."

She gaped. "It cannot be. We banned the use of such sigils."

"Yet she bears the markings. I hoped you had heard of the occasion in which it was applied and whether there is a way to remove it." He shivered, wishing for more when it came to Thugari.

"There was an entry about a sigil in the previous Arch-Magus's diary. I hadn't realized she meant the Stone Cage. An orc chief asked her to cast the sigil onto his half-breed daughter. The details escape me at present, but I do not recall her performing the spell, since it is forbidden. I can search for the text this evening. Perhaps she notes what transpired."

He slipped Thugari's lock of hair into his pocket. "Please. She believes she is without power and travels to Chaosthane as we speak."

He didn't want to focus on how much danger she was in, but Borgakh was aware of what lay beneath the Chaosthane Mountains. Since he couldn't protect Thugari, he was grateful Borgakh could.

"You care for her?" Erwana smiled.

He nodded, choosing not to lie to the most powerful magus in Kethil.

The warmth of her gaze faded as she stared at him. "You fear for her." She squeezed his forearm. "I will search the diary. You shall have your answer after you have spoken to Venec." In a flurry of draped cloth, she hurried down the stairs.

"Rukk, the chamber door has opened." Tarid waited outside Venec's chambers, his fidgeting visible from where Rukk lingered on the landing.

Shaking his head, he strode toward Tarid, entering through the door and into the smoke-filled room. Candles burned, but not enough to illuminate the room. In one corner, Venec's prized armor lay in a heap. The male himself sat in an ornate chair with one leg thrown over the armrest. He wore a stained tunic and wrinkled breeches, his feet bare. His graying hair fell in disheveled waves, his tusks yellowed, and the meticulous male who had trained him was missing. A stench permeated the room, a miasma reminiscent of a tavern.

Crossing the carved stone floor, new runes caught Rukk's eye, but he didn't focus on them, not wanting to reveal he had seen them. Someone had dared to ruin the ancient protection wards placed there with unknown runes. This was myllisan stone, mined by the dwarves. Only a coven of magi could etch such deep furrows. Erwana had sent her magi out on tasks, so there weren't many in the tower able to do this.

"At last. How dare you arrive late when I summoned you days ago." Venec sipped from his goblet. His fury and over-imbibing of wine stained his face and neck red.

"Traveling by dragon became impossible when the last one died." Rukk's comments would have garnered a chuckle from Venec had he been...*well*.

He reacted by throwing his goblet, missing Rukk who didn't dodge or flinch. The wine flew in a crimson arc, spilling onto the stone floor. The runes glowed white, soaking up the offering. Rukk had never seen them do so, unless it was with blood. He stared at the stain, kneeling to dip his fingers in and rubbing them together to test the viscosity. It was blood. What or whose blood was the question, and worse, Venec drank it.

"Blood." Rukk sent his thoughts to Tarid but didn't look at his lawbrother.

"Why? Dark magic is forbidden." He shuffled from side-to-side. *"There is power beneath our feet, but why now, why our Grand Lawmaster?"*

"Your last sounding was uninformative. You have lost your ability to perform even the simplest of tasks," Venec continued.

"Many have lost such skills," Rukk said, resting his hand on his hilt. He never entered Venec's chamber armed, but he hadn't taken the time to freshen up since arriving.

His gaze rested on Rukk's sheathed sword, and he smirked. "Do you mean to challenge me for Grand Lawmaster?" Venec scratched at a stain on his breeches with a dirty fingernail, and his shoulders remained relaxed as if he feared nothing.

"The law states only the virginal may ascend. As you are well aware, Grand Lawmaster, I am not a chaste male."

Venec unfolded his body to rise from the chair. He staggered and gripped the armrest before approaching the war table dominating half of his chambers. "I plan to send my brothers south. Let the armies of Kethil waste their time and resources chasing their tails. The Ravenous Dark consuming the dwarven lands? I don't believe it."

"The stolen bairns makes sense since the Ravenous Dark feeds on innocence." Tarid fell into position beside Rukk, also gripping his hilt.

"The koveen have stolen bairns before. Doing so now does not mean the Ravenous Dark has returned. Paranoia has consumed those in power. It ends here." Venec slammed his palm onto the table, rattling it.

"What do our scouts report?" Rukk spread his legs wider, preparing for an attack.

Of course, it meant the darkness had returned. To believe anything else was ludicrous. Yet despite what he had seen and sensed, he had to give his Grand Lawmaster the benefit of the doubt. If the scouts had reported no sign of a spreading evil, then yes, he would choose to side with Venec.

"I did not send scouts on such pointless rumors." Venec faced them, resting his backside on the edge of the table. "I sent my brethren to deal with the koveen. What have these armies done but piss in their breeches? We've been fighting koveen and hunting wylders for centuries and will continue to do so. If these cowards wish to dip their blunt blades in whatever lurks in the mountains, then I say, let them."

At Venec's violation of trust, and failing the lawbringers who revered him, fury boiled within Rukk, rising to strangle his throat. Venec spewed hatred, echoing their gripes at evening meals packed with frustration, anger, and resentment. How the lawbringers had to maintain the security for all people, feared and unappreciated, remained a sore point.

Monsters were increasing, creatures never seen before rising from the netherworld, but as lawbringers, they continued to hunt, to defend the ungrateful masses. Yet none of his brothers had acted on their disheartenment, continuing as they had vowed to do, as a matter of honor. Erwana was right to fear. Something had driven Venec to forsake his teachings and strategies when Kethil needed them the most. This was no coincidence.

"Let me understand this. You're strategizing without full knowledge of the playing field? You're tasking our lawbrothers without sending scouts?" Rukk struggled to hide his fury, his body shaking with it. What in cursed hell had happened to Venec? Running a hand over his face, he fought for control. "Forgive me, Grand Lawmaster. I'm exhausted and don't wish to offend you with my weakness. You summoned us, and I would appreciate knowing what you require us to do."

Venec nodded as if he expected nothing more from Rukk. "Rest. I will have your orders for you in the morning."

Chapter Twenty-Seven

Rukk released a long breath as the chamber door shut behind him. There was a finality to the sound it made, as if it ended a part of his life he cherished. Heaviness weighed on his heart, a mixture of fear and trepidation. Challenging Venec wouldn't be easy, and failing would cost Rukk's brothers much. Yet if they did not confront him, Kethil's fate without the aid of the lawbringers wasn't a favorable one.

"I'm sorry? What in cursed hell did we just see?" Tarid stood there, dazed, slicing glances between the stone floor and the chamber door.

"Venec was virginal when he met with the Iomhar, the last innocence in a warrior male. This has me wondering if the Ravenous Dark found him appealing, and who, in the Iomhar, still stand for Kethil?" Rukk didn't want to hover outside Venec's door. The male was unpredictable, and it was best to face him with reinforcements. He strode toward the stairs. Tarid followed.

"Will you start the summoning of our brothers? We need to gather." Rukk paused on the stairs, turning to face Tarid. *"Don't forget to go through the texts with Sharn."*

"Am I doing everything?" He threw a furious look at Rukk. *"You have missed your Thursday schedule; will you be attending to that this evening? You rutting while I save the Tower?"*

"Rut with Sharn while looking at texts, if it pleases you, brother. I must speak with Erwana. I shall find you afterward and help where you deem necessary." He flashed a smile, hoping to ease the tension solidifying his brother's shoulders.

"She hates me, as you well know." Tarid sighed. *"Very well, don't tarry."*

Rukk passed him, chuckling as he did. The sound reverberated up the stone stairwell, a fleeting moment of joy before they faced a momentous task for which they hadn't prepared.

He hurried down the stairs too, hoping Erwana had good news for him even as he brought her confirmation of her suspicions. A few magi lingered in the passageways, their expressions grim when they whispered to each other. Their presence meant some of his lawbrothers must have returned. He nodded as he went by them. They were his equals and due his respect, now more than ever since they would be fighting side-by-side.

"You may enter," Erwana said when he raised his hand to knock.

He pushed the door open, and warmth seeped through him from a fire blazing in the hearth. Her chambers were the exact size of Venec's, but candles illuminated every inch. The dense fur of a grandl lay on the stone floor, hiding the protection runes below. Scrolls lined one wall, and her narrow bed rested against the opposite side. Artifacts, tables with maps, and green plants—flourishing despite the oncoming winter—filled the remainder of the chambers. A square table held an untouched plate of food, the aroma rich and enticing.

Erwana looked up from the book she read. She gestured to the table before focusing on the pages. "I took the liberty of ordering you nourishment."

Rukk assumed the chair, raising a spoon to sample the stew. He was starving, and it was bad form to reject an Arch-Magus's kindness. As he bit off a chunk of black bread and chewed, he stared out the opened door onto her balcony. The same view as the level above greeted him, this time the stains of a setting sun painted the southern mountains in a red foreshadowing. So too would Kethil lose the light should the Ravenous Dark succeed. Blood would spill for many, soaking into the soil and feeding the darkness, empowering it. The fewer who died, the better. The upcoming battle would be harder if they had to kill without bloodshed.

"'An unusual request from the son of Nehrakgu,'" she read from the book. "'The tale the chief spins is of a conniving dark-human temptress intent on robbing his people of their wealth. She seduced him with her wiles and arrived on his doorstep with a bairn. On a personal note, expecting me, an Arch-Magus to believe this nonsense... He rutted without a care, and now regrets his actions in the light of day.'"

Rukk grimaced. Having met Varthug, he was disinclined to believe his tale of a conniving temptress, as well. He dipped his bread into the stew, soaking up the gravy before biting into it. Savory flavors bombarded his mouth, and he closed his eyes against the delicious assault.

"'I agreed to apply a Stone Cage, more to protect the child than to aid his lies. But in the darkness of night, I modified it.'" Erwana paused, giggling as she turned the page. She cast an apologetic look at Rukk. "The only way to force an Arch-Mage to cast a spell is to charm or nag her."

"I've met Chief Nehrakgu. I can see him doing what must be done to get his way."

"He's an idiot. We find ways to thwart the intention of the spell if we are manipulated." She returned her attention to the journal. "'While it is active, she will appear unattractive. It is the only additional magic the sigil would accept. The girl was but six, so thin with neglect. I wove the sigil, but took the pain upon myself.'"

That explained why Thugari couldn't remember it well. Turbulent emotion carried memories. The process inflicted excruciating agony, or so historical accounts had stated. If she had suffered in the application of the sigil, she would've remembered. Rukk sipped from the goblet, the sweet mead tart and refreshing, cleansing his tongue before he spooned in another mouthful of succulent meat.

"'Years shall pass before the sigil will require unraveling. Not to fear. The power to do so lies in her own hands, the modification I mentioned above.'" Erwana paged forward then back, her movements agitated as she flicked the stiff paper. "That's it?" She thumped the book onto the table and leaped off the chair, wringing her hands as she paced. "What did Minerva mean? 'In her own hands?'"

He scowled, frustration souring his appetite, and he dropped the spoon into the bowl, splashing gravy onto the table's patterned surface. He strode across the chambers to snatch the book. Erwana stood alongside him, turning the pages until she found the text. She tapped it and spun away, resuming her pacing.

He re-read the entry scrawled in flowing penmanship, scanning it numerous times while willing it to reveal its secrets. Pressed into it was a dead flower, its yellow hue still vibrant. A daylily.

Its finger-long petals twisted and stained the paper beneath it. "This must mean something."

"Perhaps it will trigger your female's memory." Taking the book from him, Erwana darted around her chambers, removing the flower to press it within a sheet of parchment.

She folded it with care to ensure it couldn't fall out. "How did your session with Venec go?" she asked, handing him the sealed flower.

Exhaustion, the momentous task before him, and the loss of a dearest friendship drained energy from Rukk's limbs. Darkness coated his heart as he raised his gaze to hers. "It is as you feared. He is not my Grand Lawmaster. Tarid summons our brothers. Once the lawbringers are united, Venec must concede his position. What concerns me is the Iomhar. What of their hearts and those of other leaders? How far has the Ravenous Dark spread its influence?"

"I cannot recall the archives mentioning an assault of this sort. Previous wars were aggressive and nothing this clandestine. The corruption of hearts cannot be undone." Erwana pursed her lips, her skin pale. "I do not know how to fight such an evil, Rukk."

"Let us deal with Venec and set out for Dussoum. A meeting with the Iomhar and the kings will reveal much."

Her shoulders stiffened, and she clasped her hands in front of her. "Who is Venec's replacement?"

"Janar Inaris." Rukk didn't hesitate to name him.

She grimaced, revealing her distaste for the male. "And *his* replacement?"

"Why would you ask that?" He stilled froze with the realization her expression hadn't been of distaste but despair. A sense of foreboding slithered down his spine.

"Janar's body lay sprawled at the base of the tower two days ago."

He gasped, throwing out a hand to grip the stone wall. "What? Why hasn't anyone informed me...or Tarid?"

"It was murder, and you know our procedures require silence until the investigation is complete. His last memories were of a male too familiar for words. It solidified in my heart what I had refused to accept." She rubbed her face with enough force to splay out strands of her hair. "There's more."

She strode toward a washing bowl and poured water into it from a pewter jug. With a flick of her wrist and a barked word, the water shimmered, forming images as it calmed. In the mirror's reflection was a lustful Janar sprawled before Venec with cock in hand.

Horror pooled bile in the back of Rukk's throat. What Venec did was sacrifice his virginity, taking Janar's as well, and crippling the lawbringers' leadership. This was beyond betrayal.

"No, it cannot be." Rukk stumbled, leaned against the wall, and gripped his forehead.

He staggered to the bowl to look again, to make sure he hadn't misunderstood the moving images. Drinking, rutting, and an argument followed with Venec squeezing Janar's throat. Fingers flickered in his peripherals as he fought the death grip, and seconds dragged on as his vision darkened.

Rutting or murder, either one would cost a Grand Lawmaster his authority. Venec had done both and to his second-in-command. The impact on the lawbringers was devastating.

"These were Janar's last memories. I'm sorry, Rukk. I hadn't realized Venec had lost his way."

"Only virgins can assume and retain the position of Grand Lawmaster, Erwana. Virtuous Janar was an easy choice as replacement, and Venec *is* in his prime. We have groomed no other for this position."

"Which is why I revealed this to you of all lawbringers." Erwana waited for his reaction.

"No, I will not take his place," he said. "Did Janar travel with Venec to Chaosthane?" Erwana shook her head. "Thank you for your help and the meal. Once my lawbrothers arrive, I shall inform you of our decision." With a sigh, he patted his cloak pocket where the flower rested alongside Thugari's lock of hair.

It may have looked as if he ran from Erwana's chambers, so fast did he stride along the passage leading to the archives. A part of him feared his lawbrothers' decision, while another part of him longed to hold Thugari near, to bury his face in her neck, and find peace. He could appease neither part at the moment, and since he doubted he could rest this night, he would sacrifice droplets of his blood to summon his fellow lawbringers. Doing so would free Tarid to trawl the ancient texts. Rukk groaned, startling a passing magus.

Tarid. He had to tell him about Janar, his brother. Not to mention Venec's part in his death. Tarid had coddled his brother since they left Atrar and convinced him to join the lawbringers. Pausing in the stairwell, Rukk held his palm against the cold stone, drawing strength from it even as he took in a shuddering breath.

"Tarid? Order a jug of mead, my friend. I bring terrible news." He didn't ask him to chase Sharn away. Tarid would need all the comfort she could offer.

Chapter Twenty-Eight

A THUMP JERKED THUGARI awake, and she cast a baleful glare at Borgakh, who had kicked her. Every cursed morning, Thugari would greet the dawn with crossbow lessons.

Gnash scampered across the camp to climb in by Nenneg who burrowed into her bedroll, not stirring. The fire offered no warm welcome.

Clambering to her feet to yawn, stretch, and grab her crossbow, Thugari staggered after a too-awake Borgakh. As they neared Dussoum, the orc maiden guarded more, slept less.

"Morning." Thugari fumbled with the loading mechanism.

"We reach Dussoum after breakfast. Excited to die by the Gates?"

"What?" Twitching, Thugari fired the crossbow, narrowly missing a sleeping hekle.

"Don't fret, and stay focused." Borgakh waited, patience in her stillness. "There are other ways to determine your magic or lack thereof. You need not sacrifice yourself, little one."

Thugari loaded another bolt, aimed, held her breath, then with a slow exhale, fired. It struck within the circle but nowhere near the middle. "Truly?" She lowered the crossbow. "Would these ways require something unsavory?"

Borgakh chuckled and jogged to the tree to smudge the circle before drawing a smaller one with a piece of charcoal. "Like?"

"Eating mushrooms, rutting with thirteen males, kissing a frog's ass?"

Borgakh tucked her bottom lip under the top, but her cheeks grew rosy, then she guffawed, slapping her thigh. "Mòr would like you to kiss her ass, but no, nothing that unsavory."

"Mòr?" Thugari arched a brow, but Borgakh ignored her, indicating with a swirl of a finger for her to load another bolt.

By the time Nenneg and Gnash greeted them, Thugari's arm throbbed, limp from hoisting and holding up the crossbow. Any feeling in her fingertips was burned off from loading stubborn bolts.

"Is she improving?" Nenneg offered Borgakh her cheek for a kiss.

"A little." She scooped Nenneg into her arms for a tight embrace and a tickle.

Thugari sighed, her eyes misting at the love between them. Such moments brought her aching loneliness to mind, leaving her to wonder about Rukk and what he was doing. He wasn't for her, yet he said he would see her again.

Clearing her throat, she flicked her fingers at Gnash and waited for him to escape the kissing couple and scamper up Thugari's leg. "I'll stock the fire and boil us a pot."

Not that they responded. With a shrug, she returned to the camp, fed her ravenous rat, and fetched water from the nearby stream. Her bedroll tempted her to sleep, with exhaustion making her yawn. Instead, she packed up camp, leaving out the things they would need for the morning's breakfast.

Perching her backside on a boulder, she savored the spicy tisane, relishing the heat traveling down her throat, into her belly, and adding a layer of sweat to her temple. Gnash sat beside her cleaning his whiskers, and she stroked his head, listening to his chirping.

She didn't know what awaited them in Dussoum and selfish her hadn't wanted to find Gnash a home. Still, with Borgakh alongside them, no one would dare eat him.

"When can I learn how to wield a sword or a knife?" Thugari's question gained a chuckle from Borgakh when they returned.

"A knife? Sooner rather than later if that's what you call a dagger."

Thugari smiled while pouring them each a cup of tisane, then readied the horses. Within the hour, after a quick meal of bread and cheese, they set off for Dussoum, leaving the forests for the King's Way. Carts, wagons, merchants, and riders crowded the road. The vibrant colors of garments and towers of goods snaked their way through the rolling green hills and dark rock outcroppings to the city of the dwarves sunk into the foot of the mountains. Snow painted the tips white against a pristine blue sky. Exotic and picturesque, it snatched her breath.

Excitement took hold of her, and she laughed, urging Envis into a canter. She didn't expect Dussoum to look different than Lemfor—an overpopulated town with folk darting around, attending to their business amid slapdash wooden lean-tos.

Instead, what sprawled before her were stone buildings carved deep into the bedrock. A winding gorge led in and out of the town, and the walls grew higher with each step Envis took. The rock was in variegated grays and hewn without precision, jagged chunks piercing the sky above.

Nenneg gathered her cloak around her, throwing nervous glances at any disturbance. Borgakh sat upon her horse, relaxed, but a hand rested on the hilt of her sword. Thugari's crossbow was a gift from Tarid. Its bolts nestled in the belt he had strapped around her waist that was too wide and hung at an angle off her hips. She was grateful for his thoughtfulness. Still, she didn't wrestle it out of its satchel tied to her saddle.

When they rode into the dwarven town, Atrarians, elves, and dwarves mingled in the trading markets, outside brothels and taverns. Children played among the carts, horses, and donkeys, their laughter padding the constant din of negotiations for goods or flesh. Borgakh didn't ride into the first stables on the road. She led them onward until the walls were smoother, crisper on the corners, and the colorful garments of the wealthy served as a pleasant distraction from the monochromatic stone.

Not many dwarves made it south to Haraton. Still, their adorable faces and scuttering teased a smile from Thugari.

A frantic mother chased her wayward child, running pell-mell for Borgakh's horse. She leaped off her horse and snatched up the child, tossing him into the air amid giggles before placing him into his mother's arms. Her gratitude was in the form of a smile since she was too winded to speak.

When Borgakh remained on foot, Thugari slipped off the saddle and tucked her cloak over Gnash's bulging body. Leading Envis, with his reins gripped in her hand, she straggled Borgakh and Nenneg. This near to the ground, the aromas and sounds bombarded Thugari, and she found herself with a perpetual grin by the time Borgakh halted. Thugari raised her gaze with awe. A stone house stood resolute before her. Stories high with elaborate carvings trimming the windows and corners, it blocked out the sun, casting its stables splayed out to the side in constant shadow.

The square door opened, revealing it was a foot thick. Out rushed a dwarf in golden-yellow breeches tucked into brown knee-high boots and a burgundy jerkin falling to mid-thigh. Light brown hair bounced in wild disarray. Amid this riot of color was a bright smile and a bold laugh. Thugari didn't know what the protocol was to greet a dwarf so she remained silent, stroking Envis's forehead to contain her nervousness.

Borgakh knelt, now at eye-level, to accept the barreling dwarf's hug.

"Borgakh, it is good to see you, my old friend." The voice was robust but husky.

"Mòr Guaire, your welcome always brings me to tears." She set her friend back but kept her hands on her shoulders.

"You haven't cried a day in your life." The dwarf stepped to the side and hugged Nenneg, who had also knelt. "I'm glad to see you, Nen. When you left, your sad soul worried me."

"I won't lie, Mòr, being here isn't my first choice, but it's wonderful to see you." She rose to her feet after Mòr released her.

Nenneg gestured to Thugari to step forward, and she did, she dropped the reins to kneel before the dwarf.

Not knowing how to address one, she said nothing, not wanting to offend.

Mòr ran a far-too-intelligent gaze over Thugari. "What did you bring me, Borgakh? A dark-orc in Dussoum?"

Thugari made to stand. The tone from Mòr was cold, disdainful, and for the first time since leaving Haraton, she wasn't welcomed. The dwarf laughed before dragging her into a tight hug.

"A friend of Borgakh and Nen's is welcome in my home." Releasing her in a fragrant cloud of berry tobacco and baked bread, Mòr gestured to follow.

"Where's your husband this morning?" Borgakh asked, tethering her horse to the wrought iron railing rising out of the stone road.

The dwarves had embellished it with lacework and flower buds. Thugari narrowed her focus, searching for an indication of gender within Mòr's dwarven armor, settling on two bumps in her chest plate.

"Which one?" Mòr laughed again, leading them into her home. "I seek a new one, which is why I've shaved my beard."

Thugari was the last to tether Envis and enter. She wasn't as tall as Borgakh, but she still ducked when passing through the door.

Inside, the ceiling rose high with iron chandeliers spraying out a welcoming glow from hundreds of candles. Intricate carpets lined the floors, their colors rich and—Thugari gasped—threaded with gold.

"I need your guidance, Mòr. Have you seen wagons of time-stated bairns entering Dussoum?" Borgakh remained standing, hunched over as she waited for Mòr's response.

"No, but my spies whisper of wagons stopping at Fentley, Lemfor, and Vangate before disappearing. You must have encountered them on your journey here."

She frowned. "With koveen?"

"More wylders than koveen. What is this about?" Mòr gestured for Borgakh to sit.

"The wagons we tracked headed here to Dussoum, or so we thought. Rukk and I suspect they feed the Ravenous Dark." She lowered her bulk onto the cushions strewn across a creature's pelt.

It was thick, padding the floor on top of the carpet. Silver in color, it reminded Thugari of Rukk's hair splaying around him as he moved.

Taking a deep breath, she released it, hoping to calm her erratic heartbeat. She'd missed him these past five days, more so at night, and wondered if he thought of her as much as she dwelled on the memories of him.

"The Ravenous Dark needs more than innocence." Mòr's expression hardened. "If you did not encounter those wagons, then my spies were wrong, or they reached their destination."

"They empowered someone not in Dussoum?" Nen gasped, shooting a worried glance at Borgakh.

"We were mistaken in our assessment." Her shrug was wooden, and her brow furrowed. "Can you tell me if Thugari has magic?"

Mòr hesitated, as if she had questions of her own. She rested her gaze on Thugari and sighed. "You don't want the Gates to harm her."

She sat when gestured to do so, forcing herself to relax under the dwarf's scrutiny. Mòr gathered her hair back, exposing a pretty face, then tugged a thick glove on before reaching into the blazing fire.

There, lying amid glowing embers was an amulet, the chain thick and interwoven. Vines interlaced with gems in gold looked to be from an ancient time.

Once free of the flames, Mòr wrapped her fingers around the gold links. Thugari lunged, expecting the metal to burn the dwarf.

"Fire boosts its magic, but you'll find it cold to the touch." Mòr threw the glove down and looped the amulet over Thugari's head. The weight of it bowed her shoulders, and she moaned, struggling to hold her spine erect.

"Discovered in the bowels of Chaosthane, it is one of the few artifacts that has survived the magical drain in Dussoum." Mòr stepped back and clasped her hands in front of her. "The brighter the gems glow, the more powerful the wearer."

Nenneg crawled across the fur to grip Thugari's arm, offering her support. A subtle vibration originated from the amulet, growing in strength. Fear strangled her voice, and she swallowed, unable to speak.

Gnash squeaked, bolting out of her tunic to leap onto Nenneg, burrowing into her brown hair.

The amulet pulsed gold, dimmed to pale yellow, then brightened to a blinding white. Mòr's eyes widened, and she lunged for the amulet, only to be thrown back. Borgakh grabbed Nenneg, pulling her away from where Mòr sprawled.

"Borgakh, please, what's happening?" Thugari asked, grateful she could form the words despite her rasping voice.

"Thugari, look at me." Mòr held out her hands as if she tried to placate an irate boar. "See if the amulet will let you remove it."

She reached for the chilled metal links. When she touched them, they burned her palms with a cold so hot and gripping it tore a scream from her. She swayed, fighting the darkness curling around her vision. Breathing became difficult. She struggled to suck in air, desperate to fill her lungs.

"Let go of the amulet, Thugari." Mòr stood to the side, her mouth moving, but Thugari couldn't hear all she said above the roar in her ears.

Squeezing her eyes shut, she focused on her breathing and calming the panic trembling her limbs. She didn't know much about magic and artifacts. This innocuous amulet might sense her fear.

Seconds passed, and the ringing in her ears quieted, the icy amulet's links warmed, and the vibration ceased, dimming to a pale yellow again.

She stroked the amulet in long soothing caresses. Flicking her eyes open, she rested her gaze on Mòr whose expression contorted in fear for a moment before she clapped her hands.

Thugari released a shaky breath. "Now what?"

"It's never done this before." Mòr shook her head, tendrils of her escaping strands flying outward.

"What does this mean, Mòr?" Borgakh's grip on Nenneg's shoulders softened, but she didn't release her. Instead, she kissed her temple.

Mòr didn't answer but hollered a name, "Niall."

A young dwarven male barreled into the room, bowing his head in greeting when he realized Mòr had guests.

"Summon the Geàrdan," she said. He hesitated, staring at her with his mouth gaping. "Now, Niall." He bolted, his narrow beard flowing over one shoulder as he ran. "Tea?" She grinned, gesturing to the table nearby. Upon it rested a teapot and carved pottery cups.

"Please." Borgakh relaxed, holding a dazed Nenneg next to her.

"So, a dark-orc with a mystery *and* a rat? A gift per chance?" Mòr waved a cup at Gnash sniffing the air as he took tentative steps across Nenneg's shoulder. "It's been a while since I've skewered one." She chuckled as she lined up the cups to pour the tea.

Anger burst through Thugari and started the amulet humming again. She leaped to her feet, banging her head on a chandelier. Borgakh threw out a hand to pacify her, pleading with her eyes for Thugari to trust her. She lowered her gaze to calm her emotions as she sat.

"Alas, this one is a friend too." Borgakh offered a polite smile.

Mòr studied Gnash before sighing. "Pity. That one looks like it has a bit of meat on its bones."

"Anything strange happening in Dussoum or Chaosthane?" Borgakh gathered Gnash into her hands for a stroke. She had never touched the rat before.

The emotion sweeping through Thugari summoned tears. Her friend cuddled Gnash to save him. The amulet hummed again, snagging three sets of gazes. Thugari smiled, trying to convey all was well.

"Strange? Oh, Borgakh." Mòr snorted. "You mean all those kings setting up camp north of the Chaosthane Mountains? Like we wouldn't spot thousands of armored males?"

"Yes, those males." Borgakh chuckled. "Any strange behavior from the Iomhar?"

Mòr stopped mid-pour. She put the teapot down with a thump and gripped the edge of the table. "You suspect something worse than normal, Borgakh? I thought it was but a scourge of goblins testing the boundaries, as they do every decade or so." She carried the cups to Borgakh and Nenneg, then stroked her jaw. "What could harm the Iomhar or alter their behavior?"

"Lawbringer Rukk Knaraugh sounded me last night."

Thugari sat up, her interest piqued. She longed to hear Rukk's voice, to know he was well. Scowling at having missed such an opportunity, she waited with bated breath for what he said.

At the same time, she wondered when Borgakh had spoken to him. It must have been in the middle of the night during one of her camp patrols. And yet, the orc maiden hadn't mentioned it.

"The Grand Lawmaster visited the Iomhar last month." Mòr approached Thugari with more care, holding out a cup of tea.

She reached for it, as nervous as Mòr was. When the amulet didn't react, she wrapped her fingers around the cup and brought it to her lips. A pungent aroma hit her nostrils, and she gagged, but under Mòr's observant gaze, she sipped it. A sweet earthy flavor coated her tongue, and she swallowed with a sigh of pleasure.

Nodding, Mòr ambled backward and sat on a stone cube smoothed in an indent of her backside.

"Rukk awaits his lawbrothers to challenge Venec. I pray it goes well."

"Change is constant." Mòr hummed as she savored her tea. "For the lawbringers to crumble, a great loss of power would boost whatever is behind these attacks."

"Attacks?" Nenneg asked, her voice hoarse as she rubbed her hip.

Thugari frowned, suspecting the amulet had harmed her. Stroking the metal links, she hoped it healed like Rukk's medallion but doubted it. She tried to hold herself up, but the weight of it slumped her shoulders.

"Niall brings word from his tavern visits. Certain of the deepest levels were forbidden to the miners, others seeing shifting shadows, and losing brothers, fathers, uncles, lovers."

Nenneg whimpered, dropping her chin to her chest, her body shrinking in dismay. "It's my fault." She whipped her head up, tears streaming down her cheeks. "I saw it. I heard that voice. I should've warned the Iomhar or you, Mòr, but I didn't. I ran."

"You did as you saw right, Nenneg." Borgakh gathered her sobbing form onto her lap.

"Did I?" She buried her face against Borgakh's chest, her sobs still slicing through the tension in the room. "Had I tried, none of those miners would have lost their lives."

"The Iomhar wouldn't have granted you an interview." Mòr rose to refill Nenneg's cup. "Nor would they have listened to me without evidence."

"Mòr's right. You ran to the Council, despite knowing they might kill you on sight." Borgakh cupped Nenneg's face, wiping away her tears.

"What did you see, Nen?" Mòr waddled closer.

"What is it?" A dwarven female burst into the room. Trailing her was another female with Niall behind them. All were out of breath, and the last female to enter swooned, gripping the door frame.

"The Amulet of Zylfir won't allow removal." Mòr gestured to Thugari.

As one, they gaped at her. What it all meant, she didn't want to know, as long as the thing came off.

"It's never done that before," the dark-haired dwarf panted.

"I said that, Una." Mòr placed her hands on her hips. "Don't, Isbeil."

Too late, the amulet burst into life, throwing back those nearest to Thugari. Her hair blew out with air cooling her neck. This time the amulet didn't burn her, although her skin still smarted from its previous reaction.

"Stones of Comhnall." Una struggled to her feet, gripping her forehead where blood trickled into a bushy eyebrow.

Thugari stroked the amulet, gaining confidence it wouldn't harm her. She continued to do so, hoping to calm it before chancing another removal.

Rukk's image shimmered in front of her. Gasping, she froze, as if any movement from her might disturb the illusion of him. He had never looked more handsome.

She drank in the sight of him. There were shadows under his eyes as if he hadn't found rest for days. Not once had he sounded Thugari, proving he hadn't thought of her. The urge to ignore him gripped her. She resisted, knowing she would regret not speaking to him now.

"Thugari?" His voice made her shiver, and she fought to hide her reaction. She stopped stroking the amulet and clasped her hands in her lap. Her heart thundered in her chest as if it wanted to burst free.

"Rukk, this is a surprise." She forced a smile.

"Are you well?" His tone was conversational as if he asked her about the weather.

"I am." She lingered on the gap in his tunic revealing the lines of his collarbone.

"Then tell me why my neck and hands are burning?" His obsidian gaze met hers, his tone accusatory. Moon above.

The amulet hummed and pulsed, casting off a golden glow. A hysterical giggle tumbled up her throat and escaped before she could cover her mouth. She was too late, so she lowered her hand and squared her shoulders. How dare his life bond manifest now when he was nowhere near to help her. "How can you sense that but not Devan crushing my wrist?"

"This pain is from magic, so unless you've found someone to dissolve your sigil, you're in danger again." He huffed, but she didn't care if he roared at her.

It was wonderful to feast her gaze upon him still in his lawbringer black, his silver hair spilling over his shoulders with his orcish ears peeking through.

"I miss you." Moaning, she threw a pleading gaze at Borgakh, a silent request for a rescue. The orc maiden shook her head, suppressing laughter with her eyes twinkling. "We have a situation here, Rukk." Thugari hurried to speak, louder than necessary, praying he hadn't heard her confession. "An amulet refuses to allow anyone to remove it from my neck."

He stilled. "Where in cursed hell are you?"

Him not responding to her miss-you comment not only brought on another relieved sigh, but wrenched her heart, whispering he didn't care for her like she did him.

"Dussoum." Her voice was above a whisper, hoarse with charged emotion.

"Don't lie to me, little one." He chuckled, the brightness of his smile softening his features.

She bit her inner cheek, hoping not to embarrass herself again. "Why would I lie? I'm with Borgakh and Nenneg in the lovely home of Mòr Guaire."

"Cursed hell." He turned away, hiding his face from her. His shoulders rose and fell as if he fought for control. "Don't leave there until I find you." He pointed at her, his fury clear in his hoarse voice. The sound of it had butterflies exploding in her stomach, and at that moment, she wanted to kiss him, to sample those soft lips. "I'm waiting, Thugari."

"For what?" She blinked herself back to the present, a little dazed by the heat spreading through her core.

"For your vow to await my arrival." He folded his arms across his chest, gaping the V of his tunic.

"Curse it, Rukk. Of course, I'll wait."

He nodded, and his image faded.

She slumped, her energy draining, as if she had run a mile alongside Envis. Borgakh burst into laughter ignoring Nenneg's attempts to shush her.

"So, we await the lawbringer?" Isbeil limped to a cabinet, removed a pewter jug, and drank deeply from it.

The potent scent of dragon's fire reached Thugari, and she smothered a sob at the necessity behind it. She recognized its cinnamon scent from when her father had drunk such an expensive beverage.

These females needing to consume it now was more alarming than finding Arob digging in her things. Mòr had welcomed her into her home, and Thugari had repaid her kindness with this.

"I'm so sorry," she said, flicking her tears aside while fighting to calm the amulet.

"Come, let us find the nearest inn." Borgakh rose to her full height, lifting Nenneg with her.

"You cannot leave, old friend. Not with your dark-orc wearing the Amulet of Zylfir. It cannot pass through the doors without me. It chose to remain with me, and due to this, the Iomhar has tasked me with its care." Mòr halted in front of Thugari and gathered her fingers in hers. "You shall stay with me, Thugari. My home is yours." She sighed. "And your rat's."

The floodgates burst open as sorrow and gratitude warred within Thugari. Tears gushed unhindered, and she wailed like a child, uncaring that the amulet hummed so much it made a tune of sorts.

Borgakh gathered Thugari to her chest and carried her who knew where.

The amulet didn't reject Borgakh's kindness.

CHAPTER TWENTY-NINE

RUKK GRIPPED THE RIM of the Fountain, his body trembling as he struggled to breathe. Thugari had never looked more beautiful. Not able to reach across the distance and touch her tore through him. He wanted her more than he needed sleep. Tomorrow, with the lawbringers who were able to reach the Tower, they would gather to decide Venec's fate.

After which, he needed to leave for Dussoum. Five days in the saddle loomed ahead, days where he worried over the upcoming war and yearned to hold Thugari, to listen to her voice, to bask in the joy of her smile.

Chuckling, he shook his head, finding it humorous she once again embroiled herself in some sort of danger. The Amulet of Zylfir circled her delicate throat. The thick links and embedded yellow diamonds were well-known.

He would speak to Erwana about its properties on the long journey. She had tasked her magi and spellbinders to prepare for the next week of travel.

Where they could help, his lawbringers, knights, and pages did. They too gathered supplies or purchased what they needed. The knights and pages would leave before the witching hour, driving the wagons and carts north. Due to their ponderous speed, they would need a head start. They restocked all satchels lest males became separated. All in preparation for war and done in silence. Venec need not know of their plans.

Should he gain wind of it, they were to say they headed south as he had mentioned to Rukk. Let Venec castigate Rukk for his 'eagerness' to obey. He hurried upstairs to the archives since the Fountain of Sound lay in the cellars of the Tower. He had spent hours there dripping his blood into its waters to summon his lawbrothers. Arriving lawbringers aided them in the soundings, but the Fountain had limitations. One sound at a time.

He had not asked Tarid for help. As expected, his lawbrother suffered, wasting his energy trying to spare Rukk from his sorrow. In moments when he napped or his control slipped, the rage, the utter devastation, the calling of the void was so strong, Rukk wept, unable to hold fast against such aching sadness.

He hadn't gotten to know Janar, the training of a lawmaster was separate from lawbringers. But through Tarid's fondest memories, Rukk knew Janar's character and what he had meant to the Inaris tribe. Having borne the loss of his mother alone, he longed to aid Tarid, but his lawbrother rejected any attempts Rukk made.

"Anything?" He strode across the room to where Sharn and Tarid combed through parchments and books.

Rukk had been there when his neck had burned for no reason. Failing to sense the pain Devan inflicted on Thugari, Rukk had thought their life bond broken. This incident proved him wrong. It puzzled him that his wrist hadn't throbbed. Fury must have clouded his mind for him to misinterpret the pain he was in. He now lumped it together under that volatile emotion jealousy. She had a right to question the bond's inconsistency.

Across the sounding, the soft pout of her lips tempted him, and his longing to see her showed no eagerness to dissipate. Yet another night loomed for him, his heart heavy. His medallion might ease this dull ache before he found his rest, but he doubted it.

A human magus with soft, golden hair smiled at him as she carried scrolls to Sharn. He tilted his head to admire the flow of her robes over her generous thighs. He imagined dipping his head to kiss those petal-pink lips, but as he raised his gaze, in his mental illusion it was Thugari's darker skin he stroked a finger across.

With a sigh, he adjusted his tight breeches and slumped into a chair beside a bookshelf.

"He's asleep on his feet. Let me repeat myself. We found nothing." Tarid forced a smile, but it twitched into a grimace.

Sharn had told him as soon as Erwana had informed her, breaking the vow of silence during investigations. The skin around Sharn's eyes was gray as she bore the brunt of his pain, sparing him where she could. This revealed how much she cared for him, enough to risk her magus status. He was aware of her beauty but not of her affection.

"I am aware of it." Tarid arched a brow at Rukk before rolling up a parchment and adding it to a teetering stack.

Opening the bond to communicate bombarded Rukk with a wall of anger, thoughts of vengeance, and wailings of despair Tarid didn't utter. A cacophony of intensity slammed into Rukk, roaring words, images, and intensions he struggled to sift through, to understand.

Taking a deep breath against the pressure building within him, Rukk forced a grin. *"Good. Why do you not find some rest, Tarid? Your movements are sluggish."*

"As are yours." He leveled his gaze on Rukk.

Determination squared his shoulders and once again, Rukk's insistence that Tarid rest was waved aside. What he needed was activity.

When Rukk's mother had…died, he had spent hours training recruits until he was too exhausted to think, to remember. If only there was such a task to assign to Tarid.

"Most mention the massive losses, something about the fallen fueling the Ravenous Dark." Sharn sipped her cold tea, licking her lips before lowering the cup.

"We know that, but there has to be something that defeats them." Rukk grabbed a scroll on the table beside him and unraveled it. "What's the opposite of darkness or evil?" He dragged his gaze over the intricate lettering finding it to be a cure for mortworm. He shuddered, rolled the scroll, and placed it onto the table.

"Light for darkness, love for evil?" Sharn stacked another book on a growing pile. "Or is it goodness for evil?"

"We know it feeds off innocence. Wouldn't that be the opposite of evil?" Tarid said, his gaze resting on her face and lingering there.

"So, no one in the armies can be innocent? That's a tall order," she said, balancing another scroll onto a pile.

The curvaceous magus Rukk admired earlier hurried to gather the discarded scrolls into her arms, disappearing down one of the shelf-lined passages.

He sighed, holding Thugari's lock of hair to his lips, then jerked back, surprised to find it in his hand again. "Let's hope the Iomhar have a way to battle this."

"Or King Horknuth can grant insight," Sharn said.

He grimaced. "Is he leading the orcs?"

Stilling, he dreaded her response. He hadn't seen his father in decades. Such dark circumstances forced him to be polite, to tamp down the hatred clawing its way up his throat.

Swallowing the vile words he would spew if given a chance, Rukk rose to his feet, unable to remain seated despite his body's demand for rest.

"I heard he is and the Kurdan with him."

A weight lifted off his shoulders, and he flashed a smile. "That *is* good news, Sharn."

The head of the Kurdan band of orc warriors was Keryn Yerug, an old friend and master swordsmith. Rukk had learned much of his skills from that male. Now that tension no longer kept his exhaustion at bay, he bid them goodnight and trudged to the barracks a few levels above.

"Off to bed at last?" Despite dealing with his brother's death, Tarid still cared whether Rukk found rest.

Again, a solid wall of writhing emotion slammed into Rukk. Like molten lava roiling and churning, it was a mental manifestation of grief, one that summoned forgotten promises he had once made his mother's tree.

He longed to carry more of Tarid's sorrow, to spare his lawbrother from this, but under the weight of organizing their departure, the impending Grand Lawmaster challenge, and his yearning for Thugari, Rukk was overwhelmed. He drowned in his thoughts, as they circled or spiraled downward. It might be exhaustion dragging him into the depths of his mind. He would find out soon enough.

"I bid you goodnight, did you not hear me?" Rukk couldn't resist teasing Tarid, but his smile faded. *"Do you need me to stay, brother?"*

"No, go rest. Sharn will keep me company."

"Be gentle with her. I hear she's amazing in bed but likes to cuddle afterward. We both know how much you hate those kinds of females." It wasn't true. Rukk hated clinging females, but Tarid adored them.

"Thank you for attempting to lighten my heart. I'm afraid the old Tarid is no longer." He gripped Rukk's shoulder and yanked him into a crushing hug. *"Be at peace, Rukk."*

Rukk thumped him on the back. *"Wake me if you need me."* He waited until Tarid nodded before heading for the barracks.

As Rukk readied for bed, he found himself reliving those moments when Thugari had clung to him. Perhaps he hadn't found the right female to cuddle. Kissing her lock of hair, he tucked it under his pillow. Squeezing his eyes shut, he willed himself to sleep, instead, he recalled her face when she admitted she missed him.

Heat burst in his chest, bright, bold, and breathtaking, matching his reaction when she had whispered those words. He laughed, loud in the somnolent silence of the barracks. Her declaration had surprised him, and it had taken everything within him not to respond.

"I miss you too, little doe." His words, despite their warmth, fell onto the deaf ears of night. He would tell her when he saw her. After he removed the amulet from her neck and tasted the sweet nectar of her mouth.

"GRAND LAWMASTER HAS SUMMONED you," Tarid said by way of greeting, his massive hand gripping Rukk's shoulder in a violent shake.

With a groan, he swung his legs off the side of the bed. "How many males have arrived?" He scrubbed his face, hoping to eradicate the exhaustion still clinging to him. Glancing out the window at the first tinges of dawn, he cursed. He would have preferred to rest for days, not a mere three hours.

"Enough, and all bombarding me with unceasing questions." Tarid threw a fresh tunic at him. *"This morning's challenge is to lure Venec from his chambers. We can't all enter."*

Pausing with his tunic half-on, Rukk caught his breath. The wall of emotions he expected to cross their bond had solidified into rock. Glimpses of fire beneath its surface implied something explosive awaited its moment.

"I'm aware of this. The next Grand Lawmaster must remove the new runes hindering our access." Rukk stood, dropping his breeches and pulling on the folded pair Tarid handed to him. Despite the weakness in his limbs, the clean garments refreshed him, like the kiss of sunlight on chapped cheeks.

"Sharn suggested we gather, decide Venec's fate, then reveal to him our decision. His uncharacteristic arrogance should lure him out."

"That's too risky. What if he burrows deeper, barring any of us from entering his chambers?" Rukk shook his head, pinching his lips as he considered their options. Sitting on the edge of the bed, he donned each boot, his movements methodical as he laced them.

Gazing at his boots, he smiled. There was joy to be found in completing such a simple chore when what awaited him was an unpleasant task.

"Did you find rest?" He settled his gaze on Tarid's ragged face, lingering on the circles of exhaustion and the hardened glint in his brown eyes.

"I slept well after Sharn drugged me." Tarid pursed his lips. *"I will discuss her audacity...in time."*

"A passionate female like Sharn might not take too kindly to your reprimand." Rukk strapped on his belt. *"Mmm, perhaps have me by your side lest she turn you into a grandl."*

Tarid offered Rukk his sword to sheath, twirling as he did so. *"Why not bring news of you and the Arch-Magus rutting? An opportunity like this for the Ravenous Dark to topple the magi might prove irresistible."*

"That could work, and it would reveal how much it has corrupted Venec." Rukk furrowed his brow in thought.

"You're hoping a piece of him still exists? You heard Erwana. Corruption of the heart is irreversible."

Sadness twanged through Rukk, adding to the heaviness of regret in his soul. He inhaled a calming breath. Of all the males he had known, only a few garnered great respect. Venec had been one of them.

Tarid dropped his hand on Rukk's shoulder, to remind him he was there, with him, ready to face the day together. He wore lawbringer black. Gone were his neutrals and browns. It was an auspicious sign, for nothing but ceremony would urge Tarid to align with tradition.

Slipping Thugari's lock of hair from under his pillow, Rukk kissed it and tucked it inside his pocket. They headed to the common room, a few of his brothers trailing them down the stairs. The chatter of those at their tables reached him before he entered, but it was more somber than usual. They grumbled among each other with the seriousness of the issue not yet revealed.

Silence descended as Rukk and Tarid climbed onto a trestle table. Gifts from the Iomhar, they were solid stone and able to carry the combined weight of ten orcs.

Tarid settled a tearful gaze on his lawbrothers. "Look around you. See anyone amiss?" He laughed, but it was cold and hard. "Janar, my dearest brother, was betrayed and murdered."

His announcement had them reacting in cries of dismay, disbelief, or concern. Many offered condolences while others bowed their heads in prayer.

With a flick of his wrist, he quieted them. He unsheathed his sword and stabbed the air in front of him. "I want vengeance. I demand it. Brothers, stand united with me against this evil that has pierced our hallowed ground."

"Who dared to do this?"

"In our home?" Voices rose into a cacophony urging all to act, to root out the wickedness among them. The bond between lawbrothers was sacrosanct.

"Not what I would've said but effective." Rukk tossed his thoughts at Tarid, his turn to place his palm on his shoulder. "We have found the murderer, and yet, this is not the worst of his crimes."

Rukk's words silenced their calls to bring the wrongdoer forth for justice. To his brothers, there was nothing worse than killing a lawbringer, no matter the rank. Magi glided into the room and circled his males while Erwana climbed onto the table accepting Rukk's offered hand for balance.

"Time is of the essence. I could tell you how my suspicions arose after Venec returned from Dussoum. I could reveal how crude and uncaring Venec's comments became. Instead, I will show you what Janar's last memories revealed during the investigation."

She wouldn't! This would devastate Tarid. Rukk crowded her, catching her hand. "Arch-Magus, perhaps—"

"I have seen, brother."

Rukk arched a brow at Tarid. *"Sharn?"*

At Tarid's curt nod, Rukk released Erwana's hand and stepped aside.

As one, the magi raised their arms, swirling white magic and arcing it onto the common room's stone ceiling. Water rose off tables, out of cups, from the sweat beading his males's temples, to pool above, forming a placid reflection of the room and the lawbringers' upturned faces. There, after Erwana barked the unknown word, Janar's memories played out.

"Cursed hell." Tarid gritted his teeth.

Rukk gripped his shoulders. The rock around his emotions splintered. Seeping through their bond, hatred churned and guilt that he hadn't protected his brother as he had vowed to when they were mere boys.

"The Ravenous Dark was the killer, remember that, lawbrother."

Tarid lowered his gaze to shield himself from Janar's final moments before Venec threw his body over the balcony. The room burst into an uproar, his lawbrothers, from page to knight to lawbringer, demanded justice.

A few questioned the validity of Erwana's revelation, the unspoken rivalry between the magic-users and the protectors behind their accusations.

"Lawbringer Larza, step forth." Rukk scanned the room, searching for the dwarf.

It wasn't wise to judge his power by his size, for despite his lack of physical substance, magic flowed through him with abundance—a rare talent for a dwarf. Often, his law-brothers had questioned his decision to become a lawbringer and not a magus.

The Council did allow males to become magi and an Arch-Magus, but it was the females who could better control magic's volatility and withstand the pull on their carnal appetites.

The lawbringers parted to allow Larza through, his respect well-earned. He held out his hand to Erwana, and she accepted, stepping down from the table to kneel on the stone floor. He raised his hands, spread his fingers across her face, but hovered one hand over her chest. She smiled in encouragement.

He splayed his fingers over her heart, in effect cupping a breast. No male teased him, understanding the seriousness of the task.

"Keep the mirror active." He scanned the magi, and as one, they threw their magic onto the stone ceiling once more.

Pale gold magic burst from his fingers and slammed into Erwana. She jerked, yet remained upright. Her features twisted in agony, and her body shuddered, but she didn't speak. Images flashed through the water, fleeting, showing her attending to tasks. Then it pulsed, and he halted the flow.

"Arch-Magus, we found a body…Janar's." Larza's mouthed the words, but the voice was feminine. "Janar's? Show me." Erwana's voice came through.

The images flitted as they scurried down the stairs until she approached Janar's twisted body looking like a discarded cloth doll lying in a rain puddle. She knelt beside him, pressed her fingers to his temple, and sang a lyrical spell. In the water's reflection, the same scene of Venec's betrayal played out, proving she spoke the truth.

Larza lowered his hands. He trembled with sweat dripping off his chin. The room remained silent for a second, then burst into a cacophonous uproar. Today, Venec would die.

CHAPTER THIRTY

THUGARI HAD EXPECTED A stone house to be freezing inside, or that she would need to sleep under a mountain of furs. It might have been true had the amulet not been around her neck pulsing heat through her. In the quiet hours of the night, she had tried to surprise it, snatching it to fling it off, but it clung to her sigil. Perhaps the sigil and amulet shared a commonality?

Dawn didn't dip its fingers into the depths of Dussoum before Borgakh was in her room, shoving garments at her. "What are you doing?" Thugari asked, giggling as a pair of breeches hit her in the face.

"Mòr needs to travel with the Iomhar. She goes nowhere without that amulet."

"I have to go with her?" Thugari gaped at Borgakh, then glanced at Nenneg peeking through the door.

"The Geàrdan are far more diplomatic and reasonable than the Iomhar. If you don't travel with, Mòr won't go, then the Geàrdan won't be there to stop the Iomhar and the other kings from debating their options for hours." Borgakh whacked Thugari on her fur-padded backside. "If you hurry, hot porridge awaits you. Tarry, and you shall remain hungry until mid-day meal."

Alone, Thugari rushed to dress, donning the burgundy tunic over her breeches. She wasn't sure she could take her crossbow, but did so anyway, looping the bolt belt around her hips.

With her boots on, she hurried along the passage, running her fingers through her tangled hair, cursing as she snagged on knot after knot. Her sleep must have been fraught with restlessness, but exhaustion didn't thrum through her.

Stumbling into the room, she sat to eat where Nenneg tapped the table with a finger. After resting her crossbow against her leg, Thugari spooned the sweet, blessed-warm porridge into her mouth. Nenneg wove her magic through Thugari's tresses until many braids lay heavy upon her shoulders. She should cut it but was hesitant to do so since her father had it shaven until her tenth birthday.

"As we ride out, we'll stop and purchase a back halter." Borgakh gestured to the crossbow while feeding strips of dried fruit to a chirping Gnash.

"So, where are we going?" Thugari asked between mouthfuls of porridge.

Borgakh picked up her crossbow and hitched her thumb behind her. "Grab your cloak and rat, and we'll meet you outside."

Thugari scooped Gnash onto her shoulder before striding to her room to slip on her cloak. She scanned the area, checked her pocket to ensure Rukk's coin pouch rested there, then left the house. The door shut behind her, shoving her onto the stone steps.

A saddled Envis waited with Borgakh and Nenneg mounted already. Ahead of them was a procession of mutated wolves. At half the height of a horse, obsidian beasts so dark light didn't reflect off their coats pawed the cobbled road and sniffed the air, turning as one to eye Thugari as she hurried past.

From their mounted positions on top of these dark wolves, Mòr and her Geàrdan waited as Thugari hoisted herself into the saddle. Envis was frozen in place, his ears pointing in the direction of these strange creatures. She took the time to calm him, patting his neck and whispering words of encouragement until his ears twitched then relaxed.

"I smell rat," one of the Geàrdan said.

When no one spoke, the procession inched forward, like a colossal, slinking ulipede. Armored dwarves trailed Thugari with their gazes fixed upon her as if they guarded the amulet. They gripped the reins with their left hands, and their right hands rested on the hilt of their axes. Silver and ornate matching armor and solid silver horns adorned their helms marked them as important. Tufts of hair peeked through, and their beards fell to their bellies in shades of browns to reds.

The wolves' constant presence kept Envis hopping, swishing his tail, or snorting. It took all her inconsiderable knowledge to stay in the saddle. In an attempt to calm him, she sang to him. He remained calm for a while until the snorting began again.

"What are those things?" She glared at the beasts when she and Nenneg straggled.

"Steduins," Nenneg said. "Body of a bear, head of a wolf, and from the bowels of Chaosthane. Before the last battle against the darkness, steduins were the bane of the dwarves. Many a mining team died to these ferocious beasts, but they couldn't stand against the Ravenous Dark on their own. So, they allied with the dwarves." Their rumbling interrupted Nenneg, sounding like distant thunder. "They're partial to boar and rat."

Thugari shivered and tucked Gnash deeper into her tunic. Rukk had been right. Dussoum was no place for a rat. She wanted to ask how the steduins communicated with the dwarves since talking wasn't possible. She would ask Mòr when next they spoke.

"You know, Nenneg, in the time we spent in the forests, why didn't we come across a boar?"

"Wild boars are rare in these lands. Atrar supplies all Kethil's boar meat." Nenneg leaned over to pat her horse's neck, so Thugari did the same, having forgotten to greet Envis when she had exited the house. "They grow them on farms."

"Have you seen this?" Thugari asked, imagining fields upon fields of plump beasts.

Nenneg shook her head with a dismissive flick of her wrist. Her brow was furrowed, as if something bothered her, as if she what lay ahead concerned her.

Up ahead, Borgakh led her mount to the left, halting the procession. She pointed at a stall and waited for Thugari to join her.

"We're making all these people wait?" Thugari ran up to her.

Borgakh chuckled. "Bring your crossbow."

Heat stained Thugari's cheeks, and she rushed back to remove the crossbow from the saddle. It stuck out at an odd angle since she had shoved it into a satchel any which way.

Inside the stall, hooks lined the walls with various straps, halters, and other devices hanging from them. As soon as she stopped beside Borgakh, a dwarf scurried around her, holding up a yardstick. Two dwarves joined, their hands stroking her back and chest, but when Gnash peaked out, they yelped.

One grabbed for his knife, but Borgakh stuck her hand down Thugari's tunic and yanked Gnash out. She placed him on her shoulder and nodded at the dwarves to continue. They hesitated then returned to the task, flattening Thugari's tunic and cloak or lifting her hair. With each touch, her skin tingled, and irritation grew until she had to force herself to relax her clenched jaw. The amulet hummed and fluctuated between pale yellow and gold.

"Pay the male," Borgakh said, jerking her back to the moment.

Thugari had squeezed her eyes shut and raised her face to the ceiling to focus on her breathing. Brown strips of leather strapped across her chest with buckles holding the connecting pieces together. The crossbow sat off-center, so she shrugged and jerked until its weight pressed on her spine. Then she withdrew it, checked that nothing caught on it, and the unsheathing was smooth. Once her weapon was in place and snug, she dug for the coin pouch and counted out two silvers and four coppers.

Under the procession's vigilance, Thugari softened her frown and pulled herself onto Envis. She had needed the halter, so the delay was understandable. The crowds parted, pausing to watch them pass. Amid the dwarves mounted on steduins, Borgakh, Nenneg, and herself towered above them. A human, an orc, and a dark-orc received curious stares, but it wasn't different from how the humans reacted when they rode into their towns.

Dussoum faded into the background, so Thugari twisted to face forward, then tightened the reins when Envis veered off course. Once her horizon was filled with snow-capped Chaosthane Mountains again, she patted him on the neck and sang to him, just in case. They marched west along a path cut into the rocky terrain circling the base. A jagged peak towered in the north.

Now that she had Nenneg to herself, Thugari asked the question bothering her the most. "Why do the Geàrdan have to go if the Iomhar are there?"

"The Iomhar are the law and lore council, overseeing disputes, mining, and commerce. The Geàrdan are the heart of the people, preserving culture across races, but to hear Mòr tell it, they make sure the Iomhar don't mire themselves in tradition and superstition."

"They're respected." Thugari twirled her finger, indicating the procession.

Nenneg gazed upon the steduins, but when her focus shifted to the mountain, something dark, perhaps sadness, or fear, twitched her shoulders. After that, she spoke no more, not answering Thugari's frequent questions. The last question was met with "Borgakh hasn't told me," so Thugari fell silent.

She didn't know what to expect when they rode out of the gorge. Legions upon legions of warriors filling the plains straightened her spine to see better and spinning in her saddle to do so, veering Envis off the path again. Gold and bronze armor shimmered in the sunlight, and there was perfect precision in their formation.

"Orcs from Ghorza," Nenneg said before Thugari could ask her.

Thugari dipped her chin to her chest and vowed to stop plaguing her friend. "I'm sorry."

Nenneg smiled. "You helped keep my mind off other matters."

"Do you know why we're here? Is it about the Ravenous Dark?" Thugari gaped, scanning the army they rode past. The full realization of what their presence meant settled on her shoulders like the dreshnie's piss-riddled blanket. "This is war."

Her breath rushed out of her as something squeezed her chest. She struggled to blink away the tears and the spots from her vision as heat burned her scalp. Rukk and his lawbringers would fight alongside these orcs and any other armies arriving.

"Breathe, Thugari." Nenneg gripped her forearm, holding Thugari in the saddle. She awoke to find herself clinging to Envis's neck. "You fainted. Is it the amulet?"

She wanted to say it was the amulet's fault but didn't have the energy to lie. Nor would she admit she loved a male who might die in the next few days.

"Curse it, Thugari, breathe." Borgakh cupped her shoulders, shaking her. Nenneg must have called her over.

Thugari stared at her in a daze. "I'm well, Borgakh." She threw out her arms as if to hold her friends back. Her fingers trembled, so she squeezed the reins. The leather biting into her palms grounded her.

Borgakh's head snapped up, and she grimaced, yanking on her reins before urging her horse into a gallop. Thugari followed her line of sight. Ahead of the procession stood Ghorzan orcs dressed in far more elaborate armor than the army. The one in the middle was taller, his crown merging with his helm in an extravagant headdress. Beads of glittering gems, gold, and silver draped a muscled torso. Tribal markings etched into his skin spiraled outward. There was something familiar about his stoic features.

Borgakh dismounted before her horse halted. She fell to her knees for a second in front of the king, then launched herself into an older male's arms. His armor mimicked the army's gold and bronze with a few more bones in his hair. His position to the right of the king proclaimed his authority. Thugari gaped then peeked at Nenneg whose face was pale with her white teeth dimpling her bottom lip.

When everyone dismounted, so did Thugari, scooping Gnash from between Envis's ears to stash inside her tunic. She wasn't sure what the dwarves expected from her since she was only here because of the amulet. Holding back, she gathered the discarded reins as Borgakh dragged Nenneg toward the male. Analyzing the expressions between them, Thugari guessed he was her older brother or father.

Mòr, Isbeil, and Una approached the king, bowing before trailing him inside a white and gold pavilion with the same tribal markings burned into the white leather. The dwarven warriors crowded Thugari, nudging her with a gentle touch to the guards at the tent's entrance. Their intimidation forced her to drop the reins and shuffle closer. No expressions touched the Ghorzan guards' orcish-elvish features. They stood resolute, their carved and jeweled spears crossed, barring entrance to the tent. That was fine with her since she had no intention of intruding.

Glancing back, she searched for Borgakh or Nenneg, and a sense of vulnerability hit Thugari when she didn't find them. She tensed, fidgeting with the edge of her cloak while keeping her gaze lowered. Time passed with the Ghorzan guards and the dwarven warriors not shifting or speaking.

Boredom took over, and she studied the armor of both races, and in one instance, reached to touch the guard's shimmering belt. She caught herself before making contact and huffed at her silliness.

A voice from within the tent barked out an order, and the guards reacted, uncrossing their spears. They faced each other but didn't look at her. Assuming the king and the Geàrdan were about to exit, Thugari shuffled back bumping into a horn on the nearest dwarf's helm. She squeaked, stumbling forward, rubbing her stinging backside.

"I said to enter." The king parted the drapes with a violent flick.

Heat burst across her face, traveling down her neck, and triggering the amulet to vibrate. The cursed thing was like a beacon announcing her emotions.

His obsidian gaze fell upon her hand on her backside. Spinning on his heel, he left her standing there between his guards. She hesitated, but since the drapes stayed open, she slipped inside.

"Kneel."

At his commanding tone, she obeyed, kneeling in the middle of the tent, which looked larger inside than the outside implied.

A carved wooden table dominated the space, with mountains rising in imitation of Kethil. Shifting shapes positioned enemies or allies, and for a moment, she thought she caught the placement of clouds hovering above the surface. There were other strange yet beautiful furniture pieces she didn't have the time to study. Not with the king standing before her. Over his bare torso, he draped a robe, which brushed across his bare toes. They too were exquisite on such a large orc.

"You may look upon me, dark one," he said, and she ran an admiring appraisal up his embroidered robe with silver and gold interlacing in intricate patterns depicting leaves or birds. She met his gaze, so dark a brown as to appear ebony in color. Just like Rukk's.

Holding out his hand, white tendrils left the king's long fingers, and the amulet reacted, forming a solid circle around her neck. His hair and robes blew back as the amulet fought his influence. Curling his fingers into his palm, he snuffed his magic.

"Intriguing." As he circled her kneeling form, the thick overlapping rugs softened his tread. "Gather your hair."

She did so, holding her mass of braids over one shoulder, and held her breath. He would discover her sigil and realize how he could hurt her.

His addictive bark of laughter surprised her. "That you have such a sigil alarms me, but it explains the amulet's attachment to you."

"It does, my king?" She chose to stare at Mòr than twist to look at him, hoping she had addressed him as per protocol. Forgetting to use her father's title of 'my chief,' especially when he had visitors, had led to many beatings.

"Yes, the Arch-Magus who created the amulet wove the Stone Cage."

The Geàrdan gasped as one, but Thugari ignored them. There stood a male who could answer her questions, and in doing so, free her. "Can you remove it?" She waited as he glided to stand in front of her again.

He shook his head, his waterfall of black hair not shifting with the movement. "As powerful as I am, removing it is an impossible task. However, once the sigil unravels, so too will the amulet's attachment."

Her shoulders slumped with a sigh of relief. She grinned, raising her gaze to meet his. "Rukk promised to speak to the Arch-Magus on my behalf."

He told her to wait for him too, which meant he was on his way to Dussoum. Perhaps when they returned to Mòr's house before sunset, he would be there. As scared as she was that he might die on this battlefield, eagerness to see him skittered excitement through her, raising the hairs on her arms and sending heat through her body.

"Rukk?" The king arched a delicate black brow.

"Yes, the lawbringer Rukk Knaraugh, my king."

He spun on a heel, gesturing with wild movements at the Geàrdan. "Leave us."

Thugari dared not move. She dropped her chin to her chest and waited for the killing blow. Cycling her words through her mind, she tried to understand what had angered the orc king. He fell to his knees before her, gripping her shoulders with the scent of winter engulfing her.

"Tell me, how is *Rukk?* How is my son?"

CHAPTER THIRTY-ONE

ARTE, THE PAGE DELIVERING the Grand Lawmaster's meal, planted the rumor of Erwana's affair with Rukk. Since the timing of it might raise suspicion, Rukk told him to reveal a magus had seen them arguing, and in the passionate moment, they succumbed to temptation. Magi and lawbringers alike, sat in the common room on tenterhooks, awaiting the outcome of their ruse. Erwana's pacing whipped the skirts of her robe in her agitated movements.

Arte clambering down the stone steps broke the silence. Several lawbringers asked him for an update. He said nothing until he halted in front of Rukk. "As you commanded, lawbringer."

Rukk ruffled his hair and gestured to find a meal. Erwana froze, fear twitching her narrow shoulders. She released a long breath before nodding. Her magi looped their arms around the nearest lawbringer and cloaked themselves. At first glance, there was no one, but if Rukk shifted, they shimmered for a moment before becoming invisible again.

Silence consumed the room with only the sound of Arte scraping out his bowl. Rukk rose to withdraw his sword, laying it on the stone surface of the table. He might need it close at hand, and it wasn't right to be caught wearing it when he was in the 'throes of passion.' The tension in the air thickened, and impatience had his males shuffling.

He whispered, "Silence."

They stilled.

Minutes later, the heavy footfall of Venec descended the stairs. Erwana threw herself onto Rukk's lap, her arms circling his neck as she dusted kisses along his jaw. He gripped her waist before rubbing her back, entangling his fingers in the soft waterfall of her hair.

"Cursed hell. When Arte told me, I couldn't believe it. Not frigid Erwana." Venec entered the common room sans weapon.

His arrogance would cost him. Fighting with another's sword put one at a disadvantage.

In his stained tunic from the previous evening and the undone ties of his breeches exposing him, sadness once again gripped Rukk. To see the male he had respected brought so low circled darkness in his heart, the burn of fury on its tail.

He frowned, wrapping an arm around Erwana's curvaceous form, cupping her hip in ownership, and shifted her away from his sword.

"Arte, leave us." Venec's consideration hinted at the male Rukk had once known.

"Yes, Grand Lawmaster," Arte said, grabbing an apple out of the bowl and heading for the stairs.

He wouldn't go far, and Rukk expected many pages would watch from the stairwell. After all, the Tower was their home too.

Venec strode toward Erwana, his bearing menacing. "I offered myself, but I wasn't enough for you."

Derision twisted his lips, and the shadows playing across his features made him appear possessed.

She pushed off Rukk's lap, trailing a fingertip along his jaw. "The son of an orc king is preferable, Venec, but what do you know about the pleasures of the flesh? You are as virginal as I once was."

"I would have sealed my fate to yours, Erwana. We could have ruled Kethil together." Venec gripped her upper arm as if to shake her.

Rukk rose to protect her, but she shook her head, facing Venec instead. Shimmering images in his peripherals revealed her magi shifting into position, blocking Venec's path of retreat.

"We *were* ruling together, Venec, until you killed Janar." Her voice cracked.

"You cannot lay his death at my feet when your actions are far from pure." He yanked her to him, pinning her to the length of him. "You're mine from this moment forth. If you can spread your thighs for an orc, you can do so for one of your kind."

"To lay with me will cost you the title and all its authority." Erwana struggled against him in a silent plea for release.

He barked a laugh, whether in self-loathing or mocking her, Rukk wasn't sure. "I am not virginal, *Arch-Magus*, and rutting with Janar has cost me nothing."

"What did killing him cost you, Venec?" Rukk tightened his muscles, preparing to attack or defend.

"I want to give the killing blow. Let me challenge him, Rukk." Tarid's emotions burned across Rukk's senses, volatile and self-destructive.

He had to be the one to challenge his master. To let Tarid do so might cost his lawbrother his soul. Venec's death would be swift, and Tarid's revenge unsatiated. Such hatred and unforgiveness would corrupt him until Rukk no longer recognized him.

"We will let our brothers decide the challenger."

"You have lost my respect," a lawbringer said, revealing himself.

"Mine too," another said, and one by one, the lawbringers and knights surrounded them, their disapproval on their faces. Venec shoved Erwana aside as he spun in a slow circle.

"I hereby revoke your title of Grand Lawmaster, Venec Galand. What say you?" Rukk grimaced at seeing the bruises forming on Erwana's arm.

Gone were the days when Venec would defend those abused or weak. The Ravenous Dark had taken his true self and corrupted it into the very thing he had once abhorred.

He opened his mouth to speak, but Tarid stepped forward. "I hereby accuse you of the murder of Lawmaster Janar Inaris. What say you?"

"I hereby accuse you of forsaking your lawbringer vows, succumbing to the Ravenous Dark's influence, and leading your second-in-command astray. What say you?" Erwana's expressions were a mixture of determination, sorrow, and love.

In her way, she must have loved Venec, as a friend or a male. It didn't matter now.

"I deny these allegations." Venec laughed at them.

"We have seen the evidence, Venec Galand, and judge you guilty." Rukk gestured to his lawbrothers and choruses of "ayes" filled the room. "You know the penalty of each accusation. Brothers, choose your champion."

Venec roared and lunged at Rukk, his fingers wrapping around his throat. Jerking his hands away with Venec's fingernails gouging his skin, Rukk ducked under his arms and punched him in the gut, winding him. Tarid grabbed Rukk's sword to toss it. He caught it in mid-air and raised it, catching Venec with the tip under his chin.

"Rukk, step back, let me at him." Tarid shifted but hesitated. His rock wall had melted, bombarding fury unlike anything Rukk had ever experienced.

"He will lunge for me again if I show him any quarter. I'm trapped, Tarid." Rukk thrust all his regret into the emotions he conveyed, hoping to convince Tarid of his 'sincerity,' that he would have preferred Tarid challenge Venec.

"Take my sword, Venec, and face lawbringer Rukk Knaraugh in challenge." Tarid spun his sword to offer Venec the hilt.

Venec accepted the offered weapon, dropping a hand on Tarid shoulder. Then he plunged the blade through Tarid's abdomen.

"No." Rukk leaped onto the table, swinging his sword across Venec's back as Tarid crumpled to the floor, clutching his stomach with blood seeping between his fingers.

Venec threw up his blade, meeting Rukk's downward slice. Sharn streaked across the room to kneel beside Tarid.

Rukk faced Venec's next strike, trusting Sharn to care for his lawbrother.

"You aren't virginal. You can't hope to attain the title." Venec slashed his sword, crisscrossing as he lunged, forcing Rukk to assume the defensive.

"I don't want the title, Venec. We have a duty to Kethil, one you have forgotten." He rolled across Venec's bare feet, jumping up behind him to bring his hilt down, hoping to land a blow at the back of his neck. He did, a glancing one.

"Forgotten? My eyes are open to the sacrifice and service we provide. Kethil's ingratitude has brought this upon them. They won't have the magi nor the lawbringers to defend them."

The swords met and kissed, spraying sparks until they hooked on each other's hilts. Close enough to smell the stench of old mead on Venec's breath, Rukk pushed, pulling his sword free by kicking Venec in his thigh as he vaulted backward.

"So you know." Rukk waited, hoping Venec would deny it.

"Of the Ravenous Dark? Of course." Venec laughed. "I am no fool." He angled his sword in front of him, challenging Rukk with a nudge of his chin.

"No, you are weak." Rukk's words wiped the smile from Venec's face.

He charged.

Rukk feinted to the right, but ducked under Venec's sword arm to slice his blade across Venec's stomach. He faltered and faced Rukk, clutching his chest as he lifted his sword again. A large bloodstain grew confirming Rukk had wounded him.

"You were always too lucky for your own good." Venec chuckled before slashing his sword down.

Rukk met his blow with his blade, but after unsheathing his dagger from his boot, thrust upward. With the blade buried to the hilt, Venec's eyes widened and dropped the sword. It clattered to the floor as he gripped the dagger's hilt jutting out of his stomach.

He crumpled to his knees, tilting his gaze to meet his executioner.

"That's for Tarid and Janar." Rukk slashed his sword, beheading Venec as Erwana screamed. She lunged for Venec, but it was too late. His head bounced across the floor. "That's for my lawbrothers."

"Why?" Erwana sobbed, her fluttering hands on Venec's chest.

"It is our law, Arch-Magus, as you well know." Rukk looped an arm around her waist and lifted her to her feet. "A corrupted heart is irredeemable. You said so yourself."

Her teeth dimpled her bottom lip as tears slipped free. Wiping them away, she nodded at her magi. They swarmed the room, clearing it of the execution. "Decide his replacement, and we'll tend to his burial." She marched off with bowed shoulders.

Lawbrothers didn't bother with burials for those who violated their vows. An honorable death received tribute, a pyre, and a feast with each male tossing onto the deceased's body something precious to them. Venec and Janar would receive none of that.

"It had to be done," Larza said before facing Rukk. "There are no virgins among us." His males scanned each other.

"Brothers, I'll leave you to decide on the next Grand Lawmaster." Rukk knelt beside Tarid. He arched a brow at Sharn who offered a weak smile, her hands glowing as they hovered over the wound. *Quit pretending. You have the female, so these theatrics aren't necessary.*

Tarid chuckled, then groaned. *It hurts like cursed hell, but I won't deny I like her gentle ministrations.*

The lawbringers argued, their voices soaring as they threw names about and their reasons why.

Rukk tapped Tarid's knee, forcing him to open his eyes. "Travel with Sharn so she can heal you. Dussoum awaits, and we can't delay our departure."

Sharn nodded when he looked at her.

Rukk commanded silence, and as his males faced him, he said, "We can decide this on the journey. Inform the magi we depart within the hour. The Ravenous Dark awaits."

Chapter Thirty-Two

"I CAN SEE WHY he is fond of you." King Horknuth sipped from a gold goblet. His gaze lingered on Thugari's face, igniting another round of blushes. "Your voice is lyrical, and your curves, enticing."

Not liking his avid attention, she swallowed the bile rising to gag her. "You are mistaken, my king. To Rukk, I am a debt, a bargain, nothing more." She clasped her hands in her lap, sitting cross-legged on the rug while the king sprawled in an ornate chair woven with metals, and living trees.

She couldn't decide if the lumps twinkling in the lantern light were gems or fruit. Gnash slept on her shoulder, still alive after he had startled the king.

"You wove your pleasant tale well, but I sense you've omitted parts too sensitive for my fatherly ears?" His lips curled into a smile, and she sighed, her heart fluttering from facing such beauty. Here were Rukk's features and mannerisms, yet his father lacked his brooding intensity. "You care for my son?"

"I do. He has saved me too many times for my liking, and for that, I am grateful."

He shook his head, a chuckle escaping him. "Do you think I cannot see into your heart, dark one?"

"I hoped." She flashed a teasing smile. "After all, my emotions are my own, are they not?"

"Few things are truly owned." The king traced a graceful finger along the goblet's rim. "A dark-orc siren? He believes that?"

"Yes." She unfolded her legs, stretching them out to shuffle on her backside, hoping to assuage the numbness.

The king's maidservant had offered her a goblet, but she had declined, envisioning spilling its contents on the exquisite furs. She glanced at the female, stunned by her ethereal beauty. Even if Thugari was a siren, she couldn't compete with such a creature.

There was a delicacy to the servant's features, nothing like Arob or Murzush. "What do you know of human sirens, my king?"

"You do not know?" He scowled, holding out his goblet for his maidservant to refill. "You hinted at your upbringing, opening your tale at stealing Rukk's coin pouch. What of your life before this?"

Thugari grimaced, not wanting to discuss her father, the death of her mother, and her enslavement. "It was an unpleasant time. My mother died when I was young, and I grew up alone in my father's castle."

The king unraveled his limbs, balanced his goblet on the armrest, and rose. He glided toward her, trailing his robes. "I sense your pain. Show me if the telling is unbearable."

He placed his thumbs under her eyes, and his fingers in her hair, tilting her head back. Closing his eyes, his face drained of emotion, as if a stone statue bent over her. Warmth touched her thoughts, probing her memories, and learning her deepest desires. Moisture beaded on his forehead, and his expressions twisted from sadness to fury.

There wasn't any pain where he touched her, so she studied his face, his angular jaw, sensual lips, and prominent cheekbones, all reminiscent of Rukk.

Yet, where the king was a typical male orc, tusks, furrowed brow, broad shoulders, Rukk had a little something else to his features. A slant in his eyes, the paler skin, and white hair.

"My king." A male entered the tent, thrusting aside the drapes. He halted, a hand on his sword hilt, and said no more, awaiting the king's attention.

"What is it, Furak?" King Horknuth swept strands of hair off her temples, burying his fingers deeper into her braids.

He studied her as if he considered purchasing her, tilting her head to assess her value. The temptation to bare her teeth had her gripping her thighs, holding the urge at bay. Her life lay in his hands. With a word, he could toss her to his soldiers. The life of a half-breed mattered not to a male such as he.

"The Geàrdan wish to depart but cannot without the Amulet of Zylfir."

"Which has attached itself to Thugari Nehrakgu of House Macutia." The king's gaze remained on her upturned face, a soft smile teasing his lips. "What lies before me is a mystery I did not anticipate." He removed his hands, taking the warmth with him. Leaning back, he laughed. "She must remain with me, for where she is, my son will follow."

Moon above. Thugari peeked at the shifting drapes. In the middle of an encampment, she couldn't run, and there was nowhere to hide. When leaving Haraton, all she longed for was a cabin somewhere quiet. Sitting in front of inescapable royalty was far from it.

Furak bowed. "I have invited the Geàrdan to sample our hospitality, but Mòr Guaire has declined the offer, my king."

"Talks with Keryn did not go well?" The king spun on his bare heel to resume his chair, his robes scraping over her legs. "Inform Mòr I will protect Thugari, her pet rat, and the amulet with my life."

Furak sucked in a startled breath, his cheeks darkening. He didn't respond, except with a curt bow before exiting.

Having her life decided for her was wearing thin. As an orc who must have lived centuries by now, he had to understand the concept of free will, despite his authority affording him the luxury of ignoring it. "You could have asked me first, my king, even if politeness is just an illusion."

It was his maidservant's turn to gasp, her body tensed as if she expected a beating. Thugari arched a brow, replaying her words to assess how they could offend the king. No reprimand was forthcoming.

"As I said, I can see why he is fond of you. Why should I ask when I don't need to?" He rose again and gestured to her to join him. Behind diaphanous drapes, his bed rested to the rear of the tent, but a table with chairs dominated the center. Aromas rose, tantalizing Thugari with her stomach gurgling in agreement. "Sit, eat, for it is my turn to tell a tale."

Thugari obeyed. Lowering an awake Gnash onto her lap, she accepted with tentative fingers the bowl the king held out to her. He sank onto the other chair, filling his plate from the platters between them. Roast goose, various fruit, cheeses, and fresh bread made her decision difficult. Her hunger, shooting spikes of pain at her neglect, didn't help. She wanted to bite into the goose so the juices dribbled down her chin. Yet she dined with royalty.

"I have not seen my son for decades. For an orc, that is but a drop in time." The king swirled wine in his goblet. "For a father, it is centuries."

"Was the distance out of choice or did you argue?" She stripped pieces of meat off the bone with her fingers, placing a sliver at a time onto her tongue.

She smothered a moan at the unusual yet delicious flavors. Feeding Gnash often kept him obedient, and she didn't want the king to have a reason to kill her pet. He chirped as he ate, his paws grasping each sliver of meat with gusto.

"Why do you assume an argument?" The king broke his bread with nimble fingers, sopping up the juices pooling on his plate.

"Anyone familiar with Rukk knows he can be obstinate, opinionated, and over-bearing."

"Well said, but as his father and king, I expect such traits from him." He bit into his bread, chewing with a grin.

"But not when he throws them in your face, my king." Her father had found Arob's rude comments entertaining until she targeted him. That evening her backside had burned, and Thugari had relished the pain her sister was in.

"Yes." King Horknuth laughed, then sighed, his smile lingering even as his humor dwindled. "He wanted to travel Kethil, to live as a free male. I rejected his request, and in doing so, he abandoned Ghorza."

"Why deny him the journey? Was it wrong for him to want to experience something outside of his world?"

"No, my reasons were deeper than his desires. For an orc of an ancient bloodline, living for long outside the mystical borders of our realm is a death sentence. The energy that inhabits our beings dies when not refilled by the magic of our land."

"Dies?" She returned the bread to her plate. Ash filled her mouth, and she swallowed the dry lump. When the bread lodged in her throat, she snatched the goblet and gulped down its contents.

"My spies inform me he crafted his lawbringer medallion with the soil of our homeland and asked an Arch-Magus to cast healing spells on it. With it on, he cannot flourish, but without it, this corrupted land drains his life force."

My medallion is far more precious to me. Rukk's words rose from her memories, and the icy fingers of fear squeezed her heart, spreading outward until a heaviness dragged her down. She could have killed him. Yet he had removed it to heal her, knowing the cost to his own life. *Moon above.* She owed him much more than they had agreed upon.

"Borgakh? Sharn?" Thugari frowned. "How do they prevent their life from draining?"

The king flashed a smile, softening his features. "They are not half-elf, dark one. It is Rukk's mother who weakened my son. Ancient elves are in tune with the land, so he carries a pouch of Ghorzan soil, as well."

He was a half-breed, like her? Their similarity filled her with contentment, and she sighed.

Grateful to the king for answering her, she agreed to aid him, though, had she chosen otherwise, she might have been 'locked' in a tent for who knew how long. "I will remain with you until he finds me. Should he choose to leave you again, then I must follow him."

"Fair enough." The king frowned, then gave her a polite smile. "You speak your mind without fear."

"I could lie or steal, but I've developed a conscience." She grimaced, wishing it weren't true.

Surrounding her were the most exquisite items. Rings in a bowl on a side table. Swords with jeweled hilts resting on a rack. Woven silks and soft wools draped over a garment stand, and in one corner, a full set of armor.

The king laughed again. "I have never met a human such as you. Most drip with hatred or greed."

Humans and elves were playthings to orcs.

She studied the brute, wondering why he had mated an elf—an ancient one at that. "Each race has its share of dishonorable people, my king. You were unfortunate to meet the worst of my kind."

"In that, I must agree, Thugari." He gestured to his maidservant, and she hurried across. "Dura, have Furak erect a tent for my guest. Rise, daughter, and seek rest this evening."

Thugari did so, for when a king dismissed her, it was best to leave. She hesitated. He had been kind when he needn't have been.

"Thank you for your hospitality," she said before trailing the maidservant.

The sun bleeding in farewell across the sky made her grumble. Time had flown past. She halted in mid-stride, dazzled by the dark purples to reds merging with the usual oranges and pinks staining the clouds.

The sky looked…wrong.

"Thugari." Borgakh strode toward her, a ferocious scowl marring her features. "What in cursed hell did you say to King Horknuth?"

"I mentioned Rukk in passing. I didn't know, Borgakh." Thugari held out her hands in surrender, even as Gnash scampered across to leap onto Borgakh's shoulder. The orc maiden scowled, but released a long-suffering sigh as she gave his head an awkward pat. "He's requested I stay near in the hopes Rukk will find me here."

"Mòr agreed to this?" Borgakh was as flabbergasted as Thugari, perhaps more so since she understood the dynamics between orc and dwarf better.

"The king didn't give her a choice, vowing to protect me, Gnash, and the amulet with his life." Thugari grabbed Borgakh's forearm. "You won't let him die, will you?"

Borgakh chuckled. "He's guarded by legions upon legions of warriors. Not to mention his personal guard, the Kurdan."

Thugari gaped, her mouth forming an 'oh.' Tents lined the surrounding plains, with many lanterns glowing in the growing darkness like organized fireflies. Another erected tent, smaller but no less ornate, held a prominent position alongside the king's. She supposed that was to be hers for the duration of her stay. Rukk could be weeks away. Dread drained her of energy, drooping her shoulders. Henceforth, her life would vacillate between keeping the king company or hiding in the tent.

"Who were you hugging earlier?" Thugari hurried to keep up with Borgakh's long strides.

She didn't pause when she said, "My father."

Thugari had suspected as much. A part of her was dazzled by the king's attention. Dining with him was surreal, another time, another Thugari. If she thought about it, she had dined with royalty before, with Rukk, but she hadn't known his lineage. She chewed her lip and followed Borgakh inside another tent. Whatever King Horknuth had seen in her memories, she prayed she hadn't in any way betrayed Rukk.

"Thugari, this is my father, Keryn Yerug, leader of the Kurdan, and General of King Horknuth's armies." Borgakh rested her hand on a male's shoulder.

In full regalia, the hulking male dominated the tent, rivaling Tarid and Rukk in size. His presence and authority radiated outward, suffocating the air and hiking the tension. Thugari trembled under the weight of his fury and disgust. She kept a grip on the drapes, not that leaving would save her. Borgakh had Gnash too.

"A dark human?" He unsheathed his sword and stormed toward her.

Thugari squeaked and tugged her crossbow from its holster, but by the time she leveled it on the charging male, Borgakh had leaped between them.

"My friend *and* under the protection of King Horknuth." She faced him, fearless and as commanding. The same shape of the eyes, the strong, hook noses, the stubborn chins screamed their connection.

"What?" Keryn lowered his sword, wiping the spittle off his chin with the back of his hand. His puzzled expression sliced between Thugari and Borgakh then lingered for a long time on Gnash.

"Rukk will come for her, and in doing so, see the king. Well, that's the hope." Borgakh grinned as if her father wasn't intent on spilling blood this evening.

"Why would Rukk come—?"

"If you let me finish." She rested her hands on her hips. Keryn grumbled, sheathed his sword, and stomped away. "Thugari has a Stone Cage, wears the Amulet of Zylfir, and is Rukk's friend." She gripped her father's shoulders, halting his pacing. "Look at Nenneg, Father. Not all humans are thieves and murderers."

"Do you vouch for this dark one?" Silence filled the tent at his question, the seriousness of it not lost on Thugari. She sidled toward the exit in case she needed to run but kept her crossbow raised.

"Upon my honor." Borgakh dropped to one knee, a fist pressed to her chest, then rose. "Furak readies her tent, so until then, be nice."

"A general is never nice." He sat, his gaze not leaving Thugari, as if she were a snake ready to strike. "I mean, look at her tiny tusks, and she's so...short."

"Be nice, Father." Borgakh placed her hand on Thugari's bow and pushed it down. "Put your crossbow away."

Thugari released a breath trapped within her lungs. Ice drenched her neck and shoulders as she lowered her bow, then spun it to holster it.

"I can't believe they let you enter the king's tent armed," Nenneg said, strolling through the drapes from the back of the tent. She carried a platter of sweets, which she offered around.

After her near-death experience, Thugari's stomach churned. The honeyed aroma pooled bile at the back of her throat. She remained standing, shuffling her feet, not sure whether to step farther into the tent or bid a hasty retreat.

She forced herself to slow her breathing. "It rests so well against my back I didn't feel the weight of it."

"The king must like you. To enter his tent carrying a weapon is to challenge him for the throne," Keryn said, his glare not softening. "Or do you seek a swift death, for had the Kurdan been there, we would have sliced your head off your shoulders."

He gestured with a sweep of his hand, but instead of frightening Thugari, she smiled, recognizing the graceful movements. Rukk had swept his slicing blade through the coven of wylders, his silver hair trailing him. It was one of her favorite memories.

"You trained Rukk. When he holds his sword, it's like an extension of his body, and he moves like a flowing river. It's beautiful to behold." If he had trained Rukk, then he must have taught Borgakh, as well.

It explained why she was the renowned orc maiden.

Keryn leveled his gaze on Thugari, his nostrils flaring. Under his weighted stare, the urge to escape to Tarid's cabin gripped her with a crippling longing. She had no right to be there.

Sighing, she accepted all she would ever be able to do with a knife was slice bread. The dark, persistent tendrils of fear squeezed her lungs in a vise-like grip and kept her frozen. She, an unwanted half-orc with a silly amulet around her neck, was standing in the middle of a battlefield, on the eve of war.

She had no place being here, not if it meant her friends had to protect her instead of battling the Ravenous Dark. Once Rukk arrived, she would leave for Banach Cottage.

At Furak's appearance, she and Gnash escaped Keryn, but not the tears stinging her eyes. In the privacy of her extravagant tent, she wept, crumbling to the rug with a silent wail. Her erratic breathing and the pain crushing her chest overrode her logical thoughts, bolstering her reasons for leaving. She had found a family among her friends. To spare them, she would sacrifice her need for acceptance, no matter what it cost her.

Chapter Thirty-Three

"A most intriguing development has occurred regarding the Stone Cage." Rukk threw his voice across the distance between Erwana and himself, mounted and heading west to Dussoum.

Hours crawled by, and each one passed like days inching into weeks. At night, he raised his face to the moon and hoped Thugari did the same. Peace warred with eagerness at the thought they shared the same moonlight.

They were two days into their five-day journey with his lawbrothers still undecided on leadership. It might have been faster to travel on the Berh River, but there weren't enough barges in Penven to carry all of the Tower, and leaving the wagons unguarded wasn't an option.

"Oh? Have you sounded your female?" Erwana arched a brow, even as a smile graced her lips.

His female? He hoped so. "Her name is Thugari."

Erwana winced. "Awful to be named after a monstrous father."

He had thought the same. "She wears the Amulet of Zylfir."

Erwana's slow chuckle warmed to a laugh. "I hadn't expected that. It's wonderful to finally discover the location of Minerva's amulet."

"It's around Thugari's neck and won't come off."

She nodded. "By taking on the pain of the Stone Cage, Minerva's soul bore the cost. And as you know, to craft a magical artifact, the process requires much of the crafter. She infused pieces of herself into that amulet and siphoned power from it, hence why it must be stored in fire." She faced forward. "The amulet fused with the sigil, but unraveling the latter will break the connection."

As simple as that. He pursed his lips and patted his pocket where the daylily rested. He prayed Thugari knew what it meant. The burning ache of unfulfilled desire formed a constant bombardment on his control, his mind.

Should the sigil never unravel, he would endure the onslaught for an eternity as long as he could embrace her. His magic bubbled over, volatile and demanding, seeking the release he was reluctant to perform.

He let out a breath.

Erwana arched a brow in query. "Perhaps shield yourself. Absorbing the sunlight and the wind is overloading you."

He flipped his hood up, grateful for the reminder. A little too late though, so when she held out a palm and the air wavered, rippled, melted between them, he sighed, his spine softening as the pressure of unspent magic eased.

"Holy Zetar, Rukk." She whimpered, bending over. "You...hide it well."

He grunted. "Thank you. Draining my magic shouldn't fall on your shoulders, Erwana."

She chuckled through the pain furrowing her brow and darkening her eyes. "Erwana, hey? How familiar we have become when all I did was kiss your chin."

He grinned. "Little did I know that was all it would take."

The brothers are undecided, Rukk. We need you. Tarid's plea dampened Rukk's good humor.

"On my way."

He nodded at Erwana and steered Harpax to the side, waiting for his brothers to catch up to him. Mounted magi rode abreast. Wagons carrying spellbinders and goods rumbled past. The Tower's stables didn't have enough horses for everyone, which left the novitiates and elderly magi seeing to the Tower in their absence.

None laughed, their somber expressions a prelude to what lay ahead for them. Battle, death, darkness, but also, Zetar willing, victory and life. To live through a generational defining event was to be shared with one's grandchildren.

Children? Heat stung his eyes, and he blinked to hold back the tears. He did want a child to cherish, to be a better father than his own had been. At his morbid thoughts, he shook his head, no doubt brought on by the danger they rode into. The image of a pregnant Thugari, glowing with health and happiness, snagged his focus, tormented his emotions until it was his hand in the illusion stroking her swollen belly.

"Rukk!" Tarid's face in his jerked him back from his thoughts. "What ails you, brother?"

"Daydreaming." He slapped Tarid's thigh and grinned. "So, what do you need help with?" When Rukk urged Harpax into a walk, Tarid fell in beside him. They rejoined the procession.

"Choosing the next Lawmaster."

Rukk shrugged, not knowing what Tarid expected him to do. And Rukk was too lazy to delve through their connection to find out. "I gathered as much with such a difficult choice to make."

"No, the choice is a simple one. Only your reticence stops them from making it final."

He scowled at Tarid before facing forward. "No, I'm not one to lead."

"But—"

"No, Tarid. If I wanted to lead males, I would not have left Ghorza. Let a male more worthy command the lawbringers."

"More worthy than Prince Rukk of Ghorza?"

Pulling on the reins, Rukk halted Harpax, turning in the saddle to meet Tarid's gaze. "I renounced my life, who I was, and everything I stood for when I joined the lawbringers. I am no longer a prince, nor do I claim loyalty to the Ghorzan way." He gritted his teeth and tugged his hood lower. "You know this, know how I feel, Tarid."

"I do, Rukk, but we are without leadership, with the lawbringers on the precipice of collapse."

"So desperate times cancel my sacrifices? I must make even more to please my brethren?" Fury pulsed through him, and unsummoned, white tendrils swirled around his fingers. "If I have to choose between commanding the lawbringers and life as a free male, it will be the latter."

Tarid cried out, sadness warring with anger in his brown eyes. "Impossible, you made a vow."

"I did, but asking me to do this, make this sacrifice, will force me to leave, brother." He would never lead males to their victory or doom, never command any male to kill another.

The blood on their hands was by their choice. No, he couldn't bear the responsibility, not if he had a choice. His father had decades ahead of him before Rukk would be summoned to take his rightful place. That was another battle he would need to fight and win. But not now.

"Very well, I will take this to our brothers." Tarid steered his mount around, galloping to the lawbringers trailing the wagons.

The cries and rumbles of raised voices filled the afternoon as they meandered through the rich, green farmland of northern Thoraval. The paved King's Way eased the burden of traveling with wagons, ensuring fewer wheels were lost. Up ahead, the Chaosthane Mountains curved, with their white-capped tips. Dussoum wasn't yet visible and wouldn't be for two more days. They were near, but if the battle began before they reached the city, there was nothing the lawbringers or the magi could do.

He prayed they made it there in time, that Borgakh protected Thugari, and deep within him, that the Ravenous Dark wasn't rising. It could be another evil wreaking havoc or a wizard playing with powers he didn't understand. Anything was preferable to pure evil.

He kept his gaze on the horizon, pushing Harpax into a gallop to liaise with the scouts up ahead, before falling in beside Erwana.

At camp that night after a hasty meal of stew, he stoked the fire, appreciating the warmth rolling off the flickering flames. Tarid had been absent since their 'argument,' silent too. He flicked out his bedroll, flopped down beside Rukk, and leaned back on his elbows. Rukk said nothing, choosing to bite his tongue than reiterate his point.

"I'm sorry." Tarid's simple apology drained the tension from Rukk's shoulders. "I forgot why you became a lawbringer, and my eagerness to see you succeed blinded me."

"Your intentions were of a pure heart." He offered his wineskin.

Tarid drank deeply, then wiped his mouth on his sleeve. "Well, the choice has been made. You should cast your vote."

"Who—?"

"Larza."

Rukk nodded. "A far superior male than I will ever be. And he is powerful. A wise choice, brother."

"And the first dwarf Grand Lawmaster." Tarid beamed.

Rukk snorted. "The Iomhar won't listen to him any more than they did Venec."

Tarid chuckled. "I know, but we can hope."

"It's best to cultivate the Geàrdan's ear." Larza joined them at the fire, accepting the wineskin Tarid offered. He squatted on a nearby rock and poured wine into a goblet.

"I would have preferred you lead, Rukk." The dwarf shrugged, drained his cup, then scratched with the rim at his neat honey-colored beard.

"I am pleased you were chosen, Larza. You garner far more respect than I do."

The dwarf grinned. "True, and I have not lain with a female for over a year."

Rukk laughed. "That makes you the most virginal among us."

"Well, it's as close as we're going to get." Larza rose to unbind his bedroll. "I will act in place of Venec, but we will train the next Lawmaster, and quite a few of them too. No point in putting all our rats in one bucket."

Already the male was showing his mettle. Rukk smiled, staring into the fire. More than one Lawmaster was a good decision. He sprawled onto his back, folded an arm under his head, and stared at the starlit sky.

Change was as guaranteed as death. It was how one dealt with it that determined the outcome. And perhaps, under Larza, the lawbringers wouldn't be as complacent, comfortable, and unprepared to handle the next major event. Rukk would see Thugari soon and wasn't forced to be the next Grand Lawmaster, so all was good.

"WHAT DO YOU MEAN she's not here!" Fire and disbelief barreled along his veins like a tidal wave.

The need to see Thugari, to bury his nose in her hair, to taste those sweet lips pounded his control. The moment Dussoum had come into focus, he had raced ahead, giving Harpax the lead.

"Don't you dare yell at me, Rukk Knaraugh." Mòr wagged a stumpy finger.

He pinched the bridge of his nose as he fought for calm. "My apologies. I told her to wait for me. Was I not clear on that instruction?"

"She wore the amulet, and I go nowhere without it." Mòr flopped onto her stone seat and poured a goblet of dragon's fire. "Except at the command of your father. He guards it and her with his life, or so he vowed."

"Father has her?" He grimaced, falling into a furious pacing, but ducked his head at regular intervals to dodge the low-hanging chandeliers. "So a trap?"

"That's my assessment." She offered him a goblet and gestured for him to sit. "Why didn't you tell her, Rukk? She was so innocent when she mentioned you promised to speak to the Arch-Magus on her behalf. Had she known who you were, she might not have revealed your connection. You would have found her here, feeding her fat little rat."

"I didn't want her to look at me differently." It cost him much to admit it, and he downed the dragon's fire with a wince.

Mòr chuckled. "This is Thugari you speak of. She is guileless and so trusting, she's a danger to herself. Not quite the female I imagined would snag your heart."

His breath caught, and he raised a wide-eyed gaze to Mòr's. "Does she know how I feel?"

"No. Like I said, guileless." She rubbed her palms together. "Now, can you unravel the sigil? Did you speak to your Arch-Magus?"

"We found some information leading up to its creation, but only vague directions on how to undo the spell. It's in Thugari's hands, or so the journal says."

"Stones of Comhnall." Mòr slumped onto her seat. "I was hoping for something more definite, or else a certain dark-orc will be living with me permanently."

"Well, two things will happen. The use of the amulet would be limited since you can't remove it to test others for magic. And without it being stored in fire, its powers would drain." He smiled at a realization. "That's it. If we can't unravel the sigil," he grimaced, "then we need only wait until the amulet loses strength."

"Last time it did, it took two full moons."

"Two...?" He frowned, not liking having to wait two hours, let alone two moons. But then again, if he had to wait, then the sigil hadn't unraveled yet. He shivered.

"She's in a tent beside your father's." Mòr rose to take the goblet from him. "You can sneak her here?"

"Make it look like she escaped?" He liked the idea of thwarting his father's attempt to corner him. "Thank you for—"

Mòr chuckled. "Get back my amulet."

He bolted, clambering down the steps to where he had tethered Harpax. Vaulting into the saddle, he urged his horse to take the lead again, hoping the final stretch to the battleground west of Chaosthane wouldn't overtax him. Five more hours, he could do this. Pouring his overflowing magic into Harpax, he healed and energized his horse, easing his exhaustion and any muscle strains.

It was foolish to waste his energy on shortening even an hour of his journey, but after the last five days, he couldn't bear delaying seeing Thugari.

Foolish fool in love that he was.

Chapter Thirty-Four

Days blurred, and Thugari's nights more so, spent evading the haunting images of Rukk and his healing touch. Awaking drenched in sweat and with a heaviness inside her, she tossed and turned, searching for comfort in a too-soft bed. Gripping her pillow, she circled her arm around it as if he lay beside her. Finding her reliance pathetic, she punched the pillow before throwing it across the tent. Gnash had taken to the safety of the chair, curling onto a dirty tunic she had forgotten there.

The heat was unbearable, which made no sense this close to the ice-capped mountains. She must be ill. No one else suffered like this. The camp was peaceful, and the guard at her tent's entrance silent and immobile. Yet, something rippled under her skin, heightened her senses and built in intensity as each moment passed. The amulet responded in kind, humming low to high, then dipping again when she found a small measure of peace.

In the darkness of her tent, she climbed off the bed and undid the ties of the garment. This gift, from the many strangers who sought her out, was a thin cloth and caressed her skin, but it clung to her sensitive nipples. Undone, when she paced, it fluttered open, cooling her heated skin as it tangled between her legs. This restlessness had her in its grip. Not halting her strides, she lifted the wealth of her hair off her neck, sighing in bliss.

Horknuth confused her. She may have hidden how much she loved his son, but his tale, that Rukk left home over an argument, didn't make sense. Pinching her furrowed brow, she paced, reliving each discussion with the king over the past five days. There wasn't a word or look from him that twisted her gut, only a sense of deception.

Pooling her drying cloth on the floor, she stepped onto it, slipped out of the robe, and draped it across a nearby chair. Then, with slow methodical movements, she dipped a cloth into the washbowl and dragged it from her shoulder down to her toes in one move. A moan escaped her as it cooled her body. She couldn't reach her back, so she squeezed the cloth to allow the water to run in rivulets. Droplets plopping onto the rug reached her sensitive ears.

A stray breeze teased the flaps at the entrance of the tent, and she froze, as if someone had snuck in. Scanning her empty tent, unable to pierce the darkest corners, her gaze settled on a pile of gifts beside her bed. Dwarves, human slaves, orcs, and even the Atrarian king had seen fit to bless her with bolts of cloth, cloaks, daggers she wished she could wield, jewelry she planned to sell, and even a saddle. Males smiled or stared when she passed them, hence the Ghorzan guard tasked to protect her. Even he blushed when she spoke to him. Each day, their fascination with her had grown worse. She hadn't mentioned it though, praying it would fade as swiftly as it had risen.

As she slipped the sheer robe over her damp body, she laughed at her paranoia. Horknuth loved his son, but if he was half as obstinate as Rukk, she could understand why they argued.

"Rukk, don't come here, don't find me. I don't trust your father." She whispered the words in a plea, wishing he would sound her again. The silence of the camp was her only response, not that she expected one. Her loneliness solidified thoughts of entrapment tainted by Horknuth's every word or deed.

Sprawling on her bed, she lay on her back; the parted robe granted her some relief. A sensation built inside her, as if something pressed against her skin, searching for freedom. She'd tried to ask Nenneg about the growing pressure, but words had failed Thugari. How could she explain it? Her bones ached worse than the pain Frukag had inflicted. Worse than her father withholding his love. She clenched her jaw, riding a wave of fire. Lifting her hair, so her neck caught a stray breeze, she stroked her sigil in passing. Exquisite joy darted through her.

She whimpered. Pleasure was much better than the agony she was in. She sighed as peace claimed her, but it didn't last. The tension ramped up again, lifting the hairs along her arms and puckering her nipples.

When she couldn't bear it anymore, she stroked the sigil. As she writhed and whimpered with tingles surging through her, fear squeezed her heart. But the sensations were too intense for her to bother too much with why the sigil eased her suffering.

"Rukk." She glided her hands over her breasts, searching for the ties of her robe, crying out as sparks took a direct path to her femininity. "Please, I need healing."

"Sweet Thugari, what are you doing to yourself?"

She stilled, amazed at her ability to envision his presence and the robust quality of his voice. To have him in her tent meant he saw her bathe and watched her fondle her breasts. To have him there meant the soothing trail of a finger up her thigh was his.

His touch calmed her, and she shivered, squeezing her eyes shut. *Zetar forgive me, I need his help.* She refused to look for him, trusting he was an illusion if he didn't forsake her in her time of need.

Her robe came undone, pooling beside her as his touch rose higher. "I missed you too, little doe."

A hot, hard body pushed hers deeper into the bed, and she opened her eyes, parting her mouth on a gasp. "Rukk?"

He claimed her lips with a desperation she recognized and reciprocated. Moaning, she flung her arms around him, thrusting her tongue in to duel his. Oh, the taste of him was heaven-sent—spicy, hot, and masculine. She couldn't breathe but didn't care, not with joy and pleasure mingling to vibrate through her and hold the agony at bay.

"Of all the welcomes I imagined, this was better, Thugari. I want to hold you, to taste every inch of your beautiful body." He feathered kisses down her throat and along her collarbone, his fingers lowering to cup her breasts. When he circled her nipples with his thumbs, she cried out, arching into his touch, writhing until his hips nestled between her thighs. Something delicious uncoiled there. Whatever it was kept the pain at bay. She wasn't going to look a gift horse in the mouth.

"What news of the sigil?" she asked, scraping her nails down his back.

He shivered, hissing with pleasure when she did it again.

Releasing a slow breath, he held his temple to hers. "Arch-Magus Erwana found an entry written by her previous superior. She recalls applying the sigil to your neck, taking the pain onto herself, and altering its conditions. She didn't reveal much but to say the power to unravel it lies in your hands. Also, she pressed a daylily between the pages as if it held significance."

"The wildflowers around Haraton? I would gather them and pretend a gallant beau had given them to me." She smiled, recalling the childish fantasy. "I was foolish and hopeful when I was young."

"Do they trigger a memory?" He swept her hair away from her face to feather his thumbs over her eyebrows.

"Only one. I used to sing a song about them.

Daylily, so yellow and light,

Cast thine beauty on my plight.

Where rivers and freedom flow,

So shall the mountains and my soul grow."

Cold swept through her as if a wave of water drenched her from her toes to her head. A daylily-sweet breeze swept her hair off her temples. Squeezing her eyes shut against the amulet's blinding glow, she arched off the bed on a keen, unable to hold back as the agony climbed, crested, and plummeted. The rippling energy under her skin subsided. The shuddering lessoned.

Sinking into the mattress, she sighed and cupped his cheek, relishing the weight of him on top of her.

She almost giggled at the sense of weightlessness. The intensity that had bothered her over the last few days pooled lower.

"Cursed hell." He trembled, drawing in sharp breaths. His face twisted as if he were in bliss-filled pain. "Holy Zetar, Thugari, you're beautiful." He leaned back to run his fingers to a breast before brushing his palm back and forth over a nipple.

A tremor tore through her, eliciting a deep moan. Her nipple shriveled to stone, and she was unable to slow or halt the bombardment of addictive sensations.

"What did you do?" She clung to him as wave after wave of pleasure rippled across her body. She thrust her hips at his, seeking relief of some kind, or that delicious ache from before. She burned where their bodies touched, and the sensitivity of her skin was unbearable, as was the throbbing in her core. "Am I dying, Rukk?"

"No, little one." He trailed a finger lower, running it along the seam between her legs. The spike of heat was too much, and she gripped his hand as if to stop his caresses. He ignored her, dipping a finger into her. She whimpered, releasing his wrist when he rubbed a bundle of nerves she didn't know existed.

"Please." She would beg, paw at his arms if only he eased this aching intensity.

He shifted position, more fingers coming to play, and joy slammed into her, bowing her off the bed. Unrelenting, he circled those fingers until she couldn't form words, could only react. She gaped at him, amazed at what his touch could do. When he sucked a nipple into his mouth, she cried out, unable to bear more of his onslaught.

"Look at me, Thugari."

She did, drowning in his obsidian gaze as she climbed a mountain, the height of her hips mimicking the rise. He chuckled and scraped his teeth over the nipple he tormented. It was too much, and she catapulted off the precipice, screaming and panting his name as she thrashed. Tremors hovered below the lingering sweet ecstasy, but he didn't remove his fingers. He remained still, watching her return to Kethil, to the bed, and his arms.

Stumbling away from her, he stripped off his garments and threw them aside in wild disarray. She laughed, which faded when he stood before her, the moonlight kissing his contours. He was beautiful and aroused, like a rutting horse she had seen in the stables.

She stroked a finger along the bobbing length, and when she reached the tip, dew gathered there. Hissing, he grabbed her hand and pushed her back onto the bed. He followed, nestling between her thighs while he captured her mouth for a kiss.

As distracting as tasting him was, nothing could compare to the hardness at the juncture of her thighs. She gyrated her hips, trying to find the sweet spot from earlier.

"Please." He gripped her hips. "You're making it harder for me, little doe."

"I am?" she asked, snatching a kiss from him.

"I want to pleasure you more before I take you. It will hurt."

"I'm not a stranger to pain, Rukk. If you promise it won't hurt for long, then take me." Wrapping her legs around him, she swirled her hips, licking her upper lip as she did so. His hard cock teased at her entrance, and she moaned, pleased with herself for having found the spot.

"Sweet Zetar." Trembling, he summoned his magic and held his glowing palm to her abdomen. Then he spread her thighs wide, gazing at the most private part of her body. Unwanted heat engulfed her face, but she didn't care at the moment, as long as he didn't stop.

He pressed something hard into her, and she bit her lip. Gripping her hips to hold her still, he retreated, then dipped in again. Until, with one thrust, he buried himself, his hips touching the backs of her thighs.

She whimpered as fire wrenched her pelvis despite his magic. He lowered his chest to hers to feather kisses across her lips, teasing her nipples until lust claimed her mind. She undulated her hips needing more of this wonderful sense of unity. This time, when he withdrew and thrust again, lightning licked at her core. She arched into him, unable to control her reactions.

Bliss enflamed her senses with each plunge until she thrashed beneath him. The mountain she climbed was recognizable, but more intimate now that she shared it with him. She didn't wait long, plummeting over the edge as his thrusts intensified. He roared, his hips twitching where he pinned them to her thighs. Pleasurable pain morphed his handsome features, mesmerizing her, as did the joy warming his eyes.

"You're mine, little doe. Let no male touch you but me," he said before collapsing on the bed beside her.

Resting his head on his hand, he traced lazy patterns across her abdomen, circling her breasts, up her throat to tap her chin. He dipped his head for a kiss, this one softer, lingering as if he liked the taste of her. She snuggled into the curve of his body with the weight of his arm pinning her.

"Why do I find you with my father?" he whispered the question as if he dreaded the answer.

"I mentioned you in passing, and he demanded to know how you were."

Rukk snorted. "Like he cares, Thugari. Did he tell you why I left Ghorza?"

She nodded, rubbing her cheek across his chest. "You wanted to travel, and he rejected your request." He gasped, but she held her forefinger to his lips. "I didn't believe him."

"That's my Thugari." He smiled, but sadness pooled in his eyes. "The reason why I want nothing to do with him is because he killed my mother, Celaena."

CHAPTER THIRTY-FIVE

His hypocritical father slaughtered his mother as if she were common chattel. That was what Rukk told Thugari. Fated to mate since birth, neither loved the other. They took lovers, searching for love in the wrong places, and he couldn't fault them. Yet there was one rule—no one they both knew.

When his father discovered Borgakh's brother in Celaena's arms, he had ordered the Kurdan to execute them both. Keryn, sworn to serve the king in all things, performed his duty, but not without suffering. The order had devastated the Yerug family, with Borgakh hating her father. She abandoned Ghorza as Rukk had.

Why his father needed to see him now, he didn't care. Rukk had renounced his right to the throne. He would never return as prince or king, no matter what his father said.

The drums of the Iomhar thundered in the distance, announcing their impending arrival. The rumble had woken Rukk, now bathed in contentment with Thugari sleeping curled into him. So much had happened since he last saw her, and as those thoughts and memories circled his mind, he would change none of it. He was where he needed to be.

Sneaking into his father's camp challenged him less than discovering her pacing in her tent. The darkness had been no obstacle to his elven eyes. In those unguarded moments, his doe's robe parted to reveal her nudity to his starving gaze.

She lifted her hair off her neck, thrusting out her pebbled breasts as if she yearned for his touch. He had strangled the moan tearing his throat when she bathed and fondled her breasts spread out for his enjoyment. Never a more wanton vision had he seen. When in the rutting throes, he participated and hadn't had the opportunity to watch a female's passionate movements from afar. That it was Thugari made it sweeter.

Without unraveling the sigil, he couldn't fulfill this need to be one with her. The spell required a word or a phrase as well as a blood sacrifice. Perhaps he could have sliced her palm, but the victim's virginity and high emotions prevented the spell from reforming. It was why she could sing the song as a child without breaking the sigil. When she tilted her head and the ethereal quality of her voice pierced him, blurring his vision, tightening his muscles, it confirmed his assessment.

Potent magic arched her body off the bed, and a soft light traveled under her skin toward her sigil. The Stone Cage was almost unraveled. All that was needed was her blood sacrifice. He could love her as he dreamed of doing.

Tendrils of unseen magic—not her siren's call, but older, wilder, perhaps formed in the beginning of time, with no sound and no stirring of the air but the scent of vanilla, bathed him in heat, setting his senses alight. Love and need slammed into him. His nipples pebbled and burned, so tight were they. Any movement she made, her hips rising, her breath shuddering, and her mewling cries for fulfillment spiked his arousal, building a crescendo to unknown heights.

Her soul reached out to his.

He kissed her hair, tightening his arm around her. She shifted, rising from the depths of slumber, and that same fragrance filled his nostrils, his lungs, and seeped into his skin. What she invoked in him intensified with each moment spent in her presence. A bliss so pure consumed him. This must be happiness he was feeling.

She scraped her fingers down his abdomen, feathering back and forth across the hairs below his bellybutton. Close to touching his eager cock resting on his stomach, but she didn't, torturing a deepening, aching need within him. After pressing kisses to his chest, along his jaw, and lips, she fell back with a sigh. The amulet shifted with her movements. He far preferred seeing his medallion resting between her breasts.

"Morning. I thought I dreamed your return." Her smile faded, and she squeaked, jumping away to throw at him a clothing item—a boot. He caught it but let it fall to the floor. "You have to go. Your father will come for you." She darted around the room, gathering his garments to her chest. Rukk grinned, rising on his elbows to watch her swaying hair brush her backside and her breasts bounce every time she bent to pick up an item.

He laughed. "Thugari, come back to bed."

She spun, her hair arcing around her like the tail of a celestial star. "But, Rukk, your father—"

"Let's not waste a moment on him." He held out his hand, his expectation clear. She dumped his things on the rug and slipped her fingers across his palm. Stunned, he didn't close his hold on her when she sashayed toward him, her curves and sheer femininity stealing his breath.

Coming to his senses, he yanked her onto the bed, sprawling her once more across his body. Her yelp of surprise preceded a giggle, and he snatched a kiss. One wasn't enough, could never satiate his need for her. He nipped and nibbled on her lips, flicking his tongue to soothe while burying his fingers in her hair.

She fluttered her hands up his arms to cup his neck as she tasted him, shared her life's breath with him. He trailed a path along the graceful arch of her back to knead her backside. On a gasp, she parted her legs and crawled on top of him, seating her core across his cock. The unbearable heat of her scorched him, tempting him to grip her hips, lift her, and plunge into her.

"Are you sore?" He pulled back from her lips, concern cooling his ardor enough to form words. "Did I harm you?"

"You'll harm me if you don't ease this ache, Rukk." She snagged his mouth again, trailing her fingertips down his chest, scraping her nails across his nipples. He hissed as lust's bite slammed into him. He flipped her so her back was to his torso, and with eager fingers, he stroked her seam. Her breath seized, then gushed out of her in a tortured moan.

"Why is my doe so needy, so wet?" He chuckled as he circled her bundle of nerves. Her hips gyrated, rubbing her delicious backside across his cock. "Come for me, then I will take you, dear one."

"Come for you? You say that as if I can command it." She glared at him, but her fury morphed into need and whispered pleas.

He captured a taut nipple between his fingers, drawing another cry from her. Releasing her, he pinched her chin, directing her mouth to meet his. She was sweet, growing more so with every kiss. He didn't cease the twirling of his fingers, teasing and tormenting her as he sipped from her lips. The scent of her arousal permeated the room, engulfing him in a world where he lost control amid the haze of lust.

If the Iomhar drums hadn't ceased, if the war with the Ravenous Dark wasn't on the horizon, he would remain here with her for an eternity. With a flick of his finger, she screamed, her pleasure drenching his fingers as she ground her backside against him. He was ready, had been so since he had awoken.

Sighing, she flipped onto her side, pressing those lush breasts across his chest. He needed something more today, something to remember as he battled to save Kethil, to save her. He flipped her onto her back, positioned his cock's head at her entrance, and with one thrust, buried himself to the hilt. His groan deafened his ears for a moment, his hearing returning to her chanting his name, her voice rasping, circling the pounding of his heart.

Withdrawing, he thrust again, ensuring the length of him stroked the depth of her. With each plunge, tingles intensified, rushing from his neck to his nipples, to the base of his spine, and nestled in his balls.

He grunted, striving to climb the mountain at a steady pace when his cock demanded he race for the summit. With a shake of his head, he denied this even as his cock won.

A roar shredded his throat as waves of heat, joy, and bliss flooded his senses. It was then their heartbeats synchronized. With his hips pinning her thighs, he stilled, drowning in her silver gaze. She couldn't be his valthyra. It wasn't possible unless Zetar blessed him with the other half of his soul. Or, he had taken matters into his hands and chosen for himself.

Falling beside her, he gathered her into his arms, the cooling perspiration on her body merging with his, uniting them for a moment longer. Thugari as his valthyra would explain so much. His unusual desire for her, his inability to control himself around her, his impulsive life bond, or his over protectiveness.

He brushed a damp tendril off her cheek. If she loved him, her siren's call wouldn't affect him.

Scowling, he flicked the blanket over her as a male entered the tent. Furak? Despite the joy at seeing his old friend, he hated that he had entered without permission while Thugari lay exposed.

"The king summons you both." Furak spun to face the entrance, granting them his back in respect and for decency. Such care was for Thugari, for males weren't ashamed of nudity.

"Me?" she squeaked, then glared at Rukk. "I told you to leave."

"Fear not, little one." He dropped a kiss onto her button nose. "Grant us a few minutes to prepare," he said to Furak, who left the tent as quickly as he slipped in.

She cast the blanket aside, scrambling off him while the echoes of joy still lingered.

"You can still run." She hurried to his pile of garments. "He's kept me hostage, Rukk. That's not a sign of a sane person."

"I shall face my father, more so with you by my side." He rose, striding to the washbowl, and grimaced at the soap-scummed water. "Furak, send for water."

"Very well, my prince."

Rukk cupped Thugari's face, silencing her grumbles with a kiss. "I want you to remain here when we fight the Ravenous Dark. I want you safe."

She shook her head. "I planned to travel to Tarid's cottage. You can meet me there."

"No, here, near me, yet safe, surrounded by the finest warriors in Kethil." He scowled, gliding his hands down her back to pull her into an embrace. "I don't want to chase you all over Kethil again." He stroked the amulet nestled between her breasts, then lifted it in a smooth motion. She cried out, grabbing his hands. He chuckled. "Thugari, sweetheart, your sultry singing unraveled the sigil last night."

"It did?" She gaped and released his hands, trusting him.

She did so with such ease. They had come so far since they first met with her climbing out of her window to avoid him. He draped the amulet onto the bed and claimed her lips. Words of love tangled his tongue, eager to be spoken. Perhaps now—

A cough broke the kiss, and a glance at the entrance revealed Furak hadn't violated their privacy again.

Rukk scooped up last night's discarded robe and slipped it onto Thugari, trailing a finger from her collarbone to her cleavage. He snatched his hand away and left her to do the ties. "Enter, Furak."

Chapter Thirty-Six

Thugari tightened her grip on Rukk's hand as he led her into his father's tent. Dwarves, dark-humans, and orcs crowded the limited space with the king at the center. She gritted her teeth and followed him. They would be discussing strategy, and she had no need to be here anymore than on the cursed battlefield. He gained nothing but a distraction by flaunting his dalliance with a dark-human. No, that was her anger talking.

Perhaps he didn't want to be separated from her.

She fought for air, to calm her erratic heartbeat. He faltered, pressing a hand to his chest as if his heart also misbehaved. He threw a sinful smile at her, his gaze traveling over her face to linger on her lips.

"Later," he mouthed.

The tent fell silent as he squeezed through those gathered, stopping in front of his father. His rigid shoulders and furrowed brow conveyed his emotions. Here wasn't a joyous reunion. Horknuth ignored Rukk's displeasure and hugged him, his greeting warm as expected of a father.

Against one side of the tent stood Borgakh, Nenneg, and a scowling Keryn. Nenneg rippled her fingers in a wave, and Borgakh grinned.

Thugari peeked at Keryn, wondering how he could serve a king who had instructed him to murder his son. It must have cost the male so much, to pit his honor against the life of his son.

"I see my lure worked," King Horknuth said, bringing Thugari's attention back to him.

"Well done, King Horknuth. I am here, but not for you." Rukk's tone was cutting and cold. Murmurs rippled through the tent.

A touch at her elbow gained her attention. An orc held out a chair for her. She hesitated, not sure whether it was protocol to sit before the king did.

A dwarf nudged the male out of the way and offered her his horn of mead. Another offered his cloak, as if she shivered from the cold. Three-quarters of the tent stared at her, ignoring the interaction between the king and his son. Some of them didn't blink and most had lopsided smiles on their faces.

Cursed hell, it was happening again, but now in full view of everyone. Visitors to her tent baring gifts and controlled by the guard were one thing.

Panic muddled her thoughts. This was exactly why Tarid's cottage made sense.

She tightened her grip on Rukk's hand and looped an arm through his, needing his strength. Borgakh sniggered, so Nenneg poked her with an elbow. Keryn would be furious with Thugari for disrupting the session. But his expression was soft, doting with his gaze fixed on her. Moon above, not the male who had tried to kill her just a few days ago.

"You have my amulet?" Mòr shoved males aside to reach the front.

"Furak, collect it from our tent," Rukk said, drawing a squeak from Thugari. She raised a desperate gaze to his where a smile waited for her. "I would say your siren's call is in full effect."

"What?" Groaning, she faced the king, prepared to apologize. She had chosen another robe out of respect for Rukk, but wished she had donned her breeches and boots instead. Running with skirts would hinder her movement, and the urge to escape had her in its grip.

"Ah, so Rukk spoke the truth," King Horknuth said. "I am told many have visited you bearing gifts. Your name is on my warriors' tongues, Thugari." He inhaled until it looked as if his chest would explode. "You alluring scent has deepened, dark one. Is this how you convinced my son to abandon his lawbringer duties?" He chuckled, but it was devoid of humor. "Much can be said for the fine curves of a female."

A few of the observers laughed, one or two dwarves guffawed, but Rukk pulled Thugari against his body. The frantic ticking at the base of his jaw was a warning for those who paid attention.

She stared at it, disbelieving her thundering heartbeat aligned with his. "She's my valthyra, but I don't expect you to honor it. You know nothing of such matters."

His what? She frowned, peering under her eyelashes at him.

The king flicked a dismissive wrist. "Impossible. You're a noble orc with ancient elven blood flowing in your veins and a prince of Ghorza."

"I am nothing but the son of an elf. I serve the Council and Grand Lawmaster Larza." Rukk faced the room and bowed his head to those gathered in the tent. "I return the discussion to the matter at hand. Please forgive our intrusion."

He led her to Nenneg, leaving Thugari there but greeted Keryn with a barrel hug.

Borgakh nudged her, looping an arm around Thugari's shoulders to drag her closer. Borgakh pointed out the key members, whispering their names, and humorous character traits such as Aonghas having an itchy backside, which was why he never stood still.

Thugari smothered a giggle behind her hand, picking out the fidgeting Iomhar dwarf with ease. Rukk assumed a position behind a dwarf lawbringer, but throughout the intense discussions, the determination hardening his features would soften every time he looked at her.

Sometimes he would bless her with a smile. If anyone asked her opinion on the strategy decided that day, words would elude her. With her heart thrumming, she let her love for a lawbringer warm her.

Rukk slowed his breathing, willing his thrumming heart to calm. If he smiled at Thugari one more time, he would throw her over his shoulder and flee this oppressive tent.

He wanted to pretend there was no impending battle, to bask in her sweetness and sultry voice, and to confess his love for her. He grimaced, squaring his shoulders to talk of strategy.

"The plan is to tease the Ravenous Dark's servants out into the open. Within the caves of Chaosthane, they're superior." Iomhar Seumas nodded at his wizened companions, Aonghas and Ìacob.

Gray drenched their thick and long beards. The dwarves stood side-by-side, and behind them hovered the Geàrdan, the heart of the dwarven people.

"My army shall bolster King Horknuth's." King Shertur acknowledged all present, but his admiring gaze lingered on Rukk's father.

Tall, bronzed, with gold streaking his hair, Shertur was the perfect representation of an Atrarian. His tunic and breeches were simple in comparison to Horknuth's silken robes, yet the gold thread woven into the sleeves and collar, along with the jewels stitched to the sides of his breeches, spoke of wealth.

When Shertur was but a prince, he and Rukk had trained under Keryn. Horknuth had taken a keen interest in the handsome Atrarian, but Rukk hadn't thought their affair would span decades. The mysterious death of Shertur's father had led to the crowning of Shertur as King of Atrar.

It wouldn't surprise Rukk if Horknuth had a hand in this.

"You have given this much thought." Larza bowed to the Iomhar. "Lawbringers shall enter the caves. It is what we train for. We can fight without using magic."

"Agreed, my magi have prepared for this day." Erwana stood with rigid shoulders alongside Larza, both representing a united Council.

"Still, the unanswered I must ask," Iomhar Iàcob said. "How do we kill the Dark for good? Kethil has dealt with the Ravenous Dark before, but there is no mention in our annals on how they succeeded."

"We must document this event for future generations." Erwana clasped her hands in front of her.

"Or we eradicate the threat for all time." King Horknuth withdrew an elven dagger Rukk recognized. It was the weapon his mother's father had given Horknuth on their day of union.

Iomhar Seumas snorted. "You know how, King Horknuth?"

His disrespect and disbelief brought a scowl to his father's smug features. "The Ravenous Dark threatens *my* world as well, dwarf. Do not test me. We discovered an obscure text, magic as ancient as your disrespect." He tossed the dagger to the floor. It shimmered, a glow forming around it as if the sun shone from within. "Speak the words and sunlight imbues any iron weapon with light. This is the antithesis to the dark, is it not?"

"Is it hot to the touch?" Larza knelt beside the dagger, extending a hand to hover above the metal.

"It removes all enchantments," Horknuth said by way of response.

"We are to entrust our weapons to this in the hopes it will defeat the Dark?" Iàcob twitched and gripped his ax hilt.

Rukk dropped his hand onto his shoulder, shaking his head. Iàcob released a sharp breath and lowered his arm. Every orc warrior guarding Horknuth shuffled into their vigilant positions. Allowing weapons into his presence said much of his father's concern.

"What you choose to do is up to you." Not an expression crossed the king's face. "My armies have prepared. The Ravenous Dark steals the sunlight or have you not noticed the spreading crimson clouds, a foreboding of what is to come?"

"Lawbringers will supply weapons for this blessing," Larza said.

"Our staves are not applicable, but perhaps what daggers we have?" Erwana un-sheathed a dagger from her boot, exposing the delicate curve of an ankle. She flipped the blade, offering the hilt to Horknuth.

His father accepted it, spun it on his palm to test its weight before returning it to Er-wana. "Hand over all your weapons to Furak. He will ensure they receive the enchantment and will return them to you. We strike at the witching hour."

Seumas stuttered, his voice hindered by his hand stroking his beard. "In the dark?"

"How else do we lure them out of the caves, my dear Seumas?" Horknuth raised his gaze to the group. "Lure them into our waiting armies."

"My males can see in the dark," King Shertur said. "It would be best to send in our own to bolster those brave enough to venture into the caves." He held up a hand when Horknuth would speak. "Not all of the Dark's servants will fall for the lure. We must plan for both occurrences."

"I agree." Rukk earned a scowl from his father. "This war could end in hours or years. Tossing the bulk of our armies into the first foray is foolhardy. Send the inexperienced to circle the mountains. There must be more than two entrances."

"Agreed." Horknuth nodded at Keryn.

"Never has the Ravenous Dark manipulated those in power. As you are aware, it corrupted our Grand Lawmaster Galand and Lawmaster Janar Inaris. I suggest you assess your leaders and confirm their sanity is intact." Larza ran his gaze across the fidgeting Iomhar. "It was during his visit to you he succumbed."

Gasps of surprise and outrage spiked the air.

Rukk threw his hands out, asking for silence and understanding. "Grand Lawmaster Larza is requesting an assessment, nothing more."

"We would know by now," Mòr said, but concern and fear saturated her voice.

"Had we discovered the truth sooner, Janar Inaris would not have died. Who else might need saving?" Larza scanned the room with unflinching regard. "Who else has had contact with the Ravenous Dark and has the courage to admit it?"

"Only those who know you well can reveal the corruption." Erwana's voice, echoing with sorrow, sliced through the rumblings of displeasure. "Had I reacted with more decisiveness, I might have saved Venec."

"Very well, in honor of Venec Galand, the sixteenth Grand Lawmaster, we will assess our leaders." Mòr bowed her head at Erwana, King Horknuth, and King Shertur before exiting the tent.

CHAPTER THIRTY-SEVEN

"I INSIST YOU LET me leave." Thugari thumped the table, trembling the goblets on it. "I'll be safe far from the mountain."

Rukk shot out a hand to rescue his wine. "I need you near." He rose to grip her shoulders, urging her to sit. "Stay, please."

Sheathing his glowing sword at his hip, Rukk remembered the tortured expression on her face. He was confident he had reached through to her, that she waited for him within her tent.

Yet knowing her tendencies to endanger herself, he found the youngest Ghorzan warrior and tasked him to guard her, content to believe he saved the male's life.

Rukk tightened the straps on his armguards, checked each dagger hidden on his person, and adjusted the crossbow holstered to his back. Tarid stood alongside him, readying himself for battle. They would venture into the cave together with Sharn trailing him.

Trusting her to protect them revealed how far their relationship had progressed. She had spied on them, as per Erwana's instructions, but now, when Sharn leaned across to kiss Tarid, Rukk saw the good in her. After how she had been there for Tarid, healing his wounds and anchoring him through his grief, Rukk wondered why he'd judged her harshly before.

"We have thirty teams of lawbringers entering various caves, Tarid. Alongside them are dwarves, orcs, and Atrarians." Rukk rolled his shoulders. "I am confident, lawbrother, this will end by daybreak."

"How many servants could the Ravenous Dark have?" Tarid's chuckle was dismissive.

"Koveen, wylders, and there are sightings of shedaji in full-armor." Sharn ran a cloth over her staff, polishing the wood until it gleamed.

"Shedaji? Aren't they myth?" Tarid stole her cloth to polish his sword.

"Atrarians have sharp eyes." She arched a brow. "Flocks of them arrived two days past. How the Dark gathered them to its cause, I don't know."

"A head of a human, a winged body of a lion?" Rukk shrugged. One dead creature was like another. "For them, the sharp edge of our sword will do."

Sharn huffed. "My point is, there is an army in those caves. Not to mention the usual hazardous terrain—cliffs, bottomless lakes, and such."

"Is no one mentioning dreshnies or eikusais?" Tarid sheathed his sword and looped an arm around Sharn's waist, pulling her against him. She thumped him on the chest and snatched her cloth back.

"None of our scouts have returned." Rukk scowled, admitting they were facing an unknown force with nothing but their wits and their glowing weapons. "If only we could split those mountains open, drench its innards with sunlight, and forever end—"

"Millions of innocent species," she said.

"Millions?" Tarid scoffed.

"Mushrooms, moss, algae, bats, snakes, and insects, to name a few." She ticked them off on her elegant fingers.

"Their loss is preferable to all of Kethil succumbing to the Dark," Rukk said. "If you could create an opening large enough to let in sunlight, I'll have the lawbringers plant mirrors to light the way."

"No need, magi can create indestructible mirrors." She grinned.

"There is a crevice near the Peaks of Gill-Eòin, and with a well-placed explosion, we can open it wider." Mòr entered their circle. "It's best to send dwarves since we know these mountains well." She flashed a smile. "As miners, we like to blow things up."

"We need to keep them busy for a few hours until dawn, then flood the darkness with light. It's possible," Rukk said. "Inform your people. We can fall back on this should these weapons or the lure fail."

"You are forgetting one thing, Rukk Knaraugh." Mòr raised her forefinger. "Chaosthane doesn't tolerate magic."

"Cursed hell." Sharn slumped. "Our presence would be pointless. We're reliant on those without magic, and most of them cannot fight."

"How can the Dark exist then, Mòr? Is it not a sort of magic?" Tarid sat on a crate in slumped defeat.

"It is an ancient magic, birthed into existence when Kethil formed. Our ancestors created wards to protect the mountains from today's magic. We lost the skill to weave magic since then." Mòr shrugged but twisted in despair.

"Physical mirrors and an exploded crevice will still work," Rukk said.

"Yes, but how many mirrors can we find in Dussoum? Light only travels so far, and not past solid obstacles like caves within caves. They can hide." Sharn waved her hand in front of her lit staff, blocking its white light.

"It would diminish some of the Dark's forces," Tarid said. "Any help is better than nothing."

"Don't the magi have knowledge of such magic?" Mòr asked.

"You want us to unravel the wards?" Sharn shook her head. "Orc magi are more powerful than humans or Atrarians, but we don't dabble in ancient powers. Our chronicles carry no such teachings." She snuffed her staff, leaned it against the crate, and climbed onto Tarid's lap.

Kissing her temple, he raised his head to ask, "What about Thugari?"

"What about her?" Rukk frowned, not liking where Tarid's thoughts were heading.

"You know what I mean to ask, Rukk. Can her magic not enter the cave?"

"And have her do what?" Rukk's chest burned hot as anger gripped him.

"A siren—"

"Do not speak it, Tarid Inaris." He lunged, raising a fist in warning. Tempted to punch Tarid in the face, he had to swallow the urge since Sharn was in the way.

"She's the only female here with ancient magic. I could help her." Sharn tilted her head in thought. "We can train her to use her powers."

"She's a siren, not a magi. She's not entering that mountain." Rukk glared at each person around the fire. He'd rather she traveled to Tarid's cottage than put her in the line of fire.

"She doesn't have to." Mòr stroked her stubbled chin. "What if we escort her to the crevice on top of the mountain?"

"She can't create mirrors. It's foolhardy to imply such a thing." Rukk scoffed, fighting the fear strangling his throat and squeezing the air out of his lungs.

His heartbeat pounded in his ears, engulfing the surrounding noise and muffling it. What Tarid had said was the truth. Perhaps Thugari's ancient power could speak to another just as old? They'd never had an opportunity to try.

Rukk winced. But letting her go would place her beyond his protection.

"What about water? The caves have lakes and rivers." Mòr flashed a delighted grin. "Can she enchant the water to rise and flush out or drown those inside the mountains?"

He chuckled, but it sounded high-pitched. "Enchant water? Do you hear yourself, Mòr?"

"Can't we at least test her to see if she has it within her or if it's possible?" Silence met Sharn's question. "Like this?"

She scooped water from a nearby barrel into an upturned helmet and placed it at her feet. Humming and swirling her fingers, she urged the water to rise out of a helmet, then slosh back into it when she pulled in her magic.

Rukk released a jarring breath and nodded. Let them see for themselves his Thugari couldn't do this. With how inexperienced she was, teaching her to use her magic before she reached the crevice was an impossibility.

Sharn scrambled off Tarid's lap, hurrying to fetch Thugari. No one spoke while they waited, all busying themselves with the preparations. When she entered the clearing, need, adoration, fear slammed in Rukk's chest, snatching his breath. He couldn't lose her, and he would in cursed hell not allow her to partake in this war.

"Sharn said you needed me?" She peered into the helmet, her arched brow reflected there.

"The mountains don't allow our magic, but they might accept yours." Sharn trailed her fingers down Thugari's forearm and gripped her wrist to raise her hand, hovering it over the helmet.

Thugari laughed, the sound bright, joyful, and seductive amid the readying encampment, dazzling him for a moment. "I can't cast spells, and I don't think I can control magic if it's in me."

"Try, please," Mòr said.

Thugari sighed, then straightened her arm and concentrated.

Rukk smiled, wondering what he had to fear. She was too adorable with her face scrunched and her lips parted. Nothing happened as he expected, but the dejected droop of her shoulders sliced through his fear.

He wouldn't let this destroy what confidence she had found. Part of him wanted her magic to fail, to keep her safe. The other saw her as their salvation or at least a pivotal tool in their strategy.

"Sing to it," he urged. "As if it were me."

A pink hue splashed across her cheeks, and her admiring gaze traveled the length of him, spiking warmth through his heart. With a sensual smile, she closed her eyes and sang. Silence fell across their clearing again, but this time in awe. She glowed with life, love, and everything worth fighting for. Her hair moved as if a wind caressed her neck and face.

Dragging his gaze to the water, he scowled. The surface shimmered, swirled, rose, and climbed the sides of the helmet toward her outstretched fingers. The fate of Kethil in the hands of his valthyra twisted sorrow in his chest like a plunging dagger.

"Look, little one." He kept his tone soft to not disturb her singing.

She obeyed. There before him, glowing in their gray depths of her eyes, was the Ire of Silver—a swirling silver pulsing with power. Her father had blessed her with something of worth, at last.

Her singing faltered as she gaped. The water sloshed inside the helmet. The gathering sat in stunned silence, then babbled as one. Unable to bear the distance between them, Rukk gathered her into his arms, guiding her face to the crook of his neck. She burrowed into him, her need for comfort tightening his embrace.

"The Geàrdan will escort her," Mòr said. "Guards will journey with us, not only to protect Thugari, Rukk, but also to carry the supply of explosives. Let's drown the Ravenous Dark's servants, then flood them with light by day."

"I'll speak to Larza about sending a contingent of lawbringers to Dussoum to purchase mirrors and other reflective surfaces like shields," Tarid said. "Some should stay to guard the Gates."

"She needs to practice, to strengthen her powers. A few hours won't do much, but she's all we have. I will travel with to bolster her energy or...heal her, as needed." Sharn clung to Tarid as if in farewell.

"We leave now. The journey is two hours to Dussoum, and from the base of the mountains, we'll climb the Donaidh steps on foot." Mòr hurried off, not glancing back.

Darkness circled Rukk's vision, and he struggled to control the urge to throw Thugari over his shoulder and bolt. He had lost control of the situation and his ability to protect her. "Do you want to do this?" Cupping her cheeks, he buried his fingers in her hair.

"If it helps, then yes, but...I'm just a bastard daughter, Rukk."

"Who carries her mother's magic and the influence of the moon, Thugari. As you stand here, your eyes shimmer from gray to silver. Nehrakgu is an ancient lineage, aligned with the moon and its power. While some are rejuvenated by the elements, soil, air, sun, you embrace the night.

"It must have skipped a few generations, for I sensed no such power at Haraton castle. Perhaps your father saw your potential early on and panicked. Your sigil smothered it and your mother's siren ways." Crushing Thugari in a hug, Rukk pressed his lips to her temple before pulling away. "I wish it was otherwise. It's killing me to let you go." Uncaring that others watched, he kissed her, savoring the sweetness of her mouth, and her warmth saturating his body through his armor. "I would do anything for this not to be true, but they're right, we need you." Releasing a long sigh, he tugged out his medallion. He palmed it once then slipped it off.

She jerked back, shaking her head. "No, you need your medallion. I have Sharn if things go...bad."

Bad? He raised his gaze to the stained sky. It took everything in him not to crush her against him again and confess his love. "Please, wear this for me."

Gripped in his palm, he offered her more than protection—he held out his heart.

She stared into his eyes for the longest moment, her teeth worrying her bottom lip, then she nodded. After slipping it on, he tucked it into her robe, stroking his fingers along the silkiness of her skin. His fingers twitched, revealing his need to keep her near, but Rukk allowed Sharn to drag Thugari out of his embrace. The whipping of her hair was the last glimpse he had of her.

Chapter Thirty-Eight

A VIOLENT GUST SPIRALED snow upward as it slammed Thugari against the rock wall, banging her temple on a jagged edge. She winced but didn't remove her hands from the cloak's pockets to ease the throbbing. As she struggled to lift her feet, her cyclical thoughts berated her for agreeing to this. Commanding water was an impossible task. Seducing it even more so, as if it had emotion or its own will. She would snort if she had breath.

Each step trembled her legs and weakened her knees. The icy wind lashing snow at her broke her will to continue. Thank Moon, Mòr had insisted on purchasing thicker garments, yet cold had a way of bypassing the best protection.

Thugari tucked her chin to her chest. The scarf wrapped around her head kept the fur-lined hood from opening and shielded her face. It stank of old tobacco, but she didn't care, not anymore, too grateful for its warmth.

What brought her spirits low wasn't climbing the Donaidh steps up the side of the Peaks of Gill-Eòin. It wasn't her friends' dependency on her to wield magic she had only yesterday kindled into existence.

What had the snow freezing escaped tears to her lashes was bidding Gnash farewell, along with Borgakh and Nenneg, who promised to care for him. This silly task *would* fail, killing them all. Legions would die all because she couldn't seduce water. Yes, the water in the helmet had swished. The memory replayed in disbelief. But that was a cup's worth, not a mountain full of lakes and rivers going who knew how deep.

She halted, sucking in calming breaths, fighting the urge to turn around. This was foolhardy. Any idiot could see that. The smartest and safest one among the lot of them

238

was Envis, tucked in a warm stable while the dwarven soldiers and lawbringers took formation in front of the Gates of Chaosthane. *Cursed hell.* She found herself in these absurd situations time after time.

"I can't do this," she said, forcing her words through gritted teeth.

"Thugari? Are you well?" Sharn called from ahead.

The blasted orc wasn't even wearing a cloak, standing there as if she were out on a stroll. A soft blue light shimmered around her and snowflakes melted as they touched her aura. Now that was magic worth having. Seduction? The most useless magic this side of Kethil.

"I said...I can't do this." Thugari screamed the words, as if she could project her voice above the howling wind. "I'm nobody."

"You are the female Rukk loves, and he needs you, this."

"Love?" Thugari's laugh was as cold as the snow on her nose. He hadn't said anything, and such a forthright male wouldn't hesitate to state his emotions or intentions. "What will you do when this doesn't go as hoped?" She gestured with a wild flick of her arm, almost unbalancing herself on the narrow and steep stone steps.

She peered over the edge at Dussoum far below. Warm lights shimmered and glowed as if a war wasn't on its doorstep. A pang of longing hit her, cinching her chest, and she spun on her heel, her frozen limbs compelling her to flee.

"We melt the snow and drown them from above. If that fails, we blow up the crevice and fight whatever crawls out of it." Sharn took Thugari by the shoulders and spun her to face forward. "Now walk, you're holding up the line."

She peeked over Sharn's shoulders at the dwarven soldiers carrying crates of explosives. They wore thinner garments than Thugari. She grunted and stomped up the steps, a little energy flowing into her as anger gripped her. Remaining with the dreshnie was preferable to this. She shivered as the chill of haunting memories seeped into her bones. Well, that was a lie.

Her shoulders sagged as truth took hold of her fear. Rukk had saved her from the dreshnie, from Devan, and there she was, whining like an ungrateful bairn. He *did* need her, and whether he loved her or not, she had to try. That was all he had asked her to do.

She yanked her hands out of her pockets and grabbed onto a rock jutting out of the wall. Using it to pull herself forward, she caught up with Mòr as she stepped onto a large ledge.

The wind softened, and Thugari's chapped cheeks burned when nothing lashed at her. "How much farther?" she asked, leaning against the rock wall to catch her breath. Under her cloak, her crossbow dug in her back, but its weight was comforting.

Sharn crossed the platform to where the stairs continued, tilting her head when she peered upward at the trail.

"Another hour." Mòr uncorked her flask, though the scent that reached Thugari was dragon's fire.

The dwarf offered her a taste, but she shook her head, liking her innards as they were. The soldiers grunted as they stepped onto the ledge, setting their crates down before reaching for their wineskins. Behind them struggled Isbeil and Una, collapsing in exhaustion.

Nausea coiled in Thugari's stomach, and she pressed a hand there, hoping to keep the last meal at bay. Niall had served bread and a hearty soup before they departed. It had taken no more than an hour to reach the base of the steps. According to Mòr, five hours was the expected walking time, weather permitting. The light dimmed as the sun plodded on its final journey for the day, taking with it what little warmth lingered. Her breaths huffed a cloud of vapor, and as cold as she was, she dreaded spending the night on the summit.

Without the wind, the mountain was silent, as if it held its breath in anticipation. She didn't know what animals lived in such harsh environments, but at this moment, it was as if nothing could survive up here. She mentioned as much to Mòr, who had dropped to her haunches.

"They sense the Dark and choose to hide. It is best they do. I don't want to fight the Dark *and* a grandl." She shuddered.

"A what?" Thugari arched a brow. By Mòr's horrified reaction, such an occurrence would be a hazardous one.

"It's a massive beast, feeds off rodents, snakes, and the occasional dwarf." She extended her arm still clutching her flask. "Claws from my elbow to my fingertips." She wiggled them for emphasis.

"Stop frightening her. Thugari, grandls exist in Atrar. They grow everything big there." Sharn gestured to the steps, and Thugari shoved off the wall to follow her.

"You would know." Mòr cackled, corked her wineskin, then tucked it onto her belt before starting the final leg of the march.

Thugari pushed herself to keep up. This side of the mountain shielded them from the wind, but also from the last rays of the sun. The temperatures plummeted. Her eyes stiffened as if frozen.

Keeping her palm on the wall, she squeezed them shut. Blessed warmth shot daggers of pain into her skull. Yes, frozen like the rest of her.

She blinked her eyes open and gripped the jutting rock. The faster she climbed, the quicker they could build a fire.

The icy wind slapped her face as she ascended the mountain top. She wobbled, throwing out a hand to steady herself. Snow blanketed the world around her with pearlescent flurries breathtaking against what remained of the velvet sky.

Marring the snow's pristine surface was a jagged crevice, darkness oozing outward. She stared at the black fingers clawing the edge as if the Dark tried to escape. Her breath seized.

The moon dominated the night. Crimson clouds claimed parts of the sky. They bubbled and frothed as if alive. It wouldn't be long until they smothered the moon's silver light. She stumbled after Mòr, her tired feet snagging on the ankle-deep snow. A glance behind her showed her path, where her cloak tried to smooth her tracks.

Dwarves scurried past her, as if nothing hindered their movement. With efficiency, they set up the campsite a distance away from the crevice, using the explosives-filled crates as barriers against the incessant wind. It was senseless protection when one ball of fire would incinerate everything around it.

Sharn's blue flames consumed the wood a soldier unpacked. She chatted to them as she helped them carry smaller crates to stack alongside the crevice.

Thugari closed her eyes to inhale and exhale, listening for her heartbeat. The soldiers' joking among themselves and the Geàrdan squabbling softened until the wind whispered its news, and her heart echoed in the chambers of her chest. She probed her inner core, trying to sense a change, a shift from who she was days ago. Without knowing what magic would feel like, something warm and all-consuming, or a sense of peace with new capabilities and confidence, she was wasting her time.

Pain burst from her thigh, and she yelped, flicking her eyes open to glare at Mòr, who had kicked her, judging by the footprint on her breeches.

"No time to rest. Come." Mòr forged through the snow to lean over the crevice's edge, peering into solid black.

Thugari hadn't imagined it. Ethereal fingers did claw the sides, and a faint hissing reached her ears.

"I suggest you sit or sprawl near here and hope your voice will echo far enough to awaken the waters." Mòr stamped the snow, flattening it where she expected Thugari to lie down.

"Hope? It's insane to base this all on my supposed abilities *and* hope." She rubbed her thigh, staring into the darkness beside the dwarf.

"We do have the explosives, so not everything rests on your shoulders," Mòr said with a dismissive shrug. "If you fail, more of our people will die. Then again, should you succeed, well, Death doesn't like anyone thwarting his harvest."

A hysterical giggle tickled Thugari's throat, and she swallowed it, grimacing instead. "Cursed no matter what I do." She held out her hands to another fire someone had built, praying its warmth reached the marrow of her frozen bones.

"Come, let us begin." Sharn plunged her staff into the ground alongside them, from where it cast a white circle of light.

Between Nenneg's strawberries and Sharn's ability to penetrate the cold, compacted soil, or solid rock, Thugari prayed she could learn to do the same. But she doubted it, like she viewed the success of this task.

"Mòr, guard us. Where my staff's light falls, no evil can enter. Anything else is yours to deal with." Sharn ran her gaze over the Geàrdan, each female unsheathing a yellow-glowing sword the length of Thugari's forearm.

Sharn sprawled on the blanket someone spread out. Thugari followed, sitting with crossed legs an inch from the crevice. Freezing air rose from within, the stench of rotten eggs choking her. Taking a moment to swallow bile, she studied the crevice, trying to see into the shifting shadows.

"Now?" she asked, glancing at Sharn.

Sharn nodded, blessing her with a smile. "Sing, dear Thugari, sing from the soul, spin a tale of woe and life. Entice and enchant the waters to listen, to rise, and drown those who wish harm on us all."

Thugari squeezed her eyes shut, not knowing what to expect but willing to try. Her voice croaked, her throat chilled, but as she sang, she thought of her mother, the lullaby she would serenade Thugari with each night. There, on a mountain, she gave way to her sorrow. She relived her disheartening life under her father's thumb. She sang without words of the joy of freedom, of discovering friendship. Sharn's palm rested on her neck, warmth and healing bolstered Thugari's voice. Sounds of battle reached her ears, but they were from afar, as if she were an observer and the danger not real.

Through it all, she prayed and pleaded to Moon above, and the waters below, to heed her call.

To save Kethil, herself, and Rukk, the male she loved.

Chapter Thirty-Nine

Tarid thumped Rukk on the chest, drawing him from his daze. The sun had set on a few skirmishes with koveen and shedaji striking from the cavern. Attacking, then retreating, proved they knew the armies wouldn't follow them into the mountain. He studied the jagged peaks of Gill-Eòin and the snow-blanketed plateau. Had they made it?

He prayed Thugari was well. His medallion had to heal her. This was such an idiotic plan, placing hope in an untried siren. Her immobile face and fearful eyes tormented him. He arched his back to study the sky. Eerie blood-stained clouds almost consumed the stars. Soon, with the tension in the air thickening to breaking point, the Ravenous Dark would strike.

He spun his sword, dazzled by the golden glow of trapped sunlight glimmering across the iron blade. With his bolts and daggers enchanted, as well, he couldn't help but chuckle when a dwarf pranced around in glowing armor. He could understand the novelty of it. To go from magicless to wielding or wearing enchanted items must delight them. Come morning, in the bright light of hindsight, they might feel otherwise.

"There's a rumbling from within the cave's entrance." Tarid shifted, but Rukk shook his head. "Water or another attack?"

"Too soon. Two hours to Dussoum, one hour there, and five hours up Donaidh steps would be my estimate, that is, if the journey is without peril. Once settled alongside the crevice, Thugari will sing. Whether or not the caverns carry her voice and the waters succumb will determine the success of her task. At the witching hour, Mòr will blow the crevice open, then lead the party down the mountain to Dussoum." He released a breath.

All he had to do was swing his sword. Mòr, Sharn, and Thugari had the most dangerous mission. Not only could the Dark's forces attack them along the journey, but they would need to deal with the wind and snow the higher they climbed. Should it go to plan, they would attack the Ravenous Dark from here and at the gates.

The dwarven army sent soldiers to Dussoum to cover the Gates of Chaosthane alongside lawbringers. Keryn commanded legions of archers to aid them, along with King Shertur's forces. Rukk knew not of other openings, but a mountain this immense had to have more than two. They had yet to hear from the scouts tasked to find crevices, cracks, or caves.

Tarid thumped him on the chest again, nudging his head at the valley. The tumultuous clouds, roiling and expanding, shed its shadow which flew with swift anger across the grounds, and as they watched, it engulfed the moonlight.

Silence hit them—a held breath before the strike. With war cries and wails piercing the night, swarms of shedaji and koveen burst from the mountain's innards. Glowing arrows whistled across the sky, darkening the red light emanating off the clouds.

Rukk spun, raising his sword in front of him, tightening his grip on the hilt.

"Have you seen Borgakh or Nenneg?" he asked Tarid, slicing his blade across the belly of a shedaji.

Its yellow eyes, tainted with the Dark, were coated in black. It clutched its abdomen, its gnarled fingers not stemming its tar-like intestines dribbling out. Its wings flopped long after the final throes of death.

Tarid shrugged. "Not since Sharn and Thugari left. I thought they traveled with."

Rukk scowled. He scanned the podium where his father, Keryn, Shertur, and the Iomhar stood. Borgakh was nowhere near. Something cold cinched his chest, whispering words he had heard in passing. Nenneg had seen the Ravenous Dark, but as a magic-wielder, she couldn't have been inside the mountain. Unless the entrance she discovered didn't have the ancient wards. It was possible. Mountains shifted over time, new tunnels formed, and the ground swallowed caves.

"You can't worry about them now. We have friends to greet." Tarid bellowed an Atrarian battle cry as he plunged his sword into a koveen, right between her breasts.

Rukk unholstered his crossbow to fire at a weaving shedaji. The bolt pierced its chest, dropping the creature to the ground amid tangled wings and squeals. He swung his sword with one hand, slicing across the torso of another koveen.

"Where are the wylders?" Tarid asked, scanning the attacking enemies.

"They won't be among those pouring out of the mountain with their magic. Perhaps they attack at the Gates or…" He froze, raising his eyes to Gill-Eòin as a fresh wave of fear burned through him, coating his tongue with bile.

"The Gates make sense." Tarid swept his sword across his path, then ducked, missing an arrow from a shedaji. Black ichor dripped off his glowing blade, dissolving before it hit the soil.

"It's nearing the witching hour." Rukk wiped the sweat off his brow with his gloved wrist.

They had endangered his valthyra for nothing. It had been too much to ask of Thugari, and if he had listened to her, she would be safe at Banach Cottage by now. At any moment, he expected to see fire and rock explode, up and outward. If he didn't, that would mean the Geàrdan were dead. He tried not to include Sharn and Thugari in that conclusion, tried to imagine them limping down the steps, injured but alive.

"Stop tormenting yourself." Tarid's mental voice breached his thoughts. *"Focus on surviving this and killing as many Ravenous Dark servants as possible. Want to wager?"*

"No." Rukk chuckled. *"Your luck is a magic all on its own."*

Screams from up ahead, nearer to the mountain's yawning mouth, sounded different from war cries and yawps of excitement. This was fear in its purest form. In a wave, his armies fell back, making way for the enemies pouring out. A flash of memory compared the spilled crimson blood spreading and congealing on Venec's floor to the panicking hordes.

Darkness reached out a large hand. The mutterings of a female's voice carried on its undulating contours, hurried and laced with panic. Rukk bolted forward, dodging swinging axes, ducking under sharp blades, and knocking arrows aside with his sword.

"I apologize," he roared when he used the shoulders of a dwarf to leap into the air, slicing his golden blade through the Dark's ethereal limb. A squeal pierced the chaos, and he fell to the ground in a roll, as a wave of water hit him. One moment it drenched him, and the next, the water divided around him.

Rukk, the male my enchantress loves. The water gurgled, surprise and happiness coating its words.

"Enchantress?" Rukk winced. He should be asking if he had died or embraced madness. Water didn't speak. It had no soul.

I am life.

A spray slapped him in the face as if berating him for his disbelief. As an elf, he understood the power lying beneath the soil, in the trees, in the air, and in water. Yet he had never considered water alive and something to commune with. Mòr must have known, which was in itself strange, since dwarves were magicless.

But they had made it their life's work to study magic even though they couldn't practice it.

I have killed as asked and cleansed the caverns. The rest is up to you.

The water subsided, retracting into the mountain and leaving strewn bodies in its wake.

Enemies struggling to their feet met the arrows of the Ghorzan and Atrarian archers. Drowned corpses held grotesque death masks, their mouths gaping from when they took their final breaths.

There wasn't a single wylder among them.

With his boots squishing, Rukk stomped across the sodden soil to the platform, peering up at his father. A grinning Keryn grabbed the intricate railing.

"That was fortuitous," his father said. "Now all we need to do is lure the Ravenous Dark out of the mountain."

Pride engulfed Rukk's chest at his sweet valthyra's success. "That was Thugari's doing. Mòr will open the crevice wider for sunlight to penetrate as far into the mountain as possible. We have mirrors ready to place throughout the mountain to reflect what light reaches them. Leave it for the dwarves and other magicless soldiers to do. Yet I hesitate to command they begin such a task."

"Why?" His father's face was serene, as if so many deaths meant nothing to him.

"Have you seen Borgakh or Nenneg?" Rukk ignored him, facing Keryn instead.

"What troubles you, Rukk?" Horknuth persisted, a slight furrow puckering his brow.

"There are no wylders, and there should be. We hunted them north and killed those we came across." He pursed his lips around his tusks, choosing not to mention hearing water speak its thoughts. "When I sliced through the Ravenous Dark, I heard the mutterings of a female."

"Impossible," Iomhar Iàcob said. "It has all the mannerisms of the Ravenous Dark, as documented in our annals."

"What if the Ravenous Dark has an alliance with wylders?" Iomhar Seamus said, patting Iàcob on the shoulder.

"Regardless, this was too swift an end, the sacrificing of all its pawns in the quest for a bigger prize." Rukk rubbed his temple, his other hand gripping and releasing the hilt of his sword. The black ichor covering the blade sizzled as it plopped into the puddle he stood in. "Where is Erwana and her magi?"

"They're healing the wounded." Keryn flicked a thumb behind him. "Not allowed into the mountain, she tasked her magi to help those in need."

"Did she send aid to Dussoum?" Tarid came to a standstill beside Rukk.

"Gather them together. Perhaps we have more magi than when we left the Tower." Rukk leveled his gaze on Furak, who hurried to do as he commanded.

Keryn ran a hand over his face. "Our weakest are at their mercy."

Rukk gritted his teeth. "It might be paranoia on my part, General, but something's misaligned."

A few magi approached, Erwana herding them from behind. Rukk didn't wait for her to reach him. He darted around the magi to clasp Erwana's elbow. Leaning in, he studied her familiar face, needing to make sure no black tainted her eyes. "Can you account for your spellbinders and magi?" He kept his voice low, and his gaze fixed on her.

"Of course, why...?" She studied her charges pooling around her. "Do you suspect corruption?"

"No, I search for wylders disguised as magi. I never once questioned how Nenneg made it inside the mountain." He recounted her story, shortening it to get to the heart of it. "Borgakh said they stopped at the Council and their story was disbelieved."

"They must have met with Venec. I have not heard such a tale."

Rukk frowned. "Hence my concern. Where are the wylders?"

"Magi, spellbinders, please check each other for corruption. It seems the Ravenous Dark has changed its tactics." Erwana projected her voice without having to yell.

Whispers rippled through the gathering with many glancing around, their nervous movements twitching their skirts. Fear trembled their fingers as one by one they flicked their hoods back. A figure stumbled. Her chin tucked in to hide her face. Erwana shot out an arm, and the female arched in agony as magic dragged her toward Rukk. He raised his sword, prepared to strike.

"No." Erwana flicked her wrist, and the hood fell back, revealing the matted hair and mud-smeared cheeks of a wylder.

A manic expression contorted her features, and black almost consumed the whites of her eyes.

"I am but one, *Arch-Magus*." She cackled.

He fisted her cloak at her throat. "How can wylders enter the mountain?"

She giggled with the sound too joyful for a battlefield. "Ah, at last. Unraveling the mystery will please my mistress," she said. He tightened his hold to shake her. "With an ancient text discovered in the Tower's archives and so easily dismissed. 'Leave Kethil as it is,' Arch-Magus Minerva said." Her eyes settled on Rukk. "Where's your precious Venec now? He was the first to succumb."

The wylder contorted, crying out in pain, and the black spread from her eyes, staining her face. Her mouth gaped as if she couldn't breathe. Her skin turned blue beneath the ichor. Gone was her earlier derision. Fear and pleading filled her dark gaze. Rukk released her, and she slumped to the ground.

"Her mistress wanted her silenced." Erwana gestured to her magi. "Find the wylders in our midst and kill them. Then check on the wounded. Let us pray it's not too late." A few broke off from the group, making a run for the mountain, but the archers took them down.

"Does this resolve your unease?" his father asked, standing beside him.

Keryn approached a slain wylder, flipping her over to open an eye with his large fingers. He shook his head, faced Rukk then stormed off, speaking to commanders along the way to the podium.

"No, my unease remains. Those at the Gates know nothing, and there is no time to warn them." Rukk grimaced.

Thugari was still in danger. It would take seven hours to reach her. He could do nothing but watch the magi walk away, checking each other and jabbering as they did so.

The rumble of an explosion tore through the sky, tremors shaking the mountain and the ground beneath his feet. The puddles rippled, reflecting the clouds in turmoil. Fire puffed out, catapulting debris into the air.

He smiled. Mòr was alive. A slow grumble followed, and in one smooth terrifying act, the snow capping the mountain sloughed off, plunging toward him. He twisted to roar a warning to his males. The Iomhar raised their faces to the plummeting snow. Except one. Iàcob thrust his dagger in King Shertur's back and kicked the king's sprawled body off the podium.

Rukk cried out, but a shove from the side threw him to the ground as a wall of white slammed into him.

CHAPTER FORTY

UNA DIED MINUTES AGO, succumbing to the arrow buried in her stomach. Great beasts with winged-feline bodies and human faces rained arrows upon them. They had bounced off Sharn's protective shield, but with her power waning, a few slipped through.

Staring at Una's lifeless body, Mòr's eyes glistened and her voice roughened as she offered a prayer to Moon. She rose from her haunches, then attended to her task with her usual vigor, as if death meant nothing.

Thugari peeked from behind a boulder as the dwarves planted their explosives. Mòr had explained an accident of alchemy brought them the black powder, used in dire situations only. She complained to Isbeil the necessity had never been as ominous as now.

Sharn rested her back against the rock, sucking in jarring breaths. An arrow jutted out below her collarbone, which had ended Thugari's singing. The light from the staff faded, spluttering out before re-illuminating as her magic faltered.

Thugari cupped Sharn's shoulder to brace herself, and with a nod from Sharn, yanked out the arrow. The magus screamed. Thugari threw the arrow aside, then slipped Rukk's medallion off her and onto Sharn.

She gasped and flicked her eyes open. "Oh, he is cunning," she said, a smile forming as she covered the medallion with trembling fingers. "I'll do the same with my amulet if I survive this."

"You'll survive," Thugari said, unraveling her scarf to hold it to the blood seeping from Sharn's wound. "Tarid awaits."

Her cheeks pinkened. "What's taking Mòr so long?" She inched herself up to peer over the boulder. "Reinforcements. Zetar bless Erwana." She laughed to see fellow magi climb onto the mountain top.

As the females approached the campsite, Sharn fell silent, then cupped her mouth with a blood-stained hand. Her eyes widened as she trembled.

"What is it?" Thugari squinted at the females and smiled. "Nenneg." Her voice was too hoarse to raise above a whisper.

Leading a string of magi was Nenneg in a magus robe. That wasn't alarming, not when her usual garments weren't suitable for this harsh climate. Then again, neither was a robe unless one could warm oneself with magic.

"Erwana would never allow anyone to wear a magus robe. Spellbinders work hard to earn one, and the only reason Nenneg can wear it now is if she peeled it off a dead magus."

Thugari gaped at Nenneg wading through the snow toward the crevice. No, it wasn't possible. She couldn't believe it of her friend. Yet Sharn's reaction wasn't a lie. Gauging the distance between Mòr and Nenneg, Thugari darted around the boulder, running pell-mell along the path she had forged earlier.

Grabbing Mòr by the shoulder, she fought for breath as she repeated Sharn's words with her hoarse voice.

"I'll test her. Back to the boulder for you," Mòr said then gestured for Isbeil to join her.

Diving behind the boulder, Thugari rubbed her gloved hands together and pressed her fingertips over her mouth, shielding her face from the lashing wind. Mòr waved at Nenneg as she approached, as if greeting a friend. Sharn shifted toward Thugari until their bodies touched, then clicked her fingers. In an instant, the discussion between the dwarf and the wylder was clear as if they stood inches away.

"The tasks are almost complete, but Stones of Comhnall, you're a sight for sore eyes, Nen." She turned her back on the wylder and waved for her to follow. It was a display of trust and a challenge. "Una's with the Geàrdan who have come before us, Zetar bless her soul. What news from below? How fare's the battle?"

Nenneg sighed. "Not good for us, I'm afraid."

Thugari pounded the boulder with the side of a fist. She hoped Nenneg didn't mean bad for Rukk but bad for the Ravenous Dark if she was thus aligned.

"Knowing how important this task was, Erwana sent me and a few magi to melt the snow." This was not the timid Nenneg Thugari knew.

This female was bold and confident. Borgakh wasn't with her, and the orc maiden would not have succumbed to the Dark willingly. Thugari shook her head, not prepared to believe in the teeniest possibility she might serve evil.

"Aye, and drown them from above. You have my gratitude. Where's Borgakh?" Mòr peered around Nenneg as if she searched for her. As tall as the orc maiden was, one never needed to seek her out from amid a gathering.

"I left her in Dussoum. She's ill but will recover." Nenneg held her hands out to the fire as her coven circled the crevice.

Borgakh wouldn't stand to the side and allow Nenneg to venture onto a battlefield alone. The orc maiden loved her. She would also not allow this betrayal to play out. Nenneg would have had to incapacitate her by wounding, deceiving, or killing Borgakh. Thugari couldn't believe it, searching and struggling to see the Nenneg she loved within the stranger in front of her.

"Do something, Sharn." She splayed her fingers on the boulder, needing the rock to ground her. "Nenneg's betrayed us all, and she intends to kill the Geàrdan."

"I cannot, little one. All that is left in me is wind magic." Sharn snuffed the light from her staff still planted beside the fire, taking back the last of her magic. The flames flickered as she siphoned some of its energy to replenish her stores.

Nenneg's head rose, and she met their gazes over the boulder. A cold smile formed, and she nodded, as if to say they were next.

"We have survived the last strike, so your arrival is fortuitous." Mòr gestured to Isbeil, who had approached the crevice's edge with a torch clasped in her hand.

Nenneg scrutinized Isbeil and the remaining dwarven soldiers clutching torches. As one, they lowered them with oil dripping flames to the snow, but since they didn't touch their weapons, she didn't react.

"Go." At Mòr's bellow, a soldier bolted outward, sprinting through the deep snow as if it didn't hinder his shorter legs.

Nenneg jerked from side-to-side, her mouth gaping as all the dwarves spread out, heading for cover. Mòr was the last to run, but she used Thugari's premade path and wobbled toward her, a leg shorter than the other.

A deafening roar thundered through Thugari as the ground quaked. In slow motion, the crevice widened with masses of plateau crumbling into darkness. The wylders screamed, turning to flee, but it was too late. Gulped by falling rock and snow, they fell from sight.

Behind Mòr, a fissure chased her, freezing Thugari in stunned horror. Fear gripped her limbs, numbing her more than the cold did. Alongside the fissure ran Nenneg, her fingertips almost touching Mòr's spaulder.

Thugari ran toward her, planning to snatch the dwarf and throw her to safety. Mòr waved at her to retreat, hollering dire warnings. When the fissure sucked in Nenneg, Thugari jerked to a halt a few feet away from Mòr with her boots spraying clouds of powdered snow. As soon as Mòr neared, Thugari scooped her onto her shoulders and sprinted to the camp, forcing herself not to glance back.

Sharn screamed, almost climbing over the boulder to come to their aid.

Silence engulfed them. After lowering Mòr, Thugari gripped her knees, panting for breath. Sharn giggled, despite the snow and dust still settling with Mòr grumbling as she staggered to her feet.

"Never has anyone carried me like a sack of horse shit." She slapped snow from her thighs. "You have my thanks, dark one." She strode past the boulder to peer at the gaping hole, snow still flowing over its new edges. "That went well. Freagairt? Answer."

Voices responded from various directions, having scattered as they lit the explosives. Surviving that was a miracle because, after their scramble away from the crevice, Thugari doubted any of them were miners.

"Here, Geàrdan Isbeil too." A voice penetrated the rumbling silence, reverberating out of the new chasm.

"Any wylders?" The wind whipped Mòr's words back at her.

Their voices faded to the recesses of her mind as Thugari blinked at the new crevice, at the black fingers curling over the edge. The Ravenous Dark hadn't halted its attack. Despair settled like a weight upon her shoulders, for it seemed as if there was nothing they could do to end its determination. Sunlight was the antithesis of darkness, but light couldn't reach everything. At best, it might destroy a large part of the Dark and force it to retreat. She could only hope.

"Nenneg," she said, stopping alongside Sharn to offer a hand up. "I can't believe it. How will we tell Borgakh?"

"Did anyone see her fall?" Sharn clambered to her feet, her grip crushing Thugari's fingers. "Telling Borgakh she's dead when we're not certain won't go down well."

"I saw the darkness engulf her." Thugari trembled as the fleeting image of Nenneg's twisted features flicked across her mind. "Can we return to Dussoum now?"

"We'll rest at the midpoint of Donaidh." Mòr nudged her head at Sharn.

Thugari gasped at the blood darkening Mòr's breeches. She gripped the dwarf's elbow, steering her to the boulder.

"What in cursed hell are you doing, Thugari?"

"You're bleeding. How did that happen?" Thugari replayed the last moments Nenneg was alive. She had managed to plunge a dagger into Mòr while running.

Mòr twisted, blinking at the back of her thigh where the hilt of an elegant dagger protruded. "Stones!" Her skin paled, she wavered, then bounced off the boulder as she fainted.

"She's injured," Thugari said to the dwarven soldiers and Isbeil who arrived to stare at Mòr's prostrate form.

"Can you carry her?" Sharn asked. "We need off this mountain in case more rock collapses."

Isbeil shook her head. "A dwarf is never toted around. It's an offense of the highest order."

Thugari snorted and swung Mòr's body onto her shoulders, gripping her by the forearms. "Shall we?" She arched a brow at Sharn and a furious Isbeil before nudging her head at the Donaidh steps.

Sharn giggled, shuffling through the snow to the side of the mountain. Isbeil grunted and followed. The dwarven soldiers hesitated, waving to Thugari to pass them. A tug and pull mimicked the movement of someone bandaging Mòr's thigh. A glance back confirmed this.

Going down went quicker, or it seemed like it, with the anticipation and dread no longer dragging her feet. She was grateful the explosion hadn't stripped the mountain of the carved steps, stranding them. They made the platform two hours later. She lowered Mòr with care. When she lay her down, the female grumbled, twitching as she fought unconsciousness.

A tap on Thugari's arm with the dagger snagged her attention. One of the soldiers offered the weapon, and she accepted it, too stunned to decline. "Thank you...?" She arched a brow, waiting for him to supply his name. The young dwarf's beard trembled, and he dipped his gaze as shyness overtook him.

"It's Griogal, my lady." He backed away, sneaking peeks at her before dropping to his backside.

Four soldiers remained of the dozen who'd left Dussoum with her. She tucked the dagger into her boot, grimacing at the blood still staining it. So many had died, and though her thoughts whispered it was her fault, it wasn't. The blame lay at the feet of the Ravenous Dark and sweet, angelic, and kind Nenneg.

A lump rose up Thugari's throat, scratching and choking her. *Please.* She raised her gaze, the moonlight marking silver linings around the crimson clouds. They were faded, not so intense as earlier, yet the Ravenous Dark's influence remained. She wanted to see Rukk, but returning to Dussoum didn't guarantee a sighting of him. He was hours away. With a battle on his hands, he wouldn't have the time to worry about her. The explosion had happened sooner than the witching hour, and she hoped it wasn't for nothing. All this effort made no impact in the scheme of things. Then again, there was nothing she or the Geàrdan could have done to help otherwise.

Taking a long breath and wiping her frozen tears with the fingertips of her leather gloves, she leaned against the wall, a shivering Sharn beside her. Thugari dreamed Rukk stepped onto the platform and kissed wonderful warmth into her numb lips. If she made it out of this alive, she would find a cottage in a meadow with a waterfall behind it. That's all she wanted. A place to lose and find herself many times over.

Banach Cottage would be her refuge. She would love for Rukk to go with her, but he was a prince of Ghorza and a lawbringer. Seeing him when he passed through was all she could hope for.

"Awaken, Thugari, it is time." Sharn nudged her arm.

Thugari sat up, leveling her gaze on a livid Mòr.

CHAPTER FORTY-ONE

RUKK DREW IN A harsh breath when the ice chilling his skin awakened him. He jerked, shifting the snow cocooning him. His sense of balance conflicted with the lights piercing the packed snow. Shivering, sending a dribble of melted droplets trickling into his cloak, he squeezed his eyes shut. His heartbeat deafened him. His chest tightened, crushing his lungs as he struggled to breathe.

A scream tore up his throat, but he swallowed it, forcing himself to calm his breathing and to listen for movement. That would tell him in which direction to dig. Thumps vibrated to his position, and he tilted his head. He was upside-down entombed in yards of snow.

Scooping handfuls of it, he shoved it behind him, forming a hole, so he could touch his toes and shovel toward the sound coming from under his feet. Muffled voices reverberated, and relief flooded him with warmth, his extremities no longer tingling.

"Rukk." Tarid's mental voice formed tears, and Rukk blinked them away, despite relishing their heat at the corners of his eyes.

"Tarid." He shoveled faster, ignoring the trickle of sweat on his forehead.

A shadow appeared above him, and he called out, swallowing a mouthful of soft powder before he punched his fist through the final layer. Warm hands gripped his wrist and forearm to tug him out. He crumbled to the ground, sucking in great gulps of air, and for once, the chilled breeze was refreshing across his burning cheeks.

"Are you well?" Tarid filled his vision with his concerned expression.

"Thank you. What's the status?"

Tarid's thoughts clouded over as if he hid something from him.

Clambering to his feet, his knees trembling, Rukk scanned the white surroundings. The pavilion had tilted, pushed off balance by a wave of snow. Many warriors, orcs, Atrarians, and dwarves, worked to dig others out. A magus healed Keryn, who propped up his leg. White bone shredded his breeches above his knee.

He bellowed commands for more warriors to search. Even those sporting blood-stained bandages helped where they could.

"Where's my father?" Rukk twisted, combing for the familiar face so like this own.

Tarid's gaze sliced to a pile of rocks behind him.

Rukk shook his head, his lips trembling as he struggled to form words. He pressed them together, trying to gain control. Yes, he hated his father, but he had assumed he had decades to forgive and reconcile.

"He was alongside you when the avalanche happened." Tarid draped an arm across Rukk's shoulders, holding his temple to his. "He hurled you out of the path of the falling debris."

Archers removed rocks, magi levitated them to the side—all united in the common cause—to find his father's body. Even an orc as old and powerful as he could not have survived this.

"How dare you sacrifice your life for mine! Why? You hated me, hated my mother." Rukk stumbled forward, lifting debris to throw them aside.

He tore fingernails and grazed his palms as he tackled rock after rock. Sweat drenched his body, and his hair clung to his face and neck. He threw off his cloak and worked with more vigor.

Tears burned his chapped cheeks, and an incessant keening drenched his ears. He didn't stop to find the irritation but continued to unpack the rockpile, until limb by limb, his father's crumpled body lay sprawled before him.

Erwana knelt beside him, extending her hands to heal. It was pointless. Rukk couldn't hear his father's heartbeat or sense his life force.

He leaned back onto his heels, running his fingers along the fine robe. There, under his touch and woven in silver thread, was Rukk's name. A sob escaped him, and soft arms wrapped around his neck, surrounding him in a floral scent.

He smothered his face in Erwana's thick robe, his fingers gripping her hips. He found no comfort in her embrace, expected to find none.

"Come, Rukk, now is not the time to mourn." Keryn's gravel voice tore through Rukk's grief. The older orc hobbled closer, his strapped leg not slowing him.

Tarid growled. "Give him a moment."

"The Ravenous Dark still lives. Dawn is in four hours, and we have yet to save Kethil. He can grieve when he is free to do so." Keryn slapped Rukk on his shoulder.

With a deep breath, Rukk released Erwana, nodding at her in thanks. He did not look upon his father as the Kurdan warriors prepared his body for the funeral march. They would leave within the hour for Ghorza.

"You command our armies, General Yerug." Rukk rubbed his face, willing his sorrow to bury deeper within him. His throat was raw, his voice hoarse, and he struggled to swallow. "Send the dwarves into Chaosthane, deploy the reflective surfaces, as many and as deep as they can travel."

"Alone?" Tarid offered Rukk his discarded cloak.

"No one else can enter, you know that." He raised his gaze to meet Keryn's, sadness in his old tutor's eyes. "What will you have me do?"

Keryn sighed. "Travel to Dussoum, inform Larza on what has transpired, and bring my daughter back."

"What if Borgakh has other plans?" Rukk asked. Keryn grimaced, his lips twitching between acceptance and anger. Pitying him, Rukk nodded. "I will convince her as best I can."

"Fair enough. Return here with news. Harpax is swift, and I can trust you and Tarid not to tarry."

"You cannot command me." Tarid squared his shoulders.

"I can, and I will. Your king lays dead with an Iomhar dagger in his back. It was as you said, Rukk, the Dark has corrupted many. I will deal with those alive, assess their sanity, and so forth."

"Dead? How?" Tarid stepped toward the capsized podium, but Keryn pressed a hand on his chest.

"During the avalanche, Iàcob stabbed Shertur. When Seamus realized this, he killed Iàcob, but not before seeing his eyes blacken."

"Either the explosion triggered it, or the Ravenous Dark has become intuitive, sensing an opportunity to remove two key members," Rukk said, his hands trembling as he slipped on his cloak. "We will do as you command, General Yerug, and return with news from Dussoum."

As they strode for their horses corralled far from the battle, Rukk scanned each passing soldier, peering into their eyes as fear ran a cold finger down his spine. He vaulted onto Harpax, urging him to gallop. Thugari had succeeded in enchanting the water to aid her. Mòr had exploded the crevice wider. All that remained was to bring sunlight into the mountain and destroy or at least weaken the Ravenous Dark.

Despair slumped Rukk's shoulders, and exhaustion drained what energy grief had left him. There had to be a way to kill the Ravenous Dark for good. He doubted it, and even if they could find a way, it was a momentous task. He took solace from the fact it wasn't the Dark that killed his father, but chaotic nature. Never once had they anticipated an avalanche from the explosion, which left the question, what else hadn't they considered? Their desperate plan hadn't killed his father. He wouldn't let himself follow that train of thought.

Regret wasn't a pleasant emotion. It was dark and haunting, and summoned best-forgotten memories. One day, he would sit Keryn down and hear the full saga about his mother and Donal. Bitterness, anger, and grief had prevented him from forgiving his father. There had to have been more to it for Keryn to have executed his son without question. For now, he needed to focus on finding Borgakh, Thugari, and Larza.

"What are your plans after this ends?" Tarid asked across their mental path.

"I must head for Ghorza, but I have every intention of returning to Kethil."

Tarid gaped at him. *"Won't you assume your rightful place?"*

"It is for my people to decide who should be king. If I have a choice, it won't be me." Rukk hunched over, urging Harpax to quicken his speed. *Thugari will travel with me.*

He fell silent, thinking about riding through the towering orc statues marking the Gates of Amarhei, guarding the Ghorzan royal city of Isstislaaron. He hadn't seen their pristine white beauty in decades and didn't dread the journey. He prodded his heart with a tentative mental finger. It was raw from his loss, but obligation, honor, and tradition encased it.

"I cannot believe Mòr succeeded. Even more so, water burst out of the mountain. Who would have thought a 'stableboy' would come to mean so much to...Kethil?"

Rukk snorted at Tarid's not-so-subtle dig for information when he could look inside and see how Rukk felt. But he was grateful Tarid hadn't intruded. *"So, you wish to discuss my relationship? Then we can address your intentions with Sharn."*

Tarid's thoughts clouded, drawing a bark of laughter from Rukk as surprising as it was crippling, squeezing his heart until his teeth ached. His father's death was too new for him to laugh. It felt unnatural and grated his shredded throat. The burst of joy was ineffectual at dispelling the shadows within him.

"Want to head for Donaidh steps first, along the base of Chaosthane to the Gates, then on to Dussoum?"

Rukk shook his head. *"Five hours to climb up, four to come down, and longer if they carry the wounded. Straight to the Gates of Chaosthane to see how they fare."* He was thankful when Tarid said no more.

Chapter Forty-Two

"Thugari carrying me doesn't leave this mountain." Mòr glared at everyone on the ledge until they nodded. Once that matter was settled, she knelt beside Sharn, wincing as she did. "How are you feeling?"

"Good, Rukk's medallion helped. My magic is almost restored. Want me to look at your wound?" Sharn removed the medallion to loop it over Thugari's head. She smiled her thanks.

"I'll do it," Isbeil said from the other side of the ledge.

Mòr rose and limped over, facing Thugari. With her back to the edge, Mòr had the full view of the rock wall with the steps leading up and down. Her face twisted in horror, and she threw out her hand as if to ward off an attack. Thugari sprung to her feet, bolting for Mòr, but she was too late. Mòr stumbled backward when a ball of fire hit her chest.

Following the trajectory revealed Nenneg wearing a bright, wicked smile. She must have trailed them.

Having seen her fall, Thugari gaped at her. How was this possible?

Mòr cried out, tripped over Isbeil, and in slow motion, tipped over the edge.

Isbeil dove after Mòr.

Thugari lunged for Isbeil. With her hand on Isbeil's booted ankle and Isbeil gripping Mòr by the wrist, Thugari found herself once more staring off a precipice, her body splayed out on the rock. Something heavy landed on the back of her thighs, pinning her.

"Do you have her, Isbeil?" She grimaced with the combined weight of two dwarves tearing at her shoulders. A cry of agony built in her throat, threatening to pierce through her gritted teeth.

Receiving a nod from Isbeil, she inched her up by gripping her calf, then knee, hand over hand. Chaos reigned around her, and even as the weight grounding her budged, it didn't leave her. Sharn and the remaining soldiers had to deal with Nenneg.

Once Thugari wrapped her fingers around Isbeil's belt, Thugari called out to anyone listening to help. No response came. Another soldier alongside her, adding his strength to hers, would have been helpful. Shuffling backward, made harder with the weight on her thighs, she pulled Isbeil with her, who still had a firm grip on Mòr.

With all three of them sprawled on the platform and sucking in shuddering breaths, Thugari twisted to see why the soldier still held onto her. Griogal's dead eyes stared ahead, and there was a gaping hole in his chest, singed around the edges. Swallowing a whimper, she shook him off, whispering an apology for her disrespect at his sacrifice.

Unholstering her crossbow, she aimed at the sparring magi. She couldn't dwell on the pang of sorrow fluttering through her as her mind replayed Griogal's smiling face. Sharn had a shield up, the energy to protect others draining her. The dwarven soldiers raised their axes but spent most of the time dodging Nenneg's fireballs when they ventured past Sharn's shrinking shield.

Nudging her head at the steps, Thugari said to Mòr, "She's wasting her powers protecting us. Go down the steps. I'll guard from there with my crossbow ready."

Mòr hesitated, then with a nod, two Geàrdan and three soldiers dragging Griogal disappeared down the Donaidh steps. Thugari followed but ducked until she peered over the landing. Upon it, she rested her crossbow, waiting for the perfect shot. Her bolts were sunlight-kissed, but she doubted they would work against normal magic. They would work against flesh, though.

"Why won't you die, Sharn? Draining your power to protect a half-breed? How far your kind has fallen." Nenneg laughed, and the grating sound of it raised the air on Thugari's arms. "I *paid* the dreshnie to capture you, to kill you, yet here you both stand." She flicked a hatred-filled gaze at Thugari. "I sensed the magic lying deep within you, dark one. No matter how many bairns I consumed, I could not unravel the sigil, nor could I siphon your innocence." She huffed in disgust. "But all it hid was a moonlit siren. Pathetic."

Sharn shuffled forward, her arms extended as she fired shafts of lightning. "We saw you fall into the shadows, Nenneg."

Her shield flared with each lightning strike. A smirk curled her lips. "You cannot kill me, Sharn. The Ravenous Dark fuels my power, and it is invincible. True evil lives in us all, and it saturates the soil, flowing deep into the caverns below. Your archives have knowledge of this." Nenneg twisted her hands, summoning a ball of flame. "I showed it to your precious Arch-Magus, but no, we mustn't mess with the balance. Cowards and fools."

"What are you talking about?" Sharn caught Nen's fireball. Its energy rippled along her robe before changing to blue and dissolving.

"I was a spellbinder in the Council, but when I discovered the Ravenous Dark is a living entity, I showed the ancient texts to Minerva. She laughed, said communing with such evil would lead to corruption. So, I burned the scrolls and left the Tower. Here I stand, more powerful than all the magi combined."

She launched fireball after fireball at Sharn who couldn't absorb or reflect them all. Crying out, she crumpled to a knee, but her shield held, shimmering where it weakened.

"Minerva died years ago, Nenneg. You could have spoken to Erwana. How did you convince the Dark to join with you?" Sharn asked through her clenched jaw. "How can you live with the blood of so many on your hands, Nen? This isn't you."

"Nenneg, please. You're my friend." Thugari pleaded with her, praying to Moon to help.

Nen cackled. "I promised it evil, of course. A war drenches the soil, does it not?"

"It wasn't meant to rise?" Sweat drenched Sharn's face, and she trembled as her magic failed.

"Not for centuries." Nenneg tapped her chest. "I, spellbinder Nenneg, made it stronger."

"The bairns?" Thugari asked.

"My obedient koveen and wylders buried their lifeless bodies after I fed from them. It was such a delicious plan."

Thugari frowned, ignoring the tears stinging her eyes. Something Nenneg said bothered her though. If Darkness fueled her, then she was susceptible to sunlight. Thugari didn't hesitate to fire a bolt as soon as that thought formed. Nenneg hissed when the tip sliced along her shield, tearing a hole as it traveled. It bounced off, not harming her, but it drew Nenneg's attention to Thugari.

She hurried to notch another bolt, her fingers trembling with her gaze switching between Nenneg and the crossbow. Sharn took advantage of Nenneg's distraction by firing lightning, and as it penetrated the shield, she threw a dagger. It buried in Nenneg's shoulder, staggering her back. Crying out, she clutched her wound.

Thugari didn't hesitate, firing another bolt. She aimed for the heart but hit Nenneg in the throat. Beggars couldn't be ungrateful, as long as it would weaken or wound her.

"No." She gargled the word as blood pooled at the base of her collarbone and dribbled down her chest, staining her stolen magus robe. She gripped the bolt as if to slow her impending death and fell to her knees landing in a crimson puddle on the rock. "This is not how it's supposed to end. This isn't possible. You promised." Her ability to speak diminished, but her gaze shifted, fear darkening the white of her eyes to black.

Thugari scrambled off the steps to yank the dagger out of Nenneg's shoulder and plunge it through her heart. Nenneg tried to thwart her, but her thrown-out hand was now pinned to her chest. The pool of blood beneath her seeped into the rock and faded.

Sharn stumbled back and gathered her hands to her sides, as if she pushed from deep within her. She summoned fire to engulf the wylder in molten flame. There were no cries of agony nor a body writhing on the rock. From the mountain, an eerie pain-filled wail pierced the sky. The roiling clouds dispersed with bright moonlight bathing the macabre scene. Snow showered them as tremor after tremor rippled through the rock.

Thugari shoved Sharn against the rock wall. Just in time, too, for the snow poured down like a waterfall, enshrouding them in shadow as it blocked the light.

Sharn gripped Thugari's arm, her eyes wide with circles under them. "Do you think killing her harmed the Dark?" Hope, pain, and exhaustion pooled tears at the corners of her eyes.

"I hope so. We'll only know when we reach Dussoum." She removed the medallion again, slipping it onto Sharn.

Thugari slid down the jagged rock until her backside hit the floor, with a grateful sigh escaping her. She could sleep for days. So much exhaustion, fear, trepidation burned through her that her limbs twitched. "Do you think Mòr and the soldiers made it? Survived the tremor and the avalanche?"

Sharn collapsed beside her with her eyes closed. "They're dwarves. They know these mountains well. I would say they are better at surviving than we are." She popped an eye open to meet Thugari's gaze. "Thank you, by the way. My energy drained from me faster than I anticipated. Had you not pierced her shield, who knows how long I would have held out."

"I want to make sure she's dead, Sharn. Not like last time." Thugari stared at the lump, the snow having doused the flames, then at the blood staining her palms.

The stench of burned human permeated the air, and the quicker she saw to that task, the quicker they could climb down to Dussoum.

"I don't mind the cold as much," she said. "Or am I frozen solid and don't know it?"

Sharn giggled. "You might have dwarf in you."

"Hush, don't let Mòr hear you say that." Thugari laughed and clambered up since the shower of snow had ended.

She wiped her palms on her breeches and offered Sharn a hand. The magus accepted, her shaking fingers delicate yet hot to the touch.

Approaching the corpse, Thugari crouched to sweep the snow off Nenneg's face. There was nothing there but blackened flesh, so she rolled the body until it fell off the ledge. With fresh sweat coating her face and her breaths ragged puffs, she watched Nenneg plummet. This time there wasn't the illusion of a fall. The body bounced off rocks and spires to land far below, fading into the gray tundra.

"Ready?" Sharn waited at the landing.

Thugari gestured to lead the way. "When we get to Dussoum, I think I'll try the dragon's fire."

"You might regret it," Sharn said.

Thugari chuckled. "How bad can it be?"

CHAPTER FORTY-THREE

RUKK MET LARZA ON the outskirts of Dussoum. Grins plastered on his lawbrothers's faces had to mean good news. When the wind's forlorn cry pierced the air and the mountain rumbled, he had assumed they had delivered a definitive blow. He urged Harpax to a halt alongside Larza's mount and shifted his aching backside in the saddle.

"When you suggested your dark-orc coax water to drown the mountain, I thought you were insane," Larza said by way of greeting. "Something slammed against the iron doors, then they burst open with water carrying the Dark's servants, dead or weakened." Not the most effusive of males, he thumped Rukk on the shoulder, his strength surprising for a dwarf. "I assume it played out the same for you?"

"Yes, Grand Lawmaster," Tarid said from behind Rukk. "General Yerug tasked us to journey to Dussoum to deliver the status and find his daughter, Borgakh."

Rukk scanned the party, not seeing her among them. "Any news from Gill-Eòin?" He raised his gaze to the jagged peaks and settled on the clear velvet sky and bright moon. "I heard the mountain scream. Was it your doing?"

"No. We guarded the gaping gates while darkness fought from within shadow. The cry heralded the end of the battle, the claws of the Ravenous Dark fading as moonlight pierced the clouds and into the mountain. The dwarfs deliver the mirrors as we speak. The sun will reflect off them and weaken or cancel out the Dark's power."

Rukk glanced at Tarid. "Is it over? Are we victorious?" An unknown warmth burned Rukk's chest, relief tainting it. Gratitude he need not lose another loved one shredded his breathing.

Larza continued to speak, so Rukk returned his attention to his Grand Lawmaster.

"It is done, and swifter than spoken history has recorded. I will suggest to the Iomhar they plant more mirrors in the centuries to come. Let's weaken the Dark before it forms." Larza tapped his sword. "The sunlight-blessed weapons did make a difference, harming black ether when we would normally have failed. I must speak with King Horknuth. We could use this when fighting voidwhisps."

Rukk winced, fresh pain tightened his chest and squeezed the air out of his lungs. The visage of his father, contorted in death, settled behind his eyes. "King Horknuth is no more, crushed during the avalanche. Iomhar Iàcob murdered King Shertur, so Iomhar Seamus executed him. We found the wylders spreading corruption disguised as magi and spellbinders."

As one, the party turned in the saddles to stare at the magi trailing them.

"What reveals their corruption?" a lawbringer asked.

"Would the effects remain if the Ravenous Dark has lost its influence?" Larza steered his horse to the side, urging it to canter alongside the party. He halted before the magi, his face stoic. "Please, magi and spellbinders, we have received distressing news. Dismount and kneel before me. I will attempt to make this as painless as possible." He climbed off his horse, landing on steady feet. "Le Coadic, ready your bow."

Gasps and chatter flitted through the females, then without hesitation, they dismounted, navigating through the horses to form a line in front of Larza. One by one, he flipped their hoods back. His assessing gaze traveled their features even as golden tendrils of his magic touched their chins where he tipped their faces.

When he paused, all who watched sucked in a breath. With a flick of his wrist, his dagger slipped from his forearm holster and into his hand to slice the female's throat. Another wylder tore from the line, running for Dussoum, but Le Coadic took her down.

"Only two?" Larza didn't sound disappointed. "Smaller group, fewer spies." He helped the shaking magi to remount before pulling himself into his saddle. "I haven't seen Borgakh or Nenneg," he said as he rode up to Rukk.

"Has anyone come down from the mountain?" Tarid asked on Rukk's behalf, for which he was thankful, not wanting to seem alarmed at the lack of news.

"No, although, it hasn't been five hours since the explosion." Larza arched a brow at Rukk. "You will be happy to note, I left a knight to guard the steps. Should anyone descend, he is to inform them of the Gates' status and our return to the encampment.

You are welcome to wait with him." He nudged his horse and bolted forward, ending the discussion.

"To the steps or to Mòr's? Tarid studied the party riding past him. *"I would prefer to climb those cursed steps. Not knowing if Sharn is well is killing me."*

"I agree." Rukk patted Harpax's neck. *"Going to Mòr's might not mean they would join us there. Keryn asked us to find Borgakh. We can search after seeing Mòr. Perhaps she knows of the orc maiden's location."*

"You don't need to convince me." Tarid held up his hands. "If the general asks, this was your idea." He flicked his reins to urge his warhorse on.

A fire burned bright against the dark tundra at the base of the mountain. The knight, Nazer, rose to his feet as Rukk dismounted and tethered Harpax to the iron ring embedded in the rock face.

"Lawbringers Inaris and Knaraugh, welcome." Nazer gestured to his fire and dropped onto his bedroll.

Rukk reached for his, assuming the tundra was too uncomfortable to endure for extended periods.

"Knight Nazer, we thank you for your offer." Tarid spoke the formal greeting as expected.

They grew lax with such traditions once becoming a lawbringer, but it was good for the pages and knights to learn.

"Any sign from the steps?" he asked, spreading out his bedroll and dropping his food punch in front of him.

Rukk's stomach twisted hard enough to draw a wince. He couldn't recall when last he had eaten or drunk anything. There hadn't been the time to think of sustenance.

He laid out his bedroll and lowered himself, stretching his legs with a groan after the past hours in the saddle.

"A crisp body bounced off the sides and landed a hundred yards or so."

Rukk bounded to his feet. "Where?" Fear strangled his voice and spiked his heartbeat until he couldn't breathe.

Nazer pointed. "It looks like a magus."

Relief flooded warmth through Rukk, and he released a long breath. His heartbeat calmed, but he turned to Tarid whose face had paled. "It can't be Sharn."

And Rukk believed that. Her skills were impressive, and knowing Mòr and Thugari, neither would allow harm to befall her.

Tarid broke into a sprint, skidding to a halt alongside the twisted corpse. The purple of a magus robe shimmered in the moonlight. The blackened body inside it didn't give away its identity, not by face or body shape.

Rukk opened their mental link, extending a hand to squeeze Tarid's shoulder. *"It's not her."* He grimaced, for Tarid's thoughts were like panicked bats, flittering from plausible scenario to worst.

"How can you tell?" He roared the question, his voice reverberating off the jagged cliffs.

Rukk yanked his brother into his arms, thumping him on the back. "What does your instinct say? As lawbringer and lover?"

Tarid released a rushed breath. Pulling out of Rukk's arms, he nodded in thanks and acknowledgment. "She's well." He dropped to his haunches alongside the corpse. "Do you think it's a wylder?"

"They might have discovered the same deception as we did, but how? There were no magi amid their party, excluding Sharn, of course."

Tarid rose and strode toward Nazer. *"We will find out soon enough. We need to remain patient."*

Rukk cast a gaze up the mountain. *"Doing nothing doesn't sit well with me, and if the Ravenous Dark should rise again in my lifetime, never will I allow Thugari to head into danger."*

"I might have a harder time keeping Sharn from fighting alongside me." Tarid settled on his bedroll and opened his pouch, choosing sticks of dried meat.

He passed it around, and in exchange, Nazer shared his wineskin. It wasn't long before Mòr clambered down the steps. Trailing her were Isbeil and three dwarven soldiers carrying a male. Rukk switched his gaze from her exhausted face to the steps, waiting for Thugari to reveal herself.

"Nenneg attacked us, disguised as magi reinforcements. I blew up the crevice, and it worked, but it took half my soldiers and her coven. We thought she died." Mòr snatched the wineskin out of Tarid's hands, and drank, spilling the contents down her chin.

"Thought?" He bounded to his feet before stumbling toward the steps.

"She survived. Don't ask me how. Sharn and Thugari remained behind to battle." Mòr gripped Rukk by his elbow. "Find me at my home."

Nodding, he bolted up the steps, unable to stop himself. He rested every few minutes to ease his burning thighs, calm his breathing and erratic heartbeat. Tarid's grunts as he kept pace fueled Rukk onward.

It wasn't long before joyful laughter tinkled off the rockface. Sharn came into view first, her gaze thrown over her shoulder as she spoke.

Behind her was Thugari, her body swathed in layer upon layer of garments. Her cheeks glowed red from the wind, but he had never seen a more beautiful sight. She met his gaze, stumbling to a halt. Her smile spurred an answering joy through his lungs, reminding him to breathe.

"Tarid? Rukk?" Sharn hurried forward but halted in front of Rukk. The steps were narrow, and she couldn't pass him without his assistance. "What's happened?"

Exhaustion shadowed Sharn's face, her skin lacking color. He spied his medallion around her neck and grimaced. Thugari offering it meant Sharn had drained her magic or worse.

"We saw the body." He lifted his gaze to Thugari, who shuffled closer.

Her presence soothed him. Unable to reach her with Sharn blocking the way, he looped an arm around Sharn's waist and spun her, uncaring that her legs flew over the edge.

She gasped. Before she could complain, he'd planted her safely on the steps again but facing Tarid.

Mouth gaping, Thugari scrambled down the steps. "You could have kill—"

Rukk silenced her with his lips on hers, moaning at her sweetness. "Thank Zetar, you're alive, little one." He crushed her to him, rubbing his cheek across the hair at her temple.

"This was your foolish idea, Rukk." Even as she berated him, she looped her arms around his neck, engulfing him with her scent.

"Well, it worked." He smiled, flipping her hood back with trembling fingers. There was so much to tell her.

"It did?" A tear dribbled free as her eyes widened in surprise and disbelief.

"The battle is over, Thugari." He tugged on her arm to lace his fingers through hers. "Come, Mòr awaits, and Keryn wants me to find Borgakh."

"So do we. Nenneg betrayed us all, Rukk." She huddled against his back as he led her to where Sharn and Tarid kissed. While they waited, she spewed the details. "This will devastate Borgakh."

He stilled, envisioning revealing to Borgakh Nenneg had died. But with Tarid's mourning…now Rukk's own, and how devastating the burden was, he would still be there for Borgakh.

"It will, but we won't abandon her now. She might need us." Rukk nudged Sharn's hip. *"Tarid! Move, kiss later."*

Tarid broke the kiss, threw him a glare, but spun on his heel and led them down the mountain.

Rukk snuck peeks behind him, feasting his gaze on Thugari. He consoled himself with the lie he checked for stragglers or attackers, but the truth in his heart couldn't be denied. Once he stepped onto the tundra, Nazer left for Larza. Rukk led Thugari to Harpax and lifted her into the saddle.

He vaulted up behind her, reached around her to gather the reins, and steered them toward Dussoum.

Chapter Forty-Four

Rukk standing on the steps had seemed like an illusion. Heat engulfed her cheeks, squeezed the air out of her lungs, and if she hadn't thrown out her hand to grip the rockface, she might have fainted right off the edge.

That kiss. Oh, Moon above, the way her senses came to life with him near spelled trouble. Spanning ahead for her were years of loneliness, staring at the horizon and waiting for him to visit.

He warmed the length of her back, his arm crushing her while his other hand gripped the reins. He didn't speak, and she dreaded his words. There was something different about him. A sadness pressed at him and darkened his gaze. She took a deep breath, forcing herself not to pry, to accept he would tell her if he needed to.

Outside Mòr's house, he dismounted, tethered Harpax, then lifted her down. He snatched another kiss, staring into her eyes, and there in his, lingered the sorrow she sensed.

Despite deciding not to pry, she cupped his face, stroking her thumb over his lips. "What happened, Rukk?"

"We'll talk when we're alone." He clasped her hand and led her inside.

Mòr greeted them with filled goblets, gesturing to them to find somewhere to sit. Candlelight flickered on the stone walls, painting patterns from the carved lanterns they were in. And in the fireplace, the amulet rested on the burning logs.

"Mourning lanterns." Rukk nipped at Thugari's ear, then removed her cloak and thick over-tunic.

When he grasped her hip to steer her toward a strewn pillow, his touch scorched through the cloth, made more intimate without the layers protecting her.

Sharn halted in front of him to return his medallion. He accepted it with a nod and looped it back on.

Thugari tensed, expecting him to throw a glare at her for daring to remove and give it to someone else. When he gathered her closer instead of berating her, she let her shoulders relax.

Lowering herself onto the pillow, a sigh escaped her as she sank into the softness. Exhaustion drained her and drooped her eyelids. Rukk wrapped his fingers around hers, holding the goblet, and her cheeks flushed. He arched a brow, and she smiled, raising the goblet to her mouth when he released her.

Fire burned her throat, snatching her breath, and setting her insides ablaze. Tears ran free as Rukk thumped her on the back.

When she met his gaze, he was chuckling. She wanted to throw the goblet's contents at him but couldn't bring herself to exert the energy.

Instead, she wiped her eyes with the edges of her tunic. The goblet left her hand, and she grasped for it. Rukk downed it before placing the goblet on a nearby table.

Kissing her neck, he said, "Dragon's fire isn't for you, little doe."

She blinked, dazed by his lips feathering across her skin. It raised the hairs on her arms and skittered tingles along her skin. He leaned back and smirked, confident in what he did to her. Gnash scampered into the room and bounded over everybody to reach Thugari. She caught him and hugged him. He chirped his happiness.

"Have you seen Borgakh, Mòr?" Rukk asked, without removing his sparkling eyes from Thugari's.

"No, but I haven't searched my house. Let me do so now. Niall!" Mòr's voice echoed off the walls. Niall's hurried steps preceded his entrance, the poor male. "Borgakh Yerug, find her."

"She rests in her room, Geàrdan Mòr. She is unwell." The young dwarf paled as everyone studied him, but his gaze lingered on Thugari.

Sharn leaped to her feet, grasping the male by his shoulders. "Show me."

Tarid and Mòr trailed her with Rukk and Thugari crowding them from behind. Peeking into Borgakh's room was to find her sprawled on the bed, snoring. Sharn knelt beside her bed and took Borgakh's hand.

"Well?" Rukk asked. "Does she need my medallion?"

"No." Sharn sighed and sat back on her haunches. "She sleeps. It will wear off before dawn. I feared Nenneg had killed the female she claimed to love. Turns out, she did love Borgakh." She sat on the floor and rested her back against the bed.

"Can you wake her? She needs to know Nenneg died." Mòr swept the hair off Borgakh's temple.

"The spell will unravel when it does. Seek your solace. I shall guard her." Sharn closed her eyes as if she meditated or sought peace from within. Tarid settled beside her and pulled the grumbling magus onto his lap.

Thugari's mind reeled with haunting memories, and she sighed, running her chin along Gnash's little head. Rukk laced his fingers through hers and raised their clasped hands to kiss her knuckles.

"Ready to retire?" he asked. "Come, there is much I need to tell you."

She glanced at Sharn and Borgakh before allowing him to lead her away. He hurried her along the passage with his strides too long for her shorter gait.

"The door on your right," she said when he hesitated.

He thrust it open, and pulled her inside, slamming the door behind her. After scooping a scrambling Gnash off her chest and dumping him on a pile of garments, Rukk cupped her face and kissed her.

Tentative sips from her lips and bold forays of his tongue pounded her heart in her ears. She trembled, clutching his upper arms as if her knees might crumple.

"I've missed you, Thugari."

She blinked, marveling that it had only been a day, and she said as much.

He grabbed her upper arms and spun her, pressing her against the door. This kiss he filled with so much emotion she couldn't grasp its complexity. He *had* missed her, but there was desperation behind his lips plucking at hers, as he stripped off her garments and lifted her into his arms. He sprawled her onto the bed and stepped back to remove his armor, dropping each item as he did so. Layering his body over hers, he buried his fingers in her hair for a deep kiss.

"I lost my father today." His voice was thick with sadness.

She jerked back, meeting his sorrowful eyes, then threw her arms around him, crushing him against her. "I'm so sorry, Rukk."

"I thought I hated him," he said while spreading kisses along her collarbone to her breasts.

He sucked on a nipple, hard enough to call forth a moan from her. Heat pulsed from there to her core, summoning an ache only he could assuage. His fingers slipped lower, stroking her seam, then dipping in. His shoulders slumped, and he released a strangled sob.

"You need me, little one. I am grateful for I cannot wait a moment longer. Forgive me." He flipped her over, tugging her to her knees.

She stared in a stunned stupor at the carved headboard. When he slipped a finger between her seam and rubbed the bundle of nerves, she cried out, undulating her hips, no longer caring she couldn't see his face. His touch was so good, burning and spiking her anticipation. He ran his hand from her neck along her back to knead a backside cheek. Then he held his cock at her entrance and thrust in.

Moaning with sensations too intense and beautiful, she wanted him to stop and yet couldn't bear the thought of him doing so. "Harder."

She smashed her face into the pillow. He gripped her hips added to the building fire inside her, as did his thrusts slamming into her, burying himself to the hilt. She cried out. Joy, like a heated blanket, spread out from her core, taking her to the pinnacle and flooding her with tingles. They hardened her nipples and rippled down to where each thrust sent fresh tremors through her.

Roaring, he halted on a last plunge and pinned her to the bed. He trembled, his fingers flexing where he gripped her hips. Bowed over her, he nudged her hair out of the way with his chin and kissed her shoulder.

Still inside her, he took them to the bed and held her. Ragged sobs tore from him as he mourned his father. She layered his arms wrapped around her waist, crushing her against the length of him. In the silence of the room, she waited, allowing him as much time as he needed.

Exhaustion drooped her lids, but she blinked them open, determined to be there for him. She had suffered the same when her mother had died. The shredding pain, the dazed sense of imbalance, as if something in the world wasn't right.

So she hummed the lullaby her mother used to sing to her. His breathing calmed, his tears dried, then he nuzzled her hair.

"Come with me, Thugari, to Ghorza," he said in a shredded voice. His body stilled, and her heart fluttered in her chest, as if his did.

"Why?" If only she could see his face, but not with him slipping from her body and breaking the intimacy of their connection. "Are you to assume the throne? Does that make me your concubine?"

He growled, pulling out of her to roll her over. She wiped his tear-ravaged cheeks with her thumbs, but he gripped her wrists, forcing her to meet his ebony gaze. "I don't want the throne, but I mean to—"

"Bid you farewell?" She heard the unspoken words and rushed to stop him from speaking them, from ending whatever was between them. "Then no, Rukk. I'll wait for you at Tarid's cottage. I'm done with traveling and running. I need peace, not more time in the saddle."

He pursed his lips, as if her answer distressed him. "You don't want to see the famed lands of Ghorza?" His lips curled into a playful smile, but it didn't hide that her refusal hurt him.

Taking a deep breath, she struggled to align her thoughts and fears into words he could understand. She didn't want him to have to choose between her and his obligations. That wasn't fair on either of them.

"I would go anywhere with you, Rukk, but I am me. You are a prince and a revered lawbringer. You have so many obligations with so many counting on you. I don't expect to see you often, but if I do, I'll treasure each moment you share with me."

He opened his mouth to speak, but she shook her head, freeing her hands to throw her arms around him. She couldn't bear to hear his promises. He didn't know what lay ahead for him. If this battle had taught her anything, it was that life was unpredictable.

"I want to enjoy our last night together, and if I should see you approach the cottage, know I will welcome you with open arms."

His expression darkened, his lips again parting to speak. His determination had ice squeezing her chest. He was so stubborn, and how she loved that about him.

She buried her face in his neck and pleaded with him to let her go. "I can't survive losing another person. I choose to release you now rather than to hear you have found another or returned to the Council. You owe me no allegiance."

He tightened his arms around her, his anger growing, if she judged the pulse at his jaw and her matching heartbeat. "Thugari—"

"One more word, Rukk, and I'll leave now." She struggled to pull out of his embrace, and when it looked as if he had no intention of releasing her, she went on the offensive. Pushing forward, she straddled his waist and rubbed herself across the hard length of him.

Groaning, he arched his back, and his eyes fluttered shut. "You're not playing fair." He kissed her, running his splayed hand up her back to tangle his fingers in her hair. "We'll talk about this in the morning, little one, and you won't silence me then."

She succumbed to his skilled tongue as a fleeting plan formed. Before he awoke, she would sneak out. It was cruel to place him in such a situation, knowing he couldn't chase after her when he had to leave for Ghorza. But he would insist on taking her with him, and who knew what awaited her there.

When the darkness thickened before dawn, she snuck out of the room, gathering her things as she went and shoving sleepy Gnash into her food pouch. Naked in the passage, she donned her breeches and tunic, snatching her boots with one hand. With her cloak over her forearm and her satchel thrown over a shoulder, she opened the front door, wincing at every creak as if a bell knelled.

"Going somewhere?"

She squeaked, almost dropping her boots. Borgakh sat on the steps, staring at the stars up high.

"You scared me," Thugari whispered, her heart pounding in her ears. "I thought you were—" She clamped her mouth shut, choosing instead to sit alongside her friend and lace on her boots.

"Rukk?"

"Yes, he wants me to go with him to Ghorza. He has so much on his shoulders. I would only be in his way. I am not..." With a huff, she adjusted her satchel on her shoulder, unwieldy with her crossbow and holster shoved into it.

Pausing, she dipped her head to peer at Borgakh's face, illuminated by a nearby lantern. "Are you well?" Thugari wanted to smack herself in her face. Of course Borgakh wasn't well, not after her lover drugged or enchanted her.

"I've been better," she said, her voice ice-cold and monotonous.

Unshed tears stung Thugari's eyes, and she inhaled a shuddering breath. "I'm sorry, Borgakh, for my part. If there was another way, I would have—"

"I know. I do not blame you for Nenneg's choices. It was Kethil versus the Dark, and she was the instigator." Borgakh fell silent, sorrow draped over her like a sodden blanket.

Thugari shuffled on her feet, needing to leave before the sun's rays touched the mountain top.

"Going somewhere?" Borgakh repeating the question wasn't lost on Thugari.

"To Tarid's cottage, south of here."

She rose, forcing Thugari to step back. "I'm coming with you." The orc maiden disappeared inside.

Thugari scanned the empty road, peering into the shadows while sneaking glances at the ajar door. She couldn't leave now, not with Borgakh determined to join her.

And just like that, she had an accomplice.

CHAPTER FORTY-FIVE

WAKING UP TO MÒR'S face was a shock to Rukk's system when he expected Thugari beside him. The cold linen chilled his heart even as it served as proof. She was gone.

"You best stir, Rukk." Mòr shook his shoulder. "Keryn is livid."

Rukk scrambled, yanking on his breeches, then tunic, before hopping on each foot to pull on his boots. He hurried into the front room, expecting to find Keryn bowed under Mòr's ceiling. There was no one.

"He's mounted and waiting. A few Kurdan are with him."

Rukk froze, and his shoulders slumped. So it began. He returned to Thugari's room, catching her scent in the air. Refusing to acknowledge the sting of tears behind his eyes, he gathered his things.

"I sent him word of Borgakh last night." Mòr offered Rukk a cup of steaming tisane, as consolation, as commiseration, he couldn't be certain.

"My thanks, Mòr." He downed the tea. "I forgot, and that is unforgivable of me." Hurrying along her passage, he jerked, then faced her. "Tell Tarid I'll find him at the Tower."

Mòr nodded.

The crisp morning air slapped him across his face. He grimaced and shut the door behind him, striding to where Harpax pawed the ground. The mounted Kurdan dipped their heads, acknowledging him as king.

He scowled and vaulted into the saddle. "This is but a formality, an adherence to tradition, Keryn. You know how I feel about my birthright."

A horrendous scowl twisted his old tutor's face. "You have to convince the elders, my king."

Rukk gritted his teeth against the use of that title. "So no charging after Borgakh?" He tried to hide his hope, but the slight shake of Keryn's head doused it.

"She mourns, and as her father, I must grant her the time." He flicked his reins, and the procession trudged forward.

Harpax fell into line with the Kurdan trailing. Three days it would take to reach Isstislaaron, who knew how long the elders would debate his stance, then four days to find Thugari at Talach. Days of his life wasted when all he wanted to do, to bellow from the treetops, was tell her he loved her.

Gritting his teeth, he shifted his backside, trying to find a comfortable spot. Time passed as they meandered through the markets, up along the stone pathways to where Dussoum reached level land. From there, they turned west toward the battleground, at last urging their mounts into a canter. It wouldn't shorten their journey by much, but it felt as if it did. The countryside looked serene. There were no signs of yesterday's battle. The peaks of Gill-Eòin were white-capped again, and the Chaosthane mountains steadfast and silent.

Across the Plains of Kizad they rode, where the armies had camped with the tent pikes and scarred sand showing their passing. He did not need to ask where the armies were. Keryn must have dispersed them to their garrisons across Kethil.

Rukk frowned. "Shertur had no offspring."

Keryn nodded. "Who knows who will be crowned king. You will need to guide the Atrarian council."

Rukk clenched his jaw, fighting the urge to ride in the opposite direction.

"If I had to choose, Chief Igard Bakem has a good head on his shoulders. As a warrior in his own right, strategy comes naturally to him, but his heart belongs to his people." Keryn tapped his chest. "Although, since he rules the tribes to the west in Velkond, it will take much to convince him to relocate to the royal seat in Kinargun."

Rukk listened with one ear as Keryn spoke of the males he thought had leadership qualities. What Rukk heard was Keryn's knowledge and wisdom when he listed the males' traits, both good and bad.

After setting up camp and as the sun set on the first day of their journey, an idea formed. Rukk grinned across the campfire, content to let the wind toy with his hair.

When the Kurdan had begun to set up a tent for him, he had commanded them to cease. Reaching Isstislaaron was crucial, and time would be wasted on dismantling his tent every morning.

Keryn nodded, and the Kurdan served dinner instead. The stew couldn't compare to Thugari's, but its warmth filled Rukk's belly. With a wineskin in hand, he settled onto his bedroll.

They were mounted before dawn and heading north to the town of Buzaram, which they would reach before nightfall. An inn and a soft bed awaited him. He had once complained of sleeping under the stars, but his preferences mattered no longer.

He tried to engage Keryn in conversation, but the male had awoken tightlipped and sullen. This night, over a jug of mead, Rukk would ask about his mother and Donal, Keryn's son. The plains merged into rolling hills of farmland with orchards upon orchards of apple trees.

The sweet scent filled the air, reminding him of Thugari when he first met her. Apple had been on her breath, tempting him. He plucked one now as they trotted past, biting into it with relish.

In Buzaram, the townsfolk cheered when they rode through their market square, past their Fountain of Sound to halt outside the inn. Keryn waved and slapped shoulders, but when he stopped in front of the innkeeper, his smile faded. He ordered rooms, baths, then stomped upstairs.

Rukk frowned, dreading asking Keryn to reveal the details that had broken both families. Still, he needed to know, to understand why Horknuth had ordered the executions and why Keryn had obeyed without question.

Rukk hurried through the bath, despite enjoying the hot water easing the tension in his aching muscles.

In the common room, he chose a table to the rear and waited for the meals. With a start, he couldn't recall when last he had seen his coin pouch. A chuckle slipped past his lips. His minx must have stolen it, but at least his medallion circled his neck. It proved she cared for him and wanted him well. Hope flooded him like dragon's fire hitting his stomach.

"What has you in good spirits?" Keryn sat on the bench opposite Rukk.

"Love." He grinned and took a long pull from his honeyed mead, unashamed to share how he felt.

"Her siren ways will ease negotiations." Keryn waved his fingers at a passing tavern maid, requesting mead for himself.

"I won't be king, Keryn."

"Why not?" He slapped the table with the flat of his palm. "It's what your father wanted."

Rukk met his unflinching gaze. "A true king would do what's best for the realm. Now, I'm sorry to have to ask, but tell me about my mother."

Keryn fell back, as if he tried to remove himself from the conversation. He studied Rukk while sipping his mead. Rukk didn't lower his gaze. With a grunt, Keryn dipped his chin to his chest, then slammed down the mug.

"It's time you asked, Rukk." He bellowed for another mead. "Your mother was the most beautiful female I had ever seen. With the ancient elven blood flowing through her veins, she was also powerful. Betrothed from birth, they were to unite for Ghorza. This you know." He nursed his new mug of mead. "Donal was smitten from the moment he saw her. No matter what I or Borgakh said, he wouldn't listen. He pursued Celaena, showering her with compliments, gifts, tokens of affection. His adoration was life to her starved soul, and she succumbed. I knew it would be the death of them, their tryst. I warned them when it turned serious." A tear formed at the corner of his eye. He didn't acknowledge it. "They planned to escape together, fleeing to Mythal—the southernmost town near the Salt Plains of Eral. They hoped Horknuth wouldn't track them there. She wanted to tell you, Rukk. Her love for you was pure."

Keryn's great shoulders shuddered. "I was torn. Do I warn my king, serve him as I vowed to do? Or do I let them go?" He twirled the mug, gazing into the golden liquid. "It was not I who revealed their plans, yet it was I who swung the killing blow. I pleaded with them both but to no avail. In the end, your father and mother had made a vow, and by his honor, he had to adhere to it. All would question his word, his authority."

"But what of his lover, Shertur? Surely Mother knew him?"

Keryn shook his head. "Your father visited Shertur in the barracks and never invited the young prince into the palace. Celaena never met him, not even during diplomatic feasts. Years later, Horknuth helped Shertur become king, and in his way, he loved the male."

"They still loved each other right to the end."

Keryn grinned. "Noticed that, did you?" A stew pot and a meat platter were set on the table, but neither touched them. "My son made his choice. I had to live by it, live with my honor, break my own heart...and Borgakh's."

"She expected much from you." Rukk spooned stew into his bowl. He didn't eat but kept his gaze on Keryn.

"I was a god in her eyes, as all daughters should see their fathers." He sighed. "She expected me to perform a miracle, to save everyone. It took us years to mend the bridge between us."

"I blamed my father for Mother's death." Rukk released a trembling breath.

"He understood, mourned her in his way, but loved you regardless of how you felt about him."

Rukk fought fresh sting of tears. "He saved me."

"Every parent is prepared to make such a sacrifice, but we pray we won't have to." Keryn dug into the stew, choosing strips of meat and bread for his plate. He licked his fingers. "It's good you asked, Rukk."

The unspoken reprimand settled between them. "But it should have been my father telling me."

"Yes. Now, let's discuss becoming a king."

Rukk grinned. "I plan to recommend a male for the position."

"Recommend?" Keryn spluttered. "This isn't a vote for the next Grand Lawmaster."

"Yes, it is. The best male for the realm, Keryn."

He grumbled around the bread he bit into. "Have someone in mind?"

"He's an excellent warrior, wise beyond his years, with extensive experience in strategy, both in war and politics. He has connections to most of the elders and their families. Knows the inner workings of the palace, and always has Kethil and Ghorza at heart."

Keryn chuckled, sopping his gravy with a chunk of bread. "Who is this paragon?"

"I cannot say until I have spoken with the elders. It does no good to discuss his merits if they do not agree with me."

Keryn wiped his hands on the cloth the maid had left him. "Fair enough."

Rukk shoveled stew into his mouth to drown his laughter.

The next strip of the journey was another day spent in the saddle. They pushed the horses the last five miles, needing to reach the town of Lonhuen—a pretty town with houses a mixture of dwarven stone and elvish trees.

Bypassing an inn, they boarded a barge with stables for the horses. Not a cloud marred the evening sky as they rode along the meandering Himlar River, north to the Island of Amarhei.

The great white orc statues shifted into focus the closer they sailed. With their arms touching each other's shoulder, they formed a united front, and as beautiful with their carved tribal markings, their white teeth, and long braided hair. Elvish adornments circled their wrists and ankles, and gold glimmered in the moonlight.

Leaving Himlar, they crossed the Bay of Sahtar and docked at the feet of the Gates of Amarhei in Port Menoranas. They mounted up and continued their journey to Isstislaaron, the final four hours or twenty-three miles. Rukk's backside had numbed, despite the barge granting him a reprieve.

The forests thickened the deeper into the island they traveled. Trees older than his lineage peppered the oaks and pines. Houses merged from trunks to their treetops, with shimmering lights illuminating their windows. As they neared the steps into Isstislaaron, he dismounted, unable to resist the call of the soil.

Drawing in a deep breath, unseen tendrils of magic poured into his lungs and limbs, and energy renewed his exhausted body.

He was home.

His people, a mixture of orc and elves, rushed out to greet him, waving their hands above their heads. In soft colors and dressed in robes and breeches, they glowed from the magic of the land. Beauty abounded, in their features and their graceful mannerisms. He had forgotten how breathtaking his home was.

Thugari would have loved to have seen this.

"Greetings, my king." An elder dipped her head, a golden wreath growing from within her sunlight-white hair. "We thought to crown you as soon as you stepped onto Isstislaaron soil."

He couldn't claim to be exhausted, for a true Ghorzan orc would sense the pulse of the land and heal from it.

Instead, he shook his head. "Elder, please forgive me, but I am not the male to rule."

The elder jerked back and gestured to the six other elders to join her. "He does not want the crown."

They gasped, then gathered around him, bringing with them the fragrances of soil, growth, budding spring, crisp winter, and sweet perfumes.

"Then who shall rule?" another asked, with green sprigged branches growing from his brown curls.

Rukk had an answer ready. "None is more worthy than Keryn Yerug."

As one, they faced Keryn who had just climbed the last step. He hobbled across to Rukk, his love for Ghorza and his dutiful service resting on his broad shoulders.

The elders nodded. "We see your heart is no longer with Isstislaaron, Rukk Knaraugh. And the male you have chosen is worthy."

The heat of relief swept through him. "More than any male I know."

"Your choice is acceptable." They spoke as one, linking hands to circle Rukk and Keryn.

Song broke forth, and from their feet, tendrils of magic in a kaleidoscope of colors rose to engulf them.

Keryn smiled at Rukk, his posture erect as he prepared to serve another king. The whirlpool of combined power spiraled around him, testing his heart, his honor, his strength of will, his blood.

Then, as swiftly as it had formed, it seeped into the ground at his feet, and there, on his head, rested the crown.

"Rukk," he roared, his eyes wide. "What have you done?"

Rukk smiled, unable to contain the joy pounding at his freed soul. "You are the best male for the realm, my king."

Chapter Forty-Six

Thugari lost days after she snuck out on Rukk. Endless nights of Borgakh sobbing, of loneliness plaguing Thugari until she succumbed and bought another pillow to cuddle.

After traveling northwest of Dussoum, they reached Tulach at midday on the third day with Borgakh disappearing into the tavern, as usual. Slipping through the market square, Thugari's stomach wrenched, tightening into a knot she doubted would ever unravel no matter how much she ate.

She spent her last coin on oats for Envis and Borgakh's horse, and despite the familiar weight of Rukk's coin pouch at the bottom of her satchel, Thugari was loathe to spend it. Hunger was one thing, but shelter for Envis and herself mattered more.

The baker's goods permeated the air, conquering the delicious aromas of honeyed apple and skewered hekle. Gnash sniffed the air, twittering. Guilt gripped her, and she searched around the baker for children or a pregnant wife, anything to dissuade her from stealing his livelihood. Moon heard her silent plea, and his mother, gripping a walking stick, waddled to stand beside him.

How arrogant had she been when she had first escaped the castle, believing it her right to take what she needed, that life's ill-treatment meant Kethil owed her.

Digging in her satchel, she pulled out the locket she had stolen from Arob. She would use this and save Rukk's coin for a dilapidated cottage. According to the stablemaster, Tarid's cabin was two hours north of the village of Tulach, at the base of the Gallanbour Hills.

"Here, fair lady." The baker offered her a honeyed apple, a sweet smile splitting his cherubic cheeks even as his mother hit his leg with her stick.

Thugari thanked him, then purchased other goods with the locket.

Borgakh had fallen silent since leaving Dussoum and hadn't spoken since. Once again in the tavern drowning her sorrow in mead, Thugari would need to drag her out of there at some point. She dreaded that interaction. No one could force the Orc Maiden to do something she didn't want to do.

Not many males had returned to the town, most having signed up with the dwarves when word of the Ravenous Dark had reached them. A somber mood consumed the villagers and with reason. Husbands, sons, and brothers risked their lives.

Armed with a few supplies procured or gifted, including a knife, she entered the tavern and sank onto the bench in front of Borgakh. A steaming plate of stew awaited Thugari, and she sighed, leaning over to inhale the aroma. She tore a chunk of bread off and dipped it into the gravy.

Gnash twittered, scampered across the table to Borgakh, and settled on her shoulder. Without realizing it, the orc maiden stroked his head and offered him a piece of bread.

"I have coin, you know," she said.

Heat stained Thugari's face, so she kept her gaze down. "I'm not sure what awaits us at the cottage. We might need every coin. My thanks for the meal."

Borgakh nodded, and as soon as Thugari finished the last of her mead, they rose as one. Outside, she mounted Envis and headed for the final stretch of the journey. Dealing with people as a siren meant ensuring they didn't offer what they themselves needed. Females weren't excluded from a siren's influence, but she had learned, if their hearts belonged to another, they were safe.

Lost in memories, reliving moments spent with Rukk, she followed the path through a narrow rock gorge and rounded a verge. There nestled against the base of the hills was Banach Cottage. It was smallish with what appeared to be one room tacked onto the side along with stables to the rear. Tethering Envis to a melaena branch—its silver bark reminding her of Rukk's hair—she approached the door. Borgakh chose to brush down the horses while Thugari explored.

With a solid push, the door creaked open. Afternoon sunlight lit the floor and dust motes scattered across the air, dancing in complaint at her disturbance. A stone hearth dominated the back wall, and a tired, old wooden table rested in the center of the common room with a few chairs strewn around. The tacked-on room was a bedroom with a sunken bed in the corner. On top of the table sat an old recipe book.

She squared her shoulders at the work ahead of her. Tattered cloths hung over the windows. An old pile of wood was in one corner. Groaning, she debated whether to mount Envis and seek shelter at Tulach's inn. Tomorrow, she could return with more supplies. A broken broom against the wall would aid her for now.

She needed soap and washcloths, although, the curtains would suffice for the latter. The village might have a carpenter able to check the roof and the bed for her.

Swiping the book off the table, she strode from the cottage. She yanked the door shut, fighting with its warped shape to do so.

Borgakh arched a brow.

"I'm heading to town. We need cleaning supplies and a carpenter."

"It's that bad?" Borgakh brushed her horse with long strokes with Gnash watching from beneath the horse's twitching ears. "There's no inn, so we must sleep here tonight." She dug into her cloak to offer her coin pouch.

Thugari shook her head. "I have enough for now. I stole Rukk's pouch when I left."

Borgakh chuckled, then tucked her pouch away, untethering Envis for Thugari. "I would worry you travel alone, but the hero of Chaosthane need fear no one."

Thugari snorted, flicking a dismissive hand. Borgakh laughed again, and Thugari could hear her friend do so for a while until Envis took them too far along the path. After finding the town's carpenter, she purchased what they needed from the market and strapped the packages to Envis.

As she headed back, she thumbed through the recipe book as Envis meandered the path on his own.

"A mature briar rabbit with white on its tail,

A handful of Oosmer mushrooms harvested at dawn,

A tablespoon or more of butter, preferably made the same day,

A pinch of Nesalum to burn the tongue, and kill the gout,

A pinch of ash for the savory flavor,

Salt, if you have,

A wild pink onion peeled counterclockwise,

And a jug of spring water, lightly stirred."

She tore out the page and tossed it aside. Not once in her many mushroom-finding expeditions had she stumbled upon a briar rabbit. Frowning, she wondered what the white tail added to the meal.

Regardless, the last time she ate Oosmer mushrooms, she had pleaded with Moon to kill her. Torn between insanity and bouts of shouting curses along with the cold sweats led her to never to touch the pretty blue mushrooms again. Just thinking about it churned nausea, and she paused, swallowing down bile.

Smiling, she dismounted and tucked the ruined recipe book under her arm. The cottage's gaping door was Borgakh's way of saying she was out. Thugari hadn't passed her on the trail. Perhaps Borgakh explored the surrounding area? Thugari dropped the book onto the worn table. She'd have to stable Envis and brush him down.

The old carpenter would be up to see them in the morning. She had sweet-talked the gap-toothed curmudgeon to do so. Her 'siren' skills were useful on occasion. Night settled without Borgakh returning, so Thugari tried to light the fire in the dark.

She chuckled when the flames burst into life. "Thank you, Belen."

Borgakh stomped in but collapsed on the old mattress in the room without saying a word. Gnash curled onto Borgakh's back and settled in for the night.

Thugari shrugged and left the two of them. With the flames licking the stone hearth, she set to cleaning what she could see. Exhaustion dragged at her senses, blurring her vision, but she couldn't sleep, had struggled to find peace since leaving Rukk.

She offered a prayer, once again wishing he would sound her but expecting him not to. "Moon above, please keep him safe."

Tearing the rags from the windows, she slapped them against a tree trunk relying on the moon to light her task. All the while, she kept up a steady chat with Envis, who snorted or pawed the ground depending on her tone of voice.

She slipped feed bags over the horses' heads, feeling her way to do so since the cottage shielded them from the wind and moonlight.

After drinking from her waterskin, she filled the trough she found against the wall of the cottage. She had to tilt it up to clear it out. Tomorrow, she needed to find the water source for the horses had consumed the last of her supply. Borgakh would have more, but that wouldn't last long either. Sliding the latches, Thugari bolted the door shut, then unrolled her bedroll in front of the fire.

Keeping her breeches and tunic on, she unlaced her boots and climbed into the bedroll. She tucked her hands under her cheek and stared into the flickering flames, grateful nothing had taken up residence in the chimney. This cottage would become her home and a place of refuge for her friends.

A fist pounding on the door jerked her awake. She scrambled out of her bedroll, reaching for her new cooking knife. Glaring at the door, she gripped the knife in front of her. Sleep irritated her eyes, and her hair had unraveled during the night, flying around her in disarray.

Borgakh stood at the bedroom door, as naked as when she was born, cradling Gnash in her hand.

Thugari giggled, rising hysteria blurring her logic for a moment. "Put some garments on," she said, amid choked laughter.

Borgakh huffed, and did so, disappearing into the room to yank on her breeches.

"Miss, it's Bran, the carpenter."

"Oh, one moment." Thugari stomped her boots on, then rose to unbar the door. She glanced down, waiting for Borgakh to fix her guda where one breast had popped free. "Come in, please. I need the bed repaired and a new one made. I would like an extra room or two added on, and please, circle the cottage and stables. The wind whistled through last night, which I didn't mind since it's still warm, but come winter, I don't think I would enjoy it as much."

He hobbled to the bedroom, lugging a warn wooden toolbox. Tufts of gray hair stuck through his woolen cap, and he chewed on a strip of black root, staining his teeth. He dipped his head in a silent greeting to Borgakh. Hammering soon echoed through the cottage, driving the hungover orc maiden outside.

In the bright sunlight, Thugari could see where she had missed last night. Grabbing the broom, she set to work, hissing as the splintered wooden handle irritated the blisters.

She went to find Borgakh with their food pouches in hand. Behind the cottage was a garden overrun with weeds. Vegetables, herbs, and dilligaf grew wild. Borgakh was on her knees, tugging out the weeds, while Gnash sniffed plant after plant leaving his little footprints on the churned soil. A cliff rose behind the garden, and a waterfall trickled down the rock, staining it green and black before running past the garden in a gurgling stream.

"Is that our water supply?" Thugari eyed it, certain it would be cold and sweet to the taste.

"There's a well." Borgakh flicked a thumb. "Dilligaf should earn us coin." She leaned back on her heels to nudge her head at the waterfall. "It flows well enough for a bath."

"That it does, but come winter, perhaps not."

The carpenter left mid-afternoon, granting Borgakh and her blessed silence. The continued hammering had lanced through Thugari's skull, and she winced with each strike. The following morning, he returned with a cart and quite a few males as old as he. Borgakh and Thugari chose to escape to the village and hide in the tavern until dusk.

The days blurred into weeks, and neither spoke of the darkness in their hearts. The carpenter's males gushed and stuttered whenever Thugari smiled at them, so she kept her distance. Amid the additions to the cottage, her body changed too. Her breasts grew heavy, nausea rose at odd moments, and she found herself bursting into tears for no reason like when she squashed an insect by accident. Other times, she sobbed because it was so beautiful to look upon, be it flowers, sunlight, or a butterfly landing on her shoulder.

"What's wrong?" Borgakh said, finding Thugari crying again.

"Taste this." She held out a spoon of stew, blowing on it to cool it. Borgakh opened her mouth, rolling the gravy around with her tongue before swallowing. "Isn't it delicious?"

"This is why you cry?" Borgakh grabbed her by the shoulders. "I hear two heartbeats."

"What do you mean?" She frowned, trying to understand Borgakh's implication. "Yours and mine?"

"Yes, I hear mine. Then there's yours and yours." She chuckled, shaking her head. "You're with bairn, little one."

Thugari staggered back, collapsing on a nearby chair with a jolt. "What?"

CHAPTER FORTY-SEVEN

DURING THE FESTIVITIES, RUKK stayed in his old chambers. The softest of linen was still without a warm body beside him. The hot pools soothed his muscles, but the lazy lavender-scented tendrils teasing his nose lacked the sweet vanilla of Thugari.

Happiness was elusive without her, and therein lay his dilemma—returning to life as a lawbringer. The closest Fountain of Sound to Tulach was in the southeastern town of Ainerius. Penven was fifteen hours by horse, so not an impossible distance.

Thugari wouldn't want to leave the cottage, and he couldn't force her to. After what she had endured, a home of her own meant so much to her. He didn't care where he lived, used to sleeping in strange beds or on the ground, no matter the weather. And yet, at the thought of having her waiting for him, untold bliss filled his chest to capacity.

He found sleep in bursts but was awake when the dawn kissed the tips of his mother's tree. Its silvery bark was so like a malaena tree, like his hair and hers. Thick branches cast him in shadow, and with a sigh, he held his palm to her smooth trunk. Nothing marred it, no pits or broken-off branches. Wrapping around it was an oak tree, sturdy at the base with gnarled branches.

A tear squeezed past his defenses. His father had his mother and Donal planted alongside each other. They embraced in an eternal symbol of love, their souls inhabiting the trees. Guilt should hound Rukk, at how he had mistreated his father, at his unforgiveness, but only grief remained.

"Horknuth wasn't a heartless male, Rukk." Keryn touched Donal's trunk. In a robe, embellished with gold and silver, and a crown rising from his dark hair, Keryn was as steadfast as the trees. "Now my reign is official, I have prepared Harpax for travel."

"You, my king?" Rukk smiled, ignoring the tears staining his face. There was no shame in crying.

Keryn chuckled. "Ordered it." He raised his gaze to the sunlight piercing Mother's and Donal's canopies. "I will not fail you, my son."

Harpax pawed the ground, eager to depart. Rukk allowed Keryn to steer him toward the steps of Isstislaaron.

"The ship *Gweyir* awaits at Port Menoranas to take you east to Filralad." Keryn pressed a soil-filled pouch into Rukk's palm.

It was the swiftest route. "My thanks, my king."

"The Kurdan will follow." Keryn slapped him on the shoulder. "To collect Borgakh." He grinned.

Rukk laughed. "Yes, I imagine she will be most displeased with the change in her status."

Keryn's twitching lips preceded a guffaw, as unrestrained as his daughter's laughter. Rukk vaulted into the saddle, and with a nod at Keryn, he steered Harpax south. The distance to Tulach was shorter if he traveled east along the Bay of Sahtar, disembarked at the town of Filralad, then headed south toward the Gallanbour Hills.

The town of Tulach, with its wooden and stone buildings, was quiet when he rode through it days later. Only the tavern bustled with life and raucous laughter. He continued past, unseen, as Harpax plodded onward. He had been here once before, when Tarid had first received the cottage. Then it had been ramshackle.

Grimacing at what Thugari must have discovered, he pushed Harpax into a canter, sparing a little of his magic to ease his horse's tired muscles. "Almost there, my friend."

Harpax nickered.

They rounded a bend in the trail and before him, nestled against the flat face of a towering rock stood the cottage. It was bigger than he remembered. Light flickered in the windows, calling him to rest. He tethered Harpax beside Envis and took a moment to unsaddle and feed his horse.

After splashing his face in a barrel of water beside the front door, Rukk inhaled long breaths to steady his nerves while drying himself with the hem of his tunic.

With two fingers, he pushed on the door and found it locked.

He grinned and flicked out his magic to glide the bolt to the side before slipping into the cottage. In the light from the fire—its warmth filling a common room, he crept to the door on the right. Soft snores greeted him, along with the musky scent of a drunk Borgakh.

Gathering a lantern, he veered for the other door, chasing the sweeter scent of Thugari. It was richer, full-bodied, and he rested his temple on her door, relishing the moment. A gentle touch later opened the door on silent hinges.

Sprawled on the bed was his female, with a bare leg outside of the blankets. She tossed, a moan escaping her. He faded into the shadow to admire her dark tresses spilling across the pillow, the moonlight kissing her skin, and the soft huffing noises she made when she rolled over.

Then she sat up.

A stray breeze teased his hair and engulfed him in her scent. The urge to lunge for her, to taste her sweet lips bombarded him. He gritted his teeth, not willing to succumb just yet. He needed to speak his heart.

She pushed off the bed and padded barefoot to the common room to the jug on the table. Shifting from one foot to another, she drained a cup, then poured another.

When she faced the door, his breath hitched, for covering her was the same robe she had worn the night they unraveled her sigil.

Sweet Zetar.

She glided past an arm's length away, and it took everything within him not to reach for her. Touching her from the shadows might frighten her. When she left the door open and headed for her bed, he flicked his magic at the lantern. It burst into life, and its circle of light touched on the thick rugs, the soft furnishings, her crossbow resting beside her bed, and her...the female he loved.

Chapter Forty-Eight

"Thugari." Rukk's voice penetrated the darkness as the lantern he held revealed him standing in her bedroom.

Thugari squeaked and stumbled back, tripping over the trail of her robe to land on the rug. Her limbs splayed out, and the robe parted, revealing her breasts down to her belly button to where the garment pooled between her thighs. He stared at her with something hot and intense in his eyes.

Shock trembled her cheeks, and she gasped and rolled over, hiding her curves from him.

"Rukk." Clambering to her feet, she turned her back to him to do the ties, then faced him, bumping into his chest.

He had placed the lantern on the table by her window, his tread absorbed by the thick rugs.

"Oh." She grasped his shoulders to steady herself.

He looped his arm around her waist, crushing her against his body. "You look good," he said, with a smile teasing his upper lip.

"You're well? Unharmed?" She brushed her fingers from his shoulders, down his upper arms to grip his forearms.

"You shouldn't have run." He buried his nose into her neck, drawing in a deep inhale. "I missed you, dear one."

Those lethal words skewered her with joy, like the first rays of the sun after a thunderstorm. He dusted a path of kisses along her jaw to capture her lips, granting her a fleeting taste of him before he stepped away to remove his cloak and tunic. The yellow glow of the lantern painted the valleys and peaks of his torso and his pebbled nipples.

She traced a jagged scar marring his ribs and along his etched tribal markings. He captured her fingers, pressed a scorching kiss to them, then bent to yank off his boots.

"Are you well?" He peeled off his breeches to stand naked before her.

Her throat dried, and her heart pounded so hard it deafened her. She forgot to breathe, her gaze traveling over his sculpted body, memorizing the sharp edges and the tightness of his backside.

"Thugari." He trailed his hand from her elbow to her wrist, circled it with his fingers before lacing them through hers.

She raised stunned eyes to his, every one of her senses igniting at his presence, his touch. Heat uncoiled and ached between her thighs. She glanced through her open door to Borgakh's closed one.

"Where is Tarid?"

"With Sharn at the Council." Rukk feathered his lips across hers, then with a groan, deepened the kiss until she didn't know where she began and he ended.

Gathering her into his arms, he crushed her to him, squeezing a sigh from her.

"I've missed you, this." She twisted to kiss his shoulder. "I'm sorry I left you. I didn't want you to feel torn between Ghorza, the Council, and me. Are you hungry? Can I make you anything?"

"No, stay right here." Time passed, and she let him hold her. Peace rested in his eyes. No more did sorrow linger. He scanned her garments. "You're wearing the robe." He smiled. "I have fond memories of you in this and out of it." He scooped her into his arms, carrying her to the new bed in the corner. "Remember when I told you to choose someone?"

She nodded, wiggling in his arms. He didn't lower her but released her legs. Her feet dangled inches off the floor as he pinned her to his chest.

"I have chosen for you." He claimed her mouth for another kiss, one that spiked her temperature and intensified the ache between her thighs.

She pawed his bare shoulders, urging him on. He peeled the robe off her body, a guttural growl escaping him when her bared breasts met his chest. Too sensitive in her condition, she couldn't bare his touch. She cried out and pulled away.

"I want to taste every inch of you, bury myself between your tempting thighs, and relearn what brings you pleasure even if it takes me an eternity. You enthrall me, Thugari, and tonight, I surrender to you, my doe."

Rukk lowered her until her toes touched the rug, then clasped her cheeks, holding her still for a kiss that ripped a moan from her. He dominated her, his tongue granting no mercy as his hands rubbed her back and his fingers entangled in her hair to pin her head back. He trailed wet kisses along her throat.

She whimpered, clinging to him as her knees weakened. With each kiss and caress, her core thrummed, throbbed, and demanded. She writhed, unable to halt his trek to her ear. Pursuing her, he forced her back until her calves hit the bed, and she fell. He placed a knee beside her hip and ran a finger up her thigh. She trembled, fighting the urge to cover her nudity as much as she fought her body's need to arch into his touch. His finger touched her seam, dragging a smothered gasp from her. When he dipped in, he groaned, closing his eyes as if tortured.

He flicked his eyes open to meet her gaze. Yearning and something more softened his expression. When he bent to capture her lips, he swirled his finger around a bundle of nerves. The bursts of pleasure to her core connected to her chest, affecting her ability to breathe. His kisses didn't help, tearing her attention between both onslaughts.

The burn intensified, tingling originating outward as the tension within her built to a crescendo. Oh, how she had missed this. Then he nibbled on her ear. Two darts of pleasure pebbled her nipples and sent a gush of heat to her belly. She screamed his name, thrusting her hips upward as she drowned in ecstasy so breathtaking her heart stuttered.

He plastered his body over hers, and with a flip, she found herself on top of him, her legs spread wide to brush her femininity against his cock. Shyness hit her, and her face burned as she covered her breasts. He nudged her hands away, cupping one breast and a hip with a soft chuckle.

"I dreamed of this moment, Thugari. Don't hide from me." He sat up to kiss her. His enticing lips feathered across hers, then he nipped, laughing when she cursed him in frustration. He dodged her attempts to deepen the kiss until she pushed him back, leaning over him to pin him with her body.

She stroked his jaw and kissed him, taking her time to taste his lips, press kisses to his chin, and dip into the crevices of his mouth. So had she dreamed of this moment, and she would enjoy it to the fullest. Soon she would tell him, but she shoved that thought aside when he gripped her hips to show her how to ride him. She panted, arching as he rubbed against her entrance, rekindling tremors of the previous pleasure.

Rolling her onto her back, he positioned himself and smiled. "I'm sorry, sweet Thugari, for I cannot wait."

She captured one of his hands to kiss his palm. "Neither can I, Rukk. Please, hurry. I need you."

His lips whitened, and he trembled, his hands gripping her hips again to hold her still. Then with exquisite tenderness, he held his hardness to her entrance, tearing a cry from her.

"Don't stop." She kneaded his shoulders.

In and out he thrust, each time more exquisite, more tantalizing than the last. Sweat dewed his body, and he shuddered. Then with one thrust, he buried himself. His roar drowned out her whispers.

"By Zetar, Thugari."

She smiled, caressing his hair where it curled into his neck. Looping her legs around his hips, she urged him on with her heels digging into his backside. He released a long breath, opening his eyes to meet hers before withdrawing and sliding back in. With each plunge, she succumbed to pleasure and a sense of completion she felt only with him. As if she belonged to him, as if he were her tribe.

His rhythm increased, his breathing ragged, then she climbed the mountain again, surprise parting her lips. To have him between her legs was pleasant, then it became incredible and addictive, demanding she participate.

She pawed him, running her fingers over his nipples or digging her nails into his backside. He called her name, his thrusts slamming into her, rocking the bed, but she didn't care, as long as he didn't stop. Goosebumps traveled down her back, somehow hardening her nipples. The pleasure hit her, snatching her breath, arching her into him, and clenching her thighs around him. So beautiful, a tear slipped free.

"Thugari." He drew out her name as he shuddered, a pleasurable pain contorting his features.

He stilled with his hips pressed against the back of her thighs. Small tremors rocked him, some hitching his breath.

Collapsing on top of her, he tucked his arms beneath her and rolled over, positioning her limbs so she sprawled across him as per their first night together. He buried his lips in her hair and held her against him. Contentment melted her bones, and the energy to move drained from her.

"I love you, little thief," he said, kissing her hair. "I wanted to tell you this in Dussoum. I wanted to pledge my life to yours before taking you to Isstislaaron."

"You do? You did?" She gasped, twisting to meet his gaze.

He nodded, a breathtaking smile on lips. "I want the Knaraugh tribal markings on your beautiful skin, and when next I visit the royal city, you must travel with to receive them."

Clanship? Her breath caught. To belong to something more than herself? Curses, he tempted her to keep him. "I have markings. My father gave me scars, Rukk."

"Those the medallion healed, Thugari. Your skin is as unblemished as it should be."

She clamped her lips shut to smother her surprise. Gone was the old evidence of her father's abuse. She was free, with only the memories to haunt her.

"I have spoken to Grand Lawmaster, and he has tasked lawbringers to investigate your father. If I have my way, that male will be stripped of all he holds dear and sent to mine the salt plains alongside his viper mate and selfish daughter." Rukk's upper lip curled in distaste.

Justice? A tidal wave of rioting emotions engulfed her. She threw her arms around him, kissing his chest above his heart, her eyes stinging.

"Rukk, I love you too, but—" A sob escaped her, and tears leaked without permission. He might cast her aside as her father had done to her mother. He might revoke the offer of clanship. Worse, he might leave her and never return. "I won't pin you down. I'll understand if you must leave. Borgakh has promised to remain with me, so I'll never be alone."

He frowned. "Leave? I have no intention of parting from you, Thugari."

"Oh, cursed hell. Let me speak and have done with it." She shifted out of his arms, unable to bear his gentle touch and the concern marring his brow. "I'm with bairn."

"With bairn?" He gaped, his cheeks paling, then bursting with color. "I thought the faint heartbeat was Borgakh's. I'm a father?"

"The birth is months away, and I'm not showing yet, but the midwife confirms it." She touched her belly where their bairn grew. Already, love swelled, crushing her chest as it flooded her with cold fear and heated excitement.

Rukk bolted off the bed to crumple to the floor, kneeling in front of her to plant kisses between her splayed fingers guarding her womb. Tears glistened in his obsidian eyes and gratitude claimed his features.

"I'm to be a father." He chuckled as he wept, gliding his arms around her hips to bury his face in her belly. "Daughter or son, I will adore our bairn." He tugged on her arms until she knelt before him, then claimed her mouth with his. "You have made me happy, Thugari, sweet doe, more than I deserve."

This wasn't the reaction she expected. "You won't leave me?"

"Leave you?" He shook his head. "To do so is to cut out my heart." He feathered kisses over her face as she fought disbelief.

Wanting to guard against the future, she would have preferred he admit he would abandon her. This, the certainty on his face, his delight at the news had her hoping for the best scenario, one where she was part of a family.

"I'm not your father, Thugari. He used your mother, but I gave you my love from the start *before* I knew you were a siren."

She shook her head and couldn't hold back her smile. Happiness engulfed her, like sunlight warming her upturned face and spreading to every inch of her body.

"Is the kissing done? Can I come out now?" Borgakh's voice reverberated through her bedroom door.

Rukk arched a brow as a grin conquered his features. "Do we have another bairn?"

Thugari giggled.

Borgakh growled, slamming the door open. "I heard that. Now put some garments on, Rukk Knaraugh, I wish to hear about my father."

Gnash scampered through the door, across the common room, and up his leg to curl into the curve of his neck, chirping as he did so. Reaching up, Rukk stroked his belly.

"Greetings, my princess." He laughed in the face of Borgakh's glare, despite his nudity. "I made your father king."

She gaped, then groaned. "Cursed hell."

He chuckled. "Your father and the Kurdan are en route to collect you." Brushing his lips across Thugari's sent bright bursts of joy through her. "I suggest you leave with them, Princess."

"And Thugari?" Borgakh rested her fists on her hips.

"A lawbringer taking a wife isn't unheard of. We will move to a house of her choosing in Penven." Rukk grinned. "I want my valthyra all to myself."

"Wife?" Thugari gasped.

"If you'll have me." He wrapped his arms around her and stole a quick kiss.

"And valthyra?" She struggled to hold onto her thoughts with him so near, the warmth of his body calling to hers. "You've called me that before."

"Oh, sweet Thugari." His smile faded, but he scooped Gnash onto the bed before cupping her cheeks, holding her in place for his intense gaze. "You're the joy of laughter, my will to live. You are everything to me. You have my heart, little doe."

Overwhelmed by the flood of heated emotion too powerful to contain, she could do nothing but grin through the tears. "As you have mine, Rukk."

The smile sauntering across his lips erased every negative memory. She had found where she belonged, in his arms.

About the Author

Sevannah Storm is a fiction writer who immerses herself in fantastical worlds both magical and science fiction. She has a flare for the creative having studied art and interior architecture, and spends her time drawing, oil painting, and writing. An avid reader from an early age, she finds her inspiration from various sources: games, novels, music, and the land of make-believe. The unique versus the practical has brought on numerous debates.

In her spare time, she does Krav Maga and rereads novels that snatch her breath away. Having embraced the social media world, you can find her on most platforms, and she acts as an Ambassador on Wattpad.

Her home is a land south of Wakanda, where animals roam free. Born in Zimbabwe, she grew up in South Africa. The crisp blue skies with cotton-candy sunsets expand her heart and soul, encapsulating a sense of freedom.

Words she lives by: "Know your pothole and dodge it. Don't work in a pencil factory if you're a vampire."

Sevannah loves to hear from her readers. You can find and connect with her at the links below.

Website/Blog: https://sevannahstorm.com
Facebook: https://www.facebook.com/sevannah.storm
Instagram: https://www.instagram.com/sevannah.storm/
Pinterest: https://za.pinterest.com/sevannahstorm/
Twitter: https://x.com/sevannah_storm

Thank you for taking the time to read *Ire of Silver*. If you enjoyed the story, please tell your friends, read another by Sevannah, and leave a review. Reviews support authors and ensure they continue to bring readers books to love and enjoy.

The Lady and the Assassin

Fantasy Romance

For sheltered Lady Ruvona, visiting Devenmere Manor to investigate her father's disappearance is a chance to escape her dull life. In Netherbury, the nearest town, the malevolent Lord Emil is taxing and starving the people, and a mysterious dark force is draining the land. Determined to help the townsfolk and save her father, with her magic and the skills her guardian taught her, Lady Ruvona disguises herself as the lad, Robbin.

Assassin Warric masquerades as the new Sheriff of Netherbury and is tasked to thwart Emil. What he did not expect to encounter was beautiful Lady Ruvona bathing in a moonlit river. Nor did he expect an ally in the outlaw Robbin. Aiding the lad is in line with Warric's task, but it doesn't take him long to realize who Robbin is.

Together, with magic and swords, they try to save her father, take on Emil, his ancient amulet, and the plot to destroy all they stand for. While trying not to fall in love.

Read it here:
https://books2read.com/u/bMV888

Xiaxan Fox

Fantasy Romance

An orphaned princess battles across realms to reclaim her kingdom.

Born under a calamity star, Princess Jenaso 'Joi' of Letoura survived the massacre of her family and the burning of Tennaba. Taken in by the neighboring King of Meideon, he raises her as his daughter alongside his two sons.

Years later, at a pre-coronation event, revealing her identity has old enemies once more after her, not to mention all the suitors for her hand. To secure her safety, she escapes with a Xiaxan fellow trainee and secret admirer, Prince Sohar of Greyad.

Across five realms, she battles her family's enemies, old and new, with magic and sword but must decide whether to pledge her life to her kingdom or follow her heart.

Read it here:

https://books2read.com/u/3LY6X7

The Crucible of the Eternal

Epic Fantasy

By all accounts, Zemeri deserves to take revenge. Her uncle assassinated her family, his general is hunting her for a crime she didn't commit, and for some strange reason, she cannot die.

Holy men from distant cultures and faraway lands cannot explain her immortality. This leaves her on the run, a shifting target because letting the general bring her in to face 'justice' is out of the question.

While the cure for immortality eludes her, she is not without hope. But she will need all the help she can get when she learns she is not the only one in the general's sights. When he kidnaps a gifted boy, it's her turn to hunt, and hopefully, Death has its final say.

Read it here:

https://books2read.com/u/bWlOVx

9 781067 226183